中文详注剑桥莎士比亚精选

儒略·恺撒

原版创始主编：[英] 瑞克斯·吉布森（Rex Gibson）
原版主编：[英] 瑞查德·安褚斯（Richard Andrews）
　　　　　[英] 维姬·维南德（Vicki Wienand）
原版编注：[英] 罗布·史密斯（Rob Smith）
　　　　　[英] 维姬·维南德（Vicki Wienand）
总主编：陈国华
分册主编：潘铁楠

JULIUS CAESAR

社图号 20055

Cambridge School Shakespeare: Julius Caesar [Third edition] [978-1-107-61551-9] was first published by Cambridge University Press in 2014. All rights reserved.

This Simplified Chinese edition for the People's Republic of China is published by arrangement with the Press Syndicate of the University of Cambridge, Cambridge, United Kingdom.

© Cambridge University Press & Beijing Language and Culture University Press 2020.

This book is in copyright. No reproduction of any part may take place without the written permission of Cambridge University Press or Beijing Language and Culture University Press.

本书版权由剑桥大学出版社和北京语言大学出版社共同所有。本书任何部分之文字及图片，如未获得出版者书面同意，不得用任何方式抄袭、节录或翻印。

This edition is for sale in the People's Republic of China (excluding Hong Kong SAR, Macao SAR and Taiwan Province) only.

此版本仅限在中华人民共和国境内（不包括香港特别行政区、澳门特别行政区及台湾省）销售。

北京市版权局著作权合同登记图字：01-2020-2712号

图书在版编目（CIP）数据

中文详注剑桥莎士比亚精选．儒略·恺撒 ／ 陈国华总主编；潘铁楠分册主编． -- 北京：北京语言大学出版社，2020.7

书名原文：Cambridge School Shakespeare：Julius Caesar

ISBN 978-7-5619-5663-2

Ⅰ.①中… Ⅱ.①陈… ②潘… Ⅲ.①多幕剧-剧本-英国-中世纪 Ⅳ.① I561.33

中国版本图书馆 CIP 数据核字（2020）第 092492 号

中文详注剑桥莎士比亚精选：儒略·恺撒
ZHONGWEN XIANG ZHU JIANQIAO SHASHIBIYA JINGXUAN: RULÜE KAISA

项目策划：李 亮	**责任编辑**：孙冠群
封面设计：乔 剑	**排版制作**：北京创艺涵文化发展有限公司
责任印制：武晓东	

出版发行：北京语言大学出版社

社　址：北京市海淀区学院路15号，100083
网　址：www.blcup.com
电子信箱：service@blcup.com
电　话：编辑部　8610-82301019/0178
　　　　　 发行部　8610-82303650/3591/3648
　　　　　 北语书店　8610-82303653
　　　　　 网购咨询　8610-82303908

印　刷：北京中科印刷有限公司

版　次：2020年7月第1版　　　**印　次**：2020年7月第1次印刷
开　本：787毫米×1092毫米 1/16　　**印　张**：13.75
字　数：341千字
定　价：69.00元

PRINTED IN CHINA

序

由于观察角度不同，评判标准不同，关于哪个国家哪位诗人或小说家的成就最大，世人可能难以达成一致；可是说到剧作家，大家的共识是，莎士比亚不仅是英语国家有史以来最伟大的剧作家，也是全世界最伟大的剧作家，在知名度、影响力和传世作品的数量上，没有任何一位剧作家可以与之比肩。正是由于其公认的文学成就和人文精神，在过去400多年里，莎士比亚戏剧的演出在英语国家和许多非英语国家经久不衰，莎剧的阅读和鉴赏已成为这些国家英文教学的必选内容。

莎剧进入中国，已经有100多年历史，莎士比亚全集已经有了四个中文译本。不懂英文的人可以通过译本来欣赏莎士比亚剧作。然而文学作品的语言，尤其是诗歌的语言，具有相当程度的不可译性，而几乎所有莎剧的大部分台词都是素体诗（blank verse）。例如《哈慕雷》（Hamlet）里主人翁的名言"To be, or not to be, that is the question"，不论怎样译，都难以完全再现原文的深刻内涵和形式特点。要想真正欣赏莎士比亚的语言和戏剧艺术，还得阅读其英文原作。最早由剑桥大学出版社出版的这套莎剧精选，收录了最受读者和观众喜爱的14部剧目，涵盖莎剧的各个类别，以其独具匠心的设计和编排，成为所有英文原版莎剧中最适合英语学习者阅读、最适合戏剧爱好者排演的莎剧选集。

本选集的创始主编瑞克斯·吉布森（Rex Gibson）在本书引言（Introduction）里指出："不论做什么，都要记住，莎士比亚写下他的剧本是为了演出、观看和享受的。"秉承这一宗旨，这一新版莎剧选集有四个鲜明的区别性特点：

一、书的开本和页面的宽高比例特别适合学校的老师和学生以及剧团的导演和演员在排练莎剧时把书打开，拿在手里，随时参阅，而且左边页面上有许多有关排演活动的建议。

二、书中配有大量世界各国莎剧演出的彩色剧照，为莎剧爱好者和剧团排演莎剧提供了灵感。

三、书的正文部分打开后，右页是未经删减、原汁原味的剧本原文，左页是多种不同栏目，包括导演技巧（Stagecraft）、剧中语言（Language in the play）、人物分析（Characters）、主题分析（Themes）、写作练习（Write about it）及词语注释等。每幕之间（本幕回顾）和最后一幕后（本剧回顾）有与剧情相关的各种思考题。

四、在剧本之后有各种针对全剧的专题论述，以《哈慕雷》为例，包括视角与主题（Perspectives and themes）、人物分析（Characters）、《哈慕雷》的语言（The language of Hamlet）、《哈慕雷》的演出（Hamlet in performance）、笔论莎士比亚（Writing about Shakespeare）、笔论《哈慕雷》（Writing about Hamlet），还有一份莎翁年表（William Shakespeare 1564–1616）。

左页上的栏目对于解读和排演莎剧特别有帮助，剧本后面的专题论述对于撰写有关莎士比亚的文章特别有帮助，而参加莎剧排演，背诵台词，撰写论文，又是提高英语水平的极好途径。

为了方便更多的中国读者阅读、欣赏、排演莎士比亚原作，北京语言大学出版社携手剑桥大学出版社，将这套莎剧精选引入中国。我有幸应邀担任这套书的中文版总主编，组织起一个团队，对原版进行一定程度的改编和汉化，以适应中国读者的需求。我们不仅将原版提供的关键注释基本译成了中文，而且针对中国英语学习者和莎剧爱好者阅读理解上的难点，主要做了以下四件事：

　　一、参考 *The Oxford Dictionary of Original Shakespearean Pronunciation* (David Crystal 2016)、*Oxford Dictionary of Pronunciation for Current English* (Clive Upton 2003) 和 *Shakespeare's Names: A Pronouncing Dictionary* (Helge Kökeritz 1950)，给每个剧本前面人物表里的人名加上了国际音标。为了便于读者识别，我们将第一本发音词典里一般中国读者不认识的个别音标替换成了大家熟悉的近似音标。

　　二、为左页顶端的剧情简介添加中文译文。

　　三、左页中以及剧本后面论文部分里有一些具有挑战性的词和术语（如tableau），我们为其中的大部分添加了相应的中文释义。

　　四、适当增加了原版里没有的词语注释。

　　给剧中人物的名字加了国际音标之后，我们发现，现有莎剧中文译本里一些人名的中文译名与原文的读音差别较大且互不相同。根据定名不咎、译音循本、音义兼顾、音系对应的原则，我们给出了新译名。根据前两个原则，我们将剧本 *Julius Caesar* /ˈdʒuːlɪəs ˈsiːzə(r)/ 译成《儒略·恺撒》，而没有采用《尤利/力乌斯·恺撒》《裘利/力斯·凯撒》《居里厄斯·恺撒》等现成译名中的任何一个，因为从公元前1世纪到公元16世纪西方使用的儒略历（Julian calendar）就是以这位 Julius Caesar（拉丁文读音是 /ˈjuːlɪ.ʊs ˈkaɛsar/）命名的。根据音义兼顾的原则，我们将剧本 *Hamlet* /ˈ(h)amlət/ 译成《哈慕雷》而不是《哈姆莱特》或《哈姆雷特》，因为"慕雷"比"姆莱"或"姆雷"更适合用来给男子起名，结尾的辅音 /t/ 在实际说话中往往不发音。根据音系对应的原则，我们借鉴了曹禺的译法，将剧本 *Romeo and Juliet* 译成《柔密欧与茱丽叶》，没有将 Romeo 译成更常见的"罗密欧"，因为"柔 /rou/"比"罗 /luo/"更接近原名 Romeo /ˈroːmɪoː/ 的读音；同时我们将 Juliet /ˈdʒuːlɪət/ 译成"茱丽叶"而不是"朱丽叶"，因为这样做不容易让人误以为这个女孩姓"朱"。

　　这套经过改编并且带中文注释的《中文详注剑桥莎士比亚精选》不仅可以用作中国高中和大学的英文教材，而且适合中国所有具有较高英语能力的莎剧爱好者阅读和欣赏，将戏剧从书中提升到自己心中，将剧本从课堂搬演到戏台。

　　相信《中文详注剑桥莎士比亚精选》会带给中国广大英语爱好者一个惊喜。

陈国华

北京外国语大学

2020年5月于英国剑桥家中

Contents 目录

Introduction 引言	iv
Photo gallery 剧照精选	v
Before the play begins 戏剧背景介绍	1

Julius Caesar 《儒略·恺撒》

List of characters 人物表	5
Act 1 第1幕	7
Act 2 第2幕	41
Act 3 第3幕	75
Act 4 第4幕	113
Act 5 第5幕	141
Perspectives and themes 视角与主题	166
The Roman world 罗马世界	171
Characters 人物分析	174
The language of *Julius Caesar* 《儒略·恺撒》的语言	184
Julius Caesar in performance 《儒略·恺撒》的演出	190
Writing about Shakespeare 笔论莎士比亚	198
Writing about *Julius Caesar* 笔论《儒略·恺撒》	200
William Shakespeare 1564–1616 莎翁年表	202
Acknowledgements 鸣谢	203

Introduction 引言

This *Julius Caesar* is part of the **Cambridge School Shakespeare** series. Like every other play in the series, it has been specially prepared to help all students in schools and colleges.

The **Cambridge School Shakespeare** *Julius Caesar* aims to be different. It invites you to lift the words from the page and to bring the play to life in your classroom, hall or drama studio. Through enjoyable and focused activities, you will increase your understanding of the play. Actors have created their different interpretations of the play over the centuries. Similarly, you are invited to make up your own mind about *Julius Caesar*, rather than having someone else's interpretation handed down to you.

Cambridge School Shakespeare does not offer you a cut-down or simplified version of the play. This is Shakespeare's language, filled with imaginative possibilities. You will find on every left-hand page: a summary of the action, an explanation of unfamiliar words, and a choice of activities on Shakespeare's stagecraft, characters, themes and language.

Between each act, and in the pages at the end of the play, you will find notes, illustrations and activities. These will help to encourage reflection after every act and give you insights into the background and context of the play as a whole.

This edition will be of value to you whether you are studying for an examination, reading for pleasure or thinking of putting on the play to entertain others. You can work on the activities on your own or in groups. Many of the activities suggest a particular group size, but don't be afraid to make up larger or smaller groups to suit your own purposes. Please don't think you have to do every activity: choose those that will help you most.

Although you are invited to treat *Julius Caesar* as a play, you don't need special dramatic or theatrical skills to do the activities. By choosing your activities, and by exploring and experimenting, you can make your own interpretations of Shakespeare's language, characters and stories.

Whatever you do, remember that Shakespeare wrote his plays to be acted, watched and enjoyed.

Rex Gibson
Founding editor

This new edition contains more photographs, more diversity and more supporting material than previous editions, whilst remaining true to Rex's original vision. Specifically, it contains more activities and commentary on stagecraft and writing about Shakespeare, to reflect contemporary interest. The glossary has been enlarged, too. Finally, this edition aims to reflect the best teaching and learning possible, and to represent not only Shakespeare through the ages, but also the relevance and excitement of Shakespeare today.

Richard Andrews and Vicki Wienand
Series editors

This edition of *Julius Caesar* uses the text of the play established by Marvin Spevack in **The New Cambridge Shakespeare**.

Beware the Ides of March. Shakespeare's play dramatises the political machinations (阴谋) surrounding the assassination of Julius Caesar. The action is focused on three characters: Mark Antony (left), Julius Caesar (centre) and Marcus Brutus (right).

There has been a terrible civil war. Pompey and Caesar – both formidable figures of the Roman world – have fought each other for supreme power in Rome, and Caesar has won. Caesar makes a triumphant entry into Rome.

Marcus Brutus is Caesar's close friend and military comrade. His ancestors were famed for driving the tyrannical King Tarquin from the throne and helping to found the Roman Republic.

A group of conspirators, envious of Caesar's increasing power, grow restless in Rome. They are initially led by Cassius (far right).

Brutus (right) becomes convinced that Caesar is greedy for power and intends to turn Republican Rome into a monarchy. He decides that Caesar must die for his ambition to be king, and agrees to assist in the assassination attempt planned by the conspiring senators.

PEACE
FREEDOM
LIBERTY

▲ Brutus's wife, Portia, grows fearful for his health and suspects Brutus of deviousness (歪门邪道).

▶ Meanwhile, Caesar's wife, Calpurnia, has spoken of his murder in her sleep. She orders him to stay at home, telling of frightening and ominous portents (不祥之兆). But Caesar is unmoved.

'*Et tu, Brute?*' Ignoring the Soothsayer's and his wife's premonitions (不祥的预感), Caesar resolves to go to the Senate and is caught at the mercy of the conspirators. Having declared himself the world's only constant man, he is stabbed to death. His friend Brutus's betrayal shocks him profoundly.

'Friends, Romans, countrymen, lend me your ears.'
Following Caesar's death, his friend Mark Antony delivers an eloquent and rousing speech over Caesar's corpse. He deftly turns public opinion against the assassins. The common people drive the conspirators from Rome.

Caesar's great-nephew, Octavius, arrives in Rome and forms the Triumvirate (三人团) with Antony and Lepidus. Antony and Octavius (standing, centre) decide to go to war against Brutus (seated right) and Cassius (seated left).

Brutus (left) berates (痛斥) Cassius for corruptly and dishonourably accepting bribes. He is also distressed by the news of his wife's death. Brutus and Cassius are reconciled but, as they prepare for war, Caesar's ghost appears to Brutus with a warning of defeat.

Events go badly for the conspirators during the battle. Both Cassius and Brutus (the latter pictured here with his slave Strato) choose to commit suicide rather than be captured.

The play ends with Antony's tribute (颂词) to Brutus, who has remained 'the noblest Roman of them all', and hints at the friction between Mark Antony and Octavius that will characterise another of Shakespeare's plays, *Antony and Cleopatra*.

Before the play begins 戏剧背景介绍

The origins of the Roman Republic

When the **Roman Senate** (罗马元老院) granted Julius Caesar the title of dictator (独裁官) of Rome for life, it effectively signalled the end of the **Roman Republic** that had governed the city and its territories for more than four hundred years.

The Republic had been founded when the inhabitants of Rome drove out the tyrannical **Tarquin** (塔尔昆) kings and set up their own form of government, in which they could elect their own leaders rather than being ruled by hereditary (世袭) kings.

The Republican government

At first, control of the Republic was entirely in the hands of the **patricians** (贵族), Rome's aristocratic class. Only patricians could be elected members of the Senate, or parliament, and only patricians could be chosen as heads of state, or **consuls** (执政官). To prevent any one man obtaining too much power, there were always two consuls elected at any one time, who could rule for one year only. Consuls were primarily military commanders who would lead Rome's armies in war. In times of great emergency a dictator (supreme commander) was appointed in place of the consuls, but for a period of no more than six months.

In time the **plebeians** (平民), the ordinary citizens of Rome, campaigned for and achieved the right to have their say in how they were to be ruled. They were allowed to elect two **tribunes** (护民官) to represent them in government and protect their interests. Eventually the plebeians gained their own assembly, and the right to propose laws and to require one of the two consuls to be chosen from their own class. But despite these concessions, the patricians still retained overall control of government, while the plebeians – who were far greater in number than the patricians – remained poor, discontented and ready to riot.

The size of the Roman world

As the centuries passed, the Roman Republic secured control of the rest of Italy, then Greece, Spain and North Africa, until it had conquered most of the countries surrounding the Mediterranean Sea.

But as Rome's wealth increased, so the quality of its ruling classes declined. The patrician class became more interested in luxurious living than in public service, and power gradually gravitated into the hands of a few men who could use their wealth and private armies to control the power of the Roman Senate and eliminate their political enemies.

Two such great rivals were Caesar and **Pompey**. Although for a while it suited the two men to form an uneasy political alliance, it was inevitable that they would eventually come to blows. In the bitter civil war that followed, Pompey was defeated and fled to Egypt, where he was murdered. In 48 BC, the Senate appointed Caesar as 'dictator' (i.e. made him head of government) and granted him many other powers and honours. There was even a statue of him placed in one of the Roman temples with the inscription 'To the Unconquerable God'. Caesar was now sole ruler of Rome and its territory. He was king in all but name.

Caesar was, however, surprisingly merciful to most of his defeated Roman opponents (including Brutus and Cassius) and gave a number of them responsible positions in his new regime. But the great unanswered question was how he would use his supreme power over the government of the Republic. Would he use it to reform and strengthen the old Republican system, which had so clearly failed to maintain control of Rome's vast territory? Or did he intend to establish a new monarchy with himself as the first king or emperor?

Julius Caesar
儒略·恺撒

Some of the patricians were genuinely fearful that Caesar secretly intended to return Rome to monarchical rule. One such was **Marcus Brutus**, once a supporter of Pompey but now a close friend of Caesar. Brutus was a committed Republican and boasted a distinguished ancestor who had helped expel the **Tarquin kings** and establish the original Republic. Some patricians became so desperate that in 44 BC they conspired to assassinate Caesar before he could make himself king. One of the leaders of this conspiracy was **Caius Cassius**, another former supporter of Pompey in the recent civil war.

This is the point at which Shakespeare begins his story.

◆ Working in a small group, research each of the elements of the above summary that appear in bold font. Prepare a mini-presentation on the context of the play, including additional details and images to accompany the text. Share this with your class.

Julius Caesar and the Elizabethans

The figure of Julius Caesar held a particular fascination for the Elizabethans (伊丽莎白一世时期的英国人，尤指文人). Some admired his military skill, strong leadership and generous treatment of former enemies. Others condemned him for his ruthlessness, for his weakening of the powers of the Senate and above all for his ambition.

Some Elizabethans may also have felt that the play reflected contemporary anxieties about what England might become following the death of the childless Elizabeth. They were divided in their attitude to the conspirators. If some felt Caesar's murder was justified to help preserve the Republic, others believed it to be a wicked act, or at the very least a major political misjudgement resulting in the very thing the conspirators were trying to prevent: the collapse of Rome's Republican governmental system. Brutus in particular enjoyed a double reputation. He was seen as an honest man of principle and a champion of liberty. Yet by joining the conspiracy he became also the man who treacherously murdered his friend and benefactor (恩人，赞助人).

Whatever the Elizabethans may or may not have thought of Julius Caesar and the rights or wrongs of his assassination, less than fifty years after Shakespeare wrote his play the English people executed their king and set up their own Republican form of government under Oliver Cromwell.

▼ The Roman Republic c. 44 BC

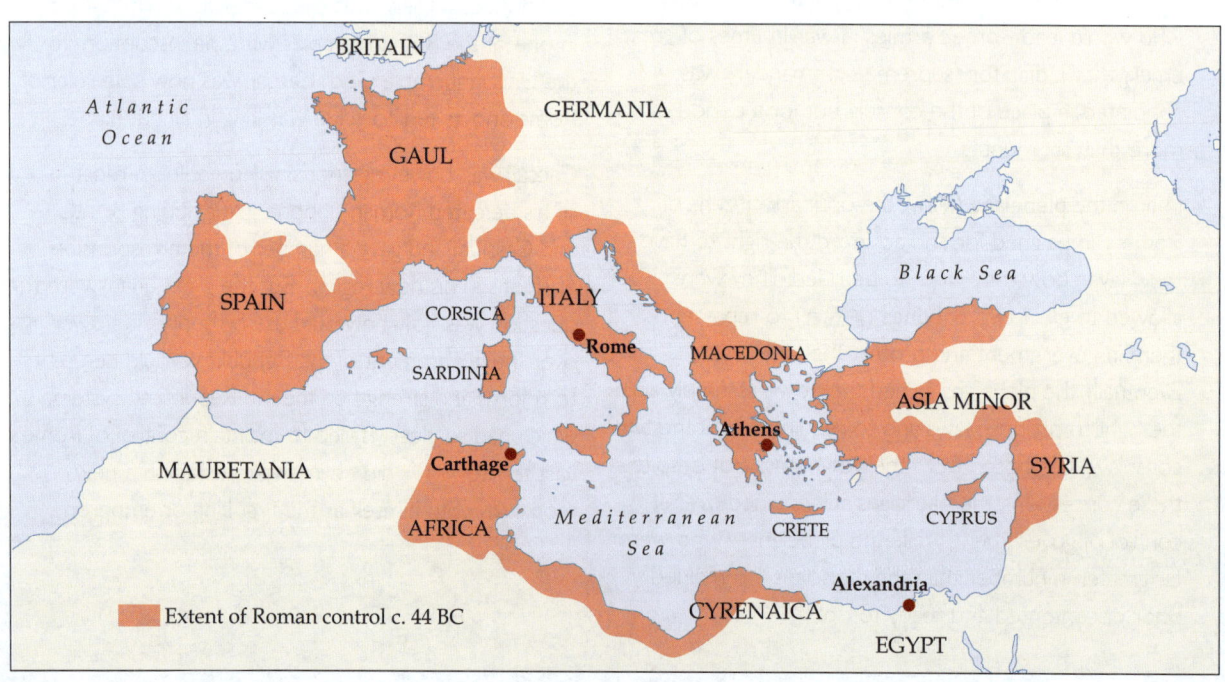

Before the play begins

Pompey and the Senate! Caesar and the people!

(in groups A and B of four or five each)

There has been a terrible civil war. Pompey and Caesar – heroes always named in one breath – have fought each other for supreme power in Rome, and Caesar has won.

All of you are Romans after the war. Group A still supports Pompey's views, believing in a more democratic type of government, through the elected assembly of the Senate. Group B supports Caesar, upholding the direct personal rule of a dictator.

- Use the opinions and details on the relevant scroll on the right to make a list of the benefits of senatorial (Group A) or one-person (Group B) rule as you see it. Include the views of both patricians and plebeians.
- After making their lists, Groups A and B should choose one person from their group who will speak at Caesar's celebratory 'triumph'. The other group members should help the nominated speaker to prepare a 60-second speech outlining the group's views to the assembled crowd.
- In your group, find and watch clips of political addresses. Suggest how the speaker might build into their own delivery any effective performance techniques that you identify. As the speaker practises the speech, the rest of the group should offer constructive feedback on what is good and what could be improved!
- Make placards, banners, badges and leaflets to distribute, or create other types of publicity material to be used at the triumph. Show clearly where your loyalties lie and either what you want to celebrate about Caesar's success or what you fear might happen under his rule.
- Then stage the triumph, allowing each group the chance to present their arguments. If you can, film it!
- Play the recording back and judge which group made the stronger case.

A: The Pompeyite (庞贝派) point of view

Pompey believed in the Senate. He fought for the Senate, he died for the Senate. One-person rule is dangerous – what's to stop Caesar becoming a tyrant now that the Senate has made him permanent head of government and granted him many special powers? Let's face it, he's even being worshipped like a god now that one of his statues has been erected in the temple. One ruler may serve us well, but what will happen when that person dies? Do we want to return to the days of the monarchy when power was handed on unopposed and we had no say in who ruled us? That's one of the reasons we killed the last king we had – four hundred years ago!

B: The Caesarite (恺撒派) point of view

People in Rome are poor. Only the rich get votes in the Senate. Yes, the rich look after themselves. But with Caesar, you ask and you get. He listens and then he takes action – and he's richer than the Senate, because he's been off on his conquests again. Yes, it's true that he saw off Pompey, but look how decent he's been in forgiving the other rebels like Brutus and Cassius. They've now taken up positions of responsibility in his government, so we can trust him to put the good of the people first. Let him rule! Let him be a dictator! We need a strong man after the wars. But we'll never let him be king, of course.

JULIUS CAESAR
儒略·恺撒

Caesar's triumph

Study this photograph from a modern production of *Julius Caesar*. How effective do you think it is in suggesting the kind of admiration that Caesar was held in by some of his public? Why?

List of characters 人物表

Caesar and his supporters 恺撒和他的支持者

JULIUS CAESAR /ˈdʒuːliəs ˈsiːzə(r)/ (儒略·恺撒)
CALPURNIA /kælˈpɜːniə/ (卡尔珀妮娅) Caesar's wife
MARK ANTONY /mɑː(r)k ˈantənəɪ/ (马克·安东尼) ⎫
OCTAVIUS CAESAR /ɒkˈteɪviəs ˈsiːzə(r)/ (屋大维·恺撒) ⎬ The ruling Triumvirate after Caesar's death
LEPIDUS /ˈlepɪdəs/ (雷丕德) ⎭

The conspirators against Caesar 谋杀恺撒的人

Conspirators 谋杀团伙成员

BRUTUS /ˈbruːtəs/ (布鲁图)　CASCA /ˈkaskə/ (喀斯柯)　CINNA /ˈsɪnə/ (希纳)
METELLUS CIMBER /məˈteləs ˈsɪmbə(r)/ (莫泰勒·欣博)　CAIUS CASSIUS /ˈkəɪəs ˈkasiəs/ (凯乌·卡休)
DECIUS BRUTUS /ˈdesiəs ˈbruːtəs/ (德休·布鲁图)　TREBONIUS /treˈboːniəs/ (绰包纽)
CAIUS LIGARIUS /ˈkəɪəs lɪˈgariəs/ (凯乌·理噶瑞欧)

Family and followers 他们的家属及手下

PORTIA /ˈpɔː(r)siə/ (鲍霞) Brutus's wife
LUCIUS /ˈluːʃəs/ (卢休) Brutus's boy servant
CLAUDIO /ˈklɔːdiːoː/ (克劳丢) ⎫　　　　　　　　　　　　　　LABEO* /ˈlabɪoː/ (拉比欧) ⎫
FLAVIUS* /ˈflaviəs/ (伏拉维欧) ⎬ Personal followers　　　 CLITUS /ˈklɪtəs/ (克里忒) ⎬
STRATO /ˈstratoː/ (斯特拉托) ⎭ of Brutus　　　　　　　　　DARDANIUS /dɑː(r)ˈdeɪniəs/ (达德纽) ⎭
VARRUS /ˈvarəs/ (瓦若)
PINDARUS /ˈpɪndərəs/ (品德若) Cassius's slave
LUCILIUS /luˈsɪliəs/ (卢希琉) ⎫　　　　　　　　　　　　　TITINIUS /tɪˈtɪniəs/ (提提纽) ⎫
MESSALA /məˈsɑːlə/ (莫撒勒) ⎬ Officers of Brutus　　　　YOUNG CATO /ˈkeɪtoː/ (小加图) ⎬
VOLUMNIUS /vəˈlʌmniəs/ (沃拉穆纽) ⎭ and Cassius　　　　STATILIUS* /stəˈtɪliəs/ (斯特提琉) ⎭

Other Romans 其他罗马人

CICERO /ˈsɪsəroː/ (西塞罗)　PUBLIUS CIMBER /ˈpʌbliəs ˈsɪmbə/ (帕布琉·欣博) ⎫
POPILLIUS LENA /pəˈpɪliəs ˈliːnə/ (珀丕琉·李讷)　OTHER SENATORS* (其他参议员) ⎬ Senators
⎭
FLAVIUS /ˈflaviəs/ (伏拉维欧) ⎫ Tribunes critical
MURELLUS /məˈrʌləs/ (莫拉勒) ⎬ of Caesar
SOOTHSAYER (预言家) ⎫ Who try to warn
ARTEMIDORUS /ɑː(r)ˌtemɪˈdɔːrəs/ (阿泰米道若) ⎬ Caesar
SERVANTS TO CAESAR, ANTONY AND OCTAVIUS (恺撒、安东尼和屋大维的仆人们)
CINNA THE POET (诗人希纳)　　　　　　　　A CYNIC POET (一位愤世嫉俗的诗人)
1ST, 2ND, 3RD, 4TH PLEBEIANS (平民甲、乙、丙、丁)　CARPENTER (木匠)
COBBLER (鞋匠)　　　　　　　　　　　　　　MESSENGER (报信儿的)
1ST, 2ND, 3RD SOLDIERS (兵丁甲、乙、丙)　　OTHER PLEBEIANS* (其他平民)

*non-speaking parts

Two Tribunes, Flavius and Murellus, ask some tradespeople why they are taking the day off. A Cobbler gives riddling replies.
剧情简介：两位护民官伏拉维欧和莫拉勒问店主们为何歇业。一个鞋匠打哑谜似的回话。

1 Tribunes versus common people (in fours)

The opening of the play immediately establishes a sense of conflict. The Tribunes Flavius and Murellus (officials of the Roman government) are loyal to the defeated Pompey. They are angry that the common people celebrate Caesar's triumph in carnival (狂欢节) mood. The Cobbler (which can also mean a person who plays with words) responds to the Tribunes' wrath with witty wordplay at their expense.

- Take the parts of Flavius, Murellus, the Cobbler and the Carpenter, and read lines 1–30 together. Experiment with different ways of bringing out the Tribunes' disapproval and the common people's celebration.

▼ Which line do you think is being spoken in the photograph below?

1	mechanical	手艺人
2	rule = ruler	（尺子）
3	apparel	衣裳
4	in respect of	和……相比
5	cobbler	鞋匠（又指笨手笨脚的人）
6	with a safe conscience	对得起自己的良心
7	soles	鞋底（sole与soul "灵魂"谐音双关）
8	naughty knave	混账的无赖
9	be not out	别撒气
10	if you be out	您要是撒气了
11	mend you	修理您
12	saucy	不知天高地厚

Stagecraft 导演技巧

Setting the scene

Shakespeare does not give any overt stage directions. The script has to be searched for references to the time of day, the location and the weather, for example, and then the director has to decide how to stage the play. They could choose to highlight in the staging a particular idea that runs throughout the play; to make the location specific, even familiar to their audience; or to go for a more neutral setting. Some directors choose to open this play with a powerful statement about the triumph of Caesar over Pompey.

- In groups, discuss your reactions to the staging shown in the picture above.
- Begin a Director's Journal to record your ideas about the staging of *Julius Caesar*, as if you were a director. Make a note in the journal outlining your discussion. Add any of your own ideas for staging afterwards.

Julius Caesar

Act 1 Scene 1
Rome   A street

Enter FLAVIUS, MURELLUS, *and certain* COMMONERS *over the stage*

FLAVIUS	Hence! Home, you idle creatures, get you home!
	Is this a holiday? What, know you not,
	Being mechanical[1], you ought not walk
	Upon a labouring day without the sign
	Of your profession? Speak, what trade art thou? 5
CARPENTER	Why, sir, a carpenter.
MURELLUS	Where is thy leather apron and thy rule[2]?
	What dost thou with thy best apparel[3] on?
	You, sir, what trade are you?
COBBLER	Truly, sir, in respect of[4] a fine workman, I am but, as you would 10
	say, a cobbler[5].
MURELLUS	But what trade art thou? Answer me directly.
COBBLER	A trade, sir, that I hope I may use with a safe conscience[6], which
	is indeed, sir, a mender of bad soles[7].
FLAVIUS	What trade, thou knave? Thou naughty knave[8], what trade? 15
COBBLER	Nay, I beseech you, sir, be not out[9] with me; yet if you be out[10], sir,
	I can mend you[11].
MURELLUS	What mean'st thou by that? Mend me, thou saucy[12] fellow?
COBBLER	Why, sir, cobble you.
FLAVIUS	Thou art a cobbler, art thou? 20

The tradespeople celebrate Caesar's triumph over Pompey. The Tribunes accuse them of ingratitude to Pompey, who was once the people's favourite.

 剧情简介：众店主要庆祝恺撒打败了庞贝。庞贝曾很受民众拥戴，因此两位护民官怒斥他们忘恩负义。

Language in the play 剧中语言

Rhetorical questions (in groups of four or five)

Murellus's lines 31–50 make much use of **rhetorical questions** (questions that do not need an answer). The questions are intended to influence the thoughts of the listeners and make them reflect on their actions.

a Share out the lines, making sure everyone has at least one rhetorical question. Practise speaking the lines, deciding where to speak harshly and where to speak softly. Surround another group and deliver the lines. Then they do the same to your group. Afterwards, talk together about the effect the lines have on the listeners.

b As you read on, keep a note of how many times rhetorical questions are used as a device to persuade a listening audience and what the effect of these questions might be.

1 Stop the party! (in large groups)

a Murellus and Flavius want to manipulate the common people and one way in which they do this is by using vivid language. They paint pictures with their words. In your group, read through Murellus's description of the crowd's reaction to Pompey (lines 36–46). Create a **tableau** (亮相，舞台造型[演员全都静止不动]) (frozen picture) of this moment. Then discuss why Murellus chose to remind them of these previous celebrations.

b Ordinary Romans were deeply superstitious (迷信). Every action or decision was taken after consultation with the augurers (古罗马的占卜师), who performed rites and sacrifices to find out the will of the gods (see p. 171). Read the Tribunes' differing accounts of what the crowd should do next in lines 52–4 and 56–9. Decide how the Tribunes are playing on the crowd's superstition in these lines and swap your ideas with another group.

2 How do the common people react? (in pairs)

The common people exit at line 59 – but Shakespeare gives no clue as to their mood. Are they subdued, resentful, angry or something else?

- Improvise (即兴表演) a conversation or write an exchange of text messages between two of the crowd after this brush with the furious Tribunes.

1 awl 锥子
2 recover 拾掇好
3 proper 英俊
4 neat's leather 牛皮
5 gone 走路
6 make holiday 放假
7 triumph （公元前45年3月，恺撒在西班牙击败庞贝的两个儿子，同年10月举行胜利大游行）
8 tributaries 纳贡的战俘
9 Pompey 罗马大将庞贝
10 oft = often
11 battlements 垛墙
12 Tiber 台伯河（流经罗马，罗马人眼中的圣河）
13 replication 回声
14 concave shores 凹陷的河岸
15 attire 衣裳
16 cull out a holiday 挑出一天作节日
17 blood 亲骨肉（恺撒打败了庞贝的两个儿子）
18 intermit 阻止
19 needs must 必将
20 light on 降临
21 Do … all （河水）漫上河岸的最高处

JULIUS CAESAR ACT 1 SCENE 1
儒略·恺撒

COBBLER   Truly, sir, all that I live by is with the awl[1]. I meddle with no tradesman's matters, nor women's matters; but withal I am indeed, sir, a surgeon to old shoes: when they are in great danger I recover[2] them. As proper[3] men as ever trod upon neat's leather[4] have gone[5] upon my handiwork.   25

FLAVIUS   But wherefore art not in thy shop today?
Why dost thou lead these men about the streets?

COBBLER   Truly, sir, to wear out their shoes, to get myself into more work. But indeed, sir, we make holiday[6] to see Caesar and to rejoice in his triumph[7].   30

MURELLUS   Wherefore rejoice? What conquest brings he home?
What tributaries[8] follow him to Rome
To grace in captive bonds his chariot wheels?
You blocks, you stones, you worse than senseless things!
O you hard hearts, you cruel men of Rome,   35
Knew you not Pompey[9]? Many a time and oft[10]
Have you climbed up to walls and battlements[11],
To towers and windows, yea, to chimney tops,
Your infants in your arms, and there have sat
The livelong day, with patient expectation,   40
To see great Pompey pass the streets of Rome.
And when you saw his chariot but appear
Have you not made an universal shout,
That Tiber[12] trembled underneath her banks
To hear the replication[13] of your sounds   45
Made in her concave shores[14]?
And do you now put on your best attire[15]?
And do you now cull out a holiday[16]?
And do you now strew flowers in his way,
That comes in triumph over Pompey's blood[17]?   50
Be gone!
Run to your houses, fall upon your knees,
Pray to the gods to intermit[18] the plague
That needs must[19] light on[20] this ingratitude.

FLAVIUS   Go, go, good countrymen, and for this fault   55
Assemble all the poor men of your sort,
Draw them to Tiber banks, and weep your tears
Into the channel till the lowest stream
Do kiss the most exalted shores of all[21].

Exeunt all the Commoners

The Tribunes leave, intending to stop further celebration. Caesar comes to the Lupercal races, in which Antony is to run. He orders Antony to touch Calpurnia in the race to cure her infertility.

剧情简介：两位护民官离开，打算去别处阻挠庆祝活动。安东尼参加牧神节上的赛跑活动，恺撒来到现场，嘱咐他赛程中打一下卡尔珀妮娅，帮助她摆脱不孕。

1 Caesar and the crowd – high and low (in threes)

Caesar does not appear in Scene 1. But the loyal Pompeyite Flavius makes clear in lines 67–8 that he plans to take all the decorations off Caesar's statues. He is also anxious that Caesar should not be allowed to 'soar above the view of men / And keep us all in servile fearfulness'. This bird image emphasises the sense of superiority that Flavius fears in Caesar.

- In your groups, make a list of all the words used by the Tribunes in this first scene to describe the 'lowness' of the common people.
- Then decide whether the Cobbler seems aptly described by these terms. In your view, is he likely to feel 'servile fearfulness'?

1	basest metal	贱胚子（metal 与mettle "品质"谐音；铅为贱金属，惰性大但易锻造）
2	tongue-tied	哑口无言
3	Capitol	朱庇特神庙，议会山（见172页）
4	Disrobe the images	扯下雕像上的彩饰
5	ceremonies	装饰
6	feast of Lupercal	牧神节（古罗马每年2月15日过牧神节；见172页）
7	trophies	战利品
8	vulgar	平民，老百姓
9	fly an ordinary pitch	飞不高
10	servile fearfulness	奴婢般的畏惧
11	barren	不孕
12	Stand … curse	（古罗马人相信，不孕妇女在牧神节上被赛跑者用鞭子抽打到就能生育了）

Stagecraft 导演技巧

Caesar's triumphal progress (in groups of six to eight)

Plan how Caesar's entrance and exit (lines 1–24) can be staged.

- How will you manage the Tribunes' exit at the end of the previous scene (to follow Caesar back on stage shortly afterwards)?
- How will you enact the stage direction at the start of this scene?
- What is the behaviour of the 'great crowd'?
- How do the different characters speak to, and about, Caesar?
- How does Caesar address his wife and how sensitive is he about her childlessness?
- What sort of person is the Soothsayer?
- How will you use music in the scene? (Consider Caesar's remark at line 16 and the *Sennet* stage direction at line 24.)

Make your choices, and then present your version of lines 1–24.

▼ Comment on the atmosphere created by the entrance of Caesar in this production.

	See where their basest metal[1] be not moved:	60
	They vanish tongue-tied[2] in their guiltiness.	
	Go you down that way towards the Capitol[3],	
	This way will I. Disrobe the images[4]	
	If you do find them decked with ceremonies[5].	
MURELLUS	May we do so?	65
	You know it is the feast of Lupercal[6].	
FLAVIUS	It is no matter; let no images	
	Be hung with Caesar's trophies[7]. I'll about	
	And drive away the vulgar[8] from the streets;	
	So do you too, where you perceive them thick.	70
	These growing feathers plucked from Caesar's wing	
	Will make him fly an ordinary pitch[9],	
	Who else would soar above the view of men	
	And keep us all in servile fearfulness[10].	

Exeunt

Act 1 Scene 2
Rome   A street

Enter CAESAR, ANTONY *for the course,* CALPURNIA, *Portia, Decius, Cicero,* BRUTUS, CASSIUS, CASCA, *a* SOOTHSAYER, [*a great crowd following*]; *after them Murellus and Flavius*

CAESAR	Calpurnia.	
CASCA	Peace ho, Caesar speaks.	
CAESAR	Calpurnia.	
CALPURNIA	Here, my lord.	
CAESAR	Stand you directly in Antonio's way	
	When he doth run his course. Antonio.	
ANTONY	Caesar, my lord.	5
CAESAR	Forget not in your speed, Antonio,	
	To touch Calpurnia, for our elders say	
	The barren[11], touchèd in this holy chase,	
	Shake off their sterile curse[12].	
ANTONY	I shall remember:	
	When Caesar says, 'Do this', it is performed.	10

Caesar is warned to beware the Ides of March. He dismisses the warning, then leaves. Cassius remains with Brutus and accuses him of being unfriendly, but Brutus says he is troubled by private problems.

 剧情简介：有人提醒恺撒3月15日要小心，他无视此人提醒，随后离去。卡休留下，抱怨布鲁图对他态度冷淡，而布鲁图解释说自己正因私事苦恼不已。

1 A break in the progress of Caesar (in small groups)

Shakespeare wrote most of his plays in **blank verse** (无韵诗，素体诗) – lines of ten syllables (see p. 188). Though shared between the Soothsayer and Caesar, line 18 is a regular blank verse line of ten syllables. Count them, and then count the syllables of other lines chosen at random.

Line 23 has only six syllables. These breaks often occur at moments of crucial importance. Shakespeare's actor must pause for four syllables (two 'beats') to think, to listen or to take action. How will Caesar, all eyes on him, play this moment of silence? The Ides, the fifteenth day of the month, are during the full moon, an unlucky time. No Roman will do business under the waning moon (月亏) that follows. Today is the Ides of February, so the Ides of March are a month away.

- From 'What man', play lines 18–24, taking it in turns to be Caesar. Imagine what Caesar would be thinking at this moment.
- When you come to the pause at line 23, hold a thought of Caesar's in your head that the others in your group must try to guess.

1 press 人群
2 *Ides of March* 3月15日
3 throng 人群
4 *Sennet* 奏木管号（演员上下场的伴奏曲）
5 gamesome 爱好运动
6 hinder 妨碍
7 was wont 以往时常
8 You ... Over 你跟……也太生分了
9 deceived 误会
10 If ... myself 我表情冷淡，是因为心里的苦衷不愿人知啊
11 Vexèd ... difference 近来我由于一些矛盾心情而烦恼不已
12 soil 坏影响
13 construe 解读，理解
14 the shows of love 友爱的表示

Themes 主题分析

Public versus private (in pairs)

With Caesar's exit, the focus shifts to Cassius and Brutus. One of the many themes explored throughout this play is the tension between what happens in public and what happens in private. Shakespeare often closely juxtaposes (并置) these two spheres of life. Caesar is publicly warned amongst 'a great crowd' in the first part of this scene. As quickly as Caesar dismisses the Soothsayer and moves on, the crowd disperses and the scene becomes more intimate. Cassius has noticed a cooling in his friendship with Brutus, and Brutus confesses that he is 'with himself at war'. Again, Shakespeare uses shortened lines (26 and 27) to allow the two men to pause reflectively at the start of their discussion.

- Take parts and read lines 25–47.
- Work together to put these lines into modern English and then write down this dialogue. Take care to use a tone and vocabulary that reflect their close friendship. Aim to tease out the meaning of Brutus's powerful phrase: 'with himself at war'.
- Read through this modern dialogue together and then share it with other pairs.

CAESAR	Set on, and leave no ceremony out.	
SOOTHSAYER	Caesar!	
CAESAR	Ha? Who calls?	
CASCA	Bid every noise be still – peace yet again!	
CAESAR	Who is it in the press[1] that calls on me?	15
	I hear a tongue shriller than all the music	
	Cry 'Caesar!' Speak, Caesar is turned to hear.	
SOOTHSAYER	Beware the Ides of March[2].	
CAESAR	What man is that?	
BRUTUS	A soothsayer bids you beware the Ides of March.	
CAESAR	Set him before me, let me see his face.	20
CASSIUS	Fellow, come from the throng[3], look upon Caesar.	
CAESAR	What say'st thou to me now? Speak once again.	
SOOTHSAYER	Beware the Ides of March.	
CAESAR	He is a dreamer, let us leave him. Pass.	

Sennet[4]. Exeunt [all but] Brutus and Cassius

CASSIUS	Will you go see the order of the course?	25
BRUTUS	Not I.	
CASSIUS	I pray you, do.	
BRUTUS	I am not gamesome[5]: I do lack some part	
	Of that quick spirit that is in Antony.	
	Let me not hinder[6], Cassius, your desires;	30
	I'll leave you.	
CASSIUS	Brutus, I do observe you now of late:	
	I have not from your eyes that gentleness	
	And show of love as I was wont[7] to have.	
	You bear too stubborn and too strange a hand	35
	Over[8] your friend that loves you.	
BRUTUS	Cassius,	
	Be not deceived[9]. If I have veiled my look	
	I turn the trouble of my countenance	
	Merely upon myself[10]. Vexèd I am	
	Of late with passions of some difference[11],	40
	Conceptions only proper to myself,	
	Which give some soil[12], perhaps, to my behaviours.	
	But let not therefore my good friends be grieved	
	(Among which number, Cassius, be you one)	
	Nor construe[13] any further my neglect	45
	Than that poor Brutus, with himself at war,	
	Forgets the shows of love[14] to other men.	

Cassius claims to help Brutus understand himself and the state of Rome. Off stage the crowd shouts. Brutus fears they want Caesar crowned.

剧情简介：卡休要帮布鲁图认识自我，认清罗马的局势。台下传来民众的欢呼声。布鲁图担心百姓要拥立恺撒为帝。

Characters 人物分析

Brutus and Cassius (in pairs)

The relationship between these two men is crucial to the development of the play.

- Cassius is at pains to point out how much he values Brutus. One of you reads through Cassius's speeches and emphasises each word in praise of Brutus. The other writes these words down. You could start a Character file at this point for all your notes relating to the characters.
- Brutus is clearly suspicious of Cassius. Look at line 63. Swap over and the other person reads the same speeches but emphasises any word that might make Brutus wary of Cassius's motives. These words should be written down, too.
- Reflect upon the speeches and your lists and decide whether Brutus is right to question Cassius's motives at this point.

1 By means whereof 因为这个误会
2 cogitations 想法
3 just 不错，对的
4 lamented 可惜
5 shadow 影像
6 respect 名望
7 yoke 枷锁
8 had his eyes 睁眼看到
9 glass 镜子
10 jealous on 怀疑
11 a common laughter 众人嘴里的笑话
12 stale 重复说，使……不再新鲜
13 fawn on 奉承，讨好
14 scandal 诽谤
15 profess myself 表真心
16 the rout 乌七八糟的人
17 Flourish 喇叭奏花腔
18 impart 告知

Stagecraft 导演技巧

A big moment – off stage

Read through lines 78–84. Why do you think Shakespeare decided to have this moment take place off stage so the audience would hear it but not see it? It would, after all, make a great public spectacle.

▶ Comment on the relationship between Brutus and Cassius (with the sword) at this moment.

Julius Caesar Act 1 Scene 2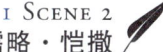
儒略・恺撒

CASSIUS	Then, Brutus, I have much mistook your passion,	
	By means whereof¹ this breast of mine hath buried	
	Thoughts of great value, worthy cogitations².	50
	Tell me, good Brutus, can you see your face?	
BRUTUS	No, Cassius, for the eye sees not itself	
	But by reflection, by some other things.	
CASSIUS	'Tis just³,	
	And it is very much lamented⁴, Brutus,	55
	That you have no such mirrors as will turn	
	Your hidden worthiness into your eye	
	That you might see your shadow⁵. I have heard	
	Where many of the best respect⁶ in Rome	
	(Except immortal Caesar), speaking of Brutus	60
	And groaning underneath this age's yoke⁷,	
	Have wished that noble Brutus had his eyes⁸.	
BRUTUS	Into what dangers would you lead me, Cassius,	
	That you would have me seek into myself	
	For that which is not in me?	65
CASSIUS	Therefore, good Brutus, be prepared to hear.	
	And since you know you cannot see yourself	
	So well as by reflection, I, your glass⁹,	
	Will modestly discover to yourself	
	That of yourself which you yet know not of.	70
	And be not jealous on¹⁰ me, gentle Brutus,	
	Were I a common laughter¹¹, or did use	
	To stale¹² with ordinary oaths my love	
	To every new protester. If you know	
	That I do fawn on¹³ men and hug them hard	75
	And after scandal¹⁴ them, or if you know	
	That I profess myself¹⁵ in banqueting	
	To all the rout¹⁶, then hold me dangerous.	

Flourish¹⁷ and shout

BRUTUS	What means this shouting? I do fear the people	
	Choose Caesar for their king.	
CASSIUS	Ay, do you fear it?	80
	Then must I think you would not have it so.	
BRUTUS	I would not, Cassius, yet I love him well.	
	But wherefore do you hold me here so long?	
	What is it that you would impart¹⁸ to me?	

Brutus demands that Cassius come to the point. Cassius proclaims that no man of honour should submit to Caesar. He is a mortal but behaves as if he were a god.

 剧情简介： 布鲁图让卡休有话直说。卡休表示，高贵之人决不能向恺撒屈服。恺撒肉体凡胎却自命天神。

Characters 人物分析

Brutus (in pairs)

Cassius has talked a great deal and Brutus is keen for him to come to the point. Briefly he outlines his principles in lines 85–9. Take it in turns to read through the lines until they are familiar. Decide where you think the emphasis should be placed. Then consider the lines from two perspectives:

- Why do you think Shakespeare wrote these lines? Discuss to what extent this seems like a character manifesto (explanation) and whether or not it might have been more effective to demonstrate these qualities in Brutus through his actions.
- Why do you think Brutus says these lines? After all, we know that Cassius knows him well. What effect do you think Brutus wants his words to have on Cassius?

Language in the play 剧中语言

What difference does rhetoric make? (in fours)

The art of **rhetoric** (see pp. 185–6) was taught in schools in Rome. This involved learning methods and techniques to make language more memorable, often in order to be more persuasive or credible when making a speech. Rhetoric should in a sense be 'invisible', as the speaker wants the effect of the speech to be significant without the methods being evident.

In his speech opposite, Cassius aims to reveal Caesar's human frailty to Brutus, but not in an obvious way. In order to gauge (测量，估计) how the rhetoric works, try the following activity:

- One person prepares a reading of Cassius's speech from line 66. Three others prepare to be the silent Brutus.
- Once the preparation is done, Cassius delivers his speech. Everyone is in character, and acts out their responses.
- Do the same again, but this time, whenever one of the Brutuses thinks Cassius is being particularly persuasive, they should raise their hand. The speech stops and Brutus explains why the word, phrase or sentence has that effect. Don't worry about technical terms at this point, just try to get a feel for the effect of the language. Cassius can comment on his own language, too, but only after Brutus has had his say.

1 aught = anything
2 indifferently 不为所动
3 speed 庇佑
4 outward favour 外在，外貌
5 as lief 宁可
6 chafing with 拍击
7 Accoutred 穿着衣服
8 buffet 划（水）
9 lusty sinews 强劲的肌腱（体力）
10 stemming it 劈波斩浪
11 hearts of controversy 昂扬的斗志
12 ere = before
13 Aeneas 埃涅阿斯（特洛伊王子，传说为罗马的建立者）
14 Anchises 安喀西斯（埃涅阿斯的父亲）
15 coward … fly 怯懦的嘴唇失去了血色

	If it be aught[1] toward the general good,	85
	Set honour in one eye and death i'th'other	
	And I will look on both indifferently[2].	
	For let the gods so speed[3] me as I love	
	The name of honour more than I fear death.	
CASSIUS	I know that virtue to be in you, Brutus,	90
	As well as I do know your outward favour[4].	
	Well, honour is the subject of my story:	
	I cannot tell what you and other men	
	Think of this life, but for my single self	
	I had as lief[5] not be as live to be	95
	In awe of such a thing as I myself.	
	I was born free as Caesar, so were you;	
	We both have fed as well, and we can both	
	Endure the winter's cold as well as he.	
	For once, upon a raw and gusty day,	100
	The troubled Tiber chafing with[6] her shores,	
	Caesar said to me, 'Dar'st thou, Cassius, now	
	Leap in with me into this angry flood	
	And swim to yonder point?' Upon the word,	
	Accoutred[7] as I was, I plungèd in	105
	And bade him follow; so indeed he did.	
	The torrent roared, and we did buffet[8] it	
	With lusty sinews[9], throwing it aside	
	And stemming it[10] with hearts of controversy[11].	
	But ere[12] we could arrive the point proposed,	110
	Caesar cried, 'Help me, Cassius, or I sink!'	
	Ay, as Aeneas[13], our great ancestor,	
	Did from the flames of Troy upon his shoulder	
	The old Anchises[14] bear, so from the waves of Tiber	
	Did I the tired Caesar. And this man	115
	Is now become a god, and Cassius is	
	A wretched creature and must bend his body	
	If Caesar carelessly but nod on him.	
	He had a fever when he was in Spain,	
	And when the fit was on him I did mark	120
	How he did shake. 'Tis true, this god did shake,	
	His coward lips did from their colour fly[15],	

Brutus thinks the offstage shouts mean honours for Caesar. Cassius mocks Caesar's greatness and tries to spur Brutus to action by reminding him that his qualities rank equally with Caesar's.
剧情简介：听到台下欢呼声的布鲁图心想一定是恺撒赢得了荣誉。卡休嘲讽恺撒的伟大，并说布鲁图样样都不比恺撒差，试图怂恿他行动起来。

Language in the play 剧中语言
Rhetoric continues – take the speech apart (in pairs)

If Cassius's last speech has been a rhetorical success, he will have made Brutus question Caesar's qualities and ambitions. In this speech he seeks to build on that.

a Read through the speech (lines 135–61) together and decide what Cassius's purpose is.

b Pick out the rhetorical techniques he uses to make his point. It may be helpful to make a copy of the speech on a large piece of paper so that you can identify the different techniques and then annotate the text. Look out for the following and highlight them on your copy of the speech:

- **Rhetorical questions.** Remember, these are questions that do not require an answer. Listeners are assumed to answer them themselves, reaching the conclusion the speaker wants them to reach.
- **Powerful imagery: similes** (明喻) or **metaphors** (隐喻) (see p. 184), which create a persuasive picture or comparison in the mind of the listener.
- **Repetition** of words or phrases for emphasis (see p. 187). For example, how many times and where do the words 'man' or 'men' appear in this speech? Why?
- **Antithesis** (对偶) – this is the opposition of words or phrases to each other (see p. 187). This technique tends to highlight contrast between one thing or person and another.
- **Exclamations**: an outburst of emotion. They are usually more planned than they appear.

c Afterwards, annotate the speech in any other ways you find helpful to bring out its persuasive qualities.

1 bend 一瞥
2 lustre 神采
3 So get the start of 这么脱颖而出
4 bear the palm 享桂冠
5 heaped on 累加给
6 Colossus 阿波罗雕像，巨型雕像
7 stars 命数
8 underlings 人下人
9 become the mouth 顺口
10 conjure 招魂
11 start 让……现形
12 great flood 神话传说中的大洪水
13 wide … man 宽阔的大路只容得下一个人
14 a Brutus once （指Lucius Junius Brutus，他建立了罗马共和国）
15 brooked 容忍

Stagecraft 导演技巧

Except for his apprehensive response to the offstage shouts for Caesar, Brutus says nothing during Cassius's long speech.

- In your Director's Journal, write notes for the actor playing Brutus, indicating how he uses movement and gesture at key points to signal his character's feelings. You may have had practice as the silent Brutus during Cassius's previous speech.

                And that same eye whose bend[1] doth awe the world
                Did lose his lustre[2]. I did hear him groan,
                Ay, and that tongue of his that bade the Romans   125
                Mark him and write his speeches in their books,
                'Alas', it cried, 'give me some drink, Titinius',
                As a sick girl. Ye gods, it doth amaze me
                A man of such a feeble temper should
                So get the start of[3] the majestic world   130
                And bear the palm[4] alone.
                          Shout. Flourish

BRUTUS   Another general shout!
                I do believe that these applauses are
                For some new honours that are heaped on[5] Caesar.

CASSIUS   Why, man, he doth bestride the narrow world   135
                Like a Colossus[6], and we petty men
                Walk under his huge legs and peep about
                To find ourselves dishonourable graves.
                Men at some time are masters of their fates:
                The fault, dear Brutus, is not in our stars[7]   140
                But in ourselves, that we are underlings[8].
                Brutus and Caesar: what should be in that 'Caesar'?
                Why should that name be sounded more than yours?
                Write them together, yours is as fair a name;
                Sound them, it doth become the mouth[9] as well;   145
                Weigh them, it is as heavy; conjure[10] with 'em,
                'Brutus' will start[11] a spirit as soon as 'Caesar'.
                Now in the names of all the gods at once,
                Upon what meat doth this our Caesar feed
                That he is grown so great? Age, thou art shamed!   150
                Rome, thou hast lost the breed of noble bloods!
                When went there by an age since the great flood[12]
                But it was famed with more than with one man?
                When could they say, till now, that talked of Rome,
                That her wide walks encompassed but one man[13]?   155
                Now is it Rome indeed and room enough
                When there is in it but one only man.
                O, you and I have heard our fathers say
                There was a Brutus once[14] that would have brooked[15]
                Th'eternal devil to keep his state in Rome   160
                As easily as a king.

Brutus says he will think about what Cassius has said. Caesar returns, looking angry. He confides to Antony that he is suspicious of Cassius.

剧情简介：布鲁图表示会考虑卡休这番话。恺撒回来后满脸怒容。他悄声告诉安东尼，要提防卡休。

1 Brutus the 'son of Rome'

To a true aristocrat, honour is more important than life, as Brutus has already said at lines 85–9. He reinforces that view at lines 172–5. As a staunch (坚定，忠诚) Republican, he will resist any tyranny that might result from Caesar's becoming king.

- Put the word HONOUR in the middle of a sheet of paper and write a definition of it. Collect around it ideas, quotations and actions drawn from this scene so far. Brutus's honour and that of the other conspirators will be tested as the play progresses. This will be useful preparation for the 'Themes' activity on page 24.

Write about it 写作练习
Caesar's secret police (in pairs)

Imagine that you are Caesar's intelligence agents. You have shadowed Brutus and Cassius through lines 25–177 and bugged their conversation, in order to make a report on them. Examine their words with care and consider how they looked and acted as they spoke the most important parts of their conversation.

- Make your report to Caesar. The report might include: a series of bullet-point notes; a list of words and phrases that are particularly incriminating (证明有罪); a conclusion explaining how dangerous you think they are and why; and a photograph of Brutus and Cassius conspiring.

1	nothing jealous	毫不怀疑
2	aim	猜测
3	recount hereafter	回头再说
4	moved	劝说
5	meet	合适
6	high	重大
7	villager	村夫（非罗马公民）
8	TRAIN	随从
9	chidden train	挨了骂的跟班
10	Cicero	西塞罗（古罗马伟大的演说家，拥护共和政体）
11	ferret	雪貂似的（雪貂眼睛为红色，似发怒）
12	crossed in conference	辩论中斗败
13	Sleek-headed … a-nights	头发油亮，晚上睡得香的人
14	Yond	那边那个
15	well given	生性善良，为人和善

▼ Which line might Caesar (left) be speaking to Antony here?

JULIUS CAESAR ACT 1 SCENE 2
儒略・恺撒

BRUTUS	That you do love me, I am nothing jealous[1];
	What you would work me to, I have some aim[2].
	How I have thought of this, and of these times,
	I shall recount hereafter[3]. For this present, 165
	I would not (so with love I might entreat you)
	Be any further moved[4]. What you have said
	I will consider; what you have to say
	I will with patience hear and find a time
	Both meet[5] to hear and answer such high[6] things. 170
	Till then, my noble friend, chew upon this:
	Brutus had rather be a villager[7]
	Than to repute himself a son of Rome
	Under these hard conditions as this time
	Is like to lay upon us. 175
CASSIUS	I am glad that my weak words
	Have struck but thus much show of fire from Brutus.

Enter CAESAR *and his* TRAIN[8]

BRUTUS	The games are done and Caesar is returning.
CASSIUS	As they pass by, pluck Casca by the sleeve
	And he will (after his sour fashion) tell you 180
	What hath proceeded worthy note today.
BRUTUS	I will do so. But look you, Cassius,
	The angry spot doth glow on Caesar's brow
	And all the rest look like a chidden train[9]:
	Calpurnia's cheek is pale, and Cicero[10] 185
	Looks with such ferret[11] and such fiery eyes
	As we have seen him in the Capitol,
	Being crossed in conference[12] by some senators.
CASSIUS	Casca will tell us what the matter is.
CAESAR	Antonio. 190
ANTONY	Caesar.
CAESAR	Let me have men about me that are fat,
	Sleek-headed men and such as sleep a-nights[13].
	Yond[14] Cassius has a lean and hungry look,
	He thinks too much: such men are dangerous. 195
ANTONY	Fear him not, Caesar, he's not dangerous,
	He is a noble Roman and well given[15].

Caesar tells Antony that Cassius is restless, brooding and dangerous. He then departs. Casca confides to Brutus and Cassius that Caesar refused a crown three times at the races.

剧情简介：恺撒告诉安东尼，卡休这个人不安分，思虑重，是个危险人物。然后恺撒离开。喀斯柯对布鲁图和卡休说起恺撒在比赛现场三拒皇冠之事。

1 Caesar in the hot-seat* (in sixes)

a Experiment with different ways of speaking everything Caesar says in lines 192–214. For example, is Caesar utterly confident and self-assured (he insists twice that he does not personally fear Cassius) or is he unsure of himself and secretly fearful of Cassius? Why do you think Shakespeare adds the detail about Caesar's deafness at line 213?

b Put Caesar in the 'hot-seat'. One of the group plays Caesar, and the others surround him to ask questions about Cassius, what happened at the Lupercal games and what it is like to have the top job.

Characters 人物分析
Cassius – 'Would he were fatter!'

a In your Director's Journal, make a list of each description of Cassius in lines 192–214 (for example 'a lean and hungry look'). Note down what these phrases tell us about his character. Have a go at sketching a likeness of him.

b Use your list to identify a modern actor (on film, television or stage) who you think would play Cassius well.

2 The people respond to Caesar (in large groups)

a Quickly read through lines 220–76, in which Casca reports what has happened at the Lupercal games. Concentrate on how the crowd (Casca calls it a 'rabblement' [暴民], line 240) responds to Caesar, especially when Caesar thrice declines the offer of a crown.

b Write down all the words and phrases that Casca uses to describe the common people, and what those words suggest about Casca's attitude to them.

c Stage this reported scene up to line 276 as a mime (哑剧). You may find it easier to choose a director who can allocate parts and who can help to shape the rhythm (节奏) of the scene. There is much scope for involvement from those playing the members of the crowd: they can be getting on with eating, chatting or whatever they feel like at first, before they begin to sense the importance of the event that is unfolding in front of them.

1　spare　瘦削
2　sort　样子
3　at heart's ease　内心安分
4　chanced　发生
5　sad　阴沉
6　put it by　推开
7　fell　爆发，开始
8　thrice　三次
9　marry　可不
10　gentler　更客气
11　manner　情形
12　gentle　好心，高贵

* hot-seat　热座位，一种课堂游戏，玩法是请一位同学坐到讲台上的一把椅子上，其他同学轮番给他/她出难题，哪个问题他/她回答不出就算输。

Julius Caesar Act 1 Scene 2

儒略·恺撒

CAESAR	Would he were fatter! But I fear him not.	
	Yet if my name were liable to fear	
	I do not know the man I should avoid	200
	So soon as that spare[1] Cassius. He reads much,	
	He is a great observer, and he looks	
	Quite through the deeds of men. He loves no plays,	
	As thou dost, Antony, he hears no music;	
	Seldom he smiles, and smiles in such a sort[2]	205
	As if he mocked himself and scorned his spirit	
	That could be moved to smile at any thing.	
	Such men as he be never at heart's ease[3]	
	Whiles they behold a greater than themselves,	
	And therefore are they very dangerous.	210
	I rather tell thee what is to be feared	
	Than what I fear: for always I am Caesar.	
	Come on my right hand, for this ear is deaf,	
	And tell me truly what thou think'st of him.	

Sennet. Exeunt Caesar and his train

CASCA	You pulled me by the cloak, would you speak with me?	215
BRUTUS	Ay, Casca, tell us what hath chanced[4] today	
	That Caesar looks so sad[5].	
CASCA	Why, you were with him, were you not?	
BRUTUS	I should not then ask, Casca, what had chanced.	
CASCA	Why, there was a crown offered him, and being offered him he put	220
	it by[6] with the back of his hand thus, and then the people fell[7]	
	a-shouting.	
BRUTUS	What was the second noise for?	
CASCA	Why, for that too.	
CASSIUS	They shouted thrice[8]; what was the last cry for?	225
CASCA	Why, for that too.	
BRUTUS	Was the crown offered him thrice?	
CASCA	Ay, marry[9], was't, and he put it by thrice, every time gentler[10] than	
	other; and at every putting-by mine honest neighbours shouted.	
CASSIUS	Who offered him the crown?	230
CASCA	Why, Antony.	
BRUTUS	Tell us the manner[11] of it, gentle[12] Casca.	

Casca describes how Caesar had an epileptic fit after Antony offered him the crown. After that, Caesar offered his bared throat for the crowd to cut.

 剧情简介: 喀斯柯讲述安东尼向恺撒献皇冠之后恺撒突发癫痫的情形。醒来后，恺撒撕开衣领让众人割自己的喉咙。

Themes 主题分析

Life, death and honour (in fours)

Romans believed that to be honourable, you must hold life lightly: 'there are conditions on which life is not worth having', as Aristotle the Greek philosopher said. Cassius and other major characters wilfully endanger or offer to give up their lives on many occasions, as Caesar does here when he 'offered them his throat to cut'.

- The status of the concept of honour varies in different cultures. In your group, discuss what honour means in your culture. It may help to think of actions that would be considered honourable and to think of people who have acted honourably. Create a list of five points about honour and be ready to contribute to a class discussion on the topic.

Write about it 写作练习

Caesar offered the crown! (in fours)

You are a team of journalists sent out to cover the dramatic events at the Lupercal games for a newspaper report. Decide who you want to interview, which angle to take on the events (are you pro- or anti-Caesar at this point?) and which details you will highlight. How will you assess Antony's actions? Will you include details of Caesar's condition, or would it be more sensible not to? You could include photographs if you want to act out part of the scene and then photograph it. Put together your report and display it. How have other groups covered the same event?

1 Caesar's epilepsy (in pairs)

Casca reports (lines 246–7) that Caesar had what sounds like an epileptic fit in the market-place (指Roman forum，即罗马广场).

a Research epilepsy in your school library or on the Internet. Then discuss what you think this detail adds to the portrait of Caesar that Shakespeare is building up in this scene.

b Look back and list any other health conditions, disabilities or physical weaknesses that Caesar is reported to have. Note down who mentioned each one and speculate on their possible motives for making the point at that time.

1 foolery 闹剧
2 fain 乐意
3 loath 不舍得
4 chopped 满是裂口
5 swounded 昏过去
6 durst not 不敢
7 the falling sickness （这里指癫痫，羊角风）
8 Marry 圣母马利亚在上（起誓）
9 plucked me ope 撕扯开 (me起加强语气的作用; ope = open)
10 doublet 衬衣
11 And ... occupation 我要是个贱人
12 taken ... word 信他的话 (a = his)
13 I would ... rogues 我情愿跟那些可怜虫一起下地狱
14 infirmity 病（指癫痫）
15 wenches 姑娘
16 no ... them 无须注意她们
17 stabbed 捅，刺（有性暗示）

Julius Caesar Act 1 Scene 2
儒略·恺撒

CASCA	I can as well be hanged as tell the manner of it. It was mere foolery[1], I did not mark it. I saw Mark Antony offer him a crown – yet 'twas not a crown neither, 'twas one of these coronets – and, as I told you, he put it by once; but for all that, to my thinking he would fain[2] have had it. Then he offered it to him again; then he put it by again; but to my thinking he was very loath[3] to lay his fingers off it. And then he offered it the third time; he put it the third time by, and still as he refused it, the rabblement hooted, and clapped their chopped[4] hands, and threw up their sweaty nightcaps, and uttered such a deal of stinking breath because Caesar refused the crown that it had, almost, choked Caesar, for he swounded[5] and fell down at it. And for mine own part I durst not[6] laugh for fear of opening my lips and receiving the bad air.
CASSIUS	But soft, I pray you; what, did Caesar swound?
CASCA	He fell down in the market-place, and foamed at mouth, and was speechless.
BRUTUS	'Tis very like, he hath the falling sickness[7].
CASSIUS	No, Caesar hath it not, but you, and I, And honest Casca, we have the falling sickness.
CASCA	I know not what you mean by that, but I am sure Caesar fell down. If the tag-rag people did not clap him and hiss him according as he pleased and displeased them, as they use to do the players in the theatre, I am no true man.
BRUTUS	What said he when he came unto himself?
CASCA	Marry[8], before he fell down, when he perceived the common herd was glad he refused the crown, he plucked me ope[9] his doublet[10] and offered them his throat to cut. And I had been a man of any occupation[11], if I would not have taken him at a word[12] I would I might go to hell among the rogues[13]. And so he fell. When he came to himself again, he said if he had done or said anything amiss, he desired their worships to think it was his infirmity[14]. Three or four wenches[15] where I stood cried, 'Alas, good soul', and forgave him with all their hearts. But there's no heed to be taken of them[16]: if Caesar had stabbed[17] their mothers they would have done no less.
BRUTUS	And after that he came thus sad away?
CASCA	Ay.
CASSIUS	Did Cicero say anything?
CASCA	Ay, he spoke Greek.
CASSIUS	To what effect?

Cassius invites Casca to supper. Brutus invites Cassius to his house. Cassius, alone, tells how he will turn Brutus against Caesar.

剧情简介：卡休邀喀斯柯一起吃晚饭。布鲁图请卡休去他家。卡休独白，说明准备如何策动布鲁图与恺撒对立。

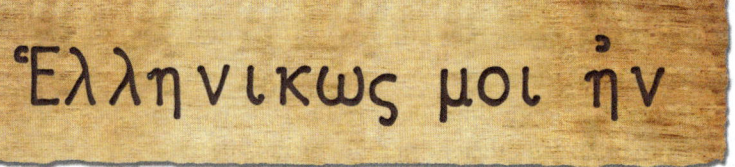
Ἑλληνικῶς μοι ἦν

1 Conspirators as future rulers – the right stuff?
(in pairs)

Old-style Republicans educated their sons at home. Intellectuals like Cicero sent their sons to Athens. They believed the Greeks were culturally superior to the proud but uncultivated citizens of Rome. Some argued that gentry (high-status persons) would be corrupted by mixing with inferior people at school and should have home tutors.

a Talk together about whether you believe it is best 'That noble minds keep ever with their likes'. Does mixing with other people corrupt or benefit those born with high status?

b Casca is introduced to Brutus as the sort of man Cassius wants to recruit for the conspiracy, but Brutus seems doubtful about him. Has the shrewd Cassius misjudged how they might get on together? What might Brutus be thinking about Casca and Cassius during the pause at the end of line 291?

1 and = if
2 it was Greek to me 我听着简直像是听天书（喀斯柯不会希腊语）
3 scarves （可能是彩带）
4 sup 吃晚饭
5 your mind hold 你不变卦
6 quick mettle 机灵
7 tardy form 迟钝的样子
8 gives men stomach 让人胃口大开
9 honourable metal 高贵品性
10 bear me hard 看我不顺眼
11 humour 煽动，影响
12 several hands 几种不同笔迹
13 tending to 关于
14 glancèd at 暗示到
15 seat him sure 坐稳当了

Characters 人物分析

Cassius's and Brutus's private thoughts (in pairs)

Cassius's **soliloquy** (独白)(a speech delivered by a character who is 'thinking aloud' and usually alone on stage) in lines 297–311 reveals his true thoughts about the noble Brutus and the way Brutus's mind can be 'seduced' into conspiring against Caesar.

a Take it in turns to try different readings of Cassius's speech and settle on one version that you think appropriately conveys Cassius's state of mind and his scheming intentions.

b What is Cassius saying about Brutus's character in lines 298–9? Why do you think he chooses to make this point using this particular metaphor?

c Imagine that Shakespeare had given Brutus his own soliloquy, in which he reflects on the events of this scene. Write it in modern English and then perform it to the class.

JULIUS CAESAR ACT 1 SCENE 2
儒略·恺撒

CASCA   Nay, and[1] I tell you that, I'll ne'er look you i'th'face again. But those that understood him smiled at one another and shook their heads; but for mine own part it was Greek to me[2]. I could tell you more news too. Murellus and Flavius, for pulling scarves[3] off Caesar's images, are put to silence. Fare you well. There was more foolery yet, if I could remember it.   275

CASSIUS   Will you sup[4] with me tonight, Casca?

CASCA   No, I am promised forth.

CASSIUS   Will you dine with me tomorrow?

CASCA   Ay, if I be alive, and your mind hold[5], and your dinner worth the eating.   280

CASSIUS   Good, I will expect you.

CASCA   Do so. Farewell both.   *Exit*

BRUTUS   What a blunt fellow is this grown to be!
He was quick mettle[6] when he went to school.   285

CASSIUS   So is he now in execution
Of any bold or noble enterprise,
However he puts on this tardy form[7].
This rudeness is a sauce to his good wit,
Which gives men stomach[8] to digest his words   290
With better appetite.

BRUTUS   And so it is. For this time I will leave you.
Tomorrow if you please to speak with me,
I will come home to you; or if you will,
Come home to me and I will wait for you.   295

CASSIUS   I will do so. Till then, think of the world.   *Exit Brutus*
Well, Brutus, thou art noble; yet I see
Thy honourable metal[9] may be wrought
From that it is disposed. Therefore it is meet
That noble minds keep ever with their likes;   300
For who so firm that cannot be seduced?
Caesar doth bear me hard[10], but he loves Brutus.
If I were Brutus now and he were Cassius,
He should not humour[11] me. I will this night,
In several hands[12], in at his windows throw,   305
As if they came from several citizens,
Writings, all tending to[13] the great opinion
That Rome holds of his name, wherein obscurely
Caesar's ambition shall be glancèd at[14].
And after this let Caesar seat him sure[15],   310
For we will shake him, or worse days endure.   *Exit*

Casca meets Cicero and describes the natural and supernatural wonders he sees in the tempest which rages. Casca thinks they are bad omens.

 剧情简介：喀斯柯路上遇到西塞罗，向他描述自己在狂风暴雨里见到的自然奇观和灵异现象。喀斯柯觉得这些异象是凶兆。

Stagecraft 导演技巧

All change (in groups of five or six)

Shakespeare's scene changes can be very dramatic moments and often highlight major themes of the plays. Here, the crowds and daylight of Scene 2 give way to night, fierce storms and solitary frightened figures.

The challenge for your group is to decide how you will stage this scene up to line 40, bringing out the turbulence of the times in the following production settings:

- **The Globe Theatre** (环球剧场) **in 1599** There seems little doubt that *Julius Caesar* was one of the first plays performed by Shakespeare's own company at the newly built Globe Theatre. There were no stage lights and very basic sound effects. How would you maximise the drama of this scene within these theatrical constraints?

- **A contemporary theatre** Most modern societies are much more sceptical of signs and supernatural events than the Romans were. Discuss how you would persuade your audience of the sheer terror the Romans would have felt as their world was turned upside down. Would there be any merit in transferring the scene to a modern apocalyptic (如世界末日般) setting?

- **On film** You have all sorts of special effects at your disposal. Make the most of the freedom of the film medium to draw up your ideas for conveying a convincing night of terror.

Write up these three sets of ideas in your Director's Journal.

1	sway	范围
2	rived	劈开
3	exalted	推上去
4	saucy	狂妄
5	incenses	激怒
6	sensible of	感觉得到
7	unscorched	未被灼伤
8	Against	在……对面
9	glazed upon	盯着
10	surly	凶巴巴，恶狠狠
11	annoying	伤害
12	drawn / Upon a heap	挤作一团
13	ghastly	吓得面如土色
14	Transformèd with their fear	吓得变了模样（面如土色）
15	prodigies	异象（通常认为是凶兆）
16	conjointly meet	一齐发生
17	portentous	预示将有大灾难，不祥
18	climate	地方

1 Prodigies on the wall (whole class in five groups)

Five prodigies (extraordinary things or events) are described by Casca (lines 15–32). Imagine they took place in your neighbourhood yesterday.

- For a wall display, each group should take a single prodigy and report it, filled out with vivid details, interviews and comments from people you know. You can add illustrations. One person in the group should be an augurer (an interpreter of signs or portents). In their part of the display, they should explain what the gods are using the prodigy to tell the people. Perhaps the augurer writes a horoscope (占星预言) column!

Act 1 Scene 3
Rome   A street   Night

Thunder and lightning. Enter [from opposite sides] CASCA *and* CICERO

CICERO	Good even, Casca, brought you Caesar home?
	Why are you breathless, and why stare you so?
CASCA	Are not you moved when all the sway[1] of earth
	Shakes like a thing unfirm? O Cicero,
	I have seen tempests when the scolding winds
	Have rived[2] the knotty oaks, and I have seen
	Th'ambitious ocean swell, and rage, and foam,
	To be exalted[3] with the threatening clouds;
	But never till tonight, never till now,
	Did I go through a tempest dropping fire.
	Either there is a civil strife in heaven,
	Or else the world, too saucy[4] with the gods,
	Incenses[5] them to send destruction.
CICERO	Why, saw you anything more wonderful?
CASCA	A common slave – you know him well by sight –
	Held up his left hand, which did flame and burn
	Like twenty torches joined, and yet his hand,
	Not sensible of[6] fire, remained unscorched[7].
	Besides – I ha' not since put up my sword –
	Against[8] the Capitol I met a lion
	Who glazed upon[9] me and went surly[10] by
	Without annoying[11] me. And there were drawn
	Upon a heap[12] a hundred ghastly[13] women,
	Transformèd with their fear[14], who swore they saw
	Men, all in fire, walk up and down the streets.
	And yesterday the bird of night did sit
	Even at noon-day upon the market-place,
	Hooting and shrieking. When these prodigies[15]
	Do so conjointly meet[16] let not men say,
	'These are their reasons, they are natural',
	For I believe they are portentous[17] things
	Unto the climate[18] that they point upon.

Cicero warns Casca that omens can be misinterpreted. Cassius enters, bare-chested. He welcomes the tempest and despises Casca's fear.

 剧情简介：西塞罗提醒喀斯柯，人们对预兆的解读可能是错的。卡休上，敞着胸膛。他表示欢迎这场暴风雨，并且鄙视喀斯柯的恐惧。

1 Cicero and Casca – conspirators? (in pairs)

Cicero and Casca's opening exchange shows a contrast in their respective characters. Cicero is calm, seeing nothing extraordinary in the storm's power, carefully avoiding political discussion. Casca is disturbed, deeply affected by the omens of the storm that he has seen, and anxious that they signify threat to Rome.

a Take parts and read lines 1–40. How will you bring out the different personalities and viewpoints of the two men?

b This is Cicero's last appearance in the play; Brutus later sees him as an unsuitable member of the conspiracy and rejects him, while Casca is accepted. Discuss how actors might play these two roles to highlight the contrasting fates of the two men.

2 The world through Cassius's eyes (in pairs)

It is hard to imagine more different reactions to the storm than those of fearful Casca, who we know from line 19 is carrying a sword, and Cassius, who says that he has been walking about offering his bare chest to the storm. Shakespeare is showing us an extreme contrast.

a Read lines 41–71. Aim to bring out the differences between the two men in the tone of voice you choose.

b Consider the contrast between the reactions of Cassius and Casca by picking out words and phrases from their speeches and putting them into a chart like the one below. Words and phrases that suggest a rational response go in one column, those that suggest an emotional response go in the other, and the speaker's name goes on the left. What observations can you make about the characters of the two men by looking at your finished chart?

Character	Rational	Emotional
Cassius	'known the earth'	
Casca		'fear and tremble'

1 strange-disposèd 动荡不安
2 Clean from 完全不顾
3 menace 威胁，发威
4 thus unbracèd 这么敞着前胸
5 thunderstone 闪电
6 cross 枝杈状的
7 tempt 顶撞
8 astonish 震慑
9 want 没有，缺少
10 from quality and kind 一反常态
11 calculate 能掐会算（连傻子、孩子都说要有灾难，说明兆头十分明显）

CICERO	Indeed, it is a strange-disposèd[1] time.
	But men may construe things after their fashion
	Clean from[2] the purpose of the things themselves. 35
	Comes Caesar to the Capitol tomorrow?
CASCA	He doth, for he did bid Antonio
	Send word to you he would be there tomorrow.
CICERO	Good night then, Casca. This disturbèd sky
	Is not to walk in.
CASCA	Farewell, Cicero. 40

Exit Cicero

Enter CASSIUS

CASSIUS	Who's there?
CASCA	A Roman.
CASSIUS	Casca, by your voice.
CASCA	Your ear is good. Cassius, what night is this!
CASSIUS	A very pleasing night to honest men.
CASCA	Who ever knew the heavens menace[3] so?
CASSIUS	Those that have known the earth so full of faults. 45
	For my part I have walked about the streets,
	Submitting me unto the perilous night,
	And, thus unbracèd[4], Casca, as you see,
	Have bared my bosom to the thunderstone[5];
	And when the cross[6] blue lightning seemed to open 50
	The breast of heaven, I did present myself
	Even in the aim and very flash of it.
CASCA	But wherefore did you so much tempt[7] the heavens?
	It is the part of men to fear and tremble
	When the most mighty gods by tokens send 55
	Such dreadful heralds to astonish[8] us.
CASSIUS	You are dull, Casca, and those sparks of life
	That should be in a Roman you do want[9],
	Or else you use not. You look pale, and gaze,
	And put on fear, and cast yourself in wonder 60
	To see the strange impatience of the heavens.
	But if you would consider the true cause
	Why all these fires, why all these gliding ghosts,
	Why birds and beasts from quality and kind[10],
	Why old men, fools, and children calculate[11], 65

Cassius hints that the tempest is a warning that should rouse the people of Rome. Casca tells him that outside Italy, Caesar will be king. Death will free me from such oppression, riddles Cassius.

 剧情简介：卡休暗示，暴风雨是要警醒罗马人民。喀斯柯告诉卡休，恺撒即将在意大利之外加冕。死亡将豁免我受此压迫，卡休话中有话。

Language in the play 剧中语言
Cassius and the art of persuasion (in pairs)

Once again, Cassius shows himself to be a powerful orator. He is out to recruit Casca to his cause. He is successful: by line 119, Casca is saying, 'I will set this foot of mine as far / As who goes farthest.' How has Cassius achieved this?

Taking parts, read carefully through lines 72–130. Follow Cassius's persuasive techniques by answering the following questions:

a In which lines does Cassius link Caesar to the strange events of the night?

b What is his view of Caesar's stature?

c Why does he not name Caesar?

d Why does he say Romans are grown 'womanish'?

e Look carefully at Cassius's speech beginning at line 89. Cassius says that he has a plan to make sure he never has to live under the reign of Caesar the king. What is that plan and how does having it make Cassius feel?

f The use of lists is a favourite rhetorical device. What is the effect of the list in lines 93–4?

g How does Casca's speech beginning at line 100 show that Cassius's persuasion is beginning to work?

h Cassius's speech beginning at line 103 is an especially clever piece of rhetoric. Looking carefully at his use of rhetorical questions, metaphors and his seeming change of attitude to Caesar, comment on how the speech works.

i It is clear the speech is well crafted, so why does he ask, 'But, O grief, / Where hast thou led me?' (lines 111–12)?

j What test does Cassius offer Casca at the end of this speech?

k How can you tell from Casca's language from line 116 onwards that he now has no doubts about joining Cassius?

l Twice in Cassius's speech beginning at line 120, he describes what they are about to embark on as highly dangerous. Identify where he does this.

m Explain the effect created by the **juxtaposition** (并置) (putting together) of the words 'honourable' and 'dangerous'.

n How does Cassius link the conspiracy to the events of the night?

1 ordinance 常态
2 performèd faculties 本性
3 state 事态，状况
4 prodigious 极其不祥
5 thews and limbs 筋骨和手脚
6 woe the while 悲哀啊，这个时代
7 yoke and sufferance 枷锁和苦难
8 save 除了
9 dismiss 解脱，释放
10 bondman 奴隶

	Why all these things change from their ordinance[1],	
	Their natures, and preformèd faculties[2],	
	To monstrous quality – why, you shall find	
	That heaven hath infused them with these spirits	
	To make them instruments of fear, and warning	70
	Unto some monstrous state[3].	
	Now could I, Casca, name to thee a man	
	Most like this dreadful night,	
	That thunders, lightens, opens graves, and roars	
	As doth the lion in the Capitol –	75
	A man no mightier than thyself, or me,	
	In personal action, yet prodigious[4] grown	
	And fearful, as these strange eruptions are.	
CASCA	'Tis Caesar that you mean, is it not, Cassius?	
CASSIUS	Let it be who it is, for Romans now	80
	Have thews and limbs[5] like to their ancestors'.	
	But, woe the while[6], our fathers' minds are dead	
	And we are governed with our mothers' spirits;	
	Our yoke and sufferance[7] show us womanish.	
CASCA	Indeed, they say the senators tomorrow	85
	Mean to establish Caesar as a king,	
	And he shall wear his crown by sea and land,	
	In every place save[8] here in Italy.	
CASSIUS	I know where I will wear this dagger then:	
	Cassius from bondage will deliver Cassius.	90
	Therein, ye gods, you make the weak most strong;	
	Therein, ye gods, you tyrants do defeat.	
	Nor stony tower, nor walls of beaten brass,	
	Nor airless dungeon, nor strong links of iron,	
	Can be retentive to the strength of spirit;	95
	But life, being weary of these worldly bars,	
	Never lacks power to dismiss[9] itself.	
	If I know this, know all the world besides,	
	That part of tyranny that I do bear	
	I can shake off at pleasure.	

Thunder still

CASCA	So can I,	100
	So every bondman[10] in his own hand bears	
	The power to cancel his captivity.	

Stung by Cassius's words, Casca commits himself to Caesar's overthrow. Cassius tells him of other conspirators he has recruited. One of them, Cinna, enters looking for Cassius.

剧情简介：被卡休的一番话刺痛，喀斯柯决心以推翻恺撒为己任。卡休告诉他已招募进来数名成员。其中一位名叫希纳的来找卡休。

Stagecraft 导演技巧
Embedded information

You might have noticed a lack of settings and stage directions in this play. Those that appear at the start of each scene were not included by Shakespeare but were added later by different editors of the play.

- Read through lines 131–8 and find the staging instructions that Shakespeare embedded within the script. In your Director's Journal, draw up a chart with two columns. Put the quotation in one column and in the other column, write down what sort of staging or movement it suggests.

1 hinds 鹿；奴仆
2 base 低贱
3 fleering tell-tale 挤眉弄眼的告密者
4 Be factious 联手造反
5 redress of all these griefs 匡正这所有的不平
6 Pompey's Porch 庞贝剧院的柱廊
7 the complexion of the element 天色
8 In favour's like 看着就像
9 Stand close 躲起来
10 gait 走路姿势
11 one incorporate / To our attempts 我们此次计划（举事）的一员
12 stayed for 等待

▼ The conspirators wait for Cassius at Pompey's Porch. What feelings do you think these actors are trying to convey?'

CASSIUS	And why should Caesar be a tyrant then?	
	Poor man, I know he would not be a wolf	
	But that he sees the Romans are but sheep;	105
	He were no lion, were not Romans hinds[1].	
	Those that with haste will make a mighty fire	
	Begin it with weak straws. What trash is Rome,	
	What rubbish and what offal, when it serves	
	For the base[2] matter to illuminate	110
	So vile a thing as Caesar? But, O grief,	
	Where hast thou led me? I perhaps speak this	
	Before a willing bondman, then I know	
	My answer must be made. But I am armed,	
	And dangers are to me indifferent.	115
CASCA	You speak to Casca, and to such a man	
	That is no fleering tell-tale[3]. Hold, my hand.	
	Be factious[4] for redress of all these griefs[5],	
	And I will set this foot of mine as far	
	As who goes farthest.	
CASSIUS	There's a bargain made.	120
	Now know you, Casca, I have moved already	
	Some certain of the noblest-minded Romans	
	To undergo with me an enterprise	
	Of honourable dangerous consequence.	
	And I do know by this they stay for me	125
	In Pompey's Porch[6]. For now, this fearful night,	
	There is no stir or walking in the streets,	
	And the complexion of the element[7]	
	In favour's like[8] the work we have in hand,	
	Most bloody, fiery, and most terrible.	130

Enter CINNA

CASCA	Stand close[9] a while, for here comes one in haste.	
CASSIUS	'Tis Cinna, I do know him by his gait[10].	
	He is a friend. Cinna, where haste you so?	
CINNA	To find out you. Who's that? Metellus Cimber?	
CASSIUS	No, it is Casca, one incorporate	135
	To our attempts[11]. Am I not stayed for[12], Cinna?	
CINNA	I am glad on't. What a fearful night is this!	
	There's two or three of us have seen strange sights.	

Cassius orders Cinna to leave letters for Brutus in places where he will find them. Cassius says Brutus will join the conspirators tonight. They leave to join the other conspirators and go to Brutus's house.

 剧情简介：卡休吩咐希纳把写给布鲁图的信放在他一定会看到的地方。卡休说布鲁图今晚一定会加入同谋的行列。他们去找别的同谋，然后一同去布鲁图家。

1 Unspoken thoughts (in threes)

Cinna's dramatic and hasty arrival signals the gathering momentum (聚积声势) of the conspiracy.

a Take parts and act out lines 131–41 with breathless speed, but emphasise the pause at the end of line 140.

b Talk about what is not said, but what is probably in the men's minds.

1	praetor	先行官（布鲁图的官职）
2	Repair	赶去
3	hie	立刻去
4	bestow … me	按您的吩咐把这些信放好
5	ere day	在天亮之前
6	yields	归顺
7	countenance	支持
8	richest alchemy	最神奇的点金术
9	conceited	考虑，理解

Stagecraft 导演技巧
Why include a tempest? (in eights)

Shakespeare often wrote or made changes in consultation with his actors. His main source for *Julius Caesar* was Plutarch's *Lives of the Noble Grecians and Romans* (see p. 166). In Plutarch's text there is only one paragraph describing the prodigies, and no tempest.

Some people today do not like 'historical facts' to be changed when made into films. Similarly, in Shakespeare's day, some people objected to the liberties taken by dramatists.

- Imagine that Shakespeare's actors meet a group of such objectors in a tavern after the opening night. Divide into two groups (actors and objectors) and plan a discussion in which you argue about whether or not Shakespeare should have inserted Scene 3, which does not advance the plot in any way. Prepare for the argument by listing justifications for, and objections to, inventing or changing historical events in plays. Then act out your discussion.

Characters 人物分析
Brutus (in threes)

There are many ways for a dramatist to establish character. Obviously how that character acts and what they say are important, but just as important in establishing their role and characteristics is what others say about them. Here, right at the end of Act 1, and just before Brutus's soliloquy in his orchard, revealing his innermost thoughts, Shakespeare has the conspirators make clear why Brutus's support is so important to them.

a Take parts and read from line 140 to the end of the scene together. Remember your meeting and business are top secret.

b In character, take it in turns to explain to the others in modern English why you think Brutus's support is vital.

CASSIUS	Am I not stayed for? Tell me.	
CINNA	Yes, you are.	
	O Cassius, if you could	140
	But win the noble Brutus to our party –	
CASSIUS	Be you content. Good Cinna, take this paper	
	And look you lay it in the praetor's[1] chair,	
	Where Brutus may but find it; and throw this	
	In at his window; set this up with wax	145
	Upon old Brutus' statue. All this done,	
	Repair[2] to Pompey's Porch, where you shall find us.	
	Is Decius Brutus and Trebonius there?	
CINNA	All but Metellus Cimber, and he's gone	
	To seek you at your house. Well, I will hie[3],	150
	And so bestow these papers as you bade me[4].	
CASSIUS	That done, repair to Pompey's Theatre.	
		Exit Cinna
	Come, Casca, you and I will yet, ere day[5],	
	See Brutus at his house. Three parts of him	
	Is ours already, and the man entire	155
	Upon the next encounter yields[6] him ours.	
CASCA	O, he sits high in all the people's hearts,	
	And that which would appear offence in us	
	His countenance[7], like richest alchemy[8],	
	Will change to virtue and to worthiness.	160
CASSIUS	Him and his worth and our great need of him	
	You have right well conceited[9]. Let us go,	
	For it is after midnight, and ere day	
	We will awake him and be sure of him.	
		Exeunt

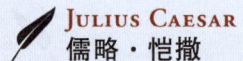

JULIUS CAESAR
儒略·恺撒

Looking back at Act 1 第1幕回顾
Activities for groups or individuals

1 A head for power?

One of the reasons for the continued appeal of this play is its examination of the nature of power.

- Discuss the personal qualities you would look for in a great leader. Find a picture of a real leader you admire, or draw a head to represent your ideal leader, and write these qualities around it. How many of these qualities does Caesar appear to have by the end of Act 1? Find an image of Caesar and write his qualities around it.

2 Caesar passes

There are twelve speaking parts in Act 1 other than Caesar. Cast yourselves in as many of these parts as there are people in your group, and choose one or two lines from the script to sum up what your character thinks of Caesar. Line up with expectant smiles. As you imagine Caesar passing in slow motion, say your line(s) about him, adding gestures and facial expressions. The rest of the class should try to identify who is playing whom.

3 Time for a speech

Cassius is highly persuasive. As we have seen, he has many clever rhetorical techniques at his disposal.

- Look back to your work on Cassius's speeches on pages 16, 18 and 32 and take inspiration. Choose a topic that you feel passionate about. Write a speech to persuade others that your point of view is the right one and include as many rhetorical techniques as you can. Deliver the speech to the class.

4 Caesar at the Lupercal

Royalty in Shakespeare's day copied the traditions of the Roman triumph. On special occasions, they paraded through the streets in a procession of elaborate floats (彩车，花车).

a Design a float that Caesar might have used at the Lupercal festival (see p. 172), emphasising his triumph and the protection of Rome from evil.

b Queen Elizabeth I was often greeted at the gate of a stately home or a city with a poem that had been written for the occasion. Write a poem to welcome Caesar to the games.

5 What do we know about Cassius?

What do you make of Cassius? Brutus's close friend seems to be the instigator of the conspiracy and the character who dominates the first act. He has a deep hatred of Caesar that is never really explained.

- Write a profile of Cassius based on his language, his behaviour and what others have said about him in Act 1. Feel free to speculate about his motives, but make it clear what is speculation and what is drawn from the text.

6 What is a true Roman?

This is a key concept in the play and Shakespeare uses Brutus and Cassius to establish it. It is crucial that this idea is familiar to the audience before the deliberations of Act 2.

- Look back at Act 1 Scene 2, lines 150–75 and Act 1 Scene 3, lines 103–15. Using the views expressed there and your reflections on them, write your answer to the question 'What is a true Roman?' Remember to use quotations in support of your points.

7 The Soothsayer

Every producer must decide how to present the Soothsayer. He is sometimes played as a kind of outsider to the society in which the political drama is taking place.

- In small groups, discuss your own ideas for the Soothsayer. Decide first whether your staging will be in modern or traditional dress. The photographs opposite may help you. Then sketch out your own costume design for the Soothsayer.

Night. In his orchard, Brutus sends Lucius to light his study. He decides that Caesar must die to prevent him from using his new power wrongly.

 剧情简介： 深夜。在果园里，布鲁图让卢休去把书房的灯点上。布鲁图决心除掉恺撒，以免日后他滥用大权。

Stagecraft 导演技巧
Public to private (in pairs)

Shakespeare retains a night-time setting for the opening of Act 2, but moves from public space (a Roman street) to a private one (Brutus's orchard). Brutus's lines 1–3 also draw attention to the thematic importance of light and darkness in the play (Lucius's name is close to the Latin word *lux*, meaning 'light', and he is sent to fetch light for Brutus's study).

- Work together to design a set for the opening of this scene in Brutus's orchard to be staged in a modern theatre. Sketch your design and show clearly how you would use lighting effects for lines 1–10. Add the annotated sketch to your Director's Journal.

1 Brutus: making his mind up (whole class)

Brutus's soliloquy charts the seesawing of his anguished thoughts as he considers the reasons why Caesar should be killed.

- First, choose a student to play Brutus. Then divide up his speech (lines 10–34) into 'sense units' (sometimes a phrase, sometimes a line or so) and allocate these to the other members of the class. Whilst Brutus is seated in the centre of the room, the others should, in turn, whisper their language extracts into Brutus's ear. Repeat the process several times, varying the volume and tone.
- Afterwards, put Brutus in the hot-seat and ask him about the impression made upon him by the thoughts of his own 'conscience'. Which words or arguments made a particular impression?

Language in the play 剧中语言
Snakes and ladders

Brutus uses two key images to describe the threat he imagines that Caesar poses. The first compares Caesar to an adder (a poisonous snake) and then a serpent; the other suggests that his ambition is like the process of his climbing a ladder.

- Find the specific images that Shakespeare creates. What do they suggest a) about Caesar and b) about Brutus's attitude to him?

1. What 喂，欸
2. I … day 看这星星我猜不出来现在是什么时辰
3. I would … to 我要是能……，挨骂也愿意
4. taper 蜡烛
5. spurn at 狠踹，猛踢
6. general 大众，老百姓
7. would 想要
8. adder 蝰蛇
9. craves wary walking 走路得小心
10. disjoins 丢掉
11. affections swayed 情感占上风
12. proof 经历，情况
13. lowliness 低姿态，谦卑
14. upmost round 最高一阶
15. base degrees 较低的台阶（指低贱的过去）
16. prevent 提早防范
17. quarrel 担忧
18. Will bear no colour 没有真凭实据
19. Fashion it thus 这样想，这样考虑
20. augmented （权势）一旦扩大

Act 2 Scene 1
Brutus' orchard   Night

Enter BRUTUS *in his orchard*

BRUTUS What[1], Lucius, ho!
I cannot by the progress of the stars
Give guess how near to day[2]. Lucius, I say!
I would it were my fault to[3] sleep so soundly.
When, Lucius, when? Awake, I say! What, Lucius!   5

Enter LUCIUS

LUCIUS Called you, my lord?
BRUTUS Get me a taper[4] in my study, Lucius.
When it is lighted, come and call me here.
LUCIUS I will, my lord.   *Exit*
BRUTUS It must be by his death. And for my part   10
I know no personal cause to spurn at[5] him
But for the general[6]. He would[7] be crowned:
How that might change his nature, there's the question.
It is the bright day that brings forth the adder[8]
And that craves wary walking[9]. Crown him that,   15
And then I grant we put a sting in him
That at his will he may do danger with.
Th'abuse of greatness is when it disjoins[10]
Remorse from power. And to speak truth of Caesar,
I have not known when his affections swayed[11]   20
More than his reason. But 'tis a common proof[12]
That lowliness[13] is young ambition's ladder,
Whereto the climber-upward turns his face;
But when he once attains the upmost round[14]
He then unto the ladder turns his back,   25
Looks in the clouds, scorning the base degrees[15]
By which he did ascend. So Caesar may.
Then lest he may, prevent[16]. And since the quarrel[17]
Will bear no colour[18] for the thing he is,
Fashion it thus[19]: that what he is, augmented[20],   30
Would run to these and these extremities.

Lucius brings Brutus one of Cassius's letters. It strengthens Brutus's resolve to kill Caesar. Lucius reports that tomorrow is 15 March – the Ides of March.

剧情简介：卢休给布鲁图拿来卡休写的一封信。这封信坚定了布鲁图除掉恺撒的决心。卢休对布鲁图说，第二天就是3月15日了。

Write about it 写作练习

Cryptic (晦涩难懂) letters (in pairs)

Lucius delivers a letter to Brutus that he has found dropped through his window. This letter gets Brutus's attention because its meaning is not clear. It is one among many ('Such instigations'), all apparently by different writers, but all in fact written by Cassius.

- Each of you, in role as Cassius, writes a letter to Brutus, prompting him to action. (Look back to pages 16, 18 and 32 for analysis of the way Cassius uses the language of persuasion.) Swap letters and comment on how persuasive and effective each one is.

Characters 人物分析

Focus on Brutus (in fours, then by yourself)

It is the eve of the Ides of March. By the end of his second soliloquy (lines 44–58), Brutus has resolved to assassinate Caesar.

a Share out Brutus's lines amongst the group. As you read through them, emphasise any shifts in tone (e.g. the movement between questions and commands). Show clearly how you think Brutus's mood gradually changes as he moves towards his final position.

b Work individually to read Brutus's first soliloquy (lines 10–34), followed instantly by his second. Write down in your own words the stages of his argument, culminating (达到顶点) in his intention to kill Caesar.

c Finally, write a paragraph in your Character file about what you think of Brutus at this point in the play. How far do you think his arguments are credible or justifiable? Is he being too idealistic or unreasonable? Use references to justify all the points you make.

1 serpent 大蛇
2 as his kind 受本性驱使
3 mischievous 害人的
4 closet 里间，里屋
5 flint 打火石
6 exhalations 流星
7 instigations 煽风点火
8 piece it out 把话补出来
9 Tarquin 塔尔昆（罗马最后两任暴君之一）
10 entreated 恳求
11 If the redress will follow 如果你们拥护我
12 thou receivest / Thy full petition 你们的诉求统统能得到满足
13 at 从（……的手中）
14 March is wasted fifteen days 3月已经过了15天了
15 whet 撺掇

◀ Describe how this actor has sought to convey Brutus's mental anguish as he considers Caesar's growing power and ambition.

JULIUS CAESAR ACT 2 SCENE 1
儒略·恺撒

And therefore think him as a serpent's[1] egg
(Which, hatched, would as his kind[2] grow mischievous[3])
And kill him in the shell.

Enter LUCIUS

LUCIUS The taper burneth in your closet[4], sir.   35
Searching the window for a flint[5], I found
This paper, thus sealed up, and I am sure
It did not lie there when I went to bed.
Gives him the letter

BRUTUS Get you to bed again, it is not day.
Is not tomorrow, boy, the Ides of March?   40

LUCIUS I know not, sir.

BRUTUS Look in the calendar and bring me word.

LUCIUS I will, sir.   *Exit*

BRUTUS The exhalations[6] whizzing in the air
Give so much light that I may read by them.   45
Opens the letter and reads
'Brutus, thou sleep'st. Awake, and see thyself!
Shall Rome, etc. Speak, strike, redress!'
'Brutus, thou sleep'st. Awake!'
Such instigations[7] have been often dropped
Where I have took them up.   50
'Shall Rome, etc.' Thus must I piece it out[8]:
Shall Rome stand under one man's awe? What, Rome?
My ancestors did from the streets of Rome
The Tarquin[9] drive when he was called a king.
'Speak, strike, redress!' Am I entreated[10]   55
To speak and strike? O Rome, I make thee promise,
If the redress will follow[11], thou receivest
Thy full petition[12] at[13] the hand of Brutus.

Enter LUCIUS

LUCIUS Sir, March is wasted fifteen days[14].
Knock within

BRUTUS 'Tis good. Go to the gate, somebody knocks.   60
[*Exit Lucius*]
Since Cassius first did whet[15] me against Caesar
I have not slept.

Brutus describes how it feels to have made up one's mind to do a fearful act. Lucius reports the arrival of the disguised conspirators. Brutus muses that conspiracy must always hide its nature.

 剧情简介：布鲁图自述决心行凶时的内心感受。卢休来报，几位乔装打扮的同谋来访。布鲁图暗自思忖，阴谋必须小心伪装起来。

Themes 主题分析

Appearance versus reality (in pairs)

The contrast between how things appear on the surface and what they are really like beneath is evident in all of Shakespeare's plays.

a Take parts and read aloud lines 72–85. Identify all the images that describe things being concealed or hidden. Write a sentence about each one, explaining how the image works to establish a contrast between appearance and reality.

b Choose one of the images to present as a tableau. Show it to other groups for them to guess which image you are portraying.

c Brutus views as shameful the need to hide his true thoughts and feelings now the conspiracy is underway. Write a short paragraph about what his choice of language suggests about his attitude to deception.

Stagecraft 导演技巧

Darkness versus light; movement versus inaction (in small groups)

Shakespeare deliberately contrasts the youthful innocence of Lucius with the dark, furtive thoughts of Brutus. The conspirators keep to the shadows with faces muffled, but Brutus feels the plotters will best 'mask' their feelings by hiding their true intentions in 'smiles and affability (和蔼可亲)'.

a Imagine that you are directing a film version of the play. Focus on the start of this scene up to the conspirators' entrance (line 85). What colours and lighting would you use? Film noir (French for 'black film') uses light to hint at the state of mind of its characters. At what point would Brutus be in the shadows? When would he be in close-up? Discuss your ideas and then write up your notes in your Director's Journal.

b Using the opening 85 lines again, focus on all Lucius's entrances and exits. Talk together about the contrasts created by the constant movements of this character and how they are set against the motionless state of Brutus. Try to come up with two or three dramatic reasons why you think Shakespeare establishes this contrast. Share your best idea with the class.

1 first motion 念头初起
2 interim 中间这段时间
3 phantasma 幻象
4 The genius and the mortal instruments 灵与肉
5 in council 争执不休
6 Like to 就像
7 insurrection 叛乱，起义
8 brother 妹夫（卡休娶的是布鲁图的妹妹）
9 mo = more
10 discover 认出
11 mark of favour 脸的样子
12 visage 脸庞
13 path 走，前行
14 native semblance 本来面目
15 Erebus 通往地狱的黑暗地带
16 prevention 阻拦
17 we … rest 我们在您休息时贸然前来

Between the acting of a dreadful thing
And the first motion¹, all the interim² is
Like a phantasma³ or a hideous dream.   65
The genius and the mortal instruments⁴
Are then in council⁵, and the state of a man,
Like to⁶ a little kingdom, suffers then
The nature of an insurrection⁷.

Enter LUCIUS

LUCIUS   Sir, 'tis your brother⁸ Cassius at the door,   70
          Who doth desire to see you.
BRUTUS   Is he alone?
LUCIUS   No, sir, there are mo⁹ with him.
BRUTUS   Do you know them?
LUCIUS   No, sir, their hats are plucked about their ears
          And half their faces buried in their cloaks,
          That by no means I may discover¹⁰ them   75
          By any mark of favour¹¹.
BRUTUS   Let 'em enter.

                                          [*Exit Lucius*]

          They are the faction. O conspiracy,
          Sham'st thou to show thy dang'rous brow by night,
          When evils are most free? O then by day
          Where wilt thou find a cavern dark enough   80
          To mask thy monstrous visage¹²? Seek none, conspiracy,
          Hide it in smiles and affability,
          For if thou path¹³, thy native semblance¹⁴ on,
          Not Erebus¹⁵ itself were dim enough
          To hide thee from prevention¹⁶.   85

          Enter the conspirators, CASSIUS, CASCA, DECIUS, CINNA,
                    METELLUS, *and* TREBONIUS

CASSIUS   I think we are too bold upon your rest¹⁷.
          Good morrow, Brutus, do we trouble you?
BRUTUS   I have been up this hour, awake all night.
          Know I these men that come along with you?
CASSIUS   Yes, every man of them; and no man here   90
          But honours you, and every one doth wish

Brutus is introduced to the conspirators. After some secret words with Cassius, he shakes their hands but he rejects the suggestion that they should all swear an oath to kill Caesar.

剧情简介：卡休把布鲁图介绍给同谋。和卡休低语几句之后，布鲁图与同谋一一握手，但拒绝了全体人员都要发誓杀死恺撒的提议。

Stagecraft 导演技巧

Watching the sun rise (in pairs)

a After line 100, Brutus and Cassius share a whispered and secret conversation. What do you think they talk about? Discuss possible ideas then work together to script their conversation in modern English.

b In your pairs, sketch a layout of the stage showing how all characters present (there are seven of them) are blocked (arranged on stage) between lines 100–112. Think carefully about the kind of relationship you want to show between the different conspirators.

c Whilst Brutus and Cassius talk out of earshot of the audience, Decius, Casca and Cinna contemplate the imminent sunrise. Remind yourself of the 'Stagecraft' activity on page 44, and think about how you would light this scene. What effects would you want to create?

d Why do you think Shakespeare chooses to include a passage of dialogue about the imminence of daybreak at this point?

1 hither 在这儿，到此处
2 Betwixt = Between
3 What … night? 什么事害得各位深更半夜不得合眼？
4 entreat a word 借一步说话
5 yon 那，那个
6 fret the clouds 在云间交错
7 growing on 朝……逼近
8 Weighing … year 考虑到现在是春天
9 sufferance 苦难
10 betimes 趁早
11 idle 空着的
12 by lottery 不知哪天
13 kindle 点着
14 prick 激励
15 palter 敷衍
16 honesty 忠诚
17 engaged 担保
18 fall 死

1 Cassius's oath

(in threes)

Cassius never gets to swear his resolution (line 113). Discuss what it might have been and write it down (in no more than two lines). Each group should share its version of Cassius's oath with the class. This will give you many ideas about Cassius and the conspiracy.

▶ Brutus (right) and Cassius: who holds the power?

Julius Caesar Act 2 Scene 1
儒略·恺撒

	You had but that opinion of yourself
	Which every noble Roman bears of you.
	This is Trebonius.
BRUTUS	He is welcome hither¹.
CASSIUS	This, Decius Brutus.
BRUTUS	He is welcome too.
CASSIUS	This, Casca; this, Cinna; and this, Metellus Cimber.
BRUTUS	They are all welcome.
	What watchful cares do interpose themselves
	Betwixt² your eyes and night?³
CASSIUS	Shall I entreat a word⁴?

They whisper

DECIUS	Here lies the east, doth not the day break here?
CASCA	No.
CINNA	O, pardon, sir, it doth, and yon⁵ grey lines
	That fret the clouds⁶ are messengers of day.
CASCA	You shall confess that you are both deceived.
	Here, as I point my sword, the sun arises,
	Which is a great way growing on⁷ the south,
	Weighing the youthful season of the year⁸.
	Some two months hence, up higher toward the north
	He first presents his fire, and the high east
	Stands, as the Capitol, directly here.
BRUTUS	[*Advancing with Cassius*] Give me your hands all over, one by one.
CASSIUS	And let us swear our resolution.
BRUTUS	No, not an oath! If not the face of men,
	The sufferance⁹ of our souls, the time's abuse –
	If these be motives weak, break off betimes¹⁰,
	And every man hence to his idle¹¹ bed;
	So let high-sighted tyranny range on,
	Till each man drop by lottery¹². But if these
	(As I am sure they do) bear fire enough
	To kindle¹³ cowards and to steel with valour
	The melting spirits of women, then, countrymen,
	What need we any spur but our own cause
	To prick¹⁴ us to redress? What other bond
	Than secret Romans that have spoke the word
	And will not palter¹⁵? And what other oath
	Than honesty¹⁶ to honesty engaged¹⁷
	That this shall be or we will fall¹⁸ for it?

No oaths – a Roman's promise is enough, says Brutus. He rejects suggestions that Cicero be approached or Antony killed.

剧情简介：无须发誓，有罗马人的承诺就足够了，布鲁图如是说。他反对拉拢西塞罗入伙，也不同意将安东尼一起除掉。

Characters 人物分析

Brutus's honour

Brutus uses his speech (lines 114–40) as a rallying cry to his fellow conspirators. To Brutus, the honour of their cause is all-important. A Roman's promise is binding and thus they do not need to swear an oath together to unite them in their enterprise.

a Read carefully through his speech. Imagine that you have to give a presentation to a group of younger students about exactly what Brutus says, what it shows about his fundamental beliefs and principles, and how he uses words to persuade and inspire his listeners. Write the text of your presentation.

b Look back at Brutus's language and behaviour so far in this scene. Produce a spider diagram of reasons why he is emerging as the natural leader of the conspirators. Link each point to evidence from the text.

1 cautelous 狡诈多疑
2 carrions 土埋到脖子的人
3 even 坚定
4 th'insuppressive mettle 不屈不挠的本性
5 a several bastardy 多重杂种（指不像罗马人一样忠义）
6 sound him 探一探他的口风
7 silver hairs 一头银发（代表睿智和成熟）
8 purchase us 为咱们争得
9 no whit 一点儿也不
10 buried in his gravity 被他的老成持重掩埋
11 break with him 让他知道，透露给他
12 well urged 问得好
13 meet 妥当
14 We … contriver 此人诡计多端，日后便知
15 means 手段，能力
16 improve 运用，发挥
17 annoy 威胁，伤害
18 envy 恶毒
19 but 不过……而已

1 Public relations (in small groups)

Metellus sees (line 145) that the conspirators have a public image problem, and so does Brutus (lines 162–83). In those lines, Brutus shows the conspirators how to think of their task in a high-minded, noble and honourable way. However, he does not show how to get the general public to think of the assassination in the same way.

- You are a public relations firm sympathetic to the Republican cause. You have secretly been asked to prepare a presentation, using all modern forms of media at your disposal (blogs, social networking, posters, adverts and so on) to give an immediate explanation and justification of the campaign against Caesar. Put together a publicity package to convince everybody that Caesar poses a genuine threat to Rome and its traditions and values.

2 What to do about Antony? (in pairs)

Cassius urges that Antony ('A shrewd contriver') should be killed along with Caesar. Brutus believes Antony will pose no threat once Caesar is dead: 'Antony is but a limb of Caesar'. Brutus quickly wins the argument here, but imagine that Cassius later decides to take up the discussion again with Brutus and argue his point further. Write an exchange of emails between the two characters.

Julius Caesar Act 2 Scene 1
儒略·恺撒

	Swear priests and cowards and men cautelous¹,	
	Old feeble carrions², and such suffering souls	130
	That welcome wrongs: unto bad causes swear	
	Such creatures as men doubt. But do not stain	
	The even³ virtue of our enterprise,	
	Nor th'insuppressive mettle⁴ of our spirits,	
	To think that or our cause or our performance	135
	Did need an oath, when every drop of blood	
	That every Roman bears, and nobly bears,	
	Is guilty of a several bastardy⁵	
	If he do break the smallest particle	
	Of any promise that hath passed from him.	140
CASSIUS	But what of Cicero? Shall we sound him⁶?	
	I think he will stand very strong with us.	
CASCA	Let us not leave him out.	
CINNA	No, by no means.	
METELLUS	O, let us have him, for his silver hairs⁷	
	Will purchase us⁸ a good opinion	145
	And buy men's voices to commend our deeds.	
	It shall be said his judgement ruled our hands;	
	Our youths and wildness shall no whit⁹ appear,	
	But all be buried in his gravity¹⁰.	
BRUTUS	O, name him not, let us not break with him¹¹,	150
	For he will never follow anything	
	That other men begin.	
CASSIUS	Then leave him out.	
CASCA	Indeed he is not fit.	
DECIUS	Shall no man else be touched but only Caesar?	
CASSIUS	Decius, well urged¹². I think it is not meet¹³	155
	Mark Antony, so well beloved of Caesar,	
	Should outlive Caesar. We shall find of him	
	A shrewd contriver¹⁴. And, you know, his means¹⁵,	
	If he improve¹⁶ them, may well stretch so far	
	As to annoy¹⁷ us all, which to prevent,	160
	Let Antony and Caesar fall together.	
BRUTUS	Our course will seem too bloody, Caius Cassius,	
	To cut the head off and then hack the limbs –	
	Like wrath in death and envy¹⁸ afterwards –	
	For Antony is but¹⁹ a limb of Caesar.	165

Brutus says Caesar must be killed, not with spite, but with regret. Again, he overrules Cassius's fears about Antony. Cassius worries that superstition may keep Caesar at home.

 剧情简介：布鲁图说，刺杀恺撒，要心怀遗憾，而不是恶意。卡休对安东尼的担忧再次遭布鲁图驳回。卡休担心，近来颇为迷信的恺撒会闭门不出。

Language in the play 剧中语言
The sacrifice of Caesar (in small groups)

'Let's be sacrificers, but not butchers', says Brutus.

a Try several group readings of Brutus's lines 162–80, taking a sentence each and then changing speaker. As you read, experiment with different tones that Brutus might employ to try to justify the conspirators' cause.

b Write down all Brutus's phrases that describe the act of killing Caesar (there may be up to ten such instances). In each case explain clearly the significance of the words he chooses. How far do you think he manages to justify or excuse the vicious act they are about to commit?

Stagecraft 导演技巧
The clock strikes three (in groups of three or four)

Brutus interrupts Cassius at line 185 and at line 192 the striking clock ends their discussion about whether Antony should also be killed.

- Talk together about the dramatic impact of the clock striking: it is 3 a.m. on the morning of the Ides of March.
- Discuss the way you would stage this moment in a modern production. What kind of 'striking' would you use to create the most powerful dramatic effect? How would you have Brutus, Cassius and Trebonius react as they listen?
- When you have settled on your ideas, try filming this dramatic moment accompanied by your chosen sound effects.

1 Conspirators caught in conspiracy (by yourself)

Imagine that you are one of Caesar's secret agents and, with or without Caesar's knowledge, you have bugged Brutus's house and listened in on this scene. Now with cast-iron (确凿) proof of conspiracy, you must report your findings to Caesar. Write up your evidence, ensuring that all the information you collect is as factual and accurate as you can make it. Compare your version with those of other students to check the validity and detail of your report.

1 come by   抓获
2 subtle   有心机，狡猾
3 Stir up their servants   挑唆仆人（将情绪比作心的仆人）
4 chide 'em   责骂他们
5 make   令……显得
6 envious   狠毒，恶毒
7 purgers   除暴安良的英雄
8 engrafted   根深蒂固
9 much he should   他做不到这份儿上
10 fear   害怕的理由
11 of late   近来
12 ceremonies   征兆
13 augurers   占卜官，占卜师
14 hold   使……闭门不出

> Let's be sacrificers, but not butchers, Caius.
> We all stand up against the spirit of Caesar,
> And in the spirit of men there is no blood.
> O, that we then could come by¹ Caesar's spirit
> And not dismember Caesar! But, alas, 170
> Caesar must bleed for it. And, gentle friends,
> Let's kill him boldly, but not wrathfully;
> Let's carve him as a dish fit for the gods,
> Not hew him as a carcass fit for hounds.
> And let our hearts, as subtle² masters do, 175
> Stir up their servants³ to an act of rage
> And after seem to chide 'em⁴. This shall make⁵
> Our purpose necessary, and not envious⁶;
> Which so appearing to the common eyes,
> We shall be called purgers⁷, not murderers. 180
> And for Mark Antony, think not of him,
> For he can do no more than Caesar's arm
> When Caesar's head is off.

CASSIUS   Yet I fear him,
> For in the engrafted⁸ love he bears to Caesar –

BRUTUS   Alas, good Cassius, do not think of him. 185
> If he love Caesar, all that he can do
> Is to himself – take thought and die for Caesar;
> And that were much he should⁹, for he is given
> To sports, to wildness, and much company.

TREBONIUS   There is no fear¹⁰ in him, let him not die, 190
> For he will live and laugh at this hereafter.

Clock strikes

BRUTUS   Peace, count the clock.

CASSIUS   The clock hath stricken three.

TREBONIUS   'Tis time to part.

CASSIUS   But it is doubtful yet
> Whether Caesar will come forth today or no,
> For he is superstitious grown of late¹¹, 195
> Quite from the main opinion he held once
> Of fantasy, of dreams, and ceremonies¹².
> It may be these apparent prodigies,
> The unaccustomed terror of this night,
> And the persuasion of his augurers¹³ 200
> May hold¹⁴ him from the Capitol today.

Decius promises to bring Caesar to the Capitol. The conspirators agree to meet at 8 a.m. at Caesar's house. They leave Brutus alone. Portia enters and Brutus questions why she has risen from her bed.

剧情简介：德休保证能让恺撒到议会山去。谋杀团伙约好上午8点在恺撒家里会合，之后他们离开布鲁图家。鲍霞上，布鲁图问她怎么起来了。

1 Justifying Brutus? (in pairs)

By the time the conspirators leave at line 228, Brutus has not only joined the conspiracy, he has taken charge of it.

a Find the three instances when Brutus overrules suggestions from Cassius and discuss how he achieves this.

b Remind yourself of the text up to line 233. Then draw up a table with two columns, headed 'Admirable decisions' and 'Questionable decisions'. Fill in the columns with details of the decisions Brutus makes. Discuss your findings and compare the kind of balance achieved.

Write about it 写作练习

Lucius the silent witness (by yourself)

Lucius has been off stage since line 76 of this scene. Since then the seven conspirators have gathered and made their plans.

- Imagine that Lucius has overheard key parts of their dialogue. Write up his thoughts as a secret diary entry in which he reflects on the conspiracy and speculates about what the future holds for him and his master. Look back at the earlier parts of the scene for clues about Lucius's character and his relationship with Brutus. Factor these into the 'voice' that you create for Lucius.

Characters 人物分析

Portia (in pairs)

Julius Caesar is dominated by men and male perspectives. The words of Portia, Brutus's wife, at line 233 mark the first speech by a woman in the play, apart from Calpurnia's 'Here, my lord' in Act 1 Scene 2.

- One of you has been cast as Portia in a new production of the play. In preparation for the role, you have asked for discussion time with your director. Plan for it by reading all Portia says in this scene before her exit at line 309. Make notes on key issues you want to discuss. For example, how do you think you should play your relationship with your husband, based on the evidence of the text? The other student is the director, who should prepare similarly.

- Run the meeting, resolve all contentious points and rehearse the episode. Another student can play Brutus if you want to work in threes.

1 o'ersway him 左右他的想法
2 That ... toils （这些都是诱捕动物的方法：独角兽的角卡在树上；熊沉迷于照镜子；大象掉进陷阱；狮子落入捕兽网）
3 give ... bent 让他回心转意
4 there （指恺撒家）
5 uttermost 最晚
6 bear Caesar hard 对恺撒怀恨在心
7 rated 训斥
8 by him 去找他
9 fashion him 劝他，做他的工作
10 put on 泄露
11 formal constancy 表面上镇定自若
12 slumber 酣睡
13 figures 幻象

JULIUS CAESAR ACT 2 SCENE 1
儒略・恺撒

DECIUS	Never fear that. If he be so resolved
	I can o'ersway him¹, for he loves to hear
	That unicorns may be betrayed with trees,
	And bears with glasses, elephants with holes, 205
	Lions with toils², and men with flatterers.
	But when I tell him he hates flatterers
	He says he does, being then most flatterèd.
	Let me work:
	For I can give his humour the true bent³, 210
	And I will bring him to the Capitol.
CASSIUS	Nay, we will all of us be there⁴ to fetch him.
BRUTUS	By the eighth hour, is that the uttermost⁵?
CINNA	Be that the uttermost, and fail not then.
METELLUS	Caius Ligarius doth bear Caesar hard⁶, 215
	Who rated⁷ him for speaking well of Pompey.
	I wonder none of you have thought of him.
BRUTUS	Now, good Metellus, go along by him⁸.
	He loves me well, and I have given him reasons.
	Send him but hither and I'll fashion him⁹. 220
CASSIUS	The morning comes upon's. We'll leave you, Brutus,
	And, friends, disperse yourselves, but all remember
	What you have said and show yourselves true Romans.
BRUTUS	Good gentlemen, look fresh and merrily:
	Let not our looks put on¹⁰ our purposes, 225
	But bear it as our Roman actors do,
	With untired spirits and formal constancy¹¹.
	And so good morrow to you every one.

Exeunt [all but] Brutus

Boy! Lucius! Fast asleep? It is no matter,
Enjoy the honey-heavy dew of slumber¹².   230
Thou hast no figures¹³ nor no fantasies
Which busy care draws in the brains of men,
Therefore thou sleep'st so sound.

Enter PORTIA

PORTIA	Brutus, my lord.
BRUTUS	Portia! What mean you? Wherefore rise you now?
	It is not for your health thus to commit 235
	Your weak condition to the raw cold morning.

Portia tells Brutus how difficult he has been in recent days. He tells her he's sick. She asks why he is out of bed, insisting on the truth.

剧情简介：鲍霞说布鲁图最近很难伺候，他解释说自己生病了。鲍霞追问实情，问他为何下了床。

1 Watching Brutus (in small groups)

One or two of you read lines 237–51, where Portia describes what happened the previous night ('yesternight'), pausing briefly after each action. In those pauses, the other members of the group act out the scene without sound, as you might see it through an uncurtained window.

2 Portia and Brutus: marriage guidance (in pairs)

Portia is clearly troubled by the changes in her husband's behaviour. In lines 252–87, she catalogues a host of her concerns.

- First, read the lines together to pick up the details, and then enact a meeting between Portia and a marriage guidance counsellor (one of you is Portia, the other the counsellor) in which Portia seeks advice about how she should respond to these difficult times in her relationship with her husband. In preparation, you will need to decide just how in love with him she is, and to consider the time in which the play was set (and written), when the role of wives was very different to what you might expect today (see p. 180).
- Follow this by staging a second 'marriage guidance' meeting, this time between the counsellor and Brutus.
- After the meeting, work together to write up an account of what was discussed and what advice was given. This could be in the style of a formal report from the counsellor.

1 Y'have = You have
2 Stole 偷偷溜走
3 across 抱着（胳膊）
4 wafture 挥动
5 too much enkindled 本来就很烦躁
6 an effect of humour 湿气的作用（喻指偶尔的情绪失常；humour指对人健康不利的湿气）
7 shape 体形
8 condition 情绪
9 come by it 治好病
10 physical 能治病，利于养病
11 wholesome 对身体好，舒舒服服
12 dare 冒着（危险）
13 contagion 侵染
14 rheumy 潮湿
15 unpurgèd 污浊
16 sick offence 疾病
17 charm 恳求
18 incorporate 使……结合

Themes 主题分析

Sickness and disease

Sickness in different forms becomes an important dramatic element in the play. Already in this scene, Brutus, concerned about his wife's health, has referred to her 'weak condition' in the early morning air.

a Read Portia's lines 261–70. Collect examples of references to sickness and disease. Write down in modern English what each one means and what it suggests about the state of Brutus's mind.

b Why do you think the theme of sickness and disease comes to prominence in this scene? (Note there are two further examples on the next two pages.)

Julius Caesar Act 2 Scene 1
儒略・恺撒

PORTIA	Nor for yours neither. Y'have[1] ungently, Brutus,
	Stole[2] from my bed; and yesternight at supper
	You suddenly arose and walked about,
	Musing and sighing, with your arms across[3], 240
	And when I asked you what the matter was,
	You stared upon me with ungentle looks.
	I urged you further, then you scratched your head
	And too impatiently stamped with your foot.
	Yet I insisted, yet you answered not, 245
	But with an angry wafture[4] of your hand
	Gave sign for me to leave you. So I did,
	Fearing to strengthen that impatience
	Which seemed too much enkindled[5], and withal
	Hoping it was but an effect of humour[6] 250
	Which sometime hath his hour with every man.
	It will not let you eat nor talk nor sleep;
	And could it work so much upon your shape[7]
	As it hath much prevailed on your condition[8],
	I should not know you, Brutus. Dear my lord, 255
	Make me acquainted with your cause of grief.
BRUTUS	I am not well in health, and that is all.
PORTIA	Brutus is wise, and were he not in health
	He would embrace the means to come by it[9].
BRUTUS	Why, so I do. Good Portia, go to bed. 260
PORTIA	Is Brutus sick? And is it physical[10]
	To walk unbracèd and suck up the humours
	Of the dank morning? What, is Brutus sick?
	And will he steal out of his wholesome[11] bed
	To dare[12] the vile contagion[13] of the night 265
	And tempt the rheumy[14] and unpurgèd[15] air
	To add unto his sickness? No, my Brutus,
	You have some sick offence[16] within your mind,
	Which by the right and virtue of my place
	I ought to know of. And upon my knees 270
	I charm[17] you, by my once commended beauty,
	By all your vows of love, and that great vow
	Which did incorporate[18] and make us one,
	That you unfold to me, your self, your half,

1 Portia's wound (in groups of four or five)

Portia makes a dramatic revelation at line 300: she has inflicted self-harm (a stab wound to her thigh). How Brutus responds to the news ('O ye gods, / Render me worthy of this noble wife') is a key moment in defining the depth of their relationship. Some productions use it to explore Brutus's tortured guilt and anguish; others suggest his words lack sincerity and that he is more preoccupied with the plot to assassinate Caesar.

a First, research the significance of this type of ritual act in Roman society in Caesar's time. Then discuss together the possible reasons for Portia committing this frightening deed. (For example, some see her capacity to 'bear' the wound 'with patience' as a mark of her love for her husband and as proof of her complete devotion to Brutus.)

b Why do you think Shakespeare chooses to reveal Portia's self-harm at this point in the play?

2 Brutus: speak the sub-text (in pairs)

Although later in the play (Act 2 Scene 4, line 9), it seems that Brutus did tell Portia the reasons for his behaviour, in this exchange with her he speaks very little (only nine lines between Portia's entrance and line 302).

- One of you reads aloud all of Brutus's words in this episode, pausing at the end of each line for the other to voice exactly what is in Brutus's mind.

▶ What does this photo suggest about the way in which Brutus and Portia relate to each other?

1 heavy　心事重重
2 resort to　来找，拜访
3 excepted　除外
4 appertain to　有关……的
5 in sort or limitation　在有限的范围内
6 Dwell … suburbs　仅仅位于……的边缘吗
7 harlot　妓女
8 ruddy drops　鲜红的血滴
9 Cato　加图（一位拥护共和制的政治家，以坚忍闻名）
10 so fathered and so husbanded　有这样的父亲和丈夫
11 counsels　心事
12 constancy　忠贞
13 Render　使成为，使变得
14 Hark　听
15 partake　得知
16 engagements　盘算的事情
17 construe　告诉
18 All … brows　眉头不展的原因

	Why you are heavy¹ and what men tonight	275
	Have had resort to² you, for here have been
	Some six or seven who did hide their faces
	Even from darkness.

BRUTUS   Kneel not, gentle Portia.
PORTIA   I should not need if you were gentle Brutus.
           Within the bond of marriage, tell me, Brutus,   280
           Is it excepted³ I should know no secrets
           That appertain to⁴ you? Am I your self
           But, as it were, in sort or limitation⁵,
           To keep with you at meals, comfort your bed,
           And talk to you sometimes? Dwell I but in the suburbs⁶   285
           Of your good pleasure? If it be no more
           Portia is Brutus' harlot⁷, not his wife.
BRUTUS   You are my true and honourable wife,
           As dear to me as are the ruddy drops⁸
           That visit my sad heart.   290
PORTIA   If this were true, then should I know this secret.
           I grant I am a woman, but withal
           A woman that Lord Brutus took to wife.
           I grant I am a woman, but withal
           A woman well reputed, Cato's⁹ daughter.   295
           Think you I am no stronger than my sex,
           Being so fathered and so husbanded¹⁰?
           Tell me your counsels¹¹, I will not disclose 'em.
           I have made strong proof of my constancy¹²,
           Giving myself a voluntary wound   300
           Here, in the thigh. Can I bear that with patience
           And not my husband's secrets?
BRUTUS   O ye gods,
           Render¹³ me worthy of this noble wife!

                        Knock

           Hark¹⁴, hark, one knocks. Portia, go in a while,
           And by and by thy bosom shall partake¹⁵   305
           The secrets of my heart.
           All my engagements¹⁶ I will construe¹⁷ to thee,
           All the charactery of my sad brows¹⁸.
           Leave me with haste.

                                      Exit Portia
                 Lucius, who's that knocks?

The sick Ligarius enters. Brutus asks for his help. Ligarius seems to find new strength in being part of the secret enterprise and swears blind obedience to Brutus.

剧情简介：理噶瑞欧着病人装束上。布鲁图请他助一臂之力。理噶瑞欧仿佛从这项秘密行动中汲取到了新的力量，他发誓无条件追随布鲁图。

Themes 主题分析

More sickness and disease (in pairs)

a There are four separate instances of sickness in this scene:

- Brutus's concerns about Portia's health
- Brutus's declining psychological health (sleepless nights, troubled mind), which is contrasted with Lucius's restful innocence
- Portia's self-inflicted wound on her thigh
- Ligarius's bodily sickness, which is covered by a bandage ('kerchief').

Talk together about the different examples of sickness in this scene and then write a series of short paragraphs exploring the dramatic importance of each one. Why do you think there are so many overt references to sickness in this act?

b Ligarius's sickness miraculously disappears once he pledges himself to Brutus's cause.

- Take it in turns to be Ligarius and try different versions of lines 320–6, during which his transformation takes place. Can you present both his physical recovery and his strength of feeling for Brutus, the 'Soul of Rome'?
- Why do you think Shakespeare chooses to place this episode at the end of the scene?

1 would　想要
2 Vouchsafe good morrow　向您问早安
3 chose out　挑出，拣出
4 wear a kerchief　勒着个头巾（生病时做此装扮）
5 healthful　健康
6 honourable loins　光荣的先祖
7 Thou … spirit　你像招魂师一样唤回了我僵死的魂魄
8 strive with　对抗
9 get the better of　战胜
10 whole　健全，痊愈
11 Set on your foot　您先请
12 it sufficeth　这就够了

Write about it 写作练习

What lies ahead?

The scene begins with Brutus wrestling agonisingly with his conscience – and ends with a resolute Brutus becoming leader of the conspirators. A dramatic and symbolic roll of thunder seems to point to Caesar's death (this technique is called **foreshadowing** [伏笔，铺垫]).

As Brutus exits, he cannot help his mind drifting ahead to what he hopes will be the outcome of that eventful day. In his private thoughts, what does he make of the plans, his fellow conspirators, the enormity of their actions, his wife and his responsibilities?

- Write a modern English dramatic monologue for Brutus to follow on from line 335.

Julius Caesar Act 2 Scene 1
儒略·恺撒

Enter LUCIUS *and* LIGARIUS

LUCIUS	Here is a sick man that would¹ speak with you.	310
BRUTUS	Caius Ligarius, that Metellus spake of.	
	Boy, stand aside.	

[*Exit Lucius*]

Caius Ligarius, how?

LIGARIUS	Vouchsafe good morrow² from a feeble tongue.	
BRUTUS	O, what a time have you chose out³, brave Caius,	
	To wear a kerchief⁴! Would you were not sick!	315
LIGARIUS	I am not sick if Brutus have in hand	
	Any exploit worthy the name of honour.	
BRUTUS	Such an exploit have I in hand, Ligarius,	
	Had you a healthful⁵ ear to hear of it.	
LIGARIUS	By all the gods that Romans bow before,	320
	I here discard my sickness!	

[*He pulls off his kerchief*]

Soul of Rome,
Brave son, derived from honourable loins⁶,
Thou, like an exorcist, hast conjured up
My mortifièd spirit.⁷ Now bid me run
And I will strive with⁸ things impossible,   325
Yea, get the better of⁹ them. What's to do?

BRUTUS	A piece of work that will make sick men whole¹⁰.	
LIGARIUS	But are not some whole that we must make sick?	
BRUTUS	That must we also. What it is, my Caius,	
	I shall unfold to thee as we are going	330
	To whom it must be done.	
LIGARIUS	Set on your foot¹¹,	
	And with a heart new fired I follow you	
	To do I know not what; but it sufficeth¹²	
	That Brutus leads me on.	

Thunder

BRUTUS	Follow me then.

Exeunt

Caesar tells how his wife Calpurnia has spoken of his murder in her sleep. She orders him to stay at home, telling of frightening portents of ill omen. Caesar is unmoved, declaring he will go out.

 剧情简介： 恺撒讲述妻子卡尔珀妮娅睡梦中大喊有人要杀他。她描述了种种骇人的凶兆，求恺撒不要出门。恺撒不为所动，执意要出去。

Stagecraft 导演技巧

The storm inside Caesar's house (in fours, then by yourself)

The first line of Scene 2 ('Nor heaven nor earth have been at peace tonight') makes it clear that the storm that ends Scene 1 carries across to the opening of this next domestic scene, this time inside Caesar's house.

a Together, work on a soundscape that could be used to accompany Caesar's lines 1–3. Think about what kind of 'storm noises' would best complement Caesar's troubled state of mind. Then have a go at recording Caesar's words accompanied by the soundscape you have designed.

b In your Director's Journal, write a paragraph on the dramatic effects created by the use of the storm and also the unnatural events that Calpurnia describes in the script opposite.

1 At home with Brutus and Caesar (in pairs)

a Remind yourselves briefly of Act 2 Scene 1, lines 233–309 (Brutus and Portia together). Then read through Act 2 Scene 2, lines 1–82 (Caesar and Calpurnia together). Act the two scenes out to another group.

b Discuss everything you notice about the ways in which Portia and Calpurnia behave with their husbands. Then create a Venn diagram (文氏图，用以表示集合或类), with 'Portia' in one circle and 'Calpurnia' in the other. Fill in the diagram with your observations about the two women. In what ways are they different? And in what ways similar?

Write about it 写作练习

'horrid sights' – two versions

Caesar's guards (the 'watch') witness some strange and supernatural events (lines 17–24).

- Imagine that you are the leader of that group. Write up in formal and accurate detail a report of exactly what you witness.
- Then, as another member of the group, take to a social networking site and describe in informal and much more personal, imaginative writing what you have seen and what you make of it.
- Compare the two texts and consider the different effects created.

---

1 *nightgown* 睡袍
2 *priests* 占卜官
3 *present* 立刻
4 *success* 结果（无论好坏）
5 *walk forth* 出门
6 *stood on ceremonies* 相信征兆
7 *fright* = frighten
8 *Recounts* 讲述
9 *watch* 守卫
10 *whelpèd* 下崽儿
11 *yawned and yielded up* 张开大嘴吐出
12 *squadrons and right form* （士兵排列的）阵式，战斗队形
13 *beyond all use* 完全不合常理
14 *purposed* 注定

Act 2 Scene 2
Caesar's house   Early morning

Thunder and lightning. Enter JULIUS CAESAR *in his nightgown*[1]

CAESAR
Nor heaven nor earth have been at peace tonight.
Thrice hath Calpurnia in her sleep cried out,
'Help ho, they murder Caesar!' Who's within?

Enter a SERVANT

SERVANT My lord?
CAESAR Go bid the priests[2] do present[3] sacrifice   5
And bring me their opinions of success[4].
SERVANT I will, my lord.   *Exit*

Enter CALPURNIA

CALPURNIA
What mean you, Caesar, think you to walk forth[5]?
You shall not stir out of your house today.
CAESAR
Caesar shall forth. The things that threatened me   10
Ne'er looked but on my back; when they shall see
The face of Caesar they are vanishèd.
CALPURNIA
Caesar, I never stood on ceremonies[6],
Yet now they fright[7] me. There is one within,
Besides the things that we have heard and seen,   15
Recounts[8] most horrid sights seen by the watch[9].
A lioness hath whelpèd[10] in the streets,
And graves have yawned and yielded up[11] their dead;
Fierce fiery warriors fight upon the clouds
In ranks and squadrons and right form[12] of war,   20
Which drizzled blood upon the Capitol;
The noise of battle hurtled in the air,
Horses did neigh and dying men did groan,
And ghosts did shriek and squeal about the streets.
O Caesar, these things are beyond all use[13],   25
And I do fear them.
CAESAR   What can be avoided
Whose end is purposed[14] by the mighty gods?
Yet Caesar shall go forth, for these predictions
Are to the world in general as to Caesar.

Although Caesar claims to have no fear of death and at first defies Calpurnia and the augurers, in the end their concerns prevail. He orders Decius to tell the Senate that Caesar will not come today.

剧情简介：恺撒虽然声称自己不怕死，起初也不听妻子和占卜官的劝告，最后还是架不住他们的担忧。恺撒让德休告诉元老院一声，他今天不去了。

Write about it 写作练习

Calpurnia's fears for Caesar

It is the morning of the Ides of March. Calpurnia has dreamt all night of her husband's murder. Now she struggles to persuade Caesar to stay at home. She even offers him a way that he can use her as the excuse ('Call it my fear / That keeps you in the house'). Finally, at line 56, he agrees to her request.

Write a short soliloquy or an aside (旁白) for Calpurnia that could be spoken to the audience after line 56. In it, try to explore her deeper feelings about Caesar, her fears for him, and her relief that he has listened to her arguments.

1. blaze forth 昭告
2. stir forth 出门
3. entrails 内脏
4. in shame of cowardice 为了羞辱懦夫
5. a beast without a heart 没胆的畜生
6. littered 产崽儿
7. Your … confidence 您的理智被自负吃光了
8. Let … this 我给您跪下，这次就依了我吧
9. for thy humour 为了照顾你的心情
10. in very happy time 正是时候

Characters 人物分析

Caesar: brave or foolish? (in pairs)

When Caesar first speaks to Calpurnia (lines 10–12), he insists that he will not be frightened into staying at home, in spite of any sense of danger that might be present. Even Calpurnia's description of the terrifying omens draws from him a firm belief that such portents are not directed at him specifically.

His famous line: 'Cowards die many times before their deaths' and an acceptance that death 'Will come when it will come' again show him resolute in the face of threat.

Finally, after the servant reports that the priests could find no heart in a sacrificed animal, Caesar puts his own gloss on that, too: he would be lacking 'heart' (courage) if he did not attend the Capitol.

- Consider each of these ideas in turn. Then make two columns on a piece of paper, one with the heading 'Brave', the other with the heading 'Foolish'. Add each detail to the appropriate column with a clear and detailed explanation of why you have put it there.

◀ How should Caesar respond to Calpurnia's pleas?

CALPURNIA	When beggars die there are no comets seen,	30
	The heavens themselves blaze forth[1] the death of princes.	
CAESAR	Cowards die many times before their deaths,	
	The valiant never taste of death but once.	
	Of all the wonders that I yet have heard	
	It seems to me most strange that men should fear,	35
	Seeing that death, a necessary end,	
	Will come when it will come.	

Enter a SERVANT

                        What say the augurers?

SERVANT	They would not have you to stir forth[2] today.	
	Plucking the entrails[3] of an offering forth,	
	They could not find a heart within the beast.	40
CAESAR	The gods do this in shame of cowardice[4].	
	Caesar should be a beast without a heart[5]	
	If he should stay at home today for fear.	
	No, Caesar shall not. Danger knows full well	
	That Caesar is more dangerous than he:	45
	We are two lions littered[6] in one day,	
	And I the elder and more terrible.	
	And Caesar shall go forth.	
CALPURNIA	Alas, my lord,	
	Your wisdom is consumed in confidence[7].	
	Do not go forth today. Call it my fear	50
	That keeps you in the house, and not your own.	
	We'll send Mark Antony to the Senate House	
	And he shall say you are not well today.	
	Let me, upon my knee, prevail in this[8].	
CAESAR	Mark Antony shall say I am not well,	55
	And for thy humour[9] I will stay at home.	

Enter DECIUS

	Here's Decius Brutus, he shall tell them so.	
DECIUS	Caesar, all hail! Good morrow, worthy Caesar,	
	I come to fetch you to the Senate House.	
CAESAR	And you are come in very happy time[10]	60
	To bear my greeting to the senators	
	And tell them that I will not come today.	
	Cannot is false, and that I dare not, falser:	
	I will not come today. Tell them so, Decius.	

Calpurnia suggests that Decius should say Caesar is sick. Caesar scorns the lie and describes Calpurnia's dream. Decius interprets it favourably and says the Senate intend to crown Caesar.

 剧情简介：卡尔珀妮娅让德休说恺撒身体不适。恺撒对撒谎很不屑，并把卡尔珀妮娅做的梦告诉了德休。德休把这个梦往好的方向解释了一番，还说元老院正打算给恺撒加冕。

Characters 人物分析

'Caesar will not come' (in pairs)

Caesar gives Decius this message for the Senate, explaining why he will not attend the Capitol that day: 'The cause is in my will. I will not come: / That is enough to satisfy the Senate' (lines 71–2).

- Read these lines several times to each other until you arrive at your preferred version. Then look back at all that Caesar says in this scene and identify every occasion on which he refers to himself not as 'I' or 'me', but as 'Caesar' (even in conversation with his wife). There are more than ten such instances.
- Discuss what these details show about Caesar's character.

1 The dream interpreted in two ways (in two groups)

Both Republican conspirators and Caesarites could make use of Calpurnia's prophetic dream to justify or condemn Caesar's assassination after the event.

- One group focuses on Calpurnia's interpretation of the dream (lines 76–82). The other concentrates on Decius's explanation (lines 83–90). Each group produces a tableau of their version. Compare versions.

Language in the play 剧中语言

Blood … and more blood

Calpurnia's dream features much blood: a statue 'with an hundred spouts' in Caesar's words; one 'spouting blood in many pipes' according to Decius.

- Create a striking drawing of Caesar's statue with its excesses of blood. Add around it all references to the word you have encountered so far: Pompey's blood (Act 1 Scene 1); Brutus speaking about the killing of Caesar (Act 2 Scene 1) and his reluctance to shed unnecessary blood in killing Antony; Portia's self-inflicted wound (Act 2 Scene 1); Calpurnia's ominous vision (the start of Act 2 Scene 2).
- Add all future references to blood as they appear. Look out specifically for those in Act 3!

1 **greybeards** 那群白胡子老头儿
2 **stays me** 拦着我
3 **evils imminent** 即将来临的灾祸
4 **all amiss** 全错了
5 **press / For** 争抢
6 **tinctures, stains, relics, and cognisance** (tinctures指可用于纹章上的颜色、金属、皮毛等, **stains**指染了恺撒鲜血的东西, **relics**指恺撒的遗物, **congnisance**指贵族家里家臣佩戴的徽章；任何物件沾染了恺撒的鲜血都变得神圣，所以人们抢来当作一种荣誉，一种忠于恺撒的标志)
7 **expounded** 解释
8 **mock / Apt to be rendered** 说出去别人会笑话
9 **meet with** 做到（好梦）

CALPURNIA	Say he is sick.	
CAESAR	Shall Caesar send a lie?	65

                Have I in conquest stretched mine arm so far
                To be afeard to tell greybeards[1] the truth?
                Decius, go tell them Caesar will not come.

DECIUS   Most mighty Caesar, let me know some cause,
                Lest I be laughed at when I tell them so.   70

CAESAR   The cause is in my will. I will not come:
                That is enough to satisfy the Senate.
                But for your private satisfaction,
                Because I love you, I will let you know:
                Calpurnia here, my wife, stays me[2] at home.   75
                She dreamt tonight she saw my statue,
                Which like a fountain with an hundred spouts
                Did run pure blood, and many lusty Romans
                Came smiling and did bathe their hands in it.
                And these does she apply for warnings and portents   80
                And evils imminent[3], and on her knee
                Hath begged that I will stay at home today.

DECIUS   This dream is all amiss[4] interpreted,
                It was a vision fair and fortunate.
                Your statue spouting blood in many pipes,   85
                In which so many smiling Romans bathed,
                Signifies that from you great Rome shall suck
                Reviving blood and that great men shall press
                For[5] tinctures, stains, relics, and cognisance[6].
                This by Calpurnia's dream is signified.   90

CAESAR   And this way have you well expounded[7] it.

DECIUS   I have, when you have heard what I can say.
                And know it now: the Senate have concluded
                To give this day a crown to mighty Caesar.
                If you shall send them word you will not come,   95
                Their minds may change. Besides, it were a mock
                Apt to be rendered[8] for someone to say,
                'Break up the Senate till another time,
                When Caesar's wife shall meet with[9] better dreams.'

Caesar finally resolves to go to the Senate. First the conspirators, then Antony arrive. Caesar offers wine while he prepares himself. The conspirators secretly confide their true intentions.

 剧情简介：最终恺撒决定去元老院。谋杀团伙的人和安东尼先后来到恺撒家。恺撒请众人品酒，他去做出门前的准备。谋杀团伙成员秘密传递他们真实的意图。

1 Decius the persuader (in threes)

Decius needs to persuade Caesar to go to the Capitol. Between lines 92 and 104 he marshals three arguments that suggest Caesar should attend.

- Read his lines to each other several times and identify the three elements of Decius's strategy. Then rank them in order: based on your knowledge of Caesar, which is the most important in changing Caesar's mind? Compare your ideas with those of other groups.

Characters 人物分析
Antony: setting the stage for the future

Prior to his vital role in Act 3, Antony has a shadowy and insubstantial part. Here he is given just five words to make an impact and remind the audience of his loyalty to, and respect for, Caesar – attributes that will be crucial later in the play. He has only five lines in total in the first two acts.

- Find all of Antony's lines so far. Write a short paragraph about what they have in common and what they show about Antony.

Themes 主题分析
Appearance versus reality (in threes)

The final dramatic episode of the scene is often used in performance to highlight the difference between the easy and assured public confidence of Caesar and the secret scheming of the conspirators. Caesar wants to share wine with his 'Good friends' (line 126); Trebonius's and Brutus's 'asides' both make clear to the audience that appearing to be Caesar's friend is nothing like actually being one.

a Write an extension of both of the asides mentioned above, in which you explore in greater detail what Trebonius and Brutus each feels about the prospect of betraying Caesar's friendship. (Note that Brutus gives a clue to his feelings by using the word 'earns', which at the time meant 'grieves'.)

b Create a tableau of the final moment of the scene, exploring the contrast between the three men's attitudes.

1 Lo 瞧，看哪
2 my … proceeding 我对您的晋升大事十分关心
3 reason … liable 理智劝言（说话不中听）也是出于敬爱
4 robe 长袍（古罗马的宽外袍）
5 ague 热病
6 lean 消瘦
7 revels long a-nights 通宵宴饮作乐
8 notwithstanding = nevertheless
9 prepare within （应该是让仆人准备酒，见126行）
10 every … same 像朋友未必真是朋友
11 earns 心酸

	If Caesar hide himself, shall they not whisper,	100
	'Lo[1], Caesar is afraid'?	
	Pardon me, Caesar, for my dear dear love	
	To your proceeding[2] bids me tell you this,	
	And reason to my love is liable[3].	
CAESAR	How foolish do your fears seem now, Calpurnia!	105
	I am ashamèd I did yield to them.	
	Give me my robe[4], for I will go.	

Enter BRUTUS, *Ligarius, Metellus, Casca,* TREBONIUS, *Cinna, and* PUBLIUS

	And look where Publius is come to fetch me.	
PUBLIUS	Good morrow, Caesar.	
CAESAR	Welcome, Publius.	
	What, Brutus, are you stirred so early too?	110
	Good morrow, Casca. Caius Ligarius,	
	Caesar was ne'er so much your enemy	
	As that same ague[5] which hath made you lean[6].	
	What is't o'clock?	
BRUTUS	Caesar, 'tis strucken eight.	
CAESAR	I thank you for your pains and courtesy.	115

Enter ANTONY

	See, Antony, that revels long a-nights[7],	
	Is notwithstanding[8] up. Good morrow, Antony.	
ANTONY	So to most noble Caesar.	
CAESAR	[*To Calpurnia*] Bid them prepare within[9],	
	[*Exit Calpurnia*]	
	I am to blame to be thus waited for.	
	Now, Cinna, now, Metellus. What, Trebonius,	120
	I have an hour's talk in store for you.	
	Remember that you call on me today;	
	Be near me that I may remember you.	
TREBONIUS	Caesar, I will. [*Aside*] And so near will I be	
	That your best friends shall wish I had been further.	125
CAESAR	Good friends, go in and taste some wine with me,	
	And we, like friends, will straightway go together.	
BRUTUS	[*Aside*] That every like is not the same[10], O Caesar,	
	The heart of Brutus earns[11] to think upon.	

Exeunt

Artemidorus reads out the warning he intends to give Caesar. Sending Lucius to the Capitol, Portia confides how she can hardly hide her worries.

 剧情简介：阿泰米道若读出了他写给恺撒的提醒。打发卢休去议会山之后，鲍霞坦言自己掩饰不住内心的焦虑。

Characters 人物分析

Focus on Artemidorus (in small groups)

This is Artemidorus's first appearance in the play, and we will see him only once more (in Act 3 Scene 1).

a Talk together about what Artemidorus adds to the dramatic structure of Act 2. Think about why Shakespeare might have given him this scene to himself, coming after the scenes involving the conspirators and then Caesar. What, for example, does he say about Caesar and how does that affect your view of the plans to assassinate him? What do you think is the importance of Artemidorus's final two lines? What is Shakespeare suggesting about the conspiracy? (You might look ahead to the start of Act 3 Scene 1 to find out what happens when he tries to give his warning letter to Caesar.)

b Imagine you are Artemidorus. Take each of the conspirators named in your paper and put together a dossier (汇编) of evidence that supports your suspicions about them. Your dossier could be a combination of witness statements, interviews, filmed or taped evidence and covert photographs. Perhaps you even have an informer amongst the conspirators! You can use your classmates to help 'stage' some of this evidence or adapt pictures and photographs from magazines. You can make up details, but keep close to the spirit of the play. Remember that you have signed the paper and your evidence may come up in court.

1 bend 指向
2 security gives way to conspiracy 自恃安全易遭人谋害
3 Thy lover 您忠心的朋友
4 suitor 上诉人，请愿人
5 laments 悲痛（不已）
6 virtue … emulation 好人总是遭嫉妒之人陷害
7 contrive 勾结
8 prithee 请，求求你
9 errand 差事
10 constancy 定力，镇定
11 'tween = between
12 keep counsel 保守秘密
13 Are thou here yet? 你怎么还不去?

1 Portia's agitation (焦虑)

Portia, like her husband Brutus in Act 2 Scene 1, has troubled thoughts jostling in her mind. Her confidential aside (lines 6–9) suggests that she is desperate to speak of something and finds it incredibly hard to restrain herself.

- What do you think is on her mind? It seems to involve sending Lucius on an errand to the Capitol. Read quickly through to the end of the scene for possible clues and then make notes on your ideas. Pool your responses as a class.

Act 2 Scene 3
Rome   A street

Enter ARTEMIDORUS [*reading a paper*]

ARTEMIDORUS 'Caesar, beware of Brutus, take heed of Cassius, come not near Casca, have an eye to Cinna, trust not Trebonius, mark well Metellus Cimber, Decius Brutus loves thee not, thou hast wronged Caius Ligarius. There is but one mind in all these men, and it is bent[1] against Caesar. If thou beest not immortal look about you: security 5 gives way to conspiracy[2]. The mighty gods defend thee!
                                                                                            Thy lover[3],
                                                                                            Artemidorus.'

Here will I stand till Caesar pass along,
And as a suitor[4] will I give him this.
My heart laments[5] that virtue cannot live   10
Out of the teeth of emulation[6].
If thou read this, O Caesar, thou mayst live;
If not, the fates with traitors do contrive[7].   *Exit*

Act 2 Scene 4
Rome   A street

Enter PORTIA *and* LUCIUS

PORTIA   I prithee[8], boy, run to the Senate House.
         Stay not to answer me but get thee gone.
         Why dost thou stay?
LUCIUS   To know my errand[9], madam.
PORTIA   I would have had thee there and here again
         Ere I can tell thee what thou shouldst do there.   5
         [*Aside*] O constancy[10], be strong upon my side,
         Set a huge mountain 'tween[11] my heart and tongue!
         I have a man's mind, but a woman's might.
         How hard it is for women to keep counsel[12]! –
         Art thou here yet?[13]
LUCIUS   Madam, what should I do?   10
         Run to the Capitol, and nothing else?
         And so return to you, and nothing else?

Portia sends Lucius to report back to her what Brutus says and does. The Soothsayer foresees harm to Caesar, but crowds make his warning difficult to deliver.

剧情简介：鲍霞派卢休去打探布鲁图说了什么、做了什么。预言者预见到恺撒要遭殃，但拥挤的人群令他很难向恺撒传达他的警告。

1 Listening to the wind (in pairs)

Sometimes, when listening for an all-important sound – the door, the telephone, a car – we can't concentrate on anything else and seem forgetful and distracted.

a Whisper lines 10–20. Leave a long listening pause at the end of line 16 and the start of line 20. One of you can make sound effects.

b Both of you are Portia, straining to hear sounds from the Capitol. As you listen, whisper your suspicions, hopes and fears for what this moment means to your life.

c Gather Portia's thoughts into a poem, in which every line starts 'Listen. In the wind I hear …'.

2 The power of the Soothsayer (in pairs)

a Act out lines 21–46, thinking hard about why Portia nearly faints after speaking to the Soothsayer. Does the Soothsayer recognise Portia as the wife of one of the conspirators?

b Write a short paragraph on the role of the Soothsayer in this scene. Consider everything he says about Caesar (e.g. 'I shall beseech him to befriend himself'). How fearful is he of what might happen?

c Write notes for the actor playing the Soothsayer about how to deliver his lines in this scene. What actions or gestures should accompany his words?

1	press to him	围着他
2	rumour	吵嚷声
3	fray	打架，争斗
4	Sooth	真的
5	take my stand	找个地儿站着
6	suit	诉求
7	beseech him	请他
8	chance	发生
9	more void	宽敞点儿的
10	Aye me	唉（表苦恼）
11	commend me	替我致意
12	merry	（心情）很好
13	severally	各自朝不同方向

Characters 人物分析

Last look at Portia

Portia's line 46 is her final line in the play. In confessing that she finds it hard to keep quiet (line 9), she displays gender stereotyping – prevalent in Shakespeare's time, but often problematic to a modern audience. In lines 39–46, as her anxiety grows, the audience is left to wonder how much she knows about Brutus's plans. What does she mean when she says: 'The heavens speed thee in thine enterprise!'?

- On page 52 you were invited to consider Portia's role in Act 2 Scene 1 (the only other scene in which she appears). As Portia, plan your rehearsal notes for a follow-up meeting with your director to work through this scene. How will you deal with the issues raised above and what final impression will you seek to make on your audience?

JULIUS CAESAR ACT 2 SCENE 4

PORTIA	Yes, bring me word, boy, if thy lord look well,
	For he went sickly forth, and take good note
	What Caesar doth, what suitors press to him¹. 15
	Hark, boy, what noise is that?
LUCIUS	I hear none, madam.
PORTIA	Prithee listen well:
	I heard a bustling rumour², like a fray³,
	And the wind brings it from the Capitol.
LUCIUS	Sooth⁴, madam, I hear nothing. 20

Enter the SOOTHSAYER

PORTIA	Come hither, fellow, which way hast thou been?
SOOTHSAYER	At mine own house, good lady.
PORTIA	What is't o'clock?
SOOTHSAYER	About the ninth hour, lady.
PORTIA	Is Caesar yet gone to the Capitol?
SOOTHSAYER	Madam, not yet. I go to take my stand⁵ 25
	To see him pass on to the Capitol.
PORTIA	Thou hast some suit⁶ to Caesar, hast thou not?
SOOTHSAYER	That I have, lady, if it will please Caesar
	To be so good to Caesar as to hear me:
	I shall beseech him⁷ to befriend himself. 30
PORTIA	Why, know'st thou any harm's intended towards him?
SOOTHSAYER	None that I know will be, much that I fear may chance⁸.
	Good morrow to you. Here the street is narrow:
	The throng that follows Caesar at the heels,
	Of senators, of praetors, common suitors, 35
	Will crowd a feeble man almost to death.
	I'll get me to a place more void⁹, and there
	Speak to great Caesar as he comes along. *Exit*
PORTIA	I must go in. [*Aside*] Ay me¹⁰, how weak a thing
	The heart of woman is! O Brutus, 40
	The heavens speed thee in thine enterprise!
	Sure the boy heard me. Brutus hath a suit
	That Caesar will not grant. O, I grow faint. –
	Run, Lucius, and commend me¹¹ to my lord,
	Say I am merry¹². Come to me again 45
	And bring me word what he doth say to thee.
	*Exeunt [severally*¹³*]*

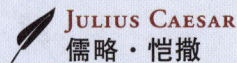
JULIUS CAESAR
儒略·恺撒

Looking back at Act 2 第2幕回顾
Activities for groups or individuals

1 Loyalties

In Scene 1 Brutus's loyalty is divided between Caesar, Cassius, Portia and himself.

- Work in four groups, each taking responsibility for one of these characters. Each group prepares the case for why its character has a claim to Brutus's loyalty.
- Each group has one minute to present its case beginning: 'You owe me loyalty because …'. Which character can make the strongest case?

2 The world through whose eyes?

Identify who you think is the more important character in each of the four scenes in Act 2. Write a short paragraph for each, saying what the character thinks about the events unfolding in Rome.

3 Focusing on female perspectives …

Act 2 is the only act to give a real insight into the domestic lives of Portia and Calpurnia.

a Imagine you are researching a radio programme on the lifestyles of important Roman wives and you have arranged an interview with the two women. Script their contributions, making clear their attitudes to their husbands. Then record your interviews.

In Elizabethan times, women were subject to rules of patriarchy (男权制), which meant that they were not allowed the freedom and responsibility that many women would reasonably expect today. Calpurnia's attempts to influence her husband's public actions are dismissed by Caesar: 'How foolish do your fears seem now, Calpurnia! / I am ashamèd I did yield to them'. Shakespeare seems to stereotype Portia by giving her the line: 'How hard it is for women to keep counsel'.

b As a group, discuss how a modern production of the play might deal with the potential problems of the presentation of the two Roman wives. (Refer to the activities you did earlier in the act.)

4 … and a male perspective

For a TV documentary programme, you plan to focus on Brutus and Caesar at home – the personal lives of the politicians. Arrange and film a television-style interview with the two men. Play the interviews back to the class for observation and comment.

5 To cut or not to cut

Some argue that the final two scenes of Act 2 are very brief and add nothing significant to the action. In pairs, one of you argues for cutting the scenes (giving all suitable reasons for doing so). The other argues for their retention (again with justifications).

6 What do you think Shakespeare made of Caesar?

Act 2 makes it clear that Caesar's days are numbered – and within the first few lines of the next scene he is dead!

a Remind yourself of how Shakespeare presented Caesar in Act 1. Then create a character map of him for Act 2 that reflects how Shakespeare consolidates and enhances his main characteristics. Put his name in the middle of a sheet of paper and group around it all key quotations and references from Act 2.

b Use all your research to help you write an essay on Shakespeare's presentation of Caesar in this act and how far you think he is sympathetic to Caesar.

7 Lucius and Artemidorus: casting the parts

Look back through Act 2 Scenes 1 and 4 (Lucius) and Act 2 Scene 3 (Artemidorus) for the contributions of these two minor characters. As a director you have to cast these small parts.

- Write a short 'casting brief' for each character, making it clear what significant qualities you are looking for in the actors who will take on these roles.

Compare the kind of relationship between Caesar and Calpurnia depicted in these two images.

Caesar ignores attempted warnings. Cassius misinterprets a senator's good wishes. Brutus reassures him. Trebonius draws Antony away.

 剧情简介：恺撒对他人的预警不予理睬。卡休误会了一位参议员的祝愿，布鲁图安抚他的情绪。绰包纽把安东尼引开。

Stagecraft 导演技巧

Caesar enters the Capitol

At least fifteen characters enter to the sound of trumpets.

- Make an enlarged sketch of the Globe Theatre, using the picture above to help you. On it, work out where everyone is at line 18, bearing in mind the change from street to Capitol at line 12. (For a description of Caesar's walk to the Capitol read Act 2 Scene 4, lines 34–6.)

1	schedule	纸条，文件
2	o'er-read	读完
3	humble suit	小小的请求
4	touches	事关
5	served	处理
6	Sirrah	伙计，小子
7	give place	让一让
8	Caesar … following	（伊丽莎白时期舞台设置细节不详，而已知的是环球剧场舞台在幕后辟出空间，这块空间有可能被布置成参议院大厅，台前做街道）
9	makes to	走向
10	sudden	尽快
11	turn back	（活着）回去
12	be constant	不要慌
13	knows his time	把握着时机

1 What is your picture of Caesar? (in threes)

Caesar's words in lines 1–26 can be delivered in different ways in order to signal key aspects of his character moments before his death. Some critics see line 8 as pivotal (关键). How does Caesar show that he is ignoring Artemidorus through his actions here?

- Try different readings of lines 1, 8 and 10. Then settle on the versions that work best.
- Present them to other groups and explain your choices.

2 Raising the tension (in pairs)

At the start of this act, Shakespeare continues to increase the dramatic tension surrounding the conspiracy.

- In your pairs, discuss and then list the ways in which he does this in the script opposite. Take time to consider the length of the lines, on whom the action focuses and whether any of the characters act out of character at this point.
- Swap and discuss your list with others.

Act 3 Scene 1
Rome   The Capitol

Flourish. Enter CAESAR, BRUTUS, CASSIUS, CASCA, DECIUS, METELLUS, TREBONIUS, CINNA, ANTONY, *Lepidus,* ARTEMIDORUS, PUBLIUS, [POPILLIUS, *Ligarius,*] *and the* SOOTHSAYER

CAESAR	The Ides of March are come.
SOOTHSAYER	Ay, Caesar, but not gone.
ARTEMIDORUS	Hail, Caesar! Read this schedule[1].
DECIUS	Trebonius doth desire you to o'er-read[2]
	(At your best leisure) this his humble suit[3]. 5
ARTEMIDORUS	O Caesar, read mine first, for mine's a suit
	That touches[4] Caesar nearer. Read it, great Caesar.
CAESAR	What touches us ourself shall be last served[5].
ARTEMIDORUS	Delay not, Caesar, read it instantly.
CAESAR	What, is the fellow mad?
PUBLIUS	Sirrah[6], give place[7]. 10
CASSIUS	What, urge you your petitions in the street?
	Come to the Capitol.
	[*Caesar enters the Capitol, the rest following*[8]]
POPILLIUS	I wish your enterprise today may thrive.
CASSIUS	What enterprise, Popillius?
POPILLIUS	Fare you well.
	[*Leaves him and joins Caesar*]
BRUTUS	What said Popillius Lena? 15
CASSIUS	He wished today our enterprise might thrive.
	I fear our purpose is discoverèd.
BRUTUS	Look how he makes to[9] Caesar, mark him.
CASSIUS	Casca, be sudden[10], for we fear prevention.
	Brutus, what shall be done? If this be known 20
	Cassius or Caesar never shall turn back[11],
	For I will slay myself.
BRUTUS	Cassius, be constant[12].
	Popillius Lena speaks not of our purposes,
	For look he smiles, and Caesar doth not change.
CASSIUS	Trebonius knows his time[13], for look you, Brutus, 25
	He draws Mark Antony out of the way.
	[*Exeunt Antony and Trebonius*]

'Repeal my brother's banishment,' Metellus begs Caesar. Brutus and Cassius support him and get nearer to Caesar. Caesar adamantly refuses them all.

 剧情简介： "请收回流放我兄弟的成命，"莫泰勒恳求恺撒。布鲁图和卡休从旁帮腔，并接近恺撒。恺撒斩钉截铁地拒绝了所有人的求情。

1 Focus on Caesar's behaviour (in fours)

- In quick succession read aloud Metellus Cimber's speech at line 33, Brutus's speech at line 52 (with Caesar's response) and Cassius's speech at line 55. Do this several times, giving everyone the chance to be Caesar.
- Now look closely at Caesar's two long speeches (beginning at lines 35 and 58) and talk together about how well he copes with the three senators' successive pleas to repeal Publius Cimber's banishment.
- Follow this up by discussing what sort of a leader Caesar presents himself as at this point. How does this suit the conspirators' intentions? Remember that Caesar drank wine with some of these people before leaving for the Capitol.

2 Caesar – dramatic irony (戏剧反讽) (in pairs)

Dramatic irony occurs when the audience knows more than a character does. Here the audience knows what is about to happen to Caesar. Caesar thinks that he is going to show off his supreme power, having put aside his fear of coming to the Capitol.

a Analyse in detail Caesar's simile in lines 60–2 and discuss the dramatic irony in the light of what is about to happen.

b Make a note in your Director's Journal outlining the directions you would give to the actor playing Caesar at this point. Which words should he emphasise and how should he stand? Would you advise any gestures to accompany these three lines?

▼ How close is this Caesar (right) to your view of him at this point in the play?

1	presently prefer	立刻呈上
2	addressed	准备好了
3	second	接应
4	rears your hand	举手
5	puissant	强大
6	couchings	卑躬屈膝
7	turn … children	把我们长久以来赖以治国的律法当作儿戏
8	Be not fond	别糊涂了
9	true quality	秉性
10	spaniel fawning	（像狗一样）摇尾讨好
11	cur	野狗
12	worthy	有分量
13	repealing	撤回
14	freedom of	准许
15	enfranchisement	赦免
16	resting	不转不移
17	fellow	同样的人，第二个人
18	firmament	天空

DECIUS	Where is Metellus Cimber? Let him go	
	And presently prefer[1] his suit to Caesar.	
BRUTUS	He is addressed[2], press near and second[3] him.	
CINNA	Casca, you are the first that rears your hand[4].	30
CAESAR	Are we all ready? What is now amiss	
	That Caesar and his Senate must redress?	
METELLUS	Most high, most mighty, and most puissant[5] Caesar,	
	Metellus Cimber throws before thy seat	
	An humble heart.	
CAESAR	I must prevent thee, Cimber.	35
	These couchings[6] and these lowly courtesies	
	Might fire the blood of ordinary men	
	And turn preordinance and first decree	
	Into the law of children[7]. Be not fond[8]	
	To think that Caesar bears such rebel blood	40
	That will be thawed from the true quality[9]	
	With that which melteth fools – I mean sweet words,	
	Low-crookèd curtsies, and base spaniel fawning[10].	
	Thy brother by decree is banishèd:	
	If thou dost bend, and pray, and fawn for him,	45
	I spurn thee like a cur[11] out of my way.	
	Know Caesar doth not wrong, nor without cause	
	Will he be satisfied.	
METELLUS	Is there no voice more worthy[12] than my own	
	To sound more sweetly in great Caesar's ear	50
	For the repealing[13] of my banished brother?	
BRUTUS	I kiss thy hand, but not in flattery, Caesar,	
	Desiring thee that Publius Cimber may	
	Have an immediate freedom of[14] repeal.	
CAESAR	What, Brutus?	
CASSIUS	Pardon, Caesar! Caesar, pardon!	55
	As low as to thy foot doth Cassius fall	
	To beg enfranchisement[15] for Publius Cimber.	
CAESAR	I could be well moved, if I were as you;	
	If I could pray to move, prayers would move me.	
	But I am constant as the northern star,	60
	Of whose true-fixed and resting[16] quality	
	There is no fellow[17] in the firmament[18].	

Having declared himself the world's only constant man, Caesar is stabbed to death. Brutus tries to reassure all who flee, but the conspirators are left alone in the Senate.

剧情简介：恺撒自称是这世上唯一始终不变的人，说完便被刺身亡。布鲁图竭力安抚惊恐而逃的人们，元老院里最终还是只剩下谋杀团伙的人。

1 The assassination (in sevens)

Brutus said, 'Let's be sacrificers, but not butchers' (Act 2 Scene 1, line 166), but the conspirators probably kill Caesar in a variety of ways.

- Each person chooses which conspirator to play. Think about which part of Caesar's body he might choose to stab, and the style in which he would stab. Notice that Brutus is the last to attack.
- Carefully stage the assassination. Then, without words, present it to the class in slow motion.

Themes 主题分析
Love and friendship (in pairs)

Caesar's death line '*Et tu, Brute?* – Then fall, Caesar!' suggests Caesar's bewilderment at what is happening. Literally translated, the first three words mean 'Even you, Brutus?' Some argue that his friend's betrayal is as mortally wounding as Brutus's blade.

a Discuss the dramatic effect of these three words. How would Caesar's death have been different without them?

b Take turns to create a 'snapshot' of Caesar at the moment of his death. Concentrate on facial expression and gesture. Hold your pose for a few seconds for your partner to look at.

Write about it 写作练习
What does Publius think?

Publius, an old senator, silently witnesses the assassination of his leader and is dumbstruck at the turn of events. Brutus is concerned that Publius is 'affrighted' and tries to reassure him.

- Imagine that you are Publius. As the conspirators usher you away, you reflect on the amazing events that have just unfolded. How will you respond to the assassins' chant: 'Liberty! Freedom! Tyranny is dead!'? Do you believe Brutus when he says 'There is no harm intended to your person'?
- Either write a diary entry describing what you have witnessed and heard today, making it as vivid as you can, or do as Brutus says – 'So tell them, Publius' (line 91). Write the speech you would make to the people to reassure them that the conspirators intend them no harm.

1	apprehensive	聪明
2	holds on his rank	坚守立场
3	Olympus	奥林匹斯山，希腊众神的聚居地
4	bootless	白白地
5	Speak hands for me!	让我的手来替我说话！
6	common pulpits	公共演讲台
7	Ambition's debt	野心的代价
8	confounded	不知所措
9	mutiny	骚乱，兵变
10	Stand fast together	团结一致
11	standing	立场一致
12	your age	您老人家
13	abide	为……负责，因……受牵连

	The skies are painted with unnumbered sparks,	
	They are all fire, and every one doth shine;	
	But there's but one in all doth hold his place.	65
	So in the world: 'tis furnished well with men,	
	And men are flesh and blood, and apprehensive¹;	
	Yet in the number I do know but one	
	That unassailable holds on his rank²,	
	Unshaked of motion, and that I am he	70
	Let me a little show it, even in this:	
	That I was constant Cimber should be banished,	
	And constant do remain to keep him so.	
CINNA	O Caesar –	
CAESAR	Hence! Wilt thou lift up Olympus³?	
DECIUS	Great Caesar –	
CAESAR	Doth not Brutus bootless⁴ kneel?	75
CASCA	Speak hands for me!⁵	
	They stab Caesar	
CAESAR	*Et tu, Brute?* – Then fall, Caesar!	*Dies*
CINNA	Liberty! Freedom! Tyranny is dead!	
	Run hence, proclaim, cry it about the streets.	
CASSIUS	Some to the common pulpits⁶, and cry out,	80
	'Liberty, freedom, and enfranchisement!'	
BRUTUS	People and senators, be not affrighted,	
	Fly not, stand still! Ambition's debt⁷ is paid.	
CASCA	Go to the pulpit, Brutus.	
DECIUS	And Cassius too.	
BRUTUS	Where's Publius?	85
CINNA	Here, quite confounded⁸ with this mutiny⁹.	
METELLUS	Stand fast together¹⁰ lest some friend of Caesar's	
	Should chance –	
BRUTUS	Talk not of standing¹¹. Publius, good cheer,	
	There is no harm intended to your person,	
	Nor to no Roman else. So tell them, Publius.	90
CASSIUS	And leave us, Publius, lest that the people,	
	Rushing on us, should do your age¹² some mischief.	
BRUTUS	Do so, and let no man abide¹³ this deed	
	But we the doers.	95

[*Exeunt all but the conspirators*]

Trebonius reports panic outside. The conspirators prepare to depart to proclaim themselves liberators, their daggers and forearms ritually bloodied. They halt as Antony's servant enters, bringing his master's message.

剧情简介：绰包纽进来说外面一片恐慌。谋杀团伙的成员郑重地将恺撒的鲜血涂在前臂和短剑上，要去向众人宣布他们是罗马的解放者。这时安东尼的小厮进来传主人的话，他们停了下来。

1 'let us bathe our hands in Caesar's blood'
(in small groups)

The photograph below shows how a 2005 production at the Barbican staged the moments following Caesar's assassination. Cassius stands at the back with his dagger out; Brutus is beside him.

a Talk together about the different thoughts and emotions that these conspirators express as they stoop to smear their hands and weapons in Caesar's blood. How many of them appear excited by Brutus's proclamation that their actions have brought 'Peace, freedom, and liberty!'?

b What is the dramatic impact of this moment?

1	amazed 惊骇，惊恐
2	doomsday 世界末日（上帝在这天对世人进行审判）
3	drawing days out 拖延时日
4	stand upon 关心，在意
5	abridged 缩减
6	accents 不同的语言
7	in sport 在娱乐表演中
8	on Pompey's basis 在庞贝雕像的底座上
9	oft = often
10	knot 群
11	grace his heels 追随他
12	Soft 等等
13	prostrate 五体投地，拜倒
14	honest 正直

Characters 人物分析
Judging Brutus

Brutus seems to take charge after the assassination. He deals with Publius and then urges the conspirators to 'bathe our hands in Caesar's blood'.

- Step into role as director. Re-read Brutus's speech at lines 103–10. How do you judge Brutus here? Is this a good decision or one that he may live to regret?
- With your judgement and what you know of Brutus in the play so far in mind, write notes in your Director's Journal advising the actor who plays Brutus how to deliver this speech.
- Include a note about how Brutus should react when he hears Antony's description of him in line 126 delivered by the servant.

Enter TREBONIUS

CASSIUS	Where is Antony?
TREBONIUS	Fled to his house amazed[1].

Men, wives, and children stare, cry out, and run
As it were doomsday[2].

BRUTUS Fates, we will know your pleasures.
That we shall die we know: 'tis but the time,
And drawing days out[3], that men stand upon[4].   100

CASCA Why, he that cuts off twenty years of life
Cuts off so many years of fearing death.

BRUTUS Grant that, and then is death a benefit.
So are we Caesar's friends, that have abridged[5]
His time of fearing death. Stoop, Romans, stoop,   105
And let us bathe our hands in Caesar's blood
Up to the elbows and besmear our swords.
Then walk we forth, even to the market-place,
And waving our red weapons o'er our heads
Let's all cry, 'Peace, freedom, and liberty!'   110

CASSIUS Stoop then and wash. How many ages hence
Shall this our lofty scene be acted over
In states unborn and accents[6] yet unknown!

BRUTUS How many times shall Caesar bleed in sport[7],
That now on Pompey's basis[8] lies along   115
No worthier than the dust!

CASSIUS So oft[9] as that shall be,
So often shall the knot[10] of us be called
The men that gave their country liberty.

DECIUS What, shall we forth?

CASSIUS Ay, every man away.
Brutus shall lead, and we will grace his heels[11]   120
With the most boldest and best hearts of Rome.

Enter a SERVANT

BRUTUS Soft[12], who comes here? A friend of Antony's.

SERVANT Thus, Brutus, did my master bid me kneel,
Thus did Mark Antony bid me fall down,
And, being prostrate[13], thus he bade me say: 125
Brutus is noble, wise, valiant, and honest[14];
Caesar was mighty, bold, royal, and loving.

Antony's servant says that if Brutus's reasons for murder are convincing, Antony will follow Brutus. Brutus grants safe access to Antony, who enters and offers to be killed with Caesar.

剧情简介：安东尼的小厮说，如果布鲁图刺杀恺撒的理由令人信服，安东尼愿意追随布鲁图。布鲁图保证安东尼的人身安全。安东尼上，求各位把他和恺撒一起杀掉。

1 Send in the servant (in pairs)

a Analyse the servant's speech (lines 123–37) closely for deliberately vague or misleading phrases, especially about Brutus and Caesar. For example, what is the impact of having 'say' at the start of lines 128 and 129?

b Discuss why Mark Antony decided to send a servant with this message for Brutus and the conspirators.

2 Antony – a lesson in sincerity? (in small groups)

Before Mark Antony's entrance, Cassius says: 'my misgiving still / Falls shrewdly to the purpose.' Antony confronts Caesar's killers while their hands are still covered in his blood (Shakespeare departed from his source material to include this moment; see p. 166). He is quick to declare his reverence for Caesar and to suggest that he would willingly die alongside his former leader. But is he telling the truth?

a How would you have Antony enter after line 146? Brutus is keen to welcome him. How does Antony respond?

b One of you reads Antony's lines 148–63, emphasising all references to blood and death. The others, as blood-soaked assassins, listen closely to his words. Afterwards, talk together about the emotive qualities of Antony's speech. Is Antony speaking from the heart, or does he want to make the conspirators squirm (羞愧)? Discuss your ideas and collect evidence to justify your conclusions.

c Consider Antony's motives for offering to die now.

d Make notes in your Director's Journal under the heading 'Antony', summing up your observations about him and his motives at this point.

1 vouchsafe 保证
2 this untrod state 这种前所未有的状况
3 presently 马上，立即
4 fears 担心，不放心
5 my ... purpose 我担心的事总是会发生
6 measure 大小
7 Who ... rank 还有谁需要放血，还有谁患病（古代西方常用放血作为医病的方法）
8 bear me hard 容不下我
9 purpled hands 染成紫色的手（安东尼意指恺撒的血是君王之色）
10 Live 就算能活
11 apt to die 情愿去死
12 mean of death 死法
13 cut off 杀死
14 The ... age 当代的精英和俊杰

▼ What is going on in this photo? Antony is in the foreground.

Julius Caesar Act 3 Scene 1
儒略·恺撒

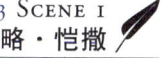

      Say I love Brutus, and I honour him;
      Say I feared Caesar, honoured him, and loved him.
      If Brutus will vouchsafe[1] that Antony   130
      May safely come to him and be resolved
      How Caesar hath deserved to lie in death,
      Mark Antony shall not love Caesar dead
      So well as Brutus living, but will follow
      The fortunes and affairs of noble Brutus   135
      Through the hazards of this untrod state[2]
      With all true faith. So says my master Antony.
BRUTUS Thy master is a wise and valiant Roman,
      I never thought him worse.
      Tell him, so please him come unto this place,   140
      He shall be satisfied and by my honour
      Depart untouched.
SERVANT   I'll fetch him presently[3].   *Exit Servant*
BRUTUS I know that we shall have him well to friend.
CASSIUS I wish we may. But yet have I a mind
      That fears[4] him much, and my misgiving still   145
      Falls shrewdly to the purpose[5].

          Enter ANTONY

BRUTUS But here comes Antony. Welcome, Mark Antony!
ANTONY O mighty Caesar! Dost thou lie so low?
      Are all thy conquests, glories, triumphs, spoils
      Shrunk to this little measure[6]? Fare thee well!   150
      I know not, gentlemen, what you intend,
      Who else must be let blood, who else is rank[7].
      If I myself, there is no hour so fit
      As Caesar's death's hour, nor no instrument
      Of half that worth as those your swords made rich   155
      With the most noble blood of all this world.
      I do beseech ye, if you bear me hard[8],
      Now, whilst your purpled hands[9] do reek and smoke,
      Fulfil your pleasure. Live[10] a thousand years,
      I shall not find myself so apt to die[11]:   160
      No place will please me so, no mean of death[12],
      As here by Caesar, and by you cut off[13],
      The choice and master spirits of this age[14].

Brutus claims that pity for Rome killed Caesar. Brutus loves Antony and loved Caesar. Antony shakes the conspirators' hands, but fears this act of friendship wrongs Caesar.

剧情简介：布鲁图称，他们杀死恺撒是出于对罗马的悲悯，他热爱安东尼，也热爱恺撒。安东尼与谋杀团伙成员握手，又担心这种友好举动对不起恺撒。

Characters 人物分析
Brutus and Cassius – two different politicians (in pairs)

a One of you reads Brutus's lines 164–76; the other reads Cassius's lines 177–8. Afterwards, talk together about how differently the two conspirators treat Antony. Make a list of the contrasting points that emerge.

b Discuss the following question: Do Brutus and Cassius respond to Antony in ways you would expect? After talking about this in pairs, pool your answers in a class discussion.

1 Outward action, secret thoughts (in eights)

At the end of Act 3 Scene 1 we have no doubt about Antony's intentions towards the conspirators, regardless of how he behaves towards them here.

- In order to explore Antony's reaction to each conspirator and theirs to him at this point, first rehearse lines 184–9. Each conspirator, although they do not speak, should think carefully about how they will react to being greeted by Antony, who was a friend of Caesar. Do they trust him? Who has the power in this encounter? How awkward is it having your hand shaken when it's covered in blood?
- Then read the lines through again, freezing the action after each greeting. Antony and then the conspirator being greeted should express how they really feel at this point. Try to bring out the tension of the moment as much as you can, as well as the contrast between appearance and reality.

Write about it 写作练习
Conspirators – why so many?

Apart from Brutus and Cassius, we do not see the seven conspirators again. Write a short paragraph in answer to the following questions:

- Why do you think Shakespeare decided to have so many conspirators, only to focus on two of them after Act 3?
- Do the other conspirators (not Brutus and Cassius) have individual characteristics? Give evidence for your view.

1 pitiful 充满怜悯
2 And pity … pity 对遭受不公的罗马民众的怜悯是大火，大火会吞噬小火
3 leaden points 铅枪头（铅质地软，不伤人）
4 Our … in 我们表面上凶狠，心里却如兄弟一般欢迎您
5 voice 意见
6 dignities 高官
7 credit 名声
8 conceit me 看待我
9 dearer 更加
10 corse = corpse（尸体）
11 close / In terms of friendship 结成朋友

BRUTUS	O Antony, beg not your death of us.	
	Though now we must appear bloody and cruel,	165
	As by our hands and this our present act	
	You see we do, yet see you but our hands	
	And this the bleeding business they have done.	
	Our hearts you see not, they are pitiful¹;	
	And pity to the general wrong of Rome –	170
	As fire drives out fire, so pity pity² –	
	Hath done this deed on Caesar. For your part,	
	To you our swords have leaden points³, Mark Antony;	
	Our arms in strength of malice, and our hearts	
	Of brothers' temper, do receive you in⁴	175
	With all kind love, good thoughts, and reverence.	
CASSIUS	Your voice⁵ shall be as strong as any man's	
	In the disposing of new dignities⁶.	
BRUTUS	Only be patient till we have appeased	
	The multitude, beside themselves with fear,	180
	And then we will deliver you the cause	
	Why I, that did love Caesar when I struck him,	
	Have thus proceeded.	
ANTONY	I doubt not of your wisdom.	
	Let each man render me his bloody hand.	
	First, Marcus Brutus, will I shake with you;	185
	Next, Caius Cassius, do I take your hand;	
	Now, Decius Brutus, yours; now yours, Metellus;	
	Yours, Cinna; and, my valiant Casca, yours;	
	Though last, not least in love, yours, good Trebonius.	
	Gentlemen all – alas, what shall I say?	190
	My credit⁷ now stands on such slippery ground	
	That one of two bad ways you must conceit me⁸,	
	Either a coward or a flatterer.	
	That I did love thee, Caesar, O, 'tis true.	
	If then thy spirit look upon us now,	195
	Shall it not grieve thee dearer⁹ than thy death	
	To see thy Antony making his peace,	
	Shaking the bloody fingers of thy foes –	
	Most noble – in the presence of thy corse¹⁰?	
	Had I as many eyes as thou hast wounds,	200
	Weeping as fast as they stream forth thy blood,	
	It would become me better than to close	
	In terms of friendship¹¹ with thine enemies.	

Antony praises Caesar. Cassius asks if Antony intends to show friendship to the conspirators. 'Yes,' replies Antony, 'if reasons for Caesar's death are given.' Cassius is uneasy about Antony speaking at Caesar's funeral.

 剧情简介：安东尼颂扬了恺撒。卡休质问他还想不想向谋杀团伙示好。安东尼回答："想，条件是给恺撒的死一个说法。"卡休对于安东尼将在恺撒的葬礼上发表演说一事很不放心。

Language in the play 剧中语言

'That I did love thee, Caesar' (in small groups)

Even though the conspirators look on, Antony is effusive (热情洋溢) in declaring his love for Caesar.

a Work through lines 194–210. What is the effect of Antony directly addressing the dead Caesar as 'Julius' and his repetition of the word 'here' three times.

b Antony's words resonate with two image patterns: blood and hunting. Caesar's wounds are like eyes that weep with blood, and Caesar the man is described as a hunted animal (a 'hart' is a deer, but it is also a pun (双关语) suggesting the word 'heart' to his audience). Work through the details of the deer image and decide what impression of Caesar Antony is aiming to give his audience by using it.

c Talk together about what you think Antony's intentions are in speaking as he does in lines 194–210 and then list them.

1. bayed 围杀
2. hart 雄鹿
3. Signed in thy spoil 身上溅的都是你的血肉
4. Lethe 忘川（希腊神话中冥界里的河，饮其水者会忘记过去）
5. cold modesty 冷静的克制
6. compact 协议
7. pricked 列为，标记为
8. full of good regard 合情合理
9. suitor 请求者
10. Produce 带去展示
11. in … funeral 在他的葬礼上
12. utter 说，讲

1 Brutus gives Antony satisfaction (in pairs)

Antony asks the conspirators to 'give me reasons / Why and wherein Caesar was dangerous' (lines 221–2). But Brutus never does explain his actions to Antony.

• Imagine Brutus has decided to offer Antony an explanation of the conspirators' actions. Improvise that conversation between them.

2 Antony – one final request (in pairs)

In lines 227–30, Antony requests that he be allowed to 'Produce his [Caesar's] body to the market-place' and speak like a 'friend' at his funeral. This is a crucial moment and it provokes differing responses in Brutus and Cassius. Cassius urgently takes Brutus aside at line 231 to talk in confidence with him.

• Take parts and read Brutus and Cassius's brief private conversation (lines 231–43). Afterwards, talk about what the lines reveal about the two men's characters. If you kept notes of your answers to the 'Characters' activity on page 84, add to them.

JULIUS CAESAR ACT 3 SCENE 1
儒略·恺撒

	Pardon me, Julius! Here wast thou bayed¹, brave hart²,	
	Here didst thou fall, and here thy hunters stand,	205
	Signed in thy spoil³ and crimsoned in thy Lethe⁴.	
	O world! Thou wast the forest to this hart,	
	And this indeed, O world, the heart of thee.	
	How like a deer strucken by many princes	
	Dost thou here lie!	210
CASSIUS	Mark Antony –	
ANTONY	Pardon me, Caius Cassius,	
	The enemies of Caesar shall say this;	
	Then, in a friend, it is cold modesty⁵.	
CASSIUS	I blame you not for praising Caesar so,	
	But what compact⁶ mean you to have with us?	215
	Will you be pricked⁷ in number of our friends,	
	Or shall we on and not depend on you?	
ANTONY	Therefore I took your hands, but was indeed	
	Swayed from the point by looking down on Caesar.	
	Friends am I with you all, and love you all,	220
	Upon this hope, that you shall give me reasons	
	Why and wherein Caesar was dangerous.	
BRUTUS	Or else were this a savage spectacle.	
	Our reasons are so full of good regard⁸	
	That were you, Antony, the son of Caesar	225
	You should be satisfied.	
ANTONY	That's all I seek,	
	And am, moreover, suitor⁹ that I may	
	Produce¹⁰ his body to the market-place,	
	And in the pulpit, as becomes a friend,	
	Speak in the order of his funeral¹¹.	230
BRUTUS	You shall, Mark Antony.	
CASSIUS	Brutus, a word with you.	
	[*Aside to Brutus*] You know not what you do. Do not consent	
	That Antony speak in his funeral.	
	Know you how much the people may be moved	
	By that which he will utter¹²?	
BRUTUS	[*Aside to Cassius*] By your pardon,	235
	I will myself into the pulpit first	
	And show the reason of our Caesar's death.	

Antony is given permission to speak at Caesar's funeral after Brutus, but not to blame the conspirators. Left alone with Caesar's body, Antony prophesies horrific civil war.

 剧情简介：安东尼得到允许，在恺撒的葬礼上可以在布鲁图之后演讲，但是不能指责谋杀团伙。台上只剩下安东尼和恺撒的尸体，安东尼预言罗马将爆发可怕的内战。

Themes 主题分析

Love and friendship (in pairs)

It is worth exploring the dramatic impact of Antony's crucial soliloquy, spoken over the mutilated (面目全非的) body of his friend. Cassius's suspicions about the potential threat posed by Antony prove correct. Now alone, Antony reveals his true feelings about Caesar's murder and the men who killed him.

- Share out the lines and read through Antony's soliloquy (lines 254–75). Find words in it that convey what he truly feels about a) Caesar, b) his murderers and c) revenge. Write them down.
- Now look back through the earlier part of the scene, starting at Antony's entrance after line 146. Compare his 'soliloquy' thoughts and feelings with those he speaks openly to the conspirators. In what ways are they similar and why? In what ways are they very different?

1	protest	宣布
2	true	正确，正当
3	advantage	对（我们）有利
4	fall	发生
5	tide of times	历史长河
6	cumber	祸害
7	in use	稀松平常
8	quartered	被撕碎，被肢解
9	choked … deeds	因见多了暴行而麻木
10	Ate	埃特（诱人犯罪、制造不和的复仇女神）
11	confines	地方
12	havoc	杀啊（战争中的口令）
13	let slip	撒开
14	carrion men	腐尸

1 Nightmare voices (in large groups)

Work out how you can present Antony's soliloquy to create the maximum horror. Use all your voices, sometimes speaking together, sometimes separately or individually. You can repeat or echo words; emphasise sound patterns and rhythms; build to a crescendo (音量渐强); fade to nothing and become suddenly loud or suddenly soft. There is no need to stick to words: you can make rhythmic, threatening noises or other sounds that the words suggest. By putting people in different parts of the room you can get quadraphonic (四声道) sound.

▶ Would you consider staging Antony's soliloquy like this? Give your reasons either way.

Julius Caesar Act 3 Scene 1
儒略·恺撒

	What Antony shall speak, I will protest¹	
	He speaks by leave and by permission,	
	And that we are contented Caesar shall	240
	Have all true² rites and lawful ceremonies.	
	It shall advantage³ more than do us wrong.	
CASSIUS	[*Aside to Brutus*] I know not what may fall⁴, I like it not.	
BRUTUS	Mark Antony, here take you Caesar's body.	
	You shall not in your funeral speech blame us,	245
	But speak all good you can devise of Caesar	
	And say you do't by our permission,	
	Else shall you not have any hand at all	
	About his funeral. And you shall speak	
	In the same pulpit whereto I am going,	250
	After my speech is ended.	
ANTONY	Be it so,	
	I do desire no more.	
BRUTUS	Prepare the body then and follow us.	
	Exeunt [all but] Antony	
ANTONY	O, pardon me, thou bleeding piece of earth,	
	That I am meek and gentle with these butchers!	255
	Thou art the ruins of the noblest man	
	That ever lived in the tide of times⁵.	
	Woe to the hand that shed this costly blood!	
	Over thy wounds now do I prophesy –	
	Which like dumb mouths do ope their ruby lips	260
	To beg the voice and utterance of my tongue –	
	A curse shall light upon the limbs of men:	
	Domestic fury and fierce civil strife	
	Shall cumber⁶ all the parts of Italy;	
	Blood and destruction shall be so in use⁷	265
	And dreadful objects so familiar	
	That mothers shall but smile when they behold	
	Their infants quartered⁸ with the hands of war,	
	All pity choked with custom of fell deeds⁹;	
	And Caesar's spirit, ranging for revenge,	270
	With Ate¹⁰ by his side come hot from hell,	
	Shall in these confines¹¹ with a monarch's voice	
	Cry havoc¹² and let slip¹³ the dogs of war,	
	That this foul deed shall smell above the earth	
	With carrion men¹⁴ groaning for burial.	275

Octavius's servant reports his master's approach. Antony suggests that Octavius waits until the people's mood has been tested. In the market-place, Brutus and Cassius prepare to speak.

 剧情简介：屋大维的小厮来报，说主人马上就到。安东尼建议屋大维不要轻举妄动，先试探了民意再说。在罗马广场，布鲁图和卡休准备开始演说。

1 The day that Caesar was killed (in small groups)

a Discuss in your groups any dramatic or significant event in your lifetime that made it feel as if time had come to a standstill. It could be a personal or a political event.

b Imagine how ordinary Romans might have felt on hearing of Caesar's death. Write a report to send to Octavius Caesar (Julius Caesar's grand-nephew [此处指甥孙] and heir) about the mood of the city after the assassination. Begin with Antony's words at line 288: 'Here is a mourning Rome, a dangerous Rome'.

2 Great speeches (in small groups)

Some of the greatest oratory (public speaking) that Shakespeare wrote is in Act 3 Scene 2. Brutus's and Mark Antony's speeches (lines 13–39 and lines 65–242) have to be read aloud and listened to in their entirety for their art to be fully appreciated.

- Two or three of you read the speeches aloud, taking a sentence each in turn while the rest listen closely without following the script. Leave out the plebeians' lines.
- Then swap over. After each speech, discuss how it felt when you spoke it and how it felt when you listened to it.

Write about it 写作练习

Cassius's speech to the people

At line 10 of Act 3 Scene 2, Cassius leaves to speak to half the crowd in another street.

- Look back at how Cassius speaks in Act 1 Scenes 2 and 3 and write the speech he might have delivered to the crowd. The Elizabethan lesson in **rhetoric** (修辞) on page 92 will help you. You could also look at the ways in which Brutus (line 13) and Antony (line 65) begin their speeches to the crowd in this scene.
- Your class could be the crowd to whom you deliver the speech. They will no doubt want to ask you questions having heard your speech.

---

1 Octavius Caesar 屋大维·恺撒（儒略·恺撒的甥孙，后被收作继子，是儒略·恺撒的继承人）
2 Passion 悲愤
3 seven leagues 约21英里，近34公里
4 Post back 火速赶回
5 Hie hence 快去
6 try 试探
7 take / The cruel issue 对这种残暴行径做出反应
8 the which （指群众的反应）
9 PLEBEIANS 民众，平民
10 be satisfied 要一个说法
11 give me audience 听我说
12 part 把……分开

Enter Octavio's SERVANT

	You serve Octavius Caesar¹, do you not?	
SERVANT	I do, Mark Antony.	
ANTONY	Caesar did write for him to come to Rome.	
SERVANT	He did receive his letters, and is coming,	
	And bid me say to you by word of mouth –	280
	[*Seeing the body*]	
	O Caesar!	
ANTONY	Thy heart is big, get thee apart and weep.	
	Passion², I see, is catching, for mine eyes,	
	Seeing those beads of sorrow stand in thine,	
	Began to water. Is thy master coming?	285
SERVANT	He lies tonight within seven leagues³ of Rome.	
ANTONY	Post back⁴ with speed and tell him what hath chanced.	
	Here is a mourning Rome, a dangerous Rome,	
	No Rome of safety for Octavius yet:	
	Hie hence⁵ and tell him so. Yet stay awhile,	290
	Thou shalt not back till I have borne this corse	
	Into the market-place. There shall I try⁶	
	In my oration how the people take	
	The cruel issue⁷ of these bloody men,	
	According to the which⁸ thou shalt discourse	295
	To young Octavius of the state of things.	
	Lend me your hand.	

Exeunt [*with Caesar's body*]

Act 3 Scene 2
Rome   The market-place

Enter BRUTUS *and Cassius with the* PLEBEIANS⁹

ALL	We will be satisfied¹⁰! Let us be satisfied!	
BRUTUS	Then follow me and give me audience¹¹, friends.	
	Cassius, go you into the other street	
	And part¹² the numbers.	
	Those that will hear me speak, let 'em stay here;	5

Brutus addresses the people. He says he loved Rome's freedom more than Caesar. The crowd accepts it. Antony enters with Caesar's corpse.

剧情简介：布鲁图对民众演说。他说他爱恺撒，但更热爱罗马的自由。群众接受了他的说法。安东尼与众人抬恺撒的尸体上。

Language in the play 剧中语言

An Elizabethan lesson in rhetoric (in threes)

Rhetoric is the art of discourse, public speaking and debate. An Elizabethan textbook on rhetoric would typically divide up a speech like this:

exordium **(introduction)** to gain the attention and approval of the hearers

narratio **(development)** so that listeners may fully understand the matter being discussed

confirmatio **(evidence)** proofs, arguments and reasons, illustrated by quotations

confutatio **(dealing with objections)** consideration of what objections may be raised and how to answer them

conclusio **(summing up)** a short recapitulation of the point(s).

a Find these five sections in lines 13–39 of Brutus's speech (they are very clear) and lines 65–242 of Antony's speech (perhaps less clear). Try reading out loud one of Brutus's sections, then the corresponding one of Antony. Note contrasts in technique, thought and behaviour.

b Identify and comment upon any other persuasive techniques Brutus uses in his speech – for example repetitions and echoes, balanced sentences, rhetorical questions and flattering his audience. How do you respond? Are you persuaded?

Stagecraft 导演技巧

Enter Mark Antony with Caesar's body

Antony likes plays and, in Act 3 Scene 1, demonstrates what a good actor he is himself!

- Imagine you are Antony, and plan your big entrance. Think carefully about: your appearance (blood?); how you relate to the corpse (would you touch it?); the corpse itself and its presentation ('coffin' at line 98?); and finally where to enter and where to stand while Brutus speaks.
- Present your ideas to the class. This could be in the form of a short talk, or you could act as director and another class member could act out your ideas as you explain them.

1 renderèd 给出（解释）
2 severally 各自，分别
3 last （讲话的）最后
4 lovers 朋友
5 have respect to 请记住
6 Censure me 评判我
7 your senses 你们的理智
8 bondman 奴隶
9 rude 愚昧
10 The question of ……的情况
11 enrolled 记录
12 extenuated 贬低
13 enforced 强调

JULIUS CAESAR ACT 3 SCENE 2
儒略·恺撒

Those that will follow Cassius, go with him;
And public reasons shall be renderèd¹
Of Caesar's death.

1 PLEBEIAN   I will hear Brutus speak.
2 PLEBEIAN   I will hear Cassius and compare their reasons
When severally² we hear them renderèd.   10
                    [*Exit Cassius with some of the Plebeians*]
                    [*Brutus goes into the pulpit*]
3 PLEBEIAN   The noble Brutus is ascended, silence!
BRUTUS   Be patient till the last³.
Romans, countrymen, and lovers⁴, hear me for my cause, and be silent that you may hear. Believe me for mine honour, and have respect to⁵ mine honour that you may believe. Censure me⁶ in your wisdom, and   15
awake your senses⁷ that you may the better judge. If there be any in this assembly, any dear friend of Caesar's, to him I say that Brutus' love to Caesar was no less than his. If then that friend demand why Brutus rose against Caesar, this is my answer: not that I loved Caesar less, but that I loved Rome more. Had you rather Caesar were living, and   20
die all slaves, than that Caesar were dead, to live all freemen? As Caesar loved me, I weep for him; as he was fortunate, I rejoice at it; as he was valiant, I honour him; but, as he was ambitious, I slew him. There is tears for his love, joy for his fortune, honour for his valour, and death for his ambition. Who is here so base that would be a   25
bondman⁸? If any, speak, for him have I offended. Who is here so rude⁹ that would not be a Roman? If any, speak, for him have I offended. Who is here so vile that will not love his country? If any, speak, for him have I offended. I pause for a reply.
ALL   None, Brutus, none.   30
BRUTUS   Then none have I offended. I have done no more to Caesar than you shall do to Brutus. The question of¹⁰ his death is enrolled¹¹ in the Capitol, his glory not extenuated¹² wherein he was worthy, nor his offences enforced¹³ for which he suffered death.

            Enter MARK ANTONY [*and others*] *with Caesar's body*

Here comes his body, mourned by Mark Antony, who, though he had   35
no hand in his death, shall receive the benefit of his dying, a place in the commonwealth, as which of you shall not? With this I depart: that, as I slew my best lover for the good of Rome, I have the same dagger for myself when it shall please my country to need my death.
                    [*Comes down*]

Hailed as a new leader, Brutus asks the crowd to hear Antony out. In the pulpit, Antony at first seems to reflect the anti-Caesar mood of the crowd.

 剧情简介：布鲁图得到群众的欢呼，已成为他们心目中新的领袖。他请众人听完安东尼的演说。在演说台上，安东尼一开始似在顺从群众的反恺撒情绪。

Characters 人物分析

Brutus's errors (in pairs)

Brutus's speech is very well received by the crowd. However, he then makes several errors of judgement.

- Read lines 45–53. Decide what Brutus's errors are.
- One of you steps into role as Brutus and the other interrogates him about his mistakes.

Stagecraft 导演技巧

Antony takes centre stage (in sixes)

Brutus descends from the pulpit to a hero's reception from the crowd. The third plebeian even shouts, 'Let him be Caesar'! But before Antony can begin his funeral oration, he must subdue the raucous (声音刺耳的，喧闹的), pro-Brutus crowd.

- Take parts (you will need four plebeians, Brutus and Antony). Start at the moment when Brutus comes down from the speaker's platform. Read through all the lines until Antony begins his speech at line 65.
- Now work out how you would stage this part of the scene. You will need to show how the mood of the plebeians changes and how Antony gradually subdues them in order to begin his address. Act it out!

1 The speaker's skill (whole class)

Antony, in his funeral oration (lines 65–99), uses many of the persuasive techniques that Brutus employed earlier. Amongst other strategies he: asks for his listeners' attention; explains his purpose; acknowledges and flatters Brutus; praises Caesar; shows his own distress.

a One person reads Antony's speech. The others line up on the opposite side of the room. Each time Antony uses one of the techniques listed, the others take a step towards him and call out the technique used.

b Between lines 65 and 151 of Antony's speech you will find five or six key words (such as ambition/ambitious) emphasised and repeated seven to fifteen times each. Find at least three of these words and work out what effects the repetitions have. Contribute your findings to a class discussion.

1 parts 品质
2 Do grace to 向……致敬
3 grace his speech 有礼貌地听他讲话
4 Tending to 关于
5 beholding to 感激
6 interrèd 入土
7 grievous fault 极其严重的错误
8 answered 为……付出代价

ALL	Live, Brutus, live, live!	40
1 PLEBEIAN	Bring him with triumph home unto his house.	
2 PLEBEIAN	Give him a statue with his ancestors.	
3 PLEBEIAN	Let him be Caesar.	
4 PLEBEIAN	Caesar's better parts[1]	
	Shall be crowned in Brutus.	
1 PLEBEIAN	We'll bring him to his house	
	With shouts and clamours.	
BRUTUS	My countrymen –	45
2 PLEBEIAN	Peace, silence, Brutus speaks!	
1 PLEBEIAN	Peace ho!	
BRUTUS	Good countrymen, let me depart alone,	
	And, for my sake, stay here with Antony.	
	Do grace to[2] Caesar's corpse, and grace his speech[3]	
	Tending to[4] Caesar's glories, which Mark Antony	50
	(By our permission) is allowed to make.	
	I do entreat you, not a man depart,	
	Save I alone, till Antony have spoke. *Exit*	
1 PLEBEIAN	Stay ho, and let us hear Mark Antony.	
3 PLEBEIAN	Let him go up into the public chair,	55
	We'll hear him. Noble Antony, go up.	
ANTONY	For Brutus' sake, I am beholding to[5] you.	
	[*Goes into the pulpit*]	
4 PLEBEIAN	What does he say of Brutus?	
3 PLEBEIAN	He says for Brutus' sake	
	He finds himself beholding to us all.	
4 PLEBEIAN	'Twere best he speak no harm of Brutus here!	60
1 PLEBEIAN	This Caesar was a tyrant.	
3 PLEBEIAN	Nay, that's certain:	
	We are blest that Rome is rid of him.	
2 PLEBEIAN	Peace, let us hear what Antony can say.	
ANTONY	You gentle Romans –	
ALL	Peace ho, let us hear him.	
ANTONY	Friends, Romans, countrymen, lend me your ears!	65
	I come to bury Caesar, not to praise him.	
	The evil that men do lives after them,	
	The good is oft interrèd[6] with their bones:	
	So let it be with Caesar. The noble Brutus	
	Hath told you Caesar was ambitious;	70
	If it were so, it was a grievous fault[7],	
	And grievously hath Caesar answered[8] it.	

While appearing to agree with Brutus's portrait of Caesar, Antony rejects it in reality by listing Caesar's virtues. The crowd becomes uncertain, swayed by Antony's grief.

剧情简介：安东尼表面上赞同布鲁图对恺撒的看法，实际却列出恺撒的种种美德加以反驳。民众被安东尼的悲痛所感染，内心开始动摇。

Stagecraft 导演技巧
Staging Antony's funeral oration

Step into role as director. By now the plebeians and the audience have heard quite a lot of speeches and there are more to come. It is crucial that they do not lose interest at this point, so they need something interesting to look at, to complement the challenging speeches they will hear. It is also important that this grand and public address is staged differently from Antony's more personal soliloquy (see p. 89).

- Remember Caesar's body is on the stage. Where would you place Antony in relation to it and why? Sketch out your staging ideas in your Director's Journal.
- Now consider the photographs below carefully. Decide which staging of the oration you prefer – you can choose your own! – and be prepared to justify your choice to the class.

1 under leave of 得到……的允许
2 general coffers 公家钱库
3 disprove 证明……是错的
4 judgement 判断力，理智
5 Bear with me 宽容我，担待我
6 dear abide it 为此付出沉重代价

　　　　　　Here, under leave of¹ Brutus and the rest –
　　　　　　For Brutus is an honourable man,
　　　　　　So are they all, all honourable men –   75
　　　　　　Come I to speak in Caesar's funeral.
　　　　　　He was my friend, faithful and just to me,
　　　　　　But Brutus says he was ambitious,
　　　　　　And Brutus is an honourable man.
　　　　　　He hath brought many captives home to Rome,   80
　　　　　　Whose ransoms did the general coffers² fill;
　　　　　　Did this in Caesar seem ambitious?
　　　　　　When that the poor have cried, Caesar hath wept:
　　　　　　Ambition should be made of sterner stuff;
　　　　　　Yet Brutus says he was ambitious,   85
　　　　　　And Brutus is an honourable man.
　　　　　　You all did see that on the Lupercal
　　　　　　I thrice presented him a kingly crown,
　　　　　　Which he did thrice refuse. Was this ambition?
　　　　　　Yet Brutus says he was ambitious,   90
　　　　　　And sure he is an honourable man.
　　　　　　I speak not to disprove³ what Brutus spoke,
　　　　　　But here I am to speak what I do know.
　　　　　　You all did love him once, not without cause;
　　　　　　What cause withholds you then to mourn for him?   95
　　　　　　O judgement⁴, thou art fled to brutish beasts,
　　　　　　And men have lost their reason! Bear with me⁵,
　　　　　　My heart is in the coffin there with Caesar,
　　　　　　And I must pause till it come back to me.
1 PLEBEIAN　　Methinks there is much reason in his sayings.   100
2 PLEBEIAN　　If thou consider rightly of the matter,
　　　　　　Caesar has had great wrong.
3 PLEBEIAN　　　　　　　　　　　　Has he, masters!
　　　　　　I fear there will a worse come in his place.
4 PLEBEIAN　　Marked ye his words? He would not take the crown,
　　　　　　Therefore 'tis certain he was not ambitious.   105
1 PLEBEIAN　　If it be found so, some will dear abide it⁶.
2 PLEBEIAN　　Poor soul, his eyes are red as fire with weeping.
3 PLEBEIAN　　There's not a nobler man in Rome than Antony.
4 PLEBEIAN　　Now mark him, he begins again to speak.

Antony pleads that the plebeians must remain loyal to the conspirators, and that he must wrong Caesar by refusing to let them know how generous his will is to them. 'Read it!' they shout.

剧情简介：安东尼恳请民众一定要忠于谋杀团伙，又说他不让他们知道恺撒在遗嘱里对他们多么慷慨，只能让恺撒蒙冤受屈。"念啊！"民众高呼。

1 'The will, the will, we will hear Caesar's will!'
(in fours)

This is perhaps Antony's masterstroke (绝招). So skilled at focusing his listeners' attention on a specific detail, in line 120 he 'just happens to' mention Caesar's will. He very probably does not have Caesar's will at this point (he sends Lepidus to fetch it from Caesar's house in Act 4 Scene 1, lines 7–9, having fled to his own house following the assassination), so this tactic is a con (骗局，诡计).

- Take parts and act out lines 120–54. Concentrate on the techniques Antony uses to 'work' his audience. How does he tease them?

1 mutiny 暴乱
2 parchment 羊皮纸
3 closet 里屋，密室
4 commons 百姓
5 testament 遗嘱
6 napkins 手巾
7 Bequeathing 遗赠
8 issue 子孙
9 o'ershot myself 超出我的本意

Antony with the will and the crowd.

Language in the play 剧中语言
Convincing the crowd (in small groups)

Antony is a skilled orator, but he does not have much time to bring the crowd around to his side. Brutus trusts him not to go beyond his remit of 'Tending to Caesar's glories'. He does, of course, but in subtle and carefully crafted ways.

- Draw up a table like the one below to help you keep track of where, how and to what effect Antony exceeds his brief.

What does Antony say?	Rhetorical techniques used	Effect on crowd
He has Caesar's will (line 120)	Concentrates on specific detail	Whips up crowd frenzy (狂暴)

- In your groups, look back to Antony's first speech ('Friends, Romans' line 65) and fill in your table with detail about it. Then turn to his speech opposite and do the same.

JULIUS CAESAR ACT 3 SCENE 2
儒略・恺撒

ANTONY	But yesterday the word of Caesar might	110
	Have stood against the world; now lies he there,	
	And none so poor to do him reverence.	
	O masters, if I were disposed to stir	
	Your hearts and minds to mutiny¹ and rage,	
	I should do Brutus wrong and Cassius wrong,	115
	Who (you all know) are honourable men.	
	I will not do them wrong; I rather choose	
	To wrong the dead, to wrong myself and you,	
	Than I will wrong such honourable men.	
	But here's a parchment² with the seal of Caesar,	120
	I found it in his closet³, 'tis his will.	
	Let but the commons⁴ hear this testament⁵ –	
	Which, pardon me, I do not mean to read –	
	And they would go and kiss dead Caesar's wounds	
	And dip their napkins⁶ in his sacred blood,	125
	Yea, beg a hair of him for memory,	
	And, dying, mention it within their wills,	
	Bequeathing⁷ it as a rich legacy	
	Unto their issue⁸.	
4 PLEBEIAN	We'll hear the will. Read it, Mark Antony.	130
ALL	The will, the will, we will hear Caesar's will!	
ANTONY	Have patience, gentle friends, I must not read it.	
	It is not meet you know how Caesar loved you:	
	You are not wood, you are not stones, but men,	
	And, being men, hearing the will of Caesar,	135
	It will inflame you, it will make you mad.	
	'Tis good you know not that you are his heirs,	
	For if you should, O, what would come of it?	
4 PLEBEIAN	Read the will, we'll hear it, Antony.	
	You shall read us the will, Caesar's will!	140
ANTONY	Will you be patient? Will you stay awhile?	
	I have o'ershot myself⁹ to tell you of it.	
	I fear I wrong the honourable men	
	Whose daggers have stabbed Caesar, I do fear it.	
4 PLEBEIAN	They were traitors. Honourable men!	145
ALL	The will! The testament!	
2 PLEBEIAN	They were villains, murderers! The will, read the will!	
ANTONY	You will compel me then to read the will?	

> Obeying the crowd, Antony comes down to show them Caesar's corpse, starting with the dagger cuts in his cloak. The plebeians weep.
>
> 剧情简介：应民众要求，安东尼走下台去，让众人看恺撒的尸体，从披风割破处的伤口看起。众人不禁落泪。

1 How well does Antony manipulate his audience? (in groups of three or four)

a Read Act 3 Scene 1 again closely and then write a precise account of what actually happened when Caesar was murdered. Compare it with Mark Antony's version in lines 160–80. What reason(s) are there to doubt the accuracy of Antony's account of the murder?

b Just as a jury has to weigh up the arguments of both the prosecuting and defending barristers (辩护律师) to arrive at a fair verdict, see if you can spot how Antony colours his account to manipulate the crowd's emotions and show the conspirators in a bad light. Note down your observations.

c **Emotive language** (有感染力的语言) is language that seeks to arouse powerful emotions such as fear, pity, anger and so on. Discuss and then write down three or four of the most emotive words or phrases that Antony uses, explaining how and why you think they spark such strong responses in the people watching and listening to him.

1 hearse 灵柩
2 far off 更远些
3 bear back 往后退
4 mantle 斗篷
5 Nervii 那尔维部落（活动于今天比利时地区，凶猛剽悍，被恺撒成功征服）
6 rent 大口子
7 envious 恶毒
8 steel 短剑，匕首
9 As rushing out 像是要冲出
10 unkindly 丧尽天良，残忍
11 most unkindest 最丧尽天良，最残忍
12 vanquished 击败，征服
13 muffling up 裹住，蒙住
14 base 底座
15 flourished 挥舞兵器（庆贺胜利）
16 dint 打击；力度
17 gracious 高贵，高尚

Themes 主题分析

Death in detail

Having come down from the pulpit, Antony gathers the crowd around Caesar's body. Rather than immediately appealing to their love of Caesar and how they feel looking at his body, he uses the opportunity to focus on the very specific details of Caesar's cloak. Like Caesar, this cloak has known victory but it is now torn and covered in blood. At the end of the speech he questions why the crowd weeps to see 'Caesar's vesture wounded' when before them is his actual body ruined by the conspirators' actions. Thus he switches their focus to the body itself.

- Read the description of the torn cloak (lines 165–80) and then make a drawing of it. Annotate the drawing with details about the damage done to the cloak by the various conspirators (you can decide whether Caesar is still in it or not). It suits Antony's purposes to mention only three conspirators, but you can draw and write about the damage done by the others as well. Be as imaginative as possible. If the wounds were 'mouths' that could speak, what would they say about the conspirator who made them and his motives?

	Then make a ring about the corpse of Caesar	
	And let me show you him that made the will.	150
	Shall I descend? And will you give me leave?	
ALL	Come down.	
2 PLEBEIAN	Descend.	
3 PLEBEIAN	You shall have leave.	

[*Antony comes down from the pulpit*]

4 PLEBEIAN	A ring, stand round.	155
1 PLEBEIAN	Stand from the hearse¹, stand from the body.	
2 PLEBEIAN	Room for Antony, most noble Antony.	
ANTONY	Nay, press not so upon me, stand far off².	
ALL	Stand back! Room, bear back³!	
ANTONY	If you have tears, prepare to shed them now.	160
	You all do know this mantle⁴. I remember	
	The first time ever Caesar put it on,	
	'Twas on a summer's evening, in his tent,	
	That day he overcame the Nervii⁵.	
	Look, in this place ran Cassius' dagger through;	165
	See what a rent⁶ the envious⁷ Casca made;	
	Through this the well-belovèd Brutus stabbed,	
	And as he plucked his cursèd steel⁸ away,	
	Mark how the blood of Caesar followed it,	
	As rushing out⁹ of doors to be resolved	170
	If Brutus so unkindly¹⁰ knocked or no,	
	For Brutus, as you know, was Caesar's angel.	
	Judge, O you gods, how dearly Caesar loved him!	
	This was the most unkindest¹¹ cut of all.	
	For when the noble Caesar saw him stab,	175
	Ingratitude, more strong than traitors' arms,	
	Quite vanquished¹² him. Then burst his mighty heart,	
	And, in his mantle muffling up¹³ his face,	
	Even at the base¹⁴ of Pompey's statue	
	(Which all the while ran blood) great Caesar fell.	180
	O, what a fall was there, my countrymen!	
	Then I, and you, and all of us fell down,	
	Whilst bloody treason flourished¹⁵ over us.	
	O, now you weep, and I perceive you feel	
	The dint¹⁶ of pity. These are gracious¹⁷ drops.	185

There are cries of grief when Antony displays the body. When he cleverly praises Brutus's oratory over his own, the enraged crowd move to attack the conspirators.

 剧情简介：安东尼给众人看恺撒的尸体时，民众放声痛哭。安东尼故意夸赞布鲁图口才比自己好，结果民众暴怒，要去打刺杀恺撒的人。

Stagecraft 导演技巧

'You blocks, you stones' / 'Good friends, sweet friends' (in large groups)

Remind yourself of how Murellus berates the crowd in Act 1 Scene 1. Now Antony calls them his friends. The crowd has an important role in this play (see p. 182). It represents the people of Rome, whose support is essential to whoever will next govern the city. But how fickle is the crowd?

- One person is the director and holds a meeting with the actors to discuss the most effective way of using the crowd in Act 3. Improvise being members of an angry crowd and then a more positive and celebratory one. Consider whether or not the numbered plebeians have individual characteristics.
- Put your improvisation into action and read lines 186–249. Members of the crowd should stay in role throughout. Remember that Antony has worked them up after his speech about Caesar's mantle, but he is able to quieten them three times before their final angry explosion at the end of the scene.
- Finally come together as one very large group and act out the response of the crowd to Antony's 'Here was a Caesar! When comes such another?'

Language in the play 剧中语言

Blaming conspirators (in small groups)

Brutus let Antony speak on the condition 'You shall not in your funeral speech blame us' (Act 3 Scene 1, line 245).

- Imagine that by Scene 2, line 220, the conspirators have found out how Antony has roused the people. They send in a force to arrest him and disperse the crowd.
- Organise your group into lawyers for the prosecution and the defence at Antony's trial. The prosecution must prove that he *did* blame the conspirators, the defence that he did not. Both sides must look closely at the language of the speech. It may be helpful to look back at the work you did in Activity 1 on page 100.
- When you have prepared your arguments, join up with another group, choose a judge, lawyers and a jury, and run the trial. Finally, get the jury to sift the evidence and arrive at a verdict.

1 vesture　衣服
2 marred ... traitors　你们都看到了，让叛贼乱剑刺成这样
3 About!　走啊！
4 private griefs　私仇
5 nor worth　无德无才
6 Action, nor utterance　不会摆手势，也没有口才
7 right on　直白，直来直去
8 ruffle up　煽动

	Kind souls, what weep you when you but behold	
	Our Caesar's vesture[1] wounded? Look you here,	
	Here is himself, marred as you see with traitors[2].	
1 PLEBEIAN	O piteous spectacle!	
2 PLEBEIAN	O noble Caesar!	190
3 PLEBEIAN	O woeful day!	
4 PLEBEIAN	O traitors, villains!	
1 PLEBEIAN	O most bloody sight!	
2 PLEBEIAN	We will be revenged!	
ALL	Revenge! About![3] Seek! Burn! Fire! Kill!	195
	Slay! Let not a traitor live!	
ANTONY	Stay, countrymen.	
1 PLEBEIAN	Peace there, hear the noble Antony.	
2 PLEBEIAN	We'll hear him, we'll follow him, we'll die with him.	
ANTONY	Good friends, sweet friends, let me not stir you up	200
	To such a sudden flood of mutiny.	
	They that have done this deed are honourable.	
	What private griefs[4] they have, alas, I know not,	
	That made them do it. They are wise and honourable,	
	And will no doubt with reasons answer you.	205
	I come not, friends, to steal away your hearts.	
	I am no orator, as Brutus is,	
	But – as you know me all – a plain blunt man	
	That love my friend, and that they know full well	
	That gave me public leave to speak of him.	210
	For I have neither wit, nor words, nor worth[5],	
	Action, nor utterance[6], nor the power of speech	
	To stir men's blood. I only speak right on[7].	
	I tell you that which you yourselves do know,	
	Show you sweet Caesar's wounds, poor, poor, dumb mouths,	215
	And bid them speak for me. But were I Brutus,	
	And Brutus Antony, there were an Antony	
	Would ruffle up[8] your spirits and put a tongue	
	In every wound of Caesar, that should move	
	The stones of Rome to rise and mutiny.	220
ALL	We'll mutiny.	
1 PLEBEIAN	We'll burn the house of Brutus.	
3 PLEBEIAN	Away then, come, seek the conspirators.	

Antony reveals how much Caesar's will left to the people. They swear vengeance on the conspirators and leave. Alone, Antony confides his satisfaction. Octavius's arrival is announced.

 剧情简介：安东尼告诉民众恺撒在遗嘱里赠送给他们丰厚的财产。他们发誓要找刺杀恺撒的人报仇。民众离开后，安东尼表示他很欣慰。来人报告屋大维已到。

Language in the play 剧中语言

How did Antony do it?

Go back to the chart you began on page 98 and fill in the details for Antony's subsequent speeches.

Themes 主题分析

Themes in focus (in small groups)

By this point in the play, all the main themes have been established. They are considered in more detail on pages 168–70.

- Choose and then write down in the middle of a large piece of paper one theme that runs through the play. Each group should choose a different theme. Already mentioned in 'Themes' boxes are:
  - death and attitudes towards it
  - public versus private life
  - sickness and disease
  - love and friendship
  - honour
  - what it is to be a Roman
- Using the charts you have drawn up to assess Antony's speeches (see pp. 98 and 104), as well as the notes you have made in your Director's Journal, cover your paper with ideas, references, quotations and thoughts about your theme.
- Either display the pieces of paper or pass them around for other groups to look at and discuss.

1 Wherein 凭什么
2 several 分别，单独
3 drachmaes 德拉克米（一种银币）
4 walks 园子
5 arbours （藤类攀缘架子而成的）凉亭
6 common pleasures 公众娱乐场所
7 holy place 圣地，圣坛
8 brands 火把
9 forms 长凳
10 windows 百叶窗
11 afoot 迈起脚步
12 thither 到那里

1 'Mischief, thou art afoot' (in pairs)

In lines 250–1, Antony makes it clear that he has deliberately worked the crowd in order to unleash their 'mischief'.

- Imagine that, with Octavius a day or so later, Antony reflects on his performance at Caesar's funeral. Improvise their conversation in which Antony runs through some of the highlights of his oration. Which strategies and ideas pleased him? Were there any surprises (either pleasant or unpleasant)? Did he feel that he accomplished all that he set out to?

ANTONY	Yet hear me, countrymen, yet hear me speak.	
ALL	Peace ho, hear Antony, most noble Antony!	
ANTONY	Why, friends, you go to do you know not what.	225
	Wherein[1] hath Caesar thus deserved your loves?	
	Alas, you know not! I must tell you then:	
	You have forgot the will I told you of.	
ALL	Most true. The will, let's stay and hear the will!	
ANTONY	Here is the will, and under Caesar's seal:	230
	To every Roman citizen he gives,	
	To every several[2] man, seventy-five drachmaes[3].	
2 PLEBEIAN	Most noble Caesar, we'll revenge his death!	
3 PLEBEIAN	O royal Caesar!	
ANTONY	Hear me with patience.	235
ALL	Peace ho!	
ANTONY	Moreover, he hath left you all his walks[4],	
	His private arbours[5] and new-planted orchards,	
	On this side Tiber; he hath left them you,	
	And to your heirs for ever – common pleasures[6],	240
	To walk abroad and recreate yourselves.	
	Here was a Caesar! When comes such another?	
1 PLEBEIAN	Never, never! Come, away, away!	
	We'll burn his body in the holy place[7]	
	And with the brands[8] fire the traitors' houses.	245
	Take up the body.	
2 PLEBEIAN	Go fetch fire!	
3 PLEBEIAN	Pluck down benches!	
4 PLEBEIAN	Pluck down forms[9], windows[10], anything!	

Exeunt Plebeians [with the body]

ANTONY	Now let it work. Mischief, thou art afoot[11],	250
	Take thou what course thou wilt!	

Enter SERVANT

	How now, fellow?	
SERVANT	Sir, Octavius is already come to Rome.	
ANTONY	Where is he?	
SERVANT	He and Lepidus are at Caesar's house.	
ANTONY	And thither[12] will I straight to visit him.	255

Octavius's servant reports that Brutus and Cassius have fled Rome. Cinna the poet is interrogated by the plebeians. 'Going where?' 'Caesar's funeral.' 'Friend or enemy?' 'Friend.'

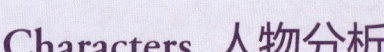剧情简介：屋大维的小厮报告说，布鲁图和卡休已逃离罗马。诗人希纳遭民众盘问。"往哪儿去？" "恺撒的葬礼。" "是朋友还是敌人？" "朋友。"

Characters 人物分析

Antony assessed (in threes)

In many of Shakespeare's plays, servants play a crucial role in overhearing important events or asides.

- One of you is a journalist covering the recent events in Rome. You have been asked to focus on Antony's role. You were present at both Brutus's and Antony's speeches in the market-place. You then manage to track down Octavius's and Antony's servants who are prepared to tell you that they overheard everything Antony said just before they entered at Act 3 Scene 1, line 276, and Scene 2, line 251. In your group improvise your conversation with the servants.
- How does what they tell you make you reassess what Antony said and did after the assassination? Write your exclusive report on 'the real Antony' for television or a newspaper.

Write about it 写作练习

This act is considered to be one of the most dramatic in all of Shakespeare's works. Think of the power shifts that have taken place: at the beginning of the act Caesar comes to the Capitol and shows how 'constant' he is, before being assassinated by the conspirators. They briefly hold power before it is taken from them by Antony, and Brutus and Cassius flee Rome.

- Write a detailed analysis of why this act is so dramatic. You could include discussion of: the nature of the events shown on stage, the use of dramatic irony (see p. 76), the use of language, the reversal of fortunes and the role the crowd plays.

1 The crowd again (in large groups)

Act 3 Scene 3 exemplifies the brutality that can take place following a political regime change.

- Prepare to act out the whole scene. Consider whether you want to experiment with locating the scene in another country and/or historical period and discuss why this might be worth doing. Then act it out, remembering that the crowd is at its most powerful and deadly.

1 upon a wish 如我所愿
2 Are rid 骑着马
3 Belike 大概，想必
4 they ... them 他们得到了消息，知道我如何煽动了民心
5 tonight 昨夜
6 things unluckily charge my fantasy 不祥的预感搅得我心神不定
7 forth of doors 出门
8 they are fools that marry 结婚的人都是傻子（伊丽莎白时代的谚语）
9 bear me a bang 吃我一拳

	He comes upon a wish¹. Fortune is merry,
	And in this mood will give us anything.
SERVANT	I heard him say Brutus and Cassius
	Are rid² like madmen through the gates of Rome.
ANTONY	Belike³ they had some notice of the people, 260
	How I had moved them⁴. Bring me to Octavius.

Exeunt

Act 3 Scene 3
Rome   A street

Enter CINNA THE POET, *and after him the* PLEBEIANS

CINNA THE POET	I dreamt tonight⁵ that I did feast with Caesar,
	And things unluckily charge my fantasy⁶.
	I have no will to wander forth of doors⁷,
	Yet something leads me forth.
1 PLEBEIAN	What is your name? 5
2 PLEBEIAN	Whither are you going?
3 PLEBEIAN	Where do you dwell?
4 PLEBEIAN	Are you a married man or a bachelor?
2 PLEBEIAN	Answer every man directly.
1 PLEBEIAN	Ay, and briefly. 10
4 PLEBEIAN	Ay, and wisely.
3 PLEBEIAN	Ay, and truly, you were best.
CINNA THE POET	What is my name? Whither am I going? Where do I dwell? Am I a married man or a bachelor? Then to answer every man directly and briefly, wisely and truly. Wisely I say I am a bachelor. 15
2 PLEBEIAN	That's as much as to say they are fools that marry⁸. You'll bear me a bang⁹ for that, I fear. Proceed directly.
CINNA THE POET	Directly I am going to Caesar's funeral.
1 PLEBEIAN	As a friend or an enemy?
CINNA THE POET	As a friend. 20
2 PLEBEIAN	That matter is answered directly.
4 PLEBEIAN	For your dwelling – briefly.
CINNA THE POET	Briefly, I dwell by the Capitol.
3 PLEBEIAN	Your name, sir, truly.

Hearing his name, the common people accuse Cinna of conspiracy; he protests he's just a poet not a conspirator. They drag him off anyway, intending to burn the conspirators' houses.

 剧情简介：民众听到名字就认定这个希纳就是刺杀团伙中的那个希纳。他辩解说自己只是个诗人，不是刺杀者。民众不分青红皂白拖走了他，并要去烧掉刺杀团伙的房子。

1 What happened that day? (in eights)

Before and during World War II, many Germans were incited by the oratory of Adolf Hitler and became involved in acts of persecution that they later regretted.

1 Pluck but 只用掏出
2 turn him going 结果了他

a Four of you are Plebeians 1–4 in old age, the other four a group of students who are investigating senior citizens' reminiscences (回忆录) about events surrounding Caesar's assassination. The plebeians describe the influence of Antony's oratory very fully, as well as how they now feel about their deeds that night. The students sharpen their memories with searching and detailed questions. Among other things, they want to know what happened to Cinna the poet – and why. Improvise their discussion.

b If you were a student, write up a report of your findings. If you were a senior citizen, write your memoirs of the events you have just discussed.

Stagecraft 导演技巧

Arguing with the director again! (in fours)

The director wants to cut Act 3 Scene 3 (as he did Act 2 Scenes 3 and 4). As before, some of the actors want to keep it.

- One of you steps into role as director, with the support of one actor. The other two take the opposing view. Each side should put a good case together and then argue it.

CINNA THE POET Truly, my name is Cinna. 25
1 PLEBEIAN Tear him to pieces, he's a conspirator.
CINNA THE POET I am Cinna the poet, I am Cinna the poet.
4 PLEBEIAN Tear him for his bad verses, tear him for his bad verses.
CINNA THE POET I am not Cinna the conspirator.
4 PLEBEIAN It is no matter, his name's Cinna. Pluck but[1] his name out of 30
his heart and turn him going[2].
3 PLEBEIAN Tear him, tear him! Come, brands ho, firebrands! To Brutus', to Cassius', burn all! Some to Decius' house, and some to Casca's, some to Ligarius'! Away, go!

Exeunt all the Plebeians [forcing out Cinna]

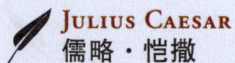
JULIUS CAESAR
儒略·恺撒

Looking back at Act 3　第3幕回顾
Activities for groups or individuals

1 Newspaper billboards
Newsagents' billboards give very brief summaries of the news. Write three of them, one for each scene in Act 3. The billboards should reflect the key aspects of the action. Full sentences are not required.

2 The coffin and the cloak
Antony is a master at using visual objects to enhance his oratory. He makes striking references to Caesar's 'coffin' and to his 'mantle' (cloak).

- All producers have to decide how to display Caesar's corpse during the funeral speeches. Write some notes for the set designer and the props (道具) manager about your own ideas. Study the photographs opposite and on pages x, 96 and 179 for help.

3 Favourite lines
Act 3 contains some of Shakespeare's most memorable lines … and most eloquent persuasion. Select a handful of your own favourites and display them strikingly: a poster, a collage (拼贴画) or a montage (蒙太奇)?

4 The crowd
Many productions seek to give the Roman crowd a dynamic and energetic presence. Some do this by having the common people dotted amongst the real audience. Some have used the audience as interactive participants in the funeral scene. The photo on page 111 (top right) shows the theatre audience mingling with cast members.

- Write two or three paragraphs summarising the strengths and weaknesses of this staging idea.
- What other ideas do you have for exploiting the crowd scenes?

5 A Caesar memorial and obituary (讣告)
a Design a striking and impressive memorial to celebrate the life of your benefactor, Caesar. It is to be installed in the newly bequeathed gardens. Present your finished idea or your work in progress as a series of sketches with explanation. Use the play to give you ideas: for example, Antony's funeral eulogies (悼词) (Act 3 Scene 2), Calpurnia's dream (Act 2 Scene 2) and Cassius's references to Caesar as Colossus.

b Now write Caesar's obituary – a written memorial. Was he a good ruler or a tyrant? Decide on your target audience and consider what impression of Caesar you wish to convey.

6 Total coverage
Create your own newspaper coverage of the assassination of Caesar and subsequent events. You can include any newspaper pieces you may have already written, if appropriate. Decide whether your newspaper is a tabloid (小报) or a broadsheet (大报) and what its political bias is, who to interview, what to comment on and what to speculate about. Display your front page and other articles for others to see.

7 Honour and friendship
Look back at Brutus's important lines 85–9 in Act 1 Scene 2. Bearing in mind the discussions about honour and friendship you have already had, write your answer to the following question, making sure you back up your points with quotations:

- Did Brutus act honourably in becoming one of the conspirators who assassinated his friend Caesar?

8 Queen Elizabeth I and Julius Caesar
When a contemporary audience saw the assassination of Caesar on stage, thoughts of the attempts on the life of their queen would have come to mind (see p. 167).

- Research the parallels between the lives and reigns of these two leaders. Display your findings so that others can benefit from them.

What are your views on the stagings of these dramatic moments from Act 3?

> The Triumvirate organises a purge which includes family relatives. Antony shows contempt for Lepidus, and Octavius defends him.
>
> 剧情简介：掌权的三人团开始清除异己，其中包括他们自己的亲族。安东尼表现出对雷丕德的鄙视，屋大维为雷丕德说好话。

1 Antony, Octavius and Lepidus: the Triumvirate
(in threes)

As Act 4 begins, the audience is introduced to the Triumvirate ('three people') who each now rule one third of the Roman Empire – Europe, North Africa and Asia (comprising modern-day Turkey, Iran and Iraq).

a This opening scene often follows an interval (幕间休息), and many directors use the opportunity to quickly establish the significance and power of the three men who will now form the direct opposition to Brutus and Cassius. Working together, suggest ways in which a modern production (in traditional costume) might quickly achieve this. Add your strongest idea to a whole-class wall display.

b In many coalition (联合执政) groups, there can be an issue about how 'equal' the members are and who might begin to emerge as its natural leader. Take parts and read this short scene aloud to each other. Experiment with different tones, pitch and volume as you seek to give your character the edge on your rivals. Use your classmates as a live audience and get them to score your performance, awarding marks when they think you are clearly dominating your fellow rulers and taking them away when you seem to be losing influence. At the end of the reading, decide together who is emerging as the natural leader, and why.

1	pricked	标出，打记号
2	spot	记号，污点
3	cut … legacies	砍掉几项遗产上的支出
4	Or	要么
5	slight, unmeritable	无足轻重，庸庸碌碌
6	Meet	适合
7	threefold world	三分天下
8	voice	意见
9	black sentence and proscription	残忍的判决和处死（**black**: 恶毒，残忍）
10	divers slanderous loads	担的许多骂名
11	where we will	咱要去的地儿
12	turn him off	打发了他
13	empty ass	卸下负担的驴子
14	graze in commons	在公地上啃草

Characters 人物分析
A new view of Antony?

Antony and his partners now control Rome. Look closely at what he says and how he behaves in the first fifteen lines. Think, too, about the significance of his having the opening line of the act and any conclusions you have reached after the activity above.

- Make notes to add to your Character file on the kind of man Antony is now revealed to be. Justify your comments by referring to the text.
- Compare the latest depiction of Antony with your earlier judgements of him. What glimpses do you recall Shakespeare providing in Act 3 of the 'new' Antony that we see in this scene?

Act 4 Scene 1
Rome

Enter ANTONY, OCTAVIUS, *and* LEPIDUS

ANTONY These many then shall die, their names are pricked[1].
OCTAVIUS Your brother too must die; consent you, Lepidus?
LEPIDUS I do consent.
OCTAVIUS   Prick him down, Antony.
LEPIDUS Upon condition Publius shall not live,
Who is your sister's son, Mark Antony.   5
ANTONY He shall not live – look, with a spot[2] I damn him.
But, Lepidus, go you to Caesar's house,
Fetch the will hither, and we shall determine
How to cut off some charge in legacies[3].
LEPIDUS What, shall I find you here?   10
OCTAVIUS Or[4] here or at the Capitol.

Exit Lepidus

ANTONY This is a slight, unmeritable[5] man,
Meet[6] to be sent on errands; is it fit,
The threefold world[7] divided, he should stand
One of the three to share it?
OCTAVIUS   So you thought him   15
And took his voice[8] who should be pricked to die
In our black sentence and proscription[9].
ANTONY Octavius, I have seen more days than you,
And though we lay these honours on this man
To ease ourselves of divers slanderous loads[10],   20
He shall but bear them as the ass bears gold,
To groan and sweat under the business,
Either led or driven, as we point the way;
And having brought our treasure where we will[11],
Then take we down his load and turn him off[12]   25
(Like to the empty ass[13]) to shake his ears
And graze in commons[14].
OCTAVIUS   You may do your will,
But he's a tried and valiant soldier.

> Antony compares Lepidus to his horse. He and Octavius prepare for war against Brutus and Cassius. In the next scene Brutus asks Pindarus to bring his master Cassius to discuss Cassius's suspected misdeeds.
>
> 剧情简介：安东尼将雷丕德比作他的马。他和屋大维准备迎战布鲁图和卡休。在接下来的一场里，布鲁图让品德若把他的主子卡休叫来，要谈一谈卡休涉嫌的不端之举。

Language in the play 剧中语言

Lepidus the 'ass' (in pairs)

Between lines 12 and 40, Antony uses powerful language to describe Lepidus. For example, he compares him to an 'ass' who should 'shake his ears / And graze in commons'.

- One of you is Antony. Read his speech aloud, pausing after the key images. The other is a staff officer in Mark Antony's army who has in the past entertained him and the rest of his staff by drawing satirical cartoon portraits of other commanders and senior officers. Using information from the script opposite, draw your cartoon portrait of the man Antony describes. Look at the political cartoon below for inspiration!

▶ A 1936 cartoon by David Low, showing Adolf Hitler goose-stepping across the 'spineless leaders of democracy'.

1 Antony and Octavius make plans (in pairs)

In line 45, Antony urges Octavius to join him in private to plan a response to Brutus and Cassius's gathering threat.

- Take parts as Antony and Octavius and script their conversation, basing their speaking styles and attitudes on the glimpses of their characterisation that Shakespeare provides in this scene.

2 Recruiting in Asia (in two groups of up to five each)

By the time Brutus and Cassius return to the stage in Act 4 Scene 2, they have raised large armies in Asia.

- One group of you is made up of Republican recruiting officers who try to explain why Brutus and Cassius must defeat Antony and Octavius. The others are Asians who challenge and ask questions. Assume that newspapers have kept the people of Asia well informed of recent events in Rome!

1 provender 草料
2 wind 拐弯
3 corporal motion 身体的运动
4 in some taste 某种程度上
5 Which … fashion 别人玩剩的、老掉牙的东西，他当稀罕物儿
6 property 道具
7 Listen = Listen to
8 levying powers 招兵买马
9 straight make head 立即集结一支军队
10 means stretched 想尽办法
11 in counsel 秘密地
12 covert 暗藏的
13 open perils 公开的严重危机
14 at … about 处境危险，被团团围住（斗熊时，熊被拴在木桩上让群狗撕咬）
15 Sardis 萨迪斯（城镇名，在今日土耳其境内）
16 Drum 军鼓声
17 In his own change 因为他自己变了（变得和布鲁图不一心）
18 ill 无能，不称职
19 worthy cause 充分的理由

Julius Caesar Act 4 Scene 2
儒略・恺撒

ANTONY	So is my horse, Octavius, and for that	
	I do appoint him store of provender¹.	30
	It is a creature that I teach to fight,	
	To wind², to stop, to run directly on,	
	His corporal motion³ governed by my spirit.	
	And, in some taste⁴, is Lepidus but so:	
	He must be taught and trained and bid go forth,	35
	A barren-spirited fellow, one that feeds	
	On objects, arts, and imitations,	
	Which, out of use and staled by other men,	
	Begin his fashion⁵. Do not talk of him	
	But as a property⁶. And now, Octavius,	40
	Listen⁷ great things. Brutus and Cassius	
	Are levying powers⁸; we must straight make head⁹.	
	Therefore let our alliance be combined,	
	Our best friends made, our means stretched¹⁰,	
	And let us presently go sit in counsel¹¹,	45
	How covert¹² matters may be best disclosed	
	And open perils¹³ surest answerèd.	
OCTAVIUS	Let us do so, for we are at the stake	
	And bayed about¹⁴ with many enemies,	
	And some that smile have in their hearts, I fear,	50
	Millions of mischiefs.	

Exeunt

Act 4 Scene 2
Brutus' camp near Sardis¹⁵ in Asia

Drum¹⁶. Enter BRUTUS, LUCILIUS, *[Lucius,] and the army. Titinius and* PINDARUS *meet them*

BRUTUS	Stand ho!	
LUCILIUS	Give the word ho, and stand!	
BRUTUS	What now, Lucilius, is Cassius near?	
LUCILIUS	He is at hand, and Pindarus is come	
	To do you salutation from his master.	5
BRUTUS	He greets me well. Your master, Pindarus,	
	In his own change¹⁷ or by ill¹⁸ officers,	
	Hath given me some worthy cause¹⁹ to wish	
	Things done undone, but if he be at hand	
	I shall be satisfied.	

Lucilius, returned from Cassius, reports that Cassius is no longer as friendly as before. Cassius enters with his army and says Brutus has wronged him. Brutus urges him to speak quietly.

 剧情简介：卢希琉从卡休处回来，报告说卡休不似以往那样友善。卡休率领部下上，说布鲁图冤枉了他。布鲁图劝他有话好好说。

Stagecraft 导演技巧

'*Enter* CASSIUS *and his powers*' (in fours)

Brutus's description of Cassius as 'A hot friend cooling' in line 19 makes it clear that there is friction between them. When Cassius enters with his military 'powers' at line 30, the tension is ratcheted up (升级) further.

- As a group, work out how to stage the arrival of Cassius and his followers to create maximum impact. Where will you position or 'block' the characters? How does Brutus deploy his soldiers? How do the men speak to each other? Use the picture of the Globe stage on page 74 if you wish. Focus on blocking* from the stage direction '*Low march within*' after line 24 to line 42. Remember that Shakespeare's company is probably only about fifteen strong.
- If you have access to a hall or stage, join forces with one or more other groups in the class and try out your different ideas for this opening confrontation. Explore how you can add sound effects to create further impact.
- Decide which group's blocking combinations you like best and then rehearse and present your staging of the beginning of Brutus and Cassius's famous quarrel scene to the rest of the class.

▶ What is this actor playing Brutus suggesting about the character's demeanour (举止，风度) at this point in the play?

| 1 | resolved （向我）说清楚
| 2 | instances （亲密的）表示
| 3 | free 坦诚的
| 4 | conference 对话，聊天
| 5 | he hath used of old 他过去那样
| 6 | enforcèd 不自然
| 7 | hot at hand 刚开始时急不可待
| 8 | gallant show 炫耀勇气
| 9 | mettle 能耐
| 10 | *Low march within* 幕后传出低沉的行军声
| 11 | fall their crests 低下头颈
| 12 | jades 劣马，驽马
| 13 | Sink in the trial 受不住考验
| 14 | horse in general 所有骑兵
| 15 | gently 缓速
| 16 | sober form 严肃的神情
| 17 | content 不生气
| 18 | griefs 不满，冤屈

* blocking 戏台调度，指导演对演员在戏台上的动作进行的设计和安排，包括演员与演员、演员与戏台景物之间的相对位置及其变化。

PINDARUS	I do not doubt	10
	But that my noble master will appear	
	Such as he is, full of regard and honour.	
BRUTUS	He is not doubted.	

[*Brutus and Lucilius draw apart*]

                A word, Lucilius,
How he received you; let me be resolved[1].

LUCILIUS	With courtesy and with respect enough,	15
	But not with such familiar instances[2],	
	Nor with such free[3] and friendly conference[4],	
	As he hath used of old[5].	
BRUTUS	Thou hast described	
	A hot friend cooling. Ever note, Lucilius,	
	When love begins to sicken and decay	20
	It useth an enforcèd[6] ceremony.	
	There are no tricks in plain and simple faith,	
	But hollow men, like horses hot at hand[7],	
	Make gallant show[8] and promise of their mettle[9].	

Low march within[10]

	But when they should endure the bloody spur	25
	They fall their crests[11], and like deceitful jades[12]	
	Sink in the trial[13]. Comes his army on?	
LUCILIUS	They mean this night in Sardis to be quartered.	
	The greater part, the horse in general[14],	
	Are come with Cassius.	

Enter CASSIUS *and his powers*

BRUTUS	Hark, he is arrived.	30
	March gently[15] on to meet him.	
CASSIUS	Stand ho!	
BRUTUS	Stand ho, speak the word along!	
1 SOLDIER	Stand!	
2 SOLDIER	Stand!	35
3 SOLDIER	Stand!	
CASSIUS	Most noble brother, you have done me wrong.	
BRUTUS	Judge me, you gods! Wrong I mine enemies?	
	And if not so, how should I wrong a brother?	
CASSIUS	Brutus, this sober form[16] of yours hides wrongs,	40
	And when you do them –	
BRUTUS	Cassius, be content[17],	
	Speak your griefs[18] softly, I do know you well.	

Brutus and Cassius enter Brutus's tent for privacy. Inside, Brutus charges Cassius with greed and corruption. Cassius says that if such accusations came from anyone but Brutus, he would kill them.

 剧情简介：布鲁图请卡休进入他的营帐密谈。帐内，布鲁图指责卡休贪财腐败。卡休表示，换作别人说这样的话，他定要取其性命。

Stagecraft 导演技巧
Quarrelling in private

In lines 43–7, Brutus urges that any heated discussion with Cassius should take place away from the watching soldiers ('in my tent').

- Sketch a set design that could quickly transform the public space of Brutus's camp (Scene 2) into the 'tent' of Scene 3. Notice that Lucilius and Titinius are instructed to 'guard our door', so they must be visible. Add your sketch to your Director's Journal.

1 Animated discussion? (in pairs)

Brutus and Cassius's quarrel holds the stage up to line 162 in a scene of strong emotion that must be carefully 'orchestrated' (精心揣摩) by the actors. Too loud and it will exhaust the audience; too restrained and it will not catch the passion of their exchange.

- Imagine you have a volume control calibrated 1–10, where normal conversation registers 4. Talk together about the scene and mark down volume levels at particular points. Remember that a big climax could be conveyed by silence, or intense emotion with a whisper.
- Record a dramatic part of the scene to match your planned version.

Write about it 写作练习
Canvas walls have ears (in fours)

Brutus and Cassius's quarrel could decide the fate of the Republican cause, which can only succeed if they are allies.

- **a** Two of you read aloud lines 1–123, pausing every so often so that the other two (as Lucilius and Titinius on guard, listening through the tent's thin walls) can reflect on what is being said and jot down their thoughts. Focus on the point where it comes dangerously near to a fight and how Brutus and Cassius manage to avoid it.
- **b** Lucilius and Titinius should use their notes to help script a conversation between the two guards. The students playing Brutus and Cassius at the same time write a summary in modern English of their grievances (委屈) against each other.
- **c** Compare all perspectives of Brutus and Cassius's quarrel. Which man has the stronger case and who handles the quarrel better? Why?

1 enlarge 详细说明
2 charges 部队
3 noted 公开点名批评
4 praying on his side 替他说情
5 slighted off 被没面子地搁置不理
6 every ... comment 芝麻大的错儿都要责罚
7 condemned to 犯下……的严重错误
8 itching palm 手痒（贪财）
9 mart your offices 出卖职位
10 honours this corruption 盖得住你的贪腐
11 chastisement 处罚

	Before the eyes of both our armies here –	
	Which should perceive nothing but love from us –	
	Let us not wrangle. Bid them move away.	45
	Then in my tent, Cassius, enlarge[1] your griefs	
	And I will give you audience.	
CASSIUS	Pindarus,	
	Bid our commanders lead their charges[2] off	
	A little from this ground.	
BRUTUS	Lucius, do you the like, and let no man	50
	Come to our tent till we have done our conference.	
	Let Lucilius and Titinius guard our door.	

Exeunt [all but] Brutus and Cassius

Act 4 Scene 3
In Brutus' tent

CASSIUS	That you have wronged me doth appear in this:	
	You have condemned and noted[3] Lucius Pella	
	For taking bribes here of the Sardians,	
	Wherein my letters, praying on his side[4],	
	Because I knew the man, was slighted off[5].	5
BRUTUS	You wronged yourself to write in such a case.	
CASSIUS	In such a time as this it is not meet	
	That every nice offence should bear his comment[6].	
BRUTUS	Let me tell you, Cassius, you yourself	
	Are much condemned to[7] have an itching palm[8],	10
	To sell and mart your offices[9] for gold	
	To undeservers.	
CASSIUS	I, an itching palm?	
	You know that you are Brutus that speaks this,	
	Or, by the gods, this speech were else your last.	
BRUTUS	The name of Cassius honours this corruption[10],	15
	And chastisement[11] doth therefore hide his head.	
CASSIUS	Chastisement?	
BRUTUS	Remember March, the Ides of March remember:	
	Did not great Julius bleed for justice' sake?	

Caesar was killed to stamp out corruption, says Brutus. Cassius claims greater experience as a soldier. Brutus scorns Cassius's bad temper.

剧情简介：布鲁图说，除掉恺撒为的就是杜绝腐败。卡休炫耀自己军旅生涯更长。布鲁图嘲笑他脾气暴躁。

Language in the play 剧中语言
The balance of power (in pairs)

When two characters quarrel, they often fire rhetorical questions (see pp. 185–6) at each other in order to score points and express indignation. There are three on the previous page and a further eleven in the script opposite.

- Take parts as Brutus and Cassius and claim your rhetorical questions. Practise speaking them aloud in a variety of ways in order to maximise their emotional impact. Then, whilst Cassius sits in the centre of the room Brutus should circle him, speaking only his questions to the silent Cassius. Swap positions so that Cassius gets his chance.
- Afterwards, talk about the effects created. It's a fair point to note that Brutus has more of the questions, but who has the more powerful ones? Why?

The rhythms of speech in this scene – as much as what is said – suggest the characters' strength or weakness. In addition, they suggest which character holds control over the dialogue at any one time.

- Read carefully from 'I am a soldier, I' (line 30) to line 42. In this passage you will find many short and broken lines. Where the pauses fall will be crucial to the balance between Brutus and Cassius. Try reading it in different ways and decide which sounds right. What do your pauses tell you about which character holds the balance of power at various points?

Write about it 写作练习
The ghost of Caesar

Later in this scene (at line 274) the ghost of Caesar appears to Brutus (see p. 136 for more detail on the apparition).

- Imagine that prior to his appearance as a ghost, Caesar witnesses all that goes on between the conspirators. As Caesar, write your thoughts as you listen to the Republicans' discussion. What do you think about the behaviour and viewpoints of the two men who were so instrumental in your downfall? Do you have any sympathy? Try to match your style of writing to the Caesar that you defined earlier.

1 And not for justice 要不是为了公正
2 the foremost 头号
3 sell … honours 出卖咱们至高的荣誉
4 trash 废物，破烂儿（这里指赃款）
5 graspèd thus 这么一把
6 bay 对着……狂吠
7 bait not 不要惹恼（bait指纵狗撕咬拴着的动物）
8 hedge me in 管制我
9 Go to 得了吧
10 health 人身安全
11 tempt 挑衅
12 choler 怒火
13 Fret 煎熬
14 budge 忍让
15 testy humour 暴脾气
16 spleen 脾脏
17 split you 把你气炸
18 mirth 开心，欢笑
19 waspish 暴躁，易怒
20 vaunting 大话，自吹

What villain touched his body, that did stab
And not for justice[1]? What, shall one of us,
That struck the foremost[2] man of all this world,
But for supporting robbers, shall we now
Contaminate our fingers with base bribes
And sell the mighty space of our large honours[3]
For so much trash[4] as may be graspèd thus[5]?
I had rather be a dog and bay[6] the moon
Than such a Roman.

CASSIUS   Brutus, bait not[7] me,
I'll not endure it. You forget yourself
To hedge me in[8]. I am a soldier, I,
Older in practice, abler than yourself
To make conditions.

BRUTUS   Go to[9], you are not, Cassius!

CASSIUS   I am.

BRUTUS   I say you are not.

CASSIUS   Urge me no more, I shall forget myself.
Have mind upon your health[10], tempt[11] me no farther!

BRUTUS   Away, slight man!

CASSIUS   Is't possible?

BRUTUS   Hear me, for I will speak.
Must I give way and room to your rash choler[12]?
Shall I be frighted when a madman stares?

CASSIUS   O ye gods, ye gods, must I endure all this?

BRUTUS   All this? Ay, more. Fret[13] till your proud heart break.
Go show your slaves how choleric you are,
And make your bondmen tremble. Must I budge[14]?
Must I observe you? Must I stand and crouch
Under your testy humour[15]? By the gods,
You shall digest the venom of your spleen[16]
Though it do split you[17]. For, from this day forth,
I'll use you for my mirth[18], yea, for my laughter,
When you are waspish[19].

CASSIUS   Is it come to this?

BRUTUS   You say you are a better soldier:
Let it appear so, make your vaunting[20] true
And it shall please me well. For mine own part
I shall be glad to learn of noble men.

Brutus shrugs off Cassius's temper but is angry that Cassius refused him gold for his troops. Cassius says friends should not magnify each other's faults.

剧情简介：布鲁图对卡休的暴脾气不屑理会，但对卡休拒绝为其供给军费感到很恼火。卡休表示，朋友之间不该放大彼此的缺点。

1 Money! Different attitudes (in pairs)

The quarrel between Brutus and Cassius in Act 4 Scene 3 is primarily over money to pay their troops. Look at what Brutus says about the matter in lines 69–82, and then in lines 100–5, where Cassius reveals something of his attitude to money.

- Read the two speeches carefully several times. Make notes on what the characters actually say, and then talk together about how Shakespeare uses the issue of money to reveal the contrasting characters of Brutus and Cassius.
- Now look back to Act 3 Scene 2, lines 120–50, and Act 4 Scene 1, lines 7–27, to see what is revealed of Antony's attitude to money. Add further details to your notes.
- Finally, write a short paragraph comparing Antony's views with those of Brutus and Cassius.

2 Design a coin (in small groups)

In Caesar's time, Roman generals often owned their armies and had to pay them out of their own pockets. Generals often minted coins with their own 'heads and tails' on them. Like today's coins, they carried designs that symbolised something important to those who minted them.

- As a design consultancy, come up with a series of designs for coin 'tails' for Brutus or Cassius. Your designs should make the soldiers think about what they are fighting for when they get paid. Write a short explanation beside each design.

1	moved me	惹我
2	honesty	正直
3	respect not	看都不看
4	vile means	歪门邪道
5	coin	（用金属）铸（币）
6	indirection	下作手段，欺诈
7	covetous	贪财，抠门儿
8	rascal counters	臭铜子儿
9	rived	撕碎

CASSIUS	You wrong me every way, you wrong me, Brutus.	55
	I said an elder soldier, not a better.	
	Did I say 'better'?	
BRUTUS	If you did, I care not.	
CASSIUS	When Caesar lived, he durst not thus have moved me[1].	
BRUTUS	Peace, peace, you durst not so have tempted him.	
CASSIUS	I durst not?	60
BRUTUS	No.	
CASSIUS	What? Durst not tempt him?	
BRUTUS	For your life you durst not.	
CASSIUS	Do not presume too much upon my love,	
	I may do that I shall be sorry for.	
BRUTUS	You have done that you should be sorry for.	65
	There is no terror, Cassius, in your threats,	
	For I am armed so strong in honesty[2]	
	That they pass by me as the idle wind,	
	Which I respect not[3]. I did send to you	
	For certain sums of gold, which you denied me,	70
	For I can raise no money by vile means[4].	
	By heaven, I had rather coin[5] my heart	
	And drop my blood for drachmaes than to wring	
	From the hard hands of peasants their vile trash	
	By any indirection[6]. I did send	75
	To you for gold to pay my legions,	
	Which you denied me. Was that done like Cassius?	
	Should I have answered Caius Cassius so?	
	When Marcus Brutus grows so covetous[7]	
	To lock such rascal counters[8] from his friends,	80
	Be ready, gods, with all your thunderbolts,	
	Dash him to pieces!	
CASSIUS	I denied you not.	
BRUTUS	You did.	
CASSIUS	I did not. He was but a fool that brought	
	My answer back. Brutus hath rived[9] my heart.	85
	A friend should bear his friend's infirmities,	
	But Brutus makes mine greater than they are.	
BRUTUS	I do not, till you practise them on me.	

Stung by Brutus's criticism, Cassius asks Brutus to kill him. Brutus relents, admits blame himself and resolves to ignore Cassius's temper in future.

 剧情简介：布鲁图的尖锐批评刺痛了卡休，他让布鲁图杀了自己。布鲁图语气缓和了下来，承认自己也有不是，并表示以后会包容卡休的暴脾气。

Characters 人物分析

Cassius: a change of heart (in pairs)

Line 93 seems to mark a turning point in Cassius and Brutus's quarrel. Cassius openly expresses his weariness at having his faults picked over, and then offers his dagger to Brutus and urges him to 'Strike as thou didst at Caesar'.

a Work through Cassius's speech (lines 93–107). Then write advice for the actor playing Cassius about how he should deliver his lines. In particular, focus on the dagger and how he offers his 'naked breast' to Brutus. Rehearse the lines and then take turns to perform the speech.

b Write a paragraph about what this speech shows about Cassius's character and his relationship with Brutus.

Write about it 写作练习

Brutus's private thoughts

After Cassius's outburst at lines 93–107, Cassius and Brutus suddenly become firm friends, and so they remain. The cultivation of friendship was an important duty in the ancient world. In the year of Caesar's death, Cicero wrote in his essay 'Of Friendship':

Take away the bond of kindly feeling from the world, and no house or city can stand. Even the fields will no longer be cultivated. If that sounds exaggerated, consider the opposite state of affairs: note the disasters that come from dissension (分歧，不合) and enmity (敌意). When there is internal hatred and division, no home or country in the world is strong enough to avoid destruction.

Suppose Brutus were to confide his thoughts in a soliloquy at the end of this scene. Brutus is seen reading a book. Imagine he is reading the passage from Cicero above. He is full of sadness as Cicero has just been killed in the purge instigated by Antony, Octavius and Lepidus.

- As you read through the rest of the scene, gather material for Brutus's additional soliloquy. In public, Brutus shows true Stoic (斯多葛派的；坚忍，坦然) self-control as he and the generals mull over (斟酌) news from Rome, but alone he can ponder aloud the whole enterprise he undertook with Cassius.
- When you reach line 274, write Brutus's additional soliloquy.

---

1 **a-weary of** 厌倦了，受够了
2 **braved** 藐视
3 **Checked** 责骂
4 **conned by rote** 牢记在心
5 **To cast into my teeth** 劈头盖脸地指责我
6 **Pluto's mine** 无尽的宝藏（罗马神话中的冥王普鲁托，拥有所有的宝藏和矿藏）
7 **If that thou beest** = If you are
8 **Sheathe** 把（刀、剑等）插入鞘中
9 **dishonour shall be humour** 你的不当行为我权当是秉性使然
10 **yokèd with a lamb** 与羊羔共轭（布鲁图说自己性情如羊羔一样温和）
11 **flint** 燧石，打火石
12 **much enforcèd** 用力敲
13 **blood ill-tempered** = ill-tempered blood （爱发火的脾气）
14 **vexeth** 使苦恼，使恼火
15 **chides** 责骂，数落

CASSIUS	You love me not.	
BRUTUS	I do not like your faults.	
CASSIUS	A friendly eye could never see such faults.	90
BRUTUS	A flatterer's would not, though they do appear	
	As huge as high Olympus.	
CASSIUS	Come, Antony, and young Octavius, come,	
	Revenge yourselves alone on Cassius,	
	For Cassius is a-weary of[1] the world:	95
	Hated by one he loves, braved[2] by his brother,	
	Checked[3] like a bondman, all his faults observed,	
	Set in a notebook, learned, and conned by rote[4],	
	To cast into my teeth[5]. O, I could weep	
	My spirit from mine eyes! There is my dagger	100
	And here my naked breast: within, a heart	
	Dearer than Pluto's mine[6], richer than gold.	
	If that thou beest[7] a Roman take it forth,	
	I that denied thee gold will give my heart:	
	Strike as thou didst at Caesar. For I know	105
	When thou didst hate him worst thou loved'st him better	
	Than ever thou loved'st Cassius.	
BRUTUS	Sheathe[8] your dagger.	
	Be angry when you will, it shall have scope;	
	Do what you will, dishonour shall be humour[9].	
	O Cassius, you are yokèd with a lamb[10]	110
	That carries anger as the flint[11] bears fire,	
	Who, much enforcèd[12], shows a hasty spark	
	And straight is cold again.	
CASSIUS	Hath Cassius lived	
	To be but mirth and laughter to his Brutus	
	When grief and blood ill-tempered[13] vexeth[14] him?	115
BRUTUS	When I spoke that, I was ill-tempered too.	
CASSIUS	Do you confess so much? Give me your hand.	
BRUTUS	And my heart too.	
CASSIUS	O Brutus!	
BRUTUS	What's the matter?	
CASSIUS	Have not you love enough to bear with me	
	When that rash humour which my mother gave me	120
	Makes me forgetful?	
BRUTUS	Yes, Cassius, and from henceforth	
	When you are over-earnest with your Brutus,	
	He'll think your mother chides[15], and leave you so.	

A poet tries to intercede and reconcile Brutus and Cassius. With uncharacteristic fury, Brutus throws him out. Cassius is surprised. Brutus explains that his wife is dead.

剧情简介：一位诗人试图劝和布鲁图和卡休。布鲁图一改往日的温和，把他吼了出去。卡休惊诧不已，布鲁图解释说因为他妻子死了。

1 Should the Poet be cut? (in threes)

The brief episode where the Poet interrupts Brutus and Cassius's conversation (lines 124–38) follows pretty closely the Greek historian Plutarch's account of events. Some argue that his intervention is used to highlight the increasing turbulence in Brutus's mind and actions. But Shakespeare could easily have left him out.

- Talk together about a) why the Poet was included and b) what the play might gain from cutting his part. Share your thoughts with other groups.

> ### Themes 主题分析
> **The importance of language**
>
> Act 3 focused closely on the power of language and its capacity to dictate the course of history (although it ended with the death of a wordsmith: Cinna the poet). Shakespeare chooses to introduce another poet in this scene, who seeks to reconcile the sparring Cassius and Brutus. Cassius labels him as a 'cynic' and Brutus exclaims: 'What should the wars do with these jigging fools?'
>
> - What do Cassius's and Brutus's attitudes to the poet and what he represents suggest about their characters? Write a short paragraph in response.

2 Portia's final moments

a **Show her death (in pairs)** The audience does not see Portia's death; Brutus reports it. One of you is Brutus, the other Portia. Brutus reads aloud lines 152–6; Portia silently enacts the events described, ending at a tableau that captures the moment of her death.

b **Portia's suicide note (in threes)** Talk together about what could have forced Portia to commit suicide and why she decided to do it this way. (Plutarch records how Portia put burning coals into her mouth and choked to death.) Each of you writes her suicide note. Then show your note to the others in your group and discuss similarities and differences.

c **Why does Portia die off stage? (in small groups)** Talk together about the reasons Shakespeare might have had for not showing Portia's death as part of the main action of the play. Be ready to contribute your strongest idea to a whole-class discussion.

---

1 stay　阻拦
2 vildly　糟糕，差劲
3 cynic　愤世嫉俗者（见172页）
4 humour　疯疯癫癫的行为
5 when he knows his time　什么时候他长了眼色
6 jigging　满口歪诗
7 your philosophy　你的哲学（指斯多葛学派哲学；见173页）
8 give place　扛不住，投降
9 accidental evils　不幸
10 scaped　免于，逃脱
11 crossed　惹恼
12 insupportable　难以承受
13 Impatient　忍受不了
14 tidings　消息
15 fell distract　精神错乱

Enter a POET, [LUCILIUS *and Titinius*]

POET	Let me go in to see the generals.
	There is some grudge between 'em, 'tis not meet	125
	They be alone.
LUCILIUS	You shall not come to them.
POET	Nothing but death shall stay¹ me.
CASSIUS	How now, what's the matter?
POET	For shame, you generals, what do you mean?	130
	Love and be friends, as two such men should be,
	For I have seen more years, I'm sure, than ye.
CASSIUS	Ha, ha, how vildly² doth this cynic³ rhyme!
BRUTUS	Get you hence, sirrah; saucy fellow, hence!
CASSIUS	Bear with him, Brutus, 'tis his fashion.	135
BRUTUS	I'll know his humour⁴ when he knows his time⁵.
	What should the wars do with these jigging⁶ fools?
	Companion, hence!
CASSIUS	Away, away, be gone!

Exit Poet

BRUTUS	Lucilius and Titinius, bid the commanders
	Prepare to lodge their companies tonight.	140
CASSIUS	And come yourselves, and bring Messala with you
	Immediately to us.

[*Exeunt Lucilius and Titinius*]

BRUTUS	[*To Lucius within*] Lucius, a bowl of wine!
CASSIUS	I did not think you could have been so angry.
BRUTUS	O Cassius, I am sick of many griefs.
CASSIUS	Of your philosophy⁷ you make no use	145
	If you give place⁸ to accidental evils⁹.
BRUTUS	No man bears sorrow better. Portia is dead.
CASSIUS	Ha? Portia?
BRUTUS	She is dead.
CASSIUS	How scaped¹⁰ I killing when I crossed¹¹ you so?	150
	O insupportable¹² and touching loss!
	Upon what sickness?
BRUTUS	Impatient¹³ of my absence,
	And grief that young Octavius with Mark Antony
	Have made themselves so strong – for with her death
	That tidings¹⁴ came. With this she fell distract¹⁵	155
	And, her attendants absent, swallowed fire.

> Reconciled, Brutus and Cassius drink wine. Titinius and Messala enter to report that the Triumvirate has executed Cicero and a hundred other senators, and now approach Philippi.
>
> 剧情简介：重归于好的布鲁图和卡休把酒对饮。提提纽和莫撒勒来报，三人团处死了西塞罗和其他一百位参议员，现在正往菲利皮进发。

1 Friends reunited (in threes)

In the gathering darkness suggested by Lucius's tapers, Brutus and Cassius drain their bowl of wine. As he would at home, Lucius brings hospitality to Cassius even though they are in a tent many hundreds of miles from Rome and Portia is dead. Perhaps Shakespeare uses this moment to echo Act 2 Scene 2, where Brutus and Caesar drank together on the morning of Caesar's assassination.

- Read and mime the actions from Lucius's entrance to his exit (lines 158–62). Feel your way into the characters' minds as you act. At the end of your mime, pause to speak aloud the exact thoughts in your character's head.

Themes 主题分析

Public versus private (in pairs)

In a play that contains many great public events, the reconciliation between Brutus and Cassius stands out as one of the more private and intimate moments.

- Discuss why you think Shakespeare focuses so intensely on this episode at this point in the play.

Write about it 写作练习

Brutus's grief

Brutus tells that he is 'sick of many griefs' at the thought of Portia's death. But he gives away very little about his deeper feelings on hearing of her agonising suicide. In fact, he dismisses talk of her with an abrupt: 'Speak no more of her.'

- Imagine that later that evening, alone in his tent, he reads Portia's suicide note, which you were asked to produce in Activity 2 on page 126. Write Brutus's deeper and more intimate reflections on the loss of his wife. Look back at their dialogue in Act 2 Scene 1 for glimpses of the kind of relationship they shared.

---

1 **o'erswell** 漫出来
2 **call in question our necessities** 商量我们必须要做的事
3 **Bending their expedition toward** 兵锋直指
4 **Philippi** 菲利皮（公元前42年，安东尼和屋大维在此击败布鲁图和卡休，取得对共和派的决定性胜利）
5 **selfsame tenor** 大同小异的消息
6 **proscription and bills of outlawry** （指判处"违法者"死刑、财产充公的处罚；见173页）

CASSIUS	And died so?
BRUTUS	Even so.
CASSIUS	O ye immortal gods!

Enter BOY [LUCIUS] *with wine and tapers*

BRUTUS	Speak no more of her. Give me a bowl of wine.	
	In this I bury all unkindness, Cassius. *Drinks*	
CASSIUS	My heart is thirsty for that noble pledge.	160
	Fill, Lucius, till the wine o'erswell¹ the cup,	
	I cannot drink too much of Brutus' love. [*Drinks*]	
	[*Exit Lucius*]	

Enter TITINIUS *and* MESSALA

BRUTUS	Come in, Titinius; welcome, good Messala.	
	Now sit we close about this taper here	
	And call in question our necessities².	165
CASSIUS	Portia, art thou gone?	
BRUTUS	No more, I pray you.	
	Messala, I have here receivèd letters	
	That young Octavius and Mark Antony	
	Come down upon us with a mighty power,	
	Bending their expedition toward³ Philippi⁴.	170
MESSALA	Myself have letters of the selfsame tenor⁵.	
BRUTUS	With what addition?	
MESSALA	That by proscription and bills of outlawry⁶	
	Octavius, Antony, and Lepidus	
	Have put to death an hundred senators.	175
BRUTUS	Therein our letters do not well agree:	
	Mine speak of seventy senators that died	
	By their proscriptions, Cicero being one.	
CASSIUS	Cicero one?	
MESSALA	Cicero is dead,	
	And by that order of proscription.	180
	Had you your letters from your wife, my lord?	
BRUTUS	No, Messala.	
MESSALA	Nor nothing in your letters writ of her?	
BRUTUS	Nothing, Messala.	
MESSALA	That, methinks, is strange.	

Brutus philosophically receives news of Portia's death, then turns to military tactics. 'Take battle to the enemy,' he says. 'Let battle come to us,' says Cassius. Brutus insists his plan is best.

剧情简介：布鲁图借助哲学之力接受了鲍霞的死，然后讨论起战争策略。"向敌人发起进攻，"他说。"我们要等敌人打过来，"卡休说。布鲁图坚信自己的方针最合理。

1 'Free Rome': social networking (in small groups)

Republicans at home and in exile stay in close touch. Those at home keep the Republican flame burning among the people; those abroad raise armies to recapture Rome.

- Imagine there is a communication network to keep all Republicans informed. Consider how you might utilise postings on social media sites, emails and text messages. Then put together a series of electronic texts that emphasise the horrors of Triumvirate rule, yet celebrate Republican achievement and give heart to those who carry on the struggle. Use excerpts from the play as part of the text you write, stage some photographs and invent interviews with leading Republicans.

2 Talking tactics (in pairs)

Although they are now reconciled as friends, Brutus and Cassius fall to a disagreement again – this time over the military tactics for the next day's battle.

a Take parts and read their discussion (lines 198–225). Then, continuing in role as the two men, improvise an extended discussion based on the core arguments you originally proposed.

b Brutus again wins the argument. In your pair, discuss how important you think this is to the way in which the scene is developing.

Language in the play 剧中语言

'a tide in the affairs of men' (in pairs)

In the days of sail, trading ships often had to wait for the right wind and tide. Too long a wait and the cargo might lose its value, especially if it were perishable. Sail at the wrong time and the ship could be wrecked. Either way investors would lose money.

a Talk together about whether what Brutus says in lines 218–24 is true of life as you know it. Can you think of any real-life examples of individuals you might mention in support of the conclusions you reach?

b Write a short paragraph analysing the effectiveness of this very famous extended metaphor about seizing the initiative at the right moment.

---

1 once 有一天
2 Even so 正是如此
3 I … you 你说的道理我都懂
4 waste 消耗
5 offence 损害
6 of force 必然，必定
7 Do … affection 表面上不得不拥护
8 new added 补充了新兵力
9 tried the utmost of 调动了最大力量
10 Omitted 一旦错过
11 bound in shallows 困在浅滩，搁浅

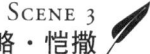

BRUTUS	Why ask you? Hear you aught of her in yours?	185
MESSALA	No, my lord.	
BRUTUS	Now as you are a Roman tell me true.	
MESSALA	Then like a Roman bear the truth I tell,	
	For certain she is dead, and by strange manner.	
BRUTUS	Why, farewell, Portia. We must die, Messala.	190
	With meditating that she must die once¹,	
	I have the patience to endure it now.	
MESSALA	Even so², great men great losses should endure.	
CASSIUS	I have as much of this in art as you³,	
	But yet my nature could not bear it so.	195
BRUTUS	Well, to our work alive. What do you think	
	Of marching to Philippi presently?	
CASSIUS	I do not think it good.	
BRUTUS	Your reason?	
CASSIUS	This it is:	
	'Tis better that the enemy seek us,	
	So shall he waste⁴ his means, weary his soldiers,	200
	Doing himself offence⁵, whilst we, lying still,	
	Are full of rest, defence, and nimbleness.	
BRUTUS	Good reasons must of force⁶ give place to better:	
	The people 'twixt Philippi and this ground	
	Do stand but in a forced affection⁷,	205
	For they have grudged us contribution.	
	The enemy, marching along by them,	
	By them shall make a fuller number up,	
	Come on refreshed, new added⁸, and encouraged,	
	From which advantage shall we cut him off	210
	If at Philippi we do face him there,	
	These people at our back.	
CASSIUS	Hear me, good brother.	
BRUTUS	Under your pardon. You must note beside	
	That we have tried the utmost of⁹ our friends,	
	Our legions are brimful, our cause is ripe;	215
	The enemy increaseth every day,	
	We, at the height, are ready to decline.	
	There is a tide in the affairs of men	
	Which, taken at the flood, leads on to fortune;	
	Omitted¹⁰, all the voyage of their life	220
	Is bound in shallows¹¹ and in miseries.	

Cassius agrees to march to face the enemy at Philippi. After a harmonious leave-taking, Brutus is left to sleep. He asks Lucius for music.

剧情简介：卡休同意部队开拔去菲利皮迎敌。二人融洽地互相道别，布鲁图准备去睡觉。他让卢休给他弹曲子听。

Stagecraft 导演技巧

The last night of the Roman Republic (in fives)

The story of what followed Julius Caesar's assassination would probably have been well known to Shakespeare's audience. Therefore they would be aware that this part of the play signals the calm before the storm – the night before the decisive battle that will destroy the Republican forces.

a In your group, read lines 226–74 (before the entrance of Caesar's ghost). What clues are there in the text that after the frenzied arguments of earlier, the mood is now of peaceful relaxation, quietness and reflection?

b A few basic stage directions have been added to Shakespeare's original script. Now, as collaborative directors, add as many more as you can in order to show how your actors will use movement, gesture and voice to enhance the mood created by the language.

c A significant number of lines 30–42 in this scene were short and broken. Here, lines 229–40 are much more regular, though nearly all shared. Read both sets of lines with careful regard for the rhythm. Talk together about the possible reasons why Shakespeare created such contrasting effects.

d Brutus begins this episode with 'The deep of night is crept upon our talk' (line 226). Produce a lighting design for the episode which clearly reflects and enhances the mood you are striving to create. Add it to your Director's Journal.

1 when it serves 机会来临时
2 ventures 所有的付出、机遇等
3 with your will go on 照您的意思前进
4 nature must obey necessity 天性也得服从必需
5 niggard （用很少的东西）打发
6 hence 出发
7 repose 睡眠
8 instrument 琴（可能是鲁特琴[lute]）
9 drowsily 昏昏然
10 Poor knave 小伙子真可怜见的
11 o'erwatched 撑太久没睡而疲倦

1 Question Cassius (whole class)

Cassius begins the scene in an angry mood, even threatening that if he were accused in such terms by anyone other than Brutus, he would kill them (lines 13–14). Just before he exits, he calls Brutus his 'dear brother' and pledges eternal companionship (lines 233–5).

- Put Cassius in the hot-seat. Question him about how he now feels about Brutus and the state of their relationship.

On such a full sea are we now afloat,
And we must take the current when it serves[1]
Or lose our ventures[2].

CASSIUS   Then with your will go on[3],
We'll along ourselves and meet them at Philippi.

BRUTUS   The deep of night is crept upon our talk,
And nature must obey necessity[4],
Which we will niggard[5] with a little rest.
There is no more to say?

CASSIUS   No more. Good night.
Early tomorrow will we rise and hence[6].

BRUTUS   Lucius!

Enter LUCIUS

My gown.

                                     [*Exit Lucius*]
                Farewell, good Messala.
Good night, Titinius. Noble, noble Cassius,
Good night and good repose[7].

CASSIUS   O my dear brother!
This was an ill beginning of the night.
Never come such division 'tween our souls!
Let it not, Brutus.

Enter LUCIUS *with the gown*

BRUTUS   Everything is well.
CASSIUS   Good night, my lord.
BRUTUS   Good night, good brother.
TITINIUS AND MESSALA   Good night, Lord Brutus.
BRUTUS   Farewell every one.
                      Exeunt [*Cassius, Titinius, Messala*]
Give me the gown. Where is thy instrument[8]?
LUCIUS   Here in the tent.
BRUTUS   What, thou speak'st drowsily[9].
Poor knave[10], I blame thee not, thou art o'erwatched[11].
Call Claudio and some other of my men,
I'll have them sleep on cushions in my tent.
LUCIUS   Varrus and Claudio!

剧情简介：布鲁图把瓦若和克劳丢叫进自己的营帐里睡觉。卢休弹着琴竟睡着了。布鲁图看书时，恺撒的灵魂上场。

1 Compose Lucius's song (in pairs)

No words or music survive for Lucius's song, and as musical directors you have to supply them.

- Think about the mood needed and the right words to express it. Compose your own music or set your words to a tune you know already. Then explain to another pair the reasons behind your choice.

1	raise	叫……起来
2	otherwise bethink me	改变我的想法
3	sought for so	好一顿找
4	strain	曲子
5	an't	= if it
6	I … might	我不该让你做力所不能及的事情
7	young bloods	血气方刚的年轻人
8	murd'rous	死神一样的（因常把睡眠与死亡作比）
9	leaden mace	沉重的权杖
10	ill	（烛光）昏暗

Characters 人物分析

Brutus: what's your reaction? (in pairs)

Brutus has dealt stoically with his wife Portia's death and is reconciled to Cassius. Again, he has overruled Cassius, urging action rather than caution. Now Shakespeare shows him treating his servant Lucius considerately and generously.

- Together, look back at this scene and consider how Brutus acts, what he says and what is said about him. Then each write a short paragraph outlining your response to the character of Brutus that Shakespeare presents. Remember to support all your points with quotations. After writing, compare your versions.

The dramatic appearance of Caesar's ghost.

Julius Caesar Act 4 Scene 3
儒略・恺撒

Enter VARRUS *and* CLAUDIO

VARRUS	Calls my lord?	245
BRUTUS	I pray you, sirs, lie in my tent and sleep,	
	It may be I shall raise¹ you by and by	
	On business to my brother Cassius.	
VARRUS	So please you, we will stand and watch your pleasure.	
BRUTUS	I will not have it so. Lie down, good sirs,	250
	It may be I shall otherwise bethink me².	

[*Varrus and Claudio lie down*]

	Look, Lucius, here's the book I sought for so³,	
	I put it in the pocket of my gown.	
LUCIUS	I was sure your lordship did not give it me.	
BRUTUS	Bear with me, good boy, I am much forgetful.	255
	Canst thou hold up thy heavy eyes awhile	
	And touch thy instrument a strain⁴ or two?	
LUCIUS	Ay, my lord, an't⁵ please you.	
BRUTUS	It does, my boy.	
	I trouble thee too much, but thou art willing.	
LUCIUS	It is my duty, sir.	260
BRUTUS	I should not urge thy duty past thy might⁶,	
	I know young bloods⁷ look for a time of rest.	
LUCIUS	I have slept, my lord, already.	
BRUTUS	It was well done and thou shalt sleep again,	
	I will not hold thee long. If I do live	265
	I will be good to thee.	

Music, and a song

	This is a sleepy tune. O murd'rous⁸ slumber,	
	Layest thou thy leaden mace⁹ upon my boy,	
	That plays thee music? Gentle knave, good night,	
	I will not do thee so much wrong to wake thee.	270
	If thou dost nod thou break'st thy instrument.	
	I'll take it from thee and, good boy, good night.	
	Let me see, let me see, is not the leaf turned down	
	Where I left reading? Here it is, I think.	

Enter the GHOST OF CAESAR

	How ill¹⁰ this taper burns! Ha, who comes here?	275

135

Promising a second appearance, the ghost disappears. Brutus wakes the servants and orders immediate preparations for marching to Philippi to do battle with Antony and Octavius.

 剧情简介： 鬼魂说他定会再来，然后消失。布鲁图叫醒小厮，下令立刻准备朝菲利皮进发，与安东尼和屋大维的军队决战。

1 Caesar's ghost

Ghosts were highly significant for Elizabethans. They believed that ghosts could be good or bad, silent or talkative, truthful or deceptive. Evil spirits could disguise themselves to mislead mortals. If you knew how to talk to a ghost, you could gain valuable (or misleading) information about the past, present or future.

a What should Caesar's ghost look like? (in small groups)
Every director must decide how to portray the 'monstrous apparition': Bloodstains? Larger than life? A floating head? Voiceover rather than physical presence? Talk together about how you could present Caesar's ghost to make the greatest impression on the audience. Then write a 'design brief' for your Director's Journal giving justification for the choices you have made.

b The first appearance of Caesar's ghost (in pairs) Read or stage lines 273–88 as dramatically as you can. The ghost has only sixteen words. Make each of them count!

c 'Art thou some god, some angel, or some devil?'
Write six more lines to add to the end of Brutus's speech (lines 275–81), beginning 'If you are a god …'

d Why does only Brutus see the ghost? (in threes)
After the ghost's exit (at line 286) Brutus is desperate to check with his companions whether they, too, have seen Caesar's spirit. But Shakespeare deliberately has the ghost appear just to Brutus (Lucius, Varro and Claudio are asleep). Try to come up with two or three possible reasons Shakespeare might have had for staging the episode in this way.

2 Fluctuating moods (in pairs)

The final scene of Act 4 is both long and varied in dramatic mood, with some episodes of heightened dramatic intensity and others more reflective.

- Split the scene into episodes. Then draw a 'mood graph', with a y-axis numbered –10 to +10 to reflect the dramatic mood in each episode. Label the x-axis with the different episodes. Allocate a number to each epidode showing its dramatic intensity (+10 for extreme dramatic intensity; –10 for extremely reflective).
- Display your graphs for other pairs to look at. How similar are they?

1 upon me　朝我
2 stare　竖起来
3 false　音不准，跑调
4 set on his powers　让他的部队拔营
5 betimes　一大早

	I think it is the weakness of mine eyes	
	That shapes this monstrous apparition.	
	It comes upon me¹. Art thou any thing?	
	Art thou some god, some angel, or some devil,	
	That mak'st my blood cold and my hair to stare²?	280
	Speak to me what thou art.	
GHOST	Thy evil spirit, Brutus.	
BRUTUS	Why com'st thou?	
GHOST	To tell thee thou shalt see me at Philippi.	
BRUTUS	Well, then I shall see thee again?	
GHOST	Ay, at Philippi.	285
BRUTUS	Why, I will see thee at Philippi then.	

[*Exit Ghost*]

	Now I have taken heart thou vanishest.	
	Ill spirit, I would hold more talk with thee.	
	Boy, Lucius! Varrus! Claudio! Sirs, awake!	
	Claudio!	290
LUCIUS	The strings, my lord, are false³.	
BRUTUS	He thinks he still is at his instrument.	
	Lucius, awake!	
LUCIUS	My lord?	
BRUTUS	Didst thou dream, Lucius, that thou so cried'st out?	295
LUCIUS	My lord, I do not know that I did cry.	
BRUTUS	Yes, that thou didst. Didst thou see anything?	
LUCIUS	Nothing, my lord.	
BRUTUS	Sleep again, Lucius. Sirrah Claudio!	
	[*To Varrus*] Fellow, thou, awake!	300
VARRUS	My lord?	
CLAUDIO	My lord?	
BRUTUS	Why did you so cry out, sirs, in your sleep?	
BOTH	Did we, my lord?	
BRUTUS	Ay. Saw you anything?	
VARRUS	No, my lord, I saw nothing.	
CLAUDIO	Nor I, my lord.	305
BRUTUS	Go and commend me to my brother Cassius.	
	Bid him set on his powers⁴ betimes⁵ before,	
	And we will follow.	
BOTH	It shall be done, my lord.	

Exeunt

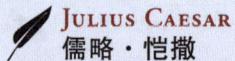

Looking back at Act 4 第4幕回顾
Activities for groups or individuals

1 From Rome to Asia

The action of the play switches at the beginning of Act 4 Scene 2 from Rome to Asia.

- Work out a set design that could quite easily accommodate the change in location required. Base your ideas on the opportunities afforded by a modern theatre. Add notes to explain how you would manage any scene-shifting so that the attention of the audience is not lost.

2 Is updating possible?

Some productions of *Julius Caesar* are given a setting in more modern times, for example Fascist Italy in the 1930s.

- Imagine that you have been invited to direct a production set in the twenty-first century. Take one of the scenes in Act 4, and talk in pairs about a possible modern setting and about appropriate costumes for the characters.

3 Comparing alliances

Act 4 shows two sets of political partnerships in operation: Antony, Octavius and Lepidus (Scene 1); Brutus and Cassius (Scenes 2 and 3).

- Look back through the act and make notes on the comparative strengths and weaknesses of the two alliances. After collecting your evidence, write a paragraph on which partnership seems the more cohesive and why.

4 Giving Octavius a presence

Octavius does not appear in the play until Act 4, yet by that time he is already established as a key member of the Triumvirate.

- How would you organise the opening of Act 4 to give Octavius a genuine stage presence and authority?

5 Keeping up the tempo

Many critics feel that the last two acts of the play are an anticlimax after the superlative assassination and funeral scenes in Act 3.

- Quickly remind yourself of the events of Act 4, and then write notes for your cast about how to sustain the dramatic energy through this act.

6 A sense of foreboding (不祥预感)

The death of Caesar marked the end of stability in Rome. The Republicans' hopes of 'Peace' are badly threatened in Act 4 and Shakespeare shows that all is not well in Brutus's world: he quarrels with Cassius, Portia commits suicide, and he is visited ominously by Caesar's ghost.

a Take these points in turn. Write a paragraph about how each is used to increase a sense of foreboding.

b Look back to earlier acts to consider how Shakespeare has used other ominous episodes to increase dramatic tension.

7 Claudio

Claudio is one of Shakespeare's near-silent characters (he has only six words in the last scene).

- Your task is to give him a voice. Study his brief appearance in the play (he enters at line 244) and then write a few entries for his diary. Express his views on life with the Republican army in Asia.

8 Brutus and Cassius

Study the photograph opposite in which Cassius (left) and Brutus argue passionately.

a How effectively does this photograph capture the moment when two friends fall out?

b In this production, Brutus and Cassius wore modern suits in the first three acts. They now dress in combat fatigues. What do you think the director had in mind?

Looking back at act 4

Octavius and Antony argue about why the enemy has come down to them, and both vie for leadership in the coming battle. Brutus and Cassius enter with their army.

剧情简介：屋大维和安东尼争论敌方主动进攻的原因，二人争夺眼前这场战斗的主导权。布鲁图和卡休率部队上。

1 Leaders disagree – again (in pairs)

The first time we saw Antony and Octavius together they argued. Here, the two men disagree over the advance of the Republican army and over which of them should lead the Triumvirate forces.

a Read lines 1–20 (missing out the Messenger's speech), bringing what you know of their characters into your performance.

b Antony and Octavius's confrontation mirrors that between Brutus and Cassius in the previous scene. Look back at Act 4 Scene 3. Then, in your Director's Journal, make a list of the similarities between:

- the issues at the centre of the arguments
- the ways in which the four men quarrel.

Stagecraft 导演技巧

a **Battle decisions (in large groups)** This scene calls for the two opposing sides to be on stage with their armies at the same time. How does a director achieve this?

- In your groups, discuss different ideas about how to stage this demanding scene. Remember they have to be practical!
- If enough space is available, act out your best idea for the entrance of both armies. You may want to appoint a director. If more actors are needed, borrow from another group.

b **Who's on the right? (in small groups)** Much has been written about how Shakespeare used his source material (see p. 166). Often the changes he made demonstrate where he wants to place the emphasis in his play. According to Plutarch, the battlefield of Philippi looked like this:

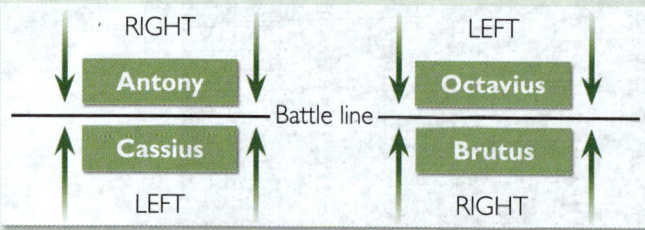

The superior general always fought on the right of the line of battle: that's why lines 16–20 are so important. Shakespeare retains who fought whom, but leaves right and left open to directors of the play to decide.

- In your groups, discuss why Shakespeare might have chosen not to specify who fought where.

1	proves	事实证明
2	battles	部队
3	warn us	向我们挑战
4	Answering … them	先发制人
5	Tut	喷（表示不耐烦或指责）
6	I am in their bosoms	我就是他们肚里的蛔虫（我清楚他们的心思）
7	could … places	巴不得往别处去
8	With fearful bravery	虚张声势以掩饰内心的恐惧
9	face	假象，（做）样子
10	fasten in our thoughts	让咱们深信
11	bloody sign	猩红的挑战旗
12	lead your battle softly on	你带着兵缓步前进
13	right hand	右翼（通常级别高的将领在右翼，故二人争右翼）
14	cross me	跟我对着干
15	exigent	节骨眼儿，紧要关头
16	I do not cross you	我不是和你作对
17	parley	和谈
18	stand fast	站定别动

Act 5 Scene 1
The battlefield at Philippi in Greece

Enter OCTAVIUS, ANTONY, *and their army*

OCTAVIUS	Now, Antony, our hopes are answerèd.	
	You said the enemy would not come down	
	But keep the hills and upper regions.	
	It proves[1] not so: their battles[2] are at hand,	
	They mean to warn us[3] at Philippi here,	5
	Answering before we do demand of them[4].	
ANTONY	Tut[5], I am in their bosoms[6], and I know	
	Wherefore they do it. They could be content	
	To visit other places[7] and come down	
	With fearful bravery[8], thinking by this face[9]	10
	To fasten in our thoughts[10] that they have courage.	
	But 'tis not so.	

Enter a MESSENGER

MESSENGER	Prepare you, generals,	
	The enemy comes on in gallant show,	
	Their bloody sign[11] of battle is hung out,	
	And something to be done immediately.	15
ANTONY	Octavius, lead your battle softly on[12]	
	Upon the left hand of the even field.	
OCTAVIUS	Upon the right hand[13] I, keep thou the left.	
ANTONY	Why do you cross me[14] in this exigent[15]?	
OCTAVIUS	I do not cross you[16], but I will do so.	20

March

Drum. Enter BRUTUS, CASSIUS, *and their army;* [LUCILIUS, *Titinius*, MESSALA, *and others*]

BRUTUS	They stand and would have parley[17].
CASSIUS	Stand fast[18], Titinius, we must out and talk.

The generals parley, trading taunts and accusations. Octavius vows vengeance for Julius Caesar's death.
剧情简介：双方主将会谈，却在阵前互相羞辱和谴责。屋大维发誓要为儒略·恺撒报仇雪恨。

Language in the play 剧中语言

Trading insults (in fours)

Before battle commences the four generals meet to parley, but quickly start taunting each other. Brutus's opening salvo (论战的开始第一炮) 'Words before blows' underlines a major issue: the importance of language to the action of the play. Remember how much plotting and planning there was before Caesar was actually killed in Act 3.

a Take parts and read lines 27–66. Begin line 27 at a whisper. With each subsequent speech, increase the volume slightly until you are virtually shouting the lines.

b Re-read lines 30–2. Work out exactly what Antony means. How do you think Brutus might react to such a description of events?

c In lines 39–44, Antony strikingly creates four powerful, insulting similes to hurl at his enemies. Two of you are Antony. Deliver the lines simultaneously (or with a slight time delay or echo effect) as you circle the seated Brutus and Cassius. How menacing can you make them? Afterwards talk about how the experience felt.

d Look back to the assassination of Caesar in Act 3. Now improvise a discussion on the accuracy of Antony's description of the event (which he did not witness) between Antony and three of the conspirators. See if you can include an accusation against Antony of hyperbole (夸张)(exaggeration).

e Choose one of Antony's similes and illustrate it.

1 answer on their charge 等敌人进攻再迎战
2 Make forth 上前去
3 posture 架势，招式
4 Hybla 希布拉（位于意大利西西里，盛产蜂蜜）
5 showed your teeth 龇牙
6 If Cassius might have ruled 如果当初听了卡休的话
7 cause 正事
8 proof （拿出）论据
9 goes up 归鞘
10 Have added slaughter to 给……再添一条人命

Write about it 写作练习

Brutus's thoughts

At line 45, things get worse for Brutus when Cassius turns upon him.

a Look back to Act 2 Scene 1 and read lines 154–65 to find out what decision by Brutus Cassius is referring to in lines 46–7.

b Imagine that that the action freezes after line 47. Write Brutus's thoughts at that point.

1 Is battle inevitable? (in pairs)

Can battle be avoided? Talk together about whether honourable negotiation might be possible and desirable after line 58.

OCTAVIUS	Mark Antony, shall we give sign of battle?	
ANTONY	No, Caesar, we will answer on their charge[1].	
	Make forth[2], the generals would have some words.	25
OCTAVIUS	Stir not until the signal.	
BRUTUS	Words before blows; is it so, countrymen?	
OCTAVIUS	Not that we love words better, as you do.	
BRUTUS	Good words are better than bad strokes, Octavius.	
ANTONY	In your bad strokes, Brutus, you give good words.	30
	Witness the hole you made in Caesar's heart,	
	Crying, 'Long live, hail, Caesar!'	
CASSIUS	Antony,	
	The posture[3] of your blows are yet unknown;	
	But for your words, they rob the Hybla[4] bees	
	And leave them honeyless.	
ANTONY	Not stingless too?	35
BRUTUS	O yes, and soundless too,	
	For you have stolen their buzzing, Antony,	
	And very wisely threat before you sting.	
ANTONY	Villains! You did not so when your vile daggers	
	Hacked one another in the sides of Caesar.	40
	You showed your teeth[5] like apes and fawned like hounds,	
	And bowed like bondmen, kissing Caesar's feet,	
	Whilst damnèd Casca, like a cur, behind	
	Struck Caesar on the neck. O you flatterers!	
CASSIUS	Flatterers? Now, Brutus, thank yourself.	45
	This tongue had not offended so today	
	If Cassius might have ruled[6].	
OCTAVIUS	Come, come, the cause[7]. If arguing make us sweat,	
	The proof[8] of it will turn to redder drops.	
	Look,	50
	I draw a sword against conspirators;	
	When think you that the sword goes up[9] again?	
	Never, till Caesar's three and thirty wounds	
	Be well avenged, or till another Caesar	
	Have added slaughter to[10] the sword of traitors.	55
BRUTUS	Caesar, thou canst not die by traitors' hands	
	Unless thou bring'st them with thee.	
OCTAVIUS	So I hope.	
	I was not born to die on Brutus' sword.	

Cassius insults the triumvirs. Octavius defies him and the triumvirs leave with their troops. Cassius, whose birthday it is, confides to Messala his newfound respect for omens.

 剧情简介：卡休羞辱三人团。屋大维反唇相讥，三人团带兵下。卡休在自己生日这天告诉莫撒勒，他新近察觉到了不祥之兆。

1 Is Cassius right?

You are a keen young war correspondent who has just overheard Cassius's summing up of the opposition, in lines 61–2. First decide whether your newspaper is objective or partisan (supporting one side). Then write your first dispatch from the front assessing the accuracy of Cassius's description. Which description matches which member of the triumvirate?

Characters 人物分析

Cassius – 'all is on the hazard' (in small groups)

Cassius seems to have become particularly superstitious. Unlike the super-confident Octavius ('If you dare fight today'), he speaks of fateful storms and chance throws of the dice ('on the hazard'). Furthermore, it's Cassius's birthday and he is conscious of powerful natural omens such as the carrion (食腐肉的) birds ('ravens, crows, and kites') that shadow his army.

- Read together lines 70–91, changing speakers at each full stop.
- One of you now becomes Cassius. The rest put him in the hot-seat. What has brought about the change in his philosophy and beliefs? How will it affect his approach to the crucial battle at Philippi? Quiz him about the assassination of Caesar and where and why it all went wrong.

Themes 主题分析

Fate and omens

Just as the battle is about to start, Cassius confesses to Messala that he has had a change of philosophical viewpoint. He had been a follower of Epicurus, who did not believe in the power of omens. In Act 1 Scene 3, he says that the tempestuous night that is terrifying others is 'a very pleasing night to honest men'. Now he says he does put some store by omens ('partly credit things that do presage') and describes two recent ones which involve birds.

- Read lines 80–8. On a large piece of paper draw an image or images inspired by Cassius's description of the omens. Then around them, write down quotations, references and ideas that relate to the theme of fate and omens in the play so far. Remember the Soothsayer? What about Julius Caesar's ghost?

1	strain	家族
2	peevish	傻，幼稚
3	masker	混迹舞场的人
4	reveller	浪荡公子
5	stomachs	胆量
6	blow … bark	风吹起来，浪涌起来，船开起来
7	on the hazard	处于危机之中
8	(As Pompey was)	（在法尔萨利亚决战时，庞贝自知胜算不大，被动迎战恺撒）
9	Epicurus	伊壁鸠鲁（古希腊哲学家，不相信神灵在乎人类的事情，也不相信征兆有什么意义；见172页）
10	partly credit	有几分相信
11	presage	预示
12	former ensign	前面的军旗
13	consorted	陪伴
14	ravens	渡鸦（一种大型乌鸦）
15	kites	黑鸢（一种黑色猛禽）
16	canopy	天篷，华盖
17	fatal	预示着死亡

BRUTUS	O, if thou wert the noblest of thy strain[1],	
	Young man, thou couldst not die more honourable.	60
CASSIUS	A peevish[2] schoolboy, worthless of such honour,	
	Joined with a masker[3] and a reveller[4]!	
ANTONY	Old Cassius still!	
OCTAVIUS	Come, Antony, away!	
	Defiance, traitors, hurl we in your teeth.	
	If you dare fight today, come to the field;	65
	If not, when you have stomachs[5].	

Exeunt Octavius, Antony, and army

CASSIUS	Why now blow wind, swell billow, and swim bark[6]!	
	The storm is up, and all is on the hazard[7].	
BRUTUS	Ho, Lucilius, hark, a word with you.	

Lucilius and Messala stand forth

LUCILIUS	My lord.	

[*Brutus speaks apart to Lucilius*]

CASSIUS	Messala!	
MESSALA	What says my general?	
CASSIUS	Messala,	70
	This is my birthday, as this very day	
	Was Cassius born. Give me thy hand, Messala.	
	Be thou my witness that against my will	
	(As Pompey was)[8] am I compelled to set	
	Upon one battle all our liberties.	75
	You know that I held Epicurus[9] strong	
	And his opinion. Now I change my mind	
	And partly credit[10] things that do presage[11].	
	Coming from Sardis, on our former ensign[12]	
	Two mighty eagles fell, and there they perched,	80
	Gorging and feeding from our soldiers' hands,	
	Who to Philippi here consorted[13] us.	
	This morning are they fled away and gone,	
	And in their steads do ravens[14], crows, and kites[15]	
	Fly o'er our heads and downward look on us	85
	As we were sickly prey. Their shadows seem	
	A canopy[16] most fatal[17] under which	
	Our army lies, ready to give up the ghost.	
MESSALA	Believe not so.	

Cassius is in high spirits despite the omens. He persuades Brutus to prefer suicide to captivity. They part in friendship and readiness for whatever the future holds.

 剧情简介：卡休不受凶兆影响，兴致颇高。他劝布鲁图宁可自杀也不能沦为俘虏。二人怀着坦然面对一切的心情友好道别。

1 Can you guess who is speaking? (in fours)

a Talk together about the differences between Cassius's and Brutus's language that we find in the play: lines 103–15 of Act 1 Scene 3 are typical of Cassius; lines 12–21 of Act 2 Scene 1 are typical of Brutus. Have a look at these lines to remind yourselves of their individual styles.

b Two of you close your eyes. The other two read aloud lines 97–125 of Act 5 Scene 1, omitting any mention of the names Brutus and Cassius. After the reading, guess who read Cassius and who Brutus, and give your reasons. Is it easy to tell who is who at this point? Explore the answers to this question in your group.

Themes 主题分析

a **What it is to be a Roman (in pairs)** Although he is a Roman, Brutus seems to be feeling his way towards the Christian doctrine condemning suicide in lines 100–7. His words seem prophetic, but after a pause for thought at line 107 he decides to take the noble Roman's way out and kill himself if he is defeated.

- Talk together about Brutus's pause for thought and speculate on what must have gone through his mind in that moment before he said 'No, Cassius, no'.

b **Friendship** Unlike many of Shakespeare's tragedies, the character after whom the play is named is not the most fully drawn. We see much more of Brutus and Cassius than we do of Caesar; hear of the changes in their view of the world and witness the fluctuations in their friendship.

- Look back at the key scenes in which Brutus and Cassius are together and draw a 'friendship graph' that charts the highs and lows of their relationship. Put the name of the scenes along one axis and use the other axis to indicate the state of their friendship.
- Bearing in mind how important male friendship was to the Romans, discuss as a class what the drama of their relationship adds to the play.
- Follow this up with a discussion of what other examples of male friendship there are in the play so far. You may want to revisit this after reading Act 5 Scene 5, when Brutus is with his 'poor remains of friends'.

1 **fresh of spirit** 精神抖擞
2 **constantly** 坚定地
3 **The gods today stand friendly** 愿神灵今天能保佑我们
4 **still incertain** 一向难料
5 **philosophy**（即斯多葛主义，支持自杀）
6 **Cato** 加图（鲍霞的父亲，自杀而亡；见56页）
7 **prevent / The time of life** 提前结束生命
8 **stay the providence** 听由……的旨意
9 **led in triumph** 被人牵着游行
10 **bound** 被捆绑着
11 **sufficeth** = suffices（足够）

CASSIUS	I but believe it partly,	
	For I am fresh of spirit¹ and resolved	90
	To meet all perils very constantly².	
BRUTUS	Even so, Lucilius. [*Advancing*]	
CASSIUS	Now, most noble Brutus,	
	The gods today stand friendly³ that we may,	
	Lovers in peace, lead on our days to age!	
	But since the affairs of men rests still incertain⁴,	95
	Let's reason with the worst that may befall.	
	If we do lose this battle, then is this	
	The very last time we shall speak together.	
	What are you then determinèd to do?	
BRUTUS	Even by the rule of that philosophy⁵	100
	By which I did blame Cato⁶ for the death	
	Which he did give himself – I know not how,	
	But I do find it cowardly and vile,	
	For fear of what might fall, so to prevent	
	The time of life⁷ – arming myself with patience	105
	To stay the providence⁸ of some high powers	
	That govern us below.	
CASSIUS	Then if we lose this battle,	
	You are contented to be led in triumph⁹	
	Through the streets of Rome?	
BRUTUS	No, Cassius, no. Think not, thou noble Roman,	110
	That ever Brutus will go bound¹⁰ to Rome:	
	He bears too great a mind. But this same day	
	Must end that work the Ides of March begun.	
	And whether we shall meet again I know not,	
	Therefore our everlasting farewell take:	115
	For ever and for ever, farewell, Cassius!	
	If we do meet again, why, we shall smile;	
	If not, why then this parting was well made.	
CASSIUS	For ever and for ever, farewell, Brutus!	
	If we do meet again, we'll smile indeed;	120
	If not, 'tis true this parting was well made.	
BRUTUS	Why then, lead on. O, that a man might know	
	The end of this day's business ere it come!	
	But it sufficeth¹¹ that the day will end,	
	And then the end is known. Come ho, away!	125

Exeunt

Battle. As Octavius weakens, Brutus orders all his troops to attack. On another part of the battlefield, Cassius reports that his soldiers have fled. 'Flee,' says Pindarus, 'Antony is in our camp.'

剧情简介：双方开战。布鲁图趁屋大维士气沉沉，命士兵全力进攻。战场另一边，卡休骂他的部下当了逃兵。"逃命吧，"品德若说，"安东尼打进了咱的营地。"

1 'Over now to our reporter at Philippi'
(in small groups)

War reporters on television tell us about:

- what is happening and the commander's overall strategy
- the state of morale, from general to footsoldier.

Devise a short national news report about the events at Philippi described opposite. Use reporters' commentary, newsreel (新闻短片), maps and interviews.

Stagecraft 导演技巧
Theatre of war (in large groups)

This activity could be planned in the classroom and then acted out in a larger space. The stage direction '*Alarum*' means that the events in this scene are preceded by a loud battle noise of drums, trumpets, voices and clashing weapons off stage.

- Start at Act 5 Scene 1, line 119, and use all the resources you have available to make the sound effects for scene changes up to Scene 3, line 4. Each scene has a different mood, and your effects must make this clear. The right volume and quality of noise take careful planning.
- While some work out sound effects, others work on the staging. How are you going to show the difference between the battlefield and the high place overlooking it? A plan of the stage area in your Director's Journal may help.
- The number of actors on stage is another crucial consideration; either restrict yourself to the four named characters, or bring on a host of soldiers. Work out blocking (where the characters move on stage) either on your stage space or on your diagram in your Journal. Have the whole field of battle in mind when you plot entrances and exits. Ensure that you show the armies' contrasting moods: thoughtful, joyful, fearful, dejected, fast, slow – or whatever you feel is appropriate.
- What would your actors wear? Perhaps you can also think of some token piece of clothing that will indicate which side they are on in your production.
- When you have seen the work of different groups, come together in one large group and discuss what was successful and what was difficult about this activity.

1 *Alarum* 开战的号角声
2 bills 军令文书
3 on the other side 另一边（即卡休的另一翼部队）
4 set on 进攻
5 cold demeanour in Octavio's wing 屋大维那一侧士气低沉
6 sudden ... overthrow 突袭准能将他们击溃
7 the villains fly 那些混蛋（卡休自己的部下）逃走了
8 ensign 扛旗手
9 did take it 扛过大旗
10 fell to spoil 开始哄抢战利品
11 tents 营帐

Act 5 Scene 2
The battlefield at Philippi

Alarum[1]. Enter BRUTUS *and Messala*

BRUTUS   Ride, ride, Messala, ride, and give these bills[2]
Unto the legions on the other side[3].
Loud alarum
Let them set on[4] at once, for I perceive
But cold demeanour in Octavio's wing[5],
And sudden push gives them the overthrow[6].   5
Ride, ride, Messala, let them all come down.

Exeunt

Act 5 Scene 3
A high place overlooking the battlefield at Philippi

Alarums. Enter CASSIUS *and* TITINIUS

CASSIUS   O, look, Titinius, look, the villains fly[7]!
Myself have to mine own turned enemy.
This ensign[8] here of mine was turning back;
I slew the coward and did take it[9] from him.

TITINIUS   O Cassius, Brutus gave the word too early,   5
Who, having some advantage on Octavius,
Took it too eagerly. His soldiers fell to spoil[10]
Whilst we by Antony are all enclosed.

Enter PINDARUS

PINDARUS   Fly further off, my lord, fly further off!
Mark Antony is in your tents[11], my lord,   10
Fly therefore, noble Cassius, fly far off.

CASSIUS   This hill is far enough. Look, look, Titinius,
Are those my tents where I perceive the fire?

149

Titinius leaves, on Cassius's orders. Pindarus reports that Titinius has been captured. Cassius decides on suicide and orders Pindarus to kill him. Pindarus obeys his command.

 剧情简介：提提纽奉卡休之命离去。品德若来报提提纽被俘。卡休决定自我了断，命品德若杀死他，品德若遵命。

Characters 人物分析

Snapshots of Cassius (in pairs)

Cassius's life has come full circle. It is his birthday:

This day I breathèd first, time is come round
And where I did begin there shall I end

Plutarch describes Cassius as a 'choleric' (angry, hot-tempered) man, with a personal hatred of Caesar, who 'even from his cradle, could not abide any manner of tyrants'. But little else is known of the historical Cassius.

a Discuss and list Cassius's main characteristics, both professional and personal. What do you think of his decisions at key points in the play? It may help to look back at previous notes you have made. Include any relevant brief quotations in your list.

b Compare your list with the brief description above of Cassius in Shakespeare's source material. Speculate on why Shakespeare developed the character in the way that he did. Make a note of your observations to share with the class.

c Cassius orders his loyal servant Pindarus to kill him (ironically with the sword that had previously killed Caesar). One of you reads Cassius's death speech (lines 33–46). The other is Pindarus. Work together on staging an effective end to Cassius's life. Finish the presentation with a tableau that 'freezes' at the instant of death.

d Cassius is a complex and passionate character. Discuss in your pair your feelings at his death.

1 even with a thought 眨眼工夫
2 thick 模糊
3 thou not'st 你看到的
4 is run his compass 就要走完一个轮回
5 make to 冲向
6 on the spur 策马
7 light 下马
8 ta'en = taken （捉住）
9 Parthia 帕提亚帝国（在如今伊朗和伊拉克的位置）
10 I swore thee 我命你发誓
11 saving of 饶（命）
12 attempt 执行
13 search 刺进
14 Stand not 别耽搁
15 hilts （刀、剑或匕首的）柄

Write about it 写作练习

Pindarus – grief and joy

Pindarus is consumed with conflicting feelings: of grief as he kills his master and of ecstasy (狂喜) at Cassius releasing him from slavery so he can begin a new life 'Where never Roman shall take note of him' (line 50).

• Pindarus does not appear again in the play. Write his diary entry once he has arrived 'far from this country'. What is his 'non-Roman' view of recent events?

TITINIUS	They are, my lord.	
CASSIUS	Titinius, if thou lovest me,	
	Mount thou my horse and hide thy spurs in him	15
	Till he have brought thee up to yonder troops	
	And here again that I may rest assured	
	Whether yond troops are friend or enemy.	
TITINIUS	I will be here again even with a thought[1]. *Exit*	
CASSIUS	Go, Pindarus, get higher on that hill,	20
	My sight was ever thick[2]: regard Titinius	
	And tell me what thou not'st[3] about the field.	
	[*Pindarus goes up*]	
	This day I breathèd first, time is come round	
	And where I did begin there shall I end:	
	My life is run his compass[4]. Sirrah, what news?	25
PINDARUS	(*Above*) O my lord!	
CASSIUS	What news?	
PINDARUS	Titinius is enclosèd round about	
	With horsemen that make to[5] him on the spur[6],	
	Yet he spurs on. Now they are almost on him.	30
	Now Titinius – Now some light[7]; O, he lights too.	
	He's ta'en[8].	
	(*Shout*)	
	And hark, they shout for joy.	
CASSIUS	Come down, behold no more.	
	O, coward that I am to live so long	
	To see my best friend ta'en before my face.	35
	Pindarus [*descends*]	
	Come hither, sirrah.	
	In Parthia[9] did I take thee prisoner,	
	And then I swore thee[10], saving of[11] thy life,	
	That whatsoever I did bid thee do	
	Thou shouldst attempt[12] it. Come now, keep thine oath.	40
	Now be a freeman, and with this good sword,	
	That ran through Caesar's bowels, search[13] this bosom.	
	Stand not[14] to answer; here, take thou the hilts[15]	
	And when my face is covered, as 'tis now,	
	Guide thou the sword.	
	[*Pindarus stabs him*]	
	Caesar, thou art revenged	45
	Even with the sword that killed thee. [*Dies*]	

Pindarus flees. Messala and Titinius enter with news of Brutus's success over Octavius. They hope to cheer Cassius but find him dead.

 剧情简介：品德若逃离。莫撒勒和提提纽上，带来布鲁图打败屋大维的消息。他们打算以此鼓舞卡休，却发现他已死。

Stagecraft 导演技巧
Pause for thought?

Several directors slow the pace of their productions after Pindarus exits, in order to allow the audience time to focus on Cassius's body.

- Write a short note in your Director's Journal to explain whether or not you would do this in your production.

1 The end of the Republic (in groups of four or five)

After five hundred years the Republic is about to end. Like millions of persecuted, defeated or outlawed people in history, Republicans anywhere in the Roman world realise that life as they knew it is over. Pindarus flees, Messala will fight on, Titinius will kill himself.

- Lines 60–4 are Titinius's lament for the Republic. Take a line each and keep repeating it, building your lament like a piece of music. Speaking the verses in any order, start softly and chime (与……和谐一致) your line into the ensemble (合奏) of voices sparingly, then increase in volume and frequency as grief deepens. Savour the sadness of the words, which reach the listener as a collage of broken phrases.

Characters 人物分析
Cassius again (in small groups)

a Lines 60–4 are also a lament for Cassius, showing that he inspired feelings of admiration and respect amongst his followers. Discuss how these lines fit with your impressions of Cassius in response to the activity on page 150.

b Is Messala right to claim that 'Mistrust of good success' (looking on the dark side of things) was responsible for Cassius's downfall?

c How do you now feel about Cassius's death, given that it was the result of a fatal error? The battle is not yet lost.

d As a final piece of work on Cassius, discuss in your group, and then write on your own, his obituary from the point of view of a friend and co-conspirator. You may want to include consideration of Brutus's lines 100–1 on page 155.

1 Durst I 如果我敢
2 change 平局
3 disconsolate 郁郁寡欢
4 Mistrust of 不相信
5 error（莫撒勒将错误拟人化，解释它的产生）
6 melancholy's child 抑郁播下的种（据说抑郁的人总会幻想出不好的事情）
7 apt thoughts 敏感脆弱的内心
8 mother（指产生错误思想的人，此处指卡休）
9 engendered 孕育
10 thrusting 刺入
11 envenomèd 淬了毒的
12 Hie 赶快

PINDARUS	So I am free, yet would not so have been	
	Durst I¹ have done my will. O Cassius,	
	Far from this country Pindarus shall run,	
	Where never Roman shall take note of him. *[Exit]*	50

Enter TITINIUS *and* MESSALA

MESSALA	It is but change², Titinius, for Octavius	
	Is overthrown by noble Brutus' power,	
	As Cassius' legions are by Antony.	
TITINIUS	These tidings will well comfort Cassius.	
MESSALA	Where did you leave him?	
TITINIUS	All disconsolate³,	55
	With Pindarus his bondman, on this hill.	
MESSALA	Is not that he that lies upon the ground?	
TITINIUS	He lies not like the living. O my heart!	
MESSALA	Is not that he?	
TITINIUS	No, this was he, Messala,	
	But Cassius is no more. O setting sun,	60
	As in thy red rays thou dost sink to night,	
	So in his red blood Cassius' day is set.	
	The sun of Rome is set. Our day is gone,	
	Clouds, dews, and dangers come. Our deeds are done.	
	Mistrust of⁴ my success hath done this deed.	65
MESSALA	Mistrust of good success hath done this deed.	
	O hateful error⁵, melancholy's child⁶,	
	Why dost thou show to the apt thoughts⁷ of men	
	The things that are not? O error, soon conceived,	
	Thou never com'st unto a happy birth	70
	But kill'st the mother⁸ that engendered⁹ thee.	
TITINIUS	What, Pindarus? Where art thou, Pindarus?	
MESSALA	Seek him, Titinius, whilst I go to meet	
	The noble Brutus, thrusting¹⁰ this report	
	Into his ears. I may say 'thrusting' it,	75
	For piercing steel and darts envenomèd¹¹	
	Shall be as welcome to the ears of Brutus	
	As tidings of this sight.	
TITINIUS	Hie¹² you, Messala,	
	And I will seek for Pindarus the while.	
	[Exit Messala]	

Titinius places a victory wreath on Cassius's head, then loyally kills himself. Brutus and others enter and mourn the two dead men. Brutus orders his fellow Romans to fight on.

 剧情简介：提提纽给卡休头上戴了一个象征胜利的花环，然后忠义地自杀。布鲁图同其他人上，为他们二人哀悼。布鲁图号令众将士战斗到底。

Themes 主题分析

Appearance and reality

Pindarus got it wrong first. Titinius was not captured by the enemy (which was what Pindarus 'saw', lines 28–32), but greeted by welcoming comrades. The victory garland (花环) sent by Brutus now becomes Cassius's funeral wreath (花圈). Titinius mourns that Cassius 'misconstrued everything'.

- Head up two columns with 'Brutus' and 'Cassius' and fill them in with details about how each character has misinterpreted or misjudged what they have 'seen' during the course of the whole play.

1. misconstrued 误会，误解
2. hold thee 您等等
3. regarded 致敬
4. By your leave, gods! （提提纽请求神灵允许自己阳寿未尽就白我了断）
5. a Roman's part 罗马人该有的死法（指自尽）
6. own proper 自己的（proper 意思同 own，这里重复使用表强调）
7. Look whe'er 看看是不是（whe'er = whether）
8. Thasos 萨索斯（菲利皮附近的一个岛）
9. discomfort us 影响我军士气
10. Labeo and Flavio （布鲁图的两位朋友）

1 The story of Cassius's sword (in small groups)

Weapons can be objects of reverence and exquisite craftsmanship. In stories they often have magical powers. Shakespeare's characters often swear on, or by, their swords. Cassius introduces us to his in Act 1 Scene 3, line 89: 'I know where I will wear this dagger then: / Cassius from bondage will deliver Cassius.' He stabs Caesar with it (Act 3 Scene 1, line 76) and invites Brutus to kill him with it (Act 4 Scene 3, lines 100–5). By the time we reach this scene, it has a life of its own. In line 45 Cassius asks Pindarus to 'Guide thou the sword'; in line 90 it is told to 'find Titinius' heart'; in lines 94–6 Brutus imagines the dead Caesar wields it 'and turns our swords / In our own proper entrails'.

- Each group takes one episode in the sword's story and works on a presentation. This could take the form of a tableau, a rewriting of the scene in which the sword has a voice or something more symbolic.
- Show your presentations in chronological order.

Write about it 写作练习

Is Brutus right?

- Read Brutus's lines 94–6, and then write two or three paragraphs analysing whether or not his assessment of events since Caesar's death is accurate. Remember to back up your points with evidence from the text and quotations.

	Why didst thou send me forth, brave Cassius?	80
	Did I not meet thy friends? And did not they	
	Put on my brows this wreath of victory	
	And bid me give it thee? Didst thou not hear their shouts?	
	Alas, thou hast misconstrued¹ everything.	
	But hold thee², take this garland on thy brow;	85
	Thy Brutus bid me give it thee, and I	
	Will do his bidding. Brutus, come apace,	
	And see how I regarded³ Caius Cassius.	
	By your leave, gods!⁴ – This is a Roman's part⁵.	
	Come, Cassius' sword, and find Titinius' heart. *Dies*	90

Alarum. Enter BRUTUS, MESSALA, YOUNG CATO, *Strato, Volumnius,*
and Lucilius, [*Labeo, and Flavius*]

BRUTUS   Where, where, Messala, doth his body lie?
MESSALA   Lo yonder, and Titinius mourning it.
BRUTUS   Titinius' face is upward.
CATO   He is slain.
BRUTUS   O Julius Caesar, thou art mighty yet,
          Thy spirit walks abroad and turns our swords   95
          In our own proper⁶ entrails.
                        Low alarums
CATO   Brave Titinius!
          Look whe'er⁷ he have not crowned dead Cassius.
BRUTUS   Are yet two Romans living such as these?
          The last of all the Romans, fare thee well!
          It is impossible that ever Rome   100
          Should breed thy fellow. Friends, I owe mo tears
          To this dead man than you shall see me pay.
          I shall find time, Cassius, I shall find time.
          Come therefore and to Thasos⁸ send his body;
          His funerals shall not be in our camp   105
          Lest it discomfort us⁹. Lucilius, come,
          And come, young Cato, let us to the field.
          Labeo and Flavio¹⁰, set our battles on.
          'Tis three o'clock, and, Romans, yet ere night
          We shall try fortune in a second fight.   110
                                                              Exeunt

Battle. Brutus encourages his troops, then leaves. Left behind, Cato is killed in combat and Lucilius (posing as Brutus) captured. Lucilius drops his pretence when Antony enters.

剧情简介：双方开战。布鲁图为众将士鼓舞士气之后下。落在后面的加图战死，卢希琉（装扮成布鲁图）被俘。安东尼上，卢希琉的冒名顶替不拆自穿。

Stagecraft 导演技巧

Time to fight (in eights)

This is the only actual fight called for by a stage direction, so it must be performed well. Display fighting was a popular entertainment in Elizabethan times. Real fighting had its place, too, and not just in Elizabeth's foreign wars. Young men used to swagger in the streets of London, shouting and banging their swords on their 'bucklers' (little shields) as a general challenge to fight. The authorities thought they were a public menace. It is reported that some women found them attractive.

- Plan how you would stage a slow-motion version of the fight, from '*Enter* SOLDIERS' to '*Young Cato is slain*'. Your fight should be convincing, but not dangerous. The golden rule of stage-fighting is safety first!
- Perform your version to the rest of the class.

1 Yet 挺住，坚持住
2 What bastard doth not? 哪个孬种没胆（战斗下去）？
3 I ... Cato 我是马库斯·加图的儿子（他是加图的儿子，鲍霞的兄弟）
4 Only I yield to die 我宁死也不会投降
5 There ... straight 我这命太值钱，你们定想即刻拿去
6 like himself 保持他的自我

1 Brutus's men (in pairs)

a Work out what is happening in the scene and what it tells us about Brutus and his men (especially Cato and Lucilius). In particular, consider why Lucilius pretends to be Brutus.

b Improvise a scenario in which one of you explains to the other, who is a younger reader of the play, what is happening in this scene.

▼ Why do you think the director decided to depart from the script and have Antony threaten Young Cato in this way?

Act 5 Scene 4
The battlefield at Philippi

Alarum. Enter BRUTUS, *Messala,* [YOUNG] CATO, LUCILIUS,
and Flavius, [*Labeo*]

BRUTUS　　Yet[1], countrymen, O, yet hold up your heads!
　　　　　　　　　　　[*Exit with Messala, Flavius, and Labeo*]

CATO　　What bastard doth not?[2] Who will go with me?
　　　　I will proclaim my name about the field.
　　　　I am the son of Marcus Cato[3], ho!
　　　　A foe to tyrants, and my country's friend.　　　　　　　　5
　　　　I am the son of Marcus Cato, ho!

Enter SOLDIERS *and fight*

LUCILIUS　　And I am Brutus, Marcus Brutus, I,
　　　　Brutus, my country's friend. Know me for Brutus!
　　　　　　　　　　　[*Young Cato is slain*]
　　　　O young and noble Cato, art thou down?
　　　　Why, now thou diest as bravely as Titinius　　　　　　　10
　　　　And mayst be honoured, being Cato's son.

1 SOLDIER　　Yield, or thou diest.

LUCILIUS　　　　　　　　　Only I yield to die[4].
　　　　There is so much that thou wilt kill me straight[5].
　　　　Kill Brutus and be honoured in his death.

1 SOLDIER　　We must not. A noble prisoner!　　　　　　　　　15

Enter ANTONY

2 SOLDIER　　Room ho! Tell Antony, Brutus is ta'en.

1 SOLDIER　　I'll tell the news. Here comes the general.
　　　　Brutus is ta'en, Brutus is ta'en, my lord!

ANTONY　　Where is he?

LUCILIUS　　Safe, Antony, Brutus is safe enough.　　　　　　　　20
　　　　I dare assure thee that no enemy
　　　　Shall ever take alive the noble Brutus.
　　　　The gods defend him from so great a shame!
　　　　When you do find him, or alive or dead,
　　　　He will be found like Brutus, like himself[6].　　　　　　　25

Antony gives safe custody to Lucilius and sends for word of Brutus. Brutus and followers enter and rest. Separately and secretly he asks them to kill him.

 剧情简介：安东尼吩咐好生对待卢希琉，并派人去打探布鲁图的情况。布鲁图和部下上场并歇息，他分别找几位部下谈话，悄悄让他们杀了自己。

Characters 人物分析
What are Antony's motives? (in small groups)
Far from being angry at Lucilius's attempt to impersonate Brutus, Antony treats him with the greatest respect and kindness (lines 26–9).

- Discuss the different motives Antony might have for doing this.

1 Contrasts of war (in large groups)
Scene 4 is all about violence, glory and action. Scene 5 opens peacefully and quietly. Some dialogue is a whisper – so quiet that the audience can't hear it. Strato falls asleep. But as the voice of battle steadily grows in volume, Brutus's plea for help in his suicide becomes urgent.

- Bring out these contrasts by making a recording of the script from the start of Act 5 Scene 4 to Act 5 Scene 5, line 57. Rehearse and coordinate sound effects and dialogue very carefully.

Themes 主题分析
Fate and omens (in pairs)
The Elizabethans were not sure what to make of ghosts. They certainly suggested unsettled times, but were they good or evil? See page 136 for more discussion of ghosts.

a Speculate on why Shakespeare has Brutus say that Caesar's ghost has appeared to him again but does not show the event on stage.

b What does it show about the state of Brutus's mind that he says 'I know my hour has come' after describing the appearance of the ghost?

c Write and stage the scene in which Caesar's ghost appears to Brutus 'here in Philippi fields'. It may help to look back to the ghost's appearance in Act 4 Scene 3, line 274. Note how the ghost speaks in simple but ominous statements. After the ghost leaves in Act 4, Brutus says 'I would hold more talk with thee'. What will he take the opportunity to say to the ghost in your scene? Finally, when writing your scene, consider what frame of mind you want Brutus to be in after the encounter. Bear in mind your answer to the question about Brutus above.

1 poor remains 可怜的还活着的人
2 showed the torchlight 用火把打暗号
3 or ta'en or slain 不是被抓就是被杀了
4 deed in fashion 正流行的做法
5 Now … grief 高贵的躯壳里满是悲伤
6 list = listen (to)
7 several 分别，单独

ANTONY	This is not Brutus, friend, but, I assure you,
	A prize no less in worth. Keep this man safe,
	Give him all kindness. I had rather have
	Such men my friends than enemies. Go on,
	And see whe'er Brutus be alive or dead, 30
	And bring us word unto Octavius' tent
	How everything is chanced.

Exeunt

Act 5 Scene 5
A rocky place near the battlefield at Philippi

Enter BRUTUS, DARDANIUS, CLITUS, STRATO, *and* VOLUMNIUS

BRUTUS	Come, poor remains[1] of friends, rest on this rock.
CLITUS	Statilius showed the torchlight[2] but, my lord,
	He came not back. He is or ta'en or slain[3].
BRUTUS	Sit thee down, Clitus. Slaying is the word,
	It is a deed in fashion[4]. Hark thee, Clitus. [*Whispering*] 5
CLITUS	What, I, my lord? No, not for all the world.
BRUTUS	Peace then, no words.
CLITUS	I'll rather kill myself.
BRUTUS	Hark thee, Dardanius. [*Whispers*]
DARDANIUS	Shall I do such a deed?
CLITUS	O Dardanius!
DARDANIUS	O Clitus! 10
CLITUS	What ill request did Brutus make to thee?
DARDANIUS	To kill him, Clitus. Look, he meditates.
CLITUS	Now is that noble vessel full of grief[5],
	That it runs over even at his eyes.
BRUTUS	Come hither, good Volumnius, list[6] a word. 15
VOLUMNIUS	What says my lord?
BRUTUS	Why, this, Volumnius:
	The ghost of Caesar hath appeared to me
	Two several[7] times by night, at Sardis once
	And this last night here in Philippi fields.
	I know my hour is come.
VOLUMNIUS	Not so, my lord. 20

Volumnius refuses to aid Brutus's suicide. Brutus bids farewell to his friends. He urges them to fly. But he detains Strato, who helps Brutus to take his own life.

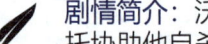 剧情简介：沃拉穆纽拒绝帮助布鲁图自杀。布鲁图向朋友们告别，劝他们赶快逃命。但他留下斯特拉托协助他自杀。

1 'Brutus' tongue' (in fives)

In taking his own life Brutus is his own biographer. He writes himself a noble death: 'Brutus' tongue / Hath almost ended his life's history'. Volumnius, an old school friend, disagrees with Brutus twice, but as usual we hear only Brutus's side of the argument.

- To let Clitus, Dardanius and Volumnius give their point of view, delay Antony's approach and have them refuse to leave at line 43. Improvise what happens as they probe the wisdom and sincerity of Brutus's motives in committing suicide both now and in the future. Brutus and Strato defend his actions and intentions.

- After your improvisation, see if you can read Brutus's part with more conviction and realism than before.

1	beat ... pit	把咱们逼到陷阱边
2	more worthy	更高贵
3	tarry	耽搁
4	vile conquest	不光彩的胜利
5	at once	彻底，永远
6	this hour	这一刻
7	good respect	受人敬重
8	smatch	几分
9	Caesar, now be still	恺撒，你可以瞑目了

Stagecraft 导演技巧

Brutus alone (in pairs)

Shakespeare deliberately increases Brutus's isolation as his death approaches. The increasing intensity of the 'alarums' (sounds of battle) suggests the Triumvirate's unstoppable advance. Brutus's last few friends flee until only Strato is left as his companion.

a Rehearse and present Brutus's lines 50–1 in slow motion, ending with a freeze-frame, then talk with other pairs about the effects you have created.

b Several critics write of the 'humiliation' of Brutus (and Cassius) at the end of the play. Discuss whether you agree with this view or whether you consider it a glorious end, as Brutus does: 'I shall have glory by this losing day'. After your discussion, consider how you would infuse your production of this scene with glory or humiliation and note your ideas in your Director's Journal.

Language in the play 剧中语言

How does Brutus persuade? (in small groups)

When Cassius was recruiting the conspirators to his cause, there was need of much persuasive language and rhetoric. In this scene, Brutus seeks to persuade one of his 'poor remains of friends' to assist him in his suicide.

- Discuss and list the techniques he uses to do this.

BRUTUS	Nay, I am sure it is, Volumnius.
	Thou seest the world, Volumnius, how it goes:
	Our enemies have beat us to the pit¹.

Low alarums

	It is more worthy² to leap in ourselves
	Than tarry³ till they push us. Good Volumnius,	25
	Thou know'st that we two went to school together;
	Even for that our love of old, I prithee
	Hold thou my sword-hilts whilst I run on it.
VOLUMNIUS	That's not an office for a friend, my lord.

Alarum still

CLITUS	Fly, fly, my lord, there is no tarrying here.	30
BRUTUS	Farewell to you, and you, and you, Volumnius.
	Strato, thou hast been all this while asleep:
	Farewell to thee too, Strato. Countrymen,
	My heart doth joy that yet in all my life
	I found no man but he was true to me.	35
	I shall have glory by this losing day
	More than Octavius and Mark Antony
	By this vile conquest⁴ shall attain unto.
	So fare you well at once⁵, for Brutus' tongue
	Hath almost ended his life's history.	40
	Night hangs upon mine eyes, my bones would rest,
	That have but laboured to attain this hour⁶.

Alarum. Cry within, 'Fly, fly, fly!'

| CLITUS | Fly, my lord, fly! |
| BRUTUS | Hence! I will follow. |

[Exeunt Clitus, Dardanius, and Volumnius]

	I prithee, Strato, stay thou by thy lord.
	Thou art a fellow of a good respect⁷,	45
	Thy life hath had some smatch⁸ of honour in it.
	Hold then my sword and turn away thy face,
	While I do run upon it. Wilt thou, Strato?
STRATO	Give me your hand first. Fare you well, my lord.
BRUTUS	Farewell, good Strato.

[Runs on his sword]

| | Caesar, now be still⁹, | 50 |
| | I killed not thee with half so good a will. | *Dies* |

To the sound of the retreating conspirators' trumpets, the triumvirs enter and accept Brutus's followers into their service. Antony honours Brutus as the only selfless conspirator.

 剧情简介：叛军撤退的号声响起，三人团上，将布鲁图的部下收为己用。安东尼敬赞布鲁图是谋杀团伙中唯一高尚无私之人。

1 Clemency – wisdom or folly? (in fours)

Octavius shows clemency (mercy) to all of Brutus's followers when he spares their lives. Julius Caesar also showed clemency to the followers of Pompey after he had defeated them. Among those same followers were Brutus and Cassius, who later assassinated the merciful Caesar. Is Octavius making the same mistake as Caesar?

- One of you takes the part of Octavius. The others play advisers who are not happy with Octavius's decision. Debate who is right.

Characters 人物分析

Brutus or Antony the hero? (in groups of five or six)

Antony's tribute to Brutus (lines 68–75) is fulsome in its praise of 'the noblest Roman of them all'. He singles out Brutus amongst the conspirators as not being driven by 'envy of great Caesar' but by a concern for the 'common good to all'.

- One person reads through Antony's final lines in the play. Discuss their dramatic impact and what they add to your opinions of Brutus's character and Antony's. Which man is the greater hero? Feed back your opinions in a class discussion. At the end, take a vote.

Stagecraft 导演技巧

An ending – but what is to come? (in large groups)

When Octavius speaks the last words of the play, he unceremoniously (but tellingly) asserts his leadership and authority. Many productions choose to suggest an irony in the ending. Caesar disposed of Pompey to become sole ruler of Rome, but will there now be a new power struggle between Antony and Octavius?

a Look carefully at the language of the final two speeches. Discuss what advice about tone, pace, emotion and gesture you would give to the actors delivering these speeches. Experiment with different actors delivering the speeches in different ways.

b Now present the play's closing moment as a tableau that suggests future hostility between the two victorious generals.

---

1 *Retreat* （撤退时击鼓或吹号）
2 can … him 也只能一把火烧了他的遗体
3 entertain them 收留他们
4 prefer 保存
5 follow 跟随
6 latest 最后的
7 envy of 对……的嫉恨
8 a … all 一身正气，为国为民
9 made one of them 加入他们（一伙）
10 gentle 君子的
11 mixed 均衡（人们认为体内各种元素均衡的人天赋高、德行好）
12 virtue 美好德行
13 use him 对待他
14 respect 敬重
15 ordered honourably 受隆重礼遇
16 part 分享

JULIUS CAESAR ACT 5 SCENE 5
儒略・恺撒

Alarum. Retreat[1]*. Enter* ANTONY, OCTAVIUS, MESSALA, LUCILIUS, *and the army*

OCTAVIUS What man is that?
MESSALA My master's man. Strato, where is thy master?
STRATO Free from the bondage you are in, Messala.
The conquerors can but make a fire of him[2]: 55
For Brutus only overcame himself,
And no man else hath honour by his death.
LUCILIUS So Brutus should be found. I thank thee, Brutus,
That thou hast proved Lucilius' saying true.
OCTAVIUS All that served Brutus I will entertain them[3]. 60
Fellow, wilt thou bestow thy time with me?
STRATO Ay, if Messala will prefer[4] me to you.
OCTAVIUS Do so, good Messala.
MESSALA How died my master, Strato?
STRATO I held the sword, and he did run on it. 65
MESSALA Octavius, then take him to follow[5] thee,
That did the latest[6] service to my master.
ANTONY This was the noblest Roman of them all:
All the conspirators, save only he,
Did that they did in envy of[7] great Caesar. 70
He only, in a general honest thought
And common good to all[8], made one of them[9].
His life was gentle[10], and the elements
So mixed[11] in him that Nature might stand up
And say to all the world, 'This was a man!' 75
OCTAVIUS According to his virtue[12] let us use him[13],
With all respect[14] and rites of burial.
Within my tent his bones tonight shall lie,
Most like a soldier, ordered honourably[15].
So call the field to rest, and let's away 80
To part[16] the glories of this happy day.

Exeunt

163

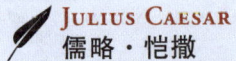

JULIUS CAESAR
儒略·恺撒

Looking back at the play 本剧回顾
Activities for groups or individuals

1 Fifteen-minute version

Divide the class into five groups, each group taking one act of the play. You are going to produce a three-minute version of your allocated act, using only the words from the script itself. When you are ready, put each of the five acts together in turn; you have created a fifteen-minute version of the whole play. As a variation, mime or perform each act in a different style (documentary investigation, soap opera, melodrama, and so on).

2 Press statement

In modern warfare, after a great victory the triumphant generals often meet the press, have their photographs taken and issue a press statement.

- Two people take the roles of Antony and Octavius, while the others prepare to be members of the press or a television crew. Question the two leaders and get as much out of them as you can. Afterwards, write the press statement issued by the victors. (They might decide to release separate statements.)

3 Octavius or Antony?

Octavius Caesar speaks the final lines of the play. As a key member of the Triumvirate he has risen slickly to power. Antony, however, is older, more experienced and arguably more likeable. Lepidus has not been seen for a while. Such a team may be unstable.

a Gather some of the plebeians together and improvise a lively discussion about which man they would prefer as leader and why. Refer to the military careers of Antony, Octavius and Lepidus, as well as to their handling of events after the death of Caesar.

b Now you have the feel of what the populace think, write a speech as either Octavius or Antony, putting their case for being sole ruler of the Roman world. Use whichever rhetorical techniques will strengthen your case. Deliver your speech to the waiting crowd.

4 Cast the play

Imagine that you are a film director about to put together a new and ambitious version of *Julius Caesar*. Go through the list of characters on page 5, and choose the eight that you think are most important in the play. Decide which well-known film actors you would cast in each part – money no object! In each case, say what it is about that particular actor that makes you think they are right for the part.

5 Julius Caesar

Julius Caesar, the character after whom the play is named, dies in Act 3. We see far more of several other characters, most notably Brutus and Cassius.

- Discuss or write answers to the questions: Why do you think Shakespeare called the play *Julius Caesar*? If you were to rename it, what would you call it? Why?

6 Women in the play

The case has been made that this is one of Shakespeare's most male plays. Female characters only appear in Acts 1 and 2, although there may be female crowd members. Answer one of the following:

- 'The female characters add nothing to the play'. Discuss.
- 'The power of Rome could not be fully understood without the female characters in *Julius Caesar*.' To what extent do you agree?

7 Why read *Julius Caesar* now?

One of the claims that is frequently made about Shakespeare is that he has something to say to everyone, whatever their age and culture.

- Explore in writing the point of studying this play in the twenty-first century and what it says to you personally. Looking back at the 'Themes' boxes may help you.

▼▶ What suggestions are being made about the future here as Octavius looks at Antony contemplating the dead Brutus?

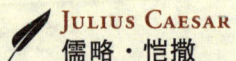
JULIUS CAESAR 儒略·恺撒

Perspectives and themes 视角与主题

What is the play about?

Julius Caesar was probably written in 1599 and first performed in the same year on the stage of the Globe Theatre on London's Bankside. Although essentially a tragedy, it is also a history play dealing with politics and war. However, unlike most of Shakespeare's other history plays, it is not drawn from English history or from Tudor England's recent past.

Shakespeare's main source for his story of *Julius Caesar* is a text that he probably studied at school: Plutarch's *Lives of the Noble Grecians and Romans*, translated into English by Thomas North in 1579. Shakespeare may have been drawn to Plutarch's *Lives* because it contained interesting, biographically detailed, rich and complex appreciations of famous people at the centre of historical events, rather than simply retelling those events. Plutarch also made studies of power and the personal dilemmas faced by political leaders. All this provided fertile source material for Shakespeare to shape and fashion in his own distinctive way. The changes that he made to Plutarch's historical account include:

- having Calpurnia present at the Lupercal festival and using Casca to report Caesar's three-time refusal of the crown (Act 1 Scene 2)
- adding Brutus's long soliloquy in Act 2 Scene 1
- having Caesar reject Artemidorus's warning about the conspiracy (Act 2 Scene 3 and Act 3 Scene 1)
- showing the assassins ritually bathing their arms in Caesar's blood (Act 3 Scene 1)
- adjusting the sequence of events so Antony's funeral oration follows directly after Brutus's speech of explanation to the Roman people; having Antony read out the details of Caesar's will (Act 3 Scene 2).

◆ **Choose one of the changes listed above. Write a paragraph discussing what the play gains from the alteration that Shakespeare made.**

To help you deepen your understanding of the narrative or **plot** of Shakespeare's *Julius Caesar,* try one or more of the following activities.

The bare bones of the script

◆ Have a go at retelling the story of the play in just one sentence, or rewrite the play as a mini-saga (exactly fifty words).

◆ Imagine you are a newspaper sub-editor. Decide what type of paper you work for ('serious' or 'popular'). Your job is to write brief, memorable headlines for each of the five acts in the play. Of course, they may include puns or clever wordplay to gain attention and interest, but they must also be accurate!

Longer versions

◆ In a group of five, each take responsibility for retelling the story of an individual act, and then put the narrative together. Display your version on the classroom wall and compare it with those of other groups. What have they included that you have missed out? Argue your case.

◆ Try writing a sentence about Act 1 Scene 1, and then pass your paper to another student who should pick up the narrative. Keep working around the group, adding a sentence about each scene until you reach the end of the play.

◆ Review the photo gallery at the start of this edition, which gives a version of the play in pictures and captions. What pictures have been missed out? Suggest three other images you would include, giving reasons for your choices.

◆ Stage a TV production meeting in which you must decide how to cut the narrative of the play to two hours ready for filming. Decide which episodes and incidents to keep and then storyboard the main elements of your newly adapted version.

Sculpture park

♦ The class divides into two groups. As one group looks away, the other half of the class — working as pairs — freezes into 'sculptures' that represent some of the key moments of the play. When the first group of students turns round, they see various statues depicting moments from the play set out before their eyes. Their task is to identify as many of the sculptures as possible.

Whose story is it?

Caesar, who gives his name to the title of the play, dies at the start of Act 3. Many critics argue that the central character is Brutus, rather than Caesar, as we witness many events from his perspective. Thus the play would be completely different if it were Cassius's story, Portia's story, Octavius's story or Antony's story.

♦ Have a go at retelling the story of *Julius Caesar* from the perspective of one of the four characters mentioned above. Choose your own text format for this (for example, letter, diary, monologue, short story, narrative poem).

Politics

The feeling that great events are happening — events that will shape all subsequent history — is unmistakable in this play. This may be ancient history, but it is told with racy vitality.

This is probably achieved by the play's mixture of old and new. Shakespeare's Rome owes much to Tudor London — its people even dress in doublets (紧身短上衣) — but it is spiced with specifically pre-Christian superstition and cruelty, such as the sacrifice of animals and the mob slaughter of the poet Cinna. The pagan world had not yet learned of the teaching of Jesus Christ, though intelligent and educated men like Cicero had brought it 'civilisation' and 'culture'.

By setting his play in ancient Rome, Shakespeare could present a debate about authority without fear of offending Queen Elizabeth I and her government or arousing religious controversy. The fact that the conspirators' attempt to save the Roman Republic actually failed was no doubt conveniently reassuring to the Tudor authorities. However, Caesar's assassination would have been an uncomfortable reminder to Elizabethans of the many attempts on the life of the queen (her Jewish physician was executed for allegedly trying to poison her). Similarly, some Elizabethans believed that the queen's power, like Caesar's, was growing too great. Others were as concerned as the ancient Romans about the threat of political upheaval and civil war when their ageing and childless queen finally died.

Tragedy

Julius Caesar is often viewed as a tragedy. Some argue that in writing the play Shakespeare was responding to a growing public demand for such types of drama, especially those that featured elements of bloody and violent revenge or retribution in their narrative structure. In the First Folio (the first published collection of Shakespeare's plays in 1623), *Julius Caesar* is placed with the other major tragedies.

In some ways, *Julius Caesar* conforms to Aristotle's model of classical Greek tragedy:

- A great man is destroyed through an error of judgement (**hamartia** [个性失误]).
- Caesar suffers from pride and arrogance (**hubris** [狂妄]).
- There are several important deaths in the play.
- The final scenes are meant to inspire pity and a release of the audience's emotion (**catharsis** [情绪净化]).

However, it is also possible to recognise that Shakespeare has added his own distinctive and individual features to this well-known model. For example, Caesar is the 'hero' after whom the play is named, yet he dies at the start of Act 3 rather than the end of the play. And Brutus is given typically 'tragic' soliloquies in which he reflects agonisingly on the prospect of murdering Caesar.

♦ Research Aristotle's views about tragedy in the library or on the Internet. Expand your research by exploring other, more recent, definitions. Then write a short essay in which you consider how closely you feel *Julius Caesar* conforms to the different possible models of tragedy.

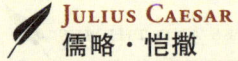

JULIUS CAESAR
儒略・恺撒

Themes in *Julius Caesar*

Another way of looking at the play is to discuss its themes. Themes are ideas, issues or topics that recur throughout the play. They suggest that Shakespeare was preoccupied by particular ideas as he wrote, and sought to explore them through a drama that would entertain his audiences – and make them think. Such major themes include: death and its physical representation; sickness and disease; public versus private; love and friendship; blood and blood ties; and appearance versus reality.

Death and its physical representation

The idea of death and its physical representation runs through the play:

- Flavius and Murellus are killed for removing the decorations from Caesar's statues (Act 1 Scene 2).
- Cassius frequently mentions the possibility of suicide. Brutus resolves to kill Caesar: 'It must be by his death' (Act 2 Scene 1).
- After the frenzied stabbing of Caesar, his bloodied body is vividly present on stage and used to rouse the crowd to an avenging fury against the 'traitors' who killed him (Act 3 Scene 2).
- The innocent poet Cinna is pointlessly killed by the Roman mob (Act 3 Scene 3).
- Antony coolly approves the execution of his nephew as the Triumvirate seek to establish control of Rome (Act 4 Scene 1).
- Portia kills herself; Caesar's ghost appears to Brutus (Act 4 Scene 3).
- Pindarus helps Cassius to commit suicide; Titinius, displaying loyalty to Cassius, takes his own life (Act 5 Scene 3).
- Strato helps Brutus to kill himself (Act 5 Scene 5).

◆ Use the examples above, and any of your own, as the basis for an essay plan on how death in *Julius Caesar* creates moments of great dramatic impact.

Sickness and disease

Disease and infection were rife in Elizabethan England. Unpleasant sexual diseases and, particularly, the bubonic plague (黑死病) were a constant threat, and epidemics were frequent. *Julius Caesar* contains many references to sickness and ill-health. When Murellus urges the common people to 'Pray to the gods to intermit (prevent) the plague' his words carry a strong contemporary resonance.

Caesar's human frailty is highlighted by focusing on his deafness and his epilepsy. Like Elizabeth I, Caesar is unable to beget an heir (Calpurnia is attending the Lupercal ceremony in an attempt to 'cure' her infertility). Cassius has poor eyesight.

Shakespeare frequently connects the sickness of the body with that of the mind. In Act 2 Scene 1, Portia asks 'Is Brutus sick?' when she witnesses his troubled sleeplessness in 'the vile contagion of the night' and concludes that her husband has 'some sick offence within [his] mind'; Ligarius's sickness is cured when he joins the conspiracy against Caesar; and to Brutus the assassination is 'A piece of work that will make sick men whole'.

◆ Research the prevalence of sickness and disease in Elizabethan England and prepare a short presentation to the class on how vulnerable and frightened Shakespeare's audiences may have been.

Public versus private

Many aspects of the play explore the dramatic tension between public and private events. At its heart are the big 'set-piece' public scenes involving Caesar's assassination and the speeches by Brutus and Antony to the Roman crowd after Caesar's death. The play begins with the common people applauding Caesar's victory over Pompey (Act 1 Scene 2), then shows the Lupercal festival where Antony is reported as offering a crown to Caesar three times; Caesar's epileptic seizure is reported to have happened publicly 'in the market-place'.

After the murder, the play focuses increasingly on the nationwide repercussions (反响) of Caesar's assassination as mob violence drives Brutus and Cassius from Rome and precipitates (使突然陷入) civil war. The play's

Perspectives and themes

final scenes show faction fighting against faction and destruction and disorder on a grand scale. Shakespeare even includes a self-indulgent reference by Cassius to the way in which future actors will re-enact 'our lofty scene'.

Yet the play is also keen to explore issues at an individual 'private' level. There is Cassius's expression of his personal hatred of Caesar (Act 1 Scene 3); Brutus's agonised soliloquy in his orchard (Act 2 Scene 1); the domestic scenes showing Portia with Brutus and Calpurnia with Caesar (Act 2 Scenes 1 and 2); the presentation of Caesar's human frailties against his grand public self-confidence (Act 2 Scene 2); Antony's private outpourings of grief ('O, pardon me, thou bleeding piece of earth') and revenge ('Now let it work. Mischief, thou art afoot') which immediately follow his apparently equally sincere public speeches to the conspirators and the Roman crowd (Act 3 Scenes 1 and 2); and Brutus and Cassius's private reconciliation (Act 4 Scene 3).

◆ Write an analysis of one scene in the play in which you think Shakespeare skilfully explores the tension between 'public' and 'private'.

Love and friendship

The nature of the male friendships presented in the play reflects Elizabethan values. The main male characters express deep and loyal affection for each other. Antony's friendship and admiration for Caesar are first suggested in Act 1 and given full dramatic play in Act 3 after Caesar's murder: 'Thou art the ruins of the noblest man / That ever livèd in the tide of times'. Brutus and Cassius share a similarly powerful friendship, even though they are not like-minded characters. In Act 4 Scene 3, after their bitter quarrel, Shakespeare stresses the importance of their reconciliation as Cassius declares 'I cannot drink too much of Brutus' love.' Brutus also inspires love and affection in Portia, his servant Lucius and his friends. This makes Brutus's betrayal of Caesar all the more treacherous. Caesar's dying words in Act 3 Scene 1 ('*Et tu, Brute*? [Even you, Brutus?] – Then fall, Caesar!') express his disbelief at what is happening. Brutus's betrayal is almost as fatal to Caesar as the conspirators' savage stab wounds.

In striking contrast, the young and inexperienced Octavius is portrayed in Acts 4 and 5 as controlled, detached and calculating. Shakespeare developed this coldly formidable, efficient character in much greater detail in his later play *Antony and Cleopatra*.

◆ Working in small groups, make a list of the main characters. For each character, write a short paragraph about their attitudes to love and friendship. Link all your comments to quotations from the play.

Julius Caesar
儒略·恺撒

Blood: loyalty, sacrifice and betrayal

Both images and actual representations of blood abound in the play. In the opening scene the common people champion Caesar 'over Pompey's blood'. Antony speaks of how Pompey's statue ran with blood as Caesar fell dead at its base. Brutus agonises about behaving like a 'butcher' during the assassination and is cautious about killing Antony lest their 'course will seem too bloody'.

After the murder the conspirators smear their arms with Caesar's blood. Portia wounds herself to prove her devotion to Brutus. Calpurnia dreams of clouds that 'drizzled blood' and of her husband's statue that 'Did run pure blood'. As Antony shakes the hand of each conspirator his own is smeared with Caesar's blood. During his funeral oration Antony makes moving use of Caesar's bloodied robe and conjures up powerful images of Caesar's blood: 'Caesar's wounds, poor, poor, dumb mouths'.

As the references to blood diminish after Act 3, we are reminded that it is Caesar's spirit rather than his body that will now dominate events. Only when Brutus dies can he declare: 'Caesar, now be still.'

◆ Find all the references to blood in the play. Display your findings as a striking presentation.

Appearance versus reality

One of Shakespeare's major preoccupations in his plays seems to have been an exploration of the difference between what things are like on the surface (appearance) and what they are really like (reality). This is a theme that is well matched to a play such as *Julius Caesar*, in which the conspirators often need to conceal their murderous intentions and sinister plotting beneath a veneer of apparent honesty, trust and friendship. In Act 2 Scene 1 Brutus, in particular, expresses his shame as he urges that the 'monstrous visage' of their conspiracy be hid 'in smiles and affability'. As the conspirators approach the assassination (Act 2 Scene 2) Caesar's assured public confidence is set against Trebonius's and Brutus's threatening asides.

◆ Look back at the 'Themes' boxes on pages 44, 66 and 154. Use the material from those boxes to help you produce a short presentation for your class on how Shakespeare uses the theme to create a range of dramatic effects in the play.

The Roman world 罗马世界

This alphabetical section provides details about some of the Roman people, places and customs that Shakespeare incorporated into his play.

Aeneas (see p. 16) was a Trojan hero, the son of Anchises and the goddess Venus. According to legend, Aeneas's journey from Troy (retold in Virgil's epic poem the *Aeneid*) led to the founding of the city that was to become Rome.

Armies At the time of the late Republic, some Roman armies were privately owned. Troops swore an oath of allegiance (效忠) to their commander and the commanders looked to their soldiers for political support.

◆ Study the image on this page and other photographs in this edition of Romans in military dress. Then conduct your own research on the equipment and fighting techniques of the Roman soldier. Suggest ways of using your information to devise suitable costumes for a modern stage production. Draw and label them to add to your Director's Journal.

Augurers (see p. 50) Any decision of importance was referred to the augurers, who had various ways of determining the will of the gods and deciding whether it was lucky or unlucky to proceed on that day. Sometimes a live animal was cut open and its insides studied. In Act 2 Scene 1, line 200, Cassius refers to Caesar's belief in the power of augurers, omens and dreams, which he fears will prevent him from going to the Capitol and thereby ruin the conspirators' plans.

◆ Look back at Act 2 Scene 2, lines 1–107, where Caesar debates whether to go to the Capitol. Describe how Shakespeare has used dreams, omens and auguries to add to the scene's dramatic tension.

◆ Remind yourself of the 'Themes' box on page 144 and use the material generated as a starting point for a mini-essay on the importance of fate and omens in the play.

Cicero (106–43 BC) (see p. 20) was the leading orator of his day. His writings were studied intensely in Elizabethan schools. His style was held up as the ideal model for students. His essays, letters and imaginary conversations between historical figures popularised the ideas of Greek philosophers, presenting them in a pleasurable and accessible style.

◆ Conduct your own research into the historical character Cicero. Then look back at Cicero's part in the play (Act 1 Scenes 2 and 3). Suggest ways in which an actor might portray something of the historical Cicero in the way he performs his role.

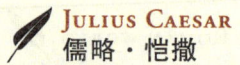

Julius Caesar
儒略·恺撒

The city of Rome was built around two locations. The forum (market-place) was the central area where commerce and the administration of justice were focused. The Capitol, on one of its seven hills, was the political and religious centre of ancient Rome.

The site of the ancient Roman forum.

The Roman Capitol seen from the Palatine Hill in the 19th century.

◆ Research what ancient Rome looked like. Choose one 'public' scene from the play and design the set and costumes for that scene. Suggest ways of bringing out the atmosphere of ancient Rome.

Colossus (see p. 18) was a giant statue of the Greek god Apollo that bestrode the harbour entrance to the Greek island of Rhodes. Over 30 metres high (the tallest statue of its time), it was known as one of the seven wonders of the ancient world.

Cynics (see p. 126) believed primarily in two key principles: that the individual was responsible for their own morality and that a person's mental determination ('will') was all-important. They rejected the social values of the time, preached the avoidance of pleasure and denied social relationships. Cynicism (愤世嫉俗论，犬儒主义) was the forerunner of Stoicism (see p. 173).

Epicurus (see p. 144) was a Greek philosopher who founded Epicureanism. He believed that seeking simple and modest pleasures was the route to tranquillity and freedom from fear.

Honour (see also **Suicide**) in ancient times and in Shakespeare's day was not the vague concept it is today. Aristotle, a famous ancient Greek philosopher, explained how the magnanimous man (the perfect ruler) made public honour his 'chief concern'.

◆ Discuss how Shakespeare explores the theme of honour in the play. Refer to the 'Themes' box on page 24 and look closely at what Brutus and Cassius say about it (e.g. in Act 1 Scene 2 and Act 3 Scene 2) and how they approach their deaths. What does 'honour' mean to them? Prepare a short talk for younger students of Shakespeare on the importance of honour to classical Romans.

The Lupercal (see p. 10) was originally a farming festival held on 15 February to ward wolves off the newborn lambs and kids in the flocks. Later it was adopted by the city of Rome to ward off evil spirits. Just as the billy goats brought fertility to the flocks, barren women thought the flick of a goatskin flail would enable them to have children.

◆ Caesar's first appearance in the play is to attend the Lupercal (Act 1 Scene 2). Sketch a set design for that scene which reflects some of the ideas above.

Octavius Caesar (63 BC–AD 14), grand-nephew to Julius Caesar, achieved high office at an early age. Caesar treated him as his heir. After Caesar's assassination (as seen in the play), Octavius established the Second Triumvirate (后三头同盟) with Antony and Lepidus, but later (as seen in *Antony and Cleopatra*) Lepidus was disposed of, and then Octavius and Antony quarrelled and battled with each other. Octavius won and became sole ruler of the Roman Empire, with the title of Emperor Caesar Augustus.

Pompey (106–48 BC) (see p. 8) was, like Caesar, a very popular general; both were members of the First Triumvirate (前三头同盟) (with Crassus). He married Caesar's daughter Julia. Pompey remained in Rome, while Caesar campaigned in Europe, becoming increasingly powerful. When Caesar returned and became dictator, Pompey fled and was finally murdered. Shakespeare's *Julius Caesar* opens after Caesar has wiped out a final pocket of resistance headed by Pompey's sons.

Proscription (see pp. 112 and 128) was the imposition of the death penalty; three hundred out of nine hundred senators were executed along with two hundred equites (aristocrats). The newly formed Triumvirate (Antony, Octavius and Lepidus) used it ruthlessly to organise a purge of their political opponents. They were even willing to sacrifice members of their own families.

Sacrifice of animals was an important ritual in Roman religious observance. Caesar shows his superstitious nature in Act 2 Scene 2 when he urges the priests to 'do present (immediate) sacrifice' on the morning of his assassination – a ceremony that threatens ill-fortune as the priests 'could not find a heart within the beast'.

Stoics (see p. 126) held to the philosophy of Stoicism(斯多葛学派，斯多葛主义). This taught that self-control, inner strength and freedom from unsettling emotions were ideal principles that made people indifferent to pleasure and pain and led to clear thinking, balanced judgement and absolute truth. If life became unendurable, it was appropriate to kill yourself.

◀ How closely does this image match the profile on the left and Shakespeare's presentation of Octavius?

Suicide was seen as a noble action in the ancient world. The Roman code of honour dictated that suicide was preferable to ignominious (可耻) death or disgrace. Brutus vows he will never 'go bound to Rome'; Cassius commits suicide remarking: 'O, coward that I am to live so long'.

◆ Many of the major characters believe their lives are not sacrosanct (神圣不可侵犯) (see the 'Themes' box on p. 24). But can suicide ever be a 'noble' act? What do you think Shakespeare's play suggests? Talk about this in a small group and be ready to offer your main conclusions in a class discussion.

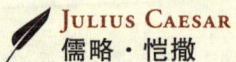

JULIUS CAESAR 儒略・恺撒

Characters 人物分析

Recent literary critical thinking has questioned the validity of considering characters in plays as 'real people'. In fact, this idea has generally been dispensed with in favour of seeing them as dramatic constructs that function only within the social and political contexts of the play. The 'identities' of these characters are also considered to be much less fixed than they were in the past, as characters may be interpreted differently in each production. They only exist for the length of the play.

It is, therefore, useful to summarise what you discover about the characters through their speech, actions and what others say about them during the course of the play. These are the three main ways in which characters are established.

Remember you are always entitled to your own views on the characters and their roles – just make sure you can back those views up with reference to the play itself.

Julius Caesar

Julius Caesar has been called Shakespeare's 'great political thriller'. Many historians agree that Caesar was a man of immense talent and great military skill, yet at the same time a mass of contradictions and complexities. Shakespeare makes great use of the paradoxical mixture of qualities chronicled by historians to portray the man whom several conspirators were desperate to wipe from the face of the Roman world.

Shakespeare's Caesar dominates the play from the start: the crowd rejoices at his triumph and the Tribunes Flavius and Murellus resentfully describe him as the man who intends to 'soar above the view of men'. It is significant that the play begins with Caesar's popularity being demonstrated by the crowd's reaction to him, as the people were a powerful force in the Republic. At the Lupercal ceremony in Act 1 Scene 2, Antony also affirms Caesar's towering authority (line 10): 'When Caesar says, "Do this", it is performed.' Any dissenting voices are ruthlessly silenced (line 275).

Yet Caesar, though powerful, betrays signs of physical weakness and emotional vulnerability. He is deaf in his left ear (a detail that Shakespeare seems to have invented), suffers from epilepsy and in Act 1 Scene 2, Caesar says that Calpurnia suffers from the 'sterile curse', but this reflects upon him too – having no heir was a weakness in a leader. Public spectacle, the 'holy chase' in celebration of the Feast of Lupercal, is mixed with personal vulnerability and susceptibility to superstition. Similarly, at the very moment when Caesar was publicly being offered a crown we are told how 'He fell down in the market-place, and foamed at mouth, and was / speechless' (Act 1 Scene 2, lines 246–7). Cassius also recounts how once he had to rescue Caesar during a swimming contest and how, during a bout (发作) of fever, he had cried out 'As a sick girl'.

However, Cassius also acknowledges Caesar to 'bestride the narrow world / Like a Colossus'. Arrogant enough to constantly talk of himself in the third person (as 'Caesar' rather than 'I'), nineteen times in total in fact, Caesar is at one moment a shrewd and astute (精明) judge of character, warning Antony to be on his guard against Cassius with his 'lean and hungry look', then moments later boasting of his own immunity from fear: 'I rather tell thee what is to be feared / Than what I fear: for always I am Caesar' (Act 1 Scene 2, lines 211–12).

Perhaps foolhardy (有勇无谋), perhaps fearless, Caesar finally ignores his wife's pleas for him not to go to the Capitol, and in the lead-up to his assassination many of his more unattractive traits are given prominence. Adamantly refusing to repeal the order to banish Metellus's brother, Caesar spurns Metellus 'like a cur (dog)', declaring himself 'constant as the northern star'. This inflexible pride seals his fate.

But Caesar's spirit lives on. Antony's moving funeral oration, the blood-drenched corpse, the appearance of his ghost and the fact that both Cassius and Brutus die with Caesar's name on their lips – all help keep Caesar clearly in the audience's mind to the end of the play.

CHARACTERS

◆ In order to help your thinking about Caesar, discuss or write about the following questions:

   a In your own production of *Julius Caesar* would you stress Caesar's weakness or his power? Justify your answer.
   b What would the effect be of having a female Caesar in a production with male conspirators?
   c Is it fierce courage or dangerous pride that makes Caesar say, 'Danger knows full well / That Caesar is more dangerous than he' (Act 2 Scene 2, lines 44–5)? Justify your answer.
   d In a review of a recent production, the actor's performance of Caesar was described as 'thuggish' (凶狠，粗野). Is there evidence in the play to suggest that this is a valid interpretation?
   e Do you find Caesar a likeable leader? Why or why not?
   f 'In dramatising the character of Caesar, Shakespeare avoids soliciting sympathy for him or arousing alienation towards him.' Discuss.

◆ 'Could the way in which Julius Caesar is portrayed as somewhat petulant (暴躁，任性) and past his prime, almost the old maid, have offered a whispered suggestion of Queen Elizabeth at the end of her life, fearful of conspiracy and assassination?' Try acting out a few scenes, with Caesar being 'petulant and past his prime'. Follow this up with an analysis of how successful you think this interpretation is.

▼ Which of these two photos better captures your impressions of Caesar? Give reasons for your answer.

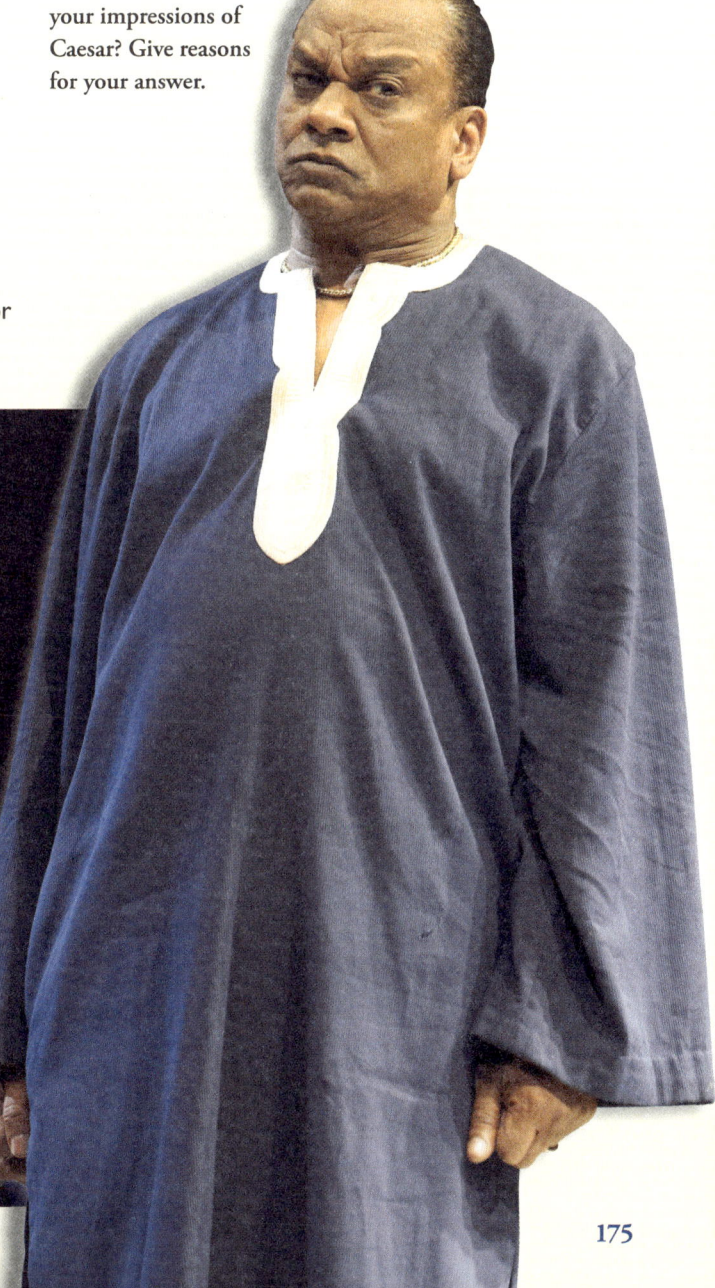

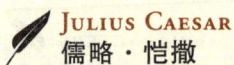

JULIUS CAESAR
儒略·恺撒

Brutus

Brutus was a highly educated man from a distinguished family; an ancestor of his overthrew the tyrannous Tarquin royal family and established the Roman Republic. He fought with Pompey against Caesar, but was pardoned and became Caesar's trusted and close friend. He now sees Caesar's increasing power and the rumoured impending coronation as a danger to his Republican idealism and Rome itself.

Perhaps the key to Shakespeare's presentation of Brutus is the sense of conflict that haunts him. By his own admission he is 'Brutus, with himself at war'. In his soliloquy (Act 2 Scene 1, lines 10–34) he reasons very carefully why Caesar must die, concerned to justify all his actions to the highest ethical standard. He believes passionately in the power of rational and logical argument, yet his judgement is sometimes flawed. He fails to see how Cassius manipulates him, suggests conspirators dip their hands in Caesar's blood, spares Antony's life, and then lets Antony speak at Caesar's funeral. He heads the conspirators with unquestioned authority, overruling the others on the need to swear an oath, Cicero's suitability as a fellow conspirator and the best way to do battle.

Brutus's integrity and reputation are admired by his colleagues and he brings respectability to the conspiracy. Cassius judges: 'Well, Brutus, thou art noble'. Casca remarks that he 'sits high in all the people's hearts'. To Ligarius he is the 'Soul of Rome'. Brutus himself boasts: 'Set honour in one eye and death i'th'other / And I will look on both indifferently.'

Although these traits lend him a pompous and self-righteous air (perhaps most clearly seen in his quarrel with Cassius in Act 4 Scene 3), his idealism often makes him tragically vulnerable. He has a soft and caring side, which surfaces in the domestic scenes where he shows tenderness and concern for his wife, Portia and his servant, Lucius. It is noticeable that Cassius has no comparable scenes, and consequently Brutus can be said to show greater emotional range than Cassius.

At the end of the play, even though he is presented as increasingly isolated, he is still seen with the 'remains of friends', who loyally refuse to help him die. Antony's epitaph (悼文) celebrates powerfully 'the noblest Roman of them all', motivated only by 'common good' rather than 'envy of great Caesar'.

Below are some comments from critics about Brutus.

I used to think Brutus was the idealist in a world of realpolitik: [the actor] excellently shows him to be a self-righteous blunderer.
Michael Billington, 2012

Brutus's vision is obscured by Utopian assumptions (his belief that people can be persuaded by rational argument and that they are as consistent and trustworthy as he believes himself to be).
Anthony Davies, 2002

[Brutus] is a man who thinks much, but none too well; a man whose assumptions about the world he lives in are almost all mistaken; a man who, acting on these assumptions, achieves the exact opposite of what he intended. He is a political disaster – and yet he is not without a certain nobility.
John Nettles, 2000

It cannot be seriously doubted that Brutus is the focus – dramatically, psychologically, politically, and morally.
Marvin Spevack, 2004

Shakespeare treats him [Brutus] with delicate sympathy.
Frank Kermode, 1974

- ◆ Choose one of the above quotations and, having discussed your ideas about it in a group, write up your answer making clear whether or not you agree with the view expressed. Make sure you back up your points with evidence and quotations from the text.

- ◆ Look back at all the work you did on Brutus throughout your study of the play. Make the case for him being the most interesting and sympathetic character in the whole play. You could do this in the form of a speech and then take questions.

Characters

- Without going back to your notes, write down all the times you can remember that Brutus and Cassius disagree and what they disagree about. What is the significance of these arguments?

- Imagine a production of the play without Brutus. What difference would his absence make?

▼ Which of Brutus's qualities does this actor show in his expression and gesture?

Cassius

Cassius fought with Pompey against Caesar and was pardoned, but he did not receive Caesar's favour. It is he who drives the initial stages of the conspiracy. Like Brutus, he is troubled by the thoughts of what Caesar has become: 'Upon what meat doth this our Caesar feed / That he is grown so great?'

Cassius is prompted by personal resentment and antagonism (敌意). These feelings surface powerfully in the way he tries to 'seduce' Brutus to the cause of toppling Caesar. In Act 1 Scene 2, in particular, his words seethe with energy and passion as he compares 'we petty men' to the demi-god Caesar. Although Shakespeare does not elaborate on his motives, Cassius expresses his contempt for 'So vile a thing as Caesar' because he 'doth bear me hard' (has a grudge against me). Later in the play (Act 4 Scene 3) Shakespeare suggests that Cassius's temper was inherited from his mother.

Caesar's assessment of Cassius (Act 1 Scene 2) is astute and accurate. Cassius looks predatory (掠夺成性) and he 'thinks too much'. A shrewd judge of character, he rarely smiles and abjures entertainment. But he is particularly dangerous because such men will forever be restless: 'Whiles they behold a greater than themselves'.

In contrast to Brutus, Cassius has political acumen (敏锐) and cleverness. He knows that the conspiracy will only be successful if all threats are removed (Brutus is obsessed by the need to be 'sacrificers' rather than 'butchers'). However, Cassius knows that he needs Brutus's support in order to lend dignity and nobility to their enterprise and to quash any accusations of self-interest on the part of the conspirators.

A key aspect of Cassius's presentation is the change that his character undergoes. He becomes much more sympathetic after the assassination. Like Brutus, he attracts loyal followers and shows the deep value of friendship (his reconciliation with Brutus in Act 4 Scene 3 is very moving). Frenzied outbursts give way to calmness. Brutus pays a mournful tribute to him: 'The last of all the Romans'. But perhaps Titinius's ironic comment ('thou hast misconstrued everything'), capping Cassius's impetuous suicide, is the more appropriate assessment.

Julius Caesar
儒略·恺撒

- A theatre critic wrote of Cassius in the 2012 RSC production: 'Wary and sly, scared and manipulative, Mr Nri is an excellent Cassius.' Would you want the Cassius in your production to show these characteristics?

- 'Cassius is branded as a figure of disorder on both the personal and political levels.' Is this an accurate way of considering Cassius, in your view?

- Consider Cassius the leader:
    a Why is Cassius so successful in binding the conspirators together?
    b If you had been in Rome at the time and had harboured feelings against Caesar, do you think you would have joined Cassius? Give reasons for your answer. Compare your answer with others'.

- In the course of the play, Cassius refers to himself fourteen times in the third person. Explore the significance of this, bearing in mind that Brutus (thirteen times) and Caesar (nineteen times) also refer to themselves in this way.

- You are the director of a new production of the play. What advice would you offer the actor playing Cassius about how to make the change in his character after the assassination plausible? With a partner, perform a role play – what ideas does Cassius have?

Cassius and Brutus could be said to be dramatic 'foils' for each other. This means that the contrasting qualities and actions of one help to highlight the qualities and actions of the other.

- Using the list of disagreements you compiled for the activity on page 177 to help you, draw up a table to show how their qualities and actions contrast.

- 'The conspiracy would not have gone ahead if Brutus had refused to join it.' Do you agree? Improvise a discussion between two conspirators who hold different views.

- Brutus and Cassius are the two most important conspirators. They need to be considered separately, but it is also useful to compare their roles and traits, as you have been offered the opportunity to do on some of the left-hand pages. How would the play be different if there were no dramatic contrast between these two characters?

Antony

Antony was a soldier with a reputation for womanising and riotous (放荡) living. Shakespeare stresses his virility (男子气概) and social pursuits – he is a Lupercalian runner 'given / To sports, to wildness, and much company'. This reputation endures into Act 5, where Cassius labels him 'a masker and a reveller'. He campaigned with Caesar, reaching high government office through Caesar's favour. Prior to Caesar's assassination Antony speaks only five lines; in his first appearance he is presented as Caesar's close friend, a man who respects his absolute authority: 'When Caesar says, "Do this", it is performed.' Like Brutus, his judgement is seen to be flawed, and he mistakenly rates Cassius as harmless.

After Caesar's death Antony really comes into his own. As a deeply grieving friend, master tactician and political opportunist, he holds the stage during the pivotal 'funeral' scene in a mesmerising (施催眠术) way.

First he must engage with the murderers. Whilst holding loyally to his love for Caesar, he skilfully negotiates with the assassins, shaking their bloodied hands in an ironic gesture of friendship and respect. But his main objective is to set up his funeral oration to Caesar, and his soliloquy (from Act 3 Scene 1, line 254) shows how false his earlier words have been, the true depth of his grief and the anticipated fury of his revenge.

His funeral speech (from Act 3 Scene 2, line 65), widely regarded as the climactic moment of the play, shows off all Antony's rhetorical skills. Careful not to antagonise (引起反感) the crowd, he first denies he has come to praise Caesar. Dealing with claims about Caesar's ambition, he shows ironic respect for Brutus and sets up memorable choruses and refrains ('honourable man').

CHARACTERS

The pause to allow the common people to digest his message is a masterstroke. By the time he has re-established Caesar's greatness, planted ideas of mutiny in the minds of the crowd and made reference to the violation of Caesar's cloak, it remains only for him to mention the munificence (慷慨) of Caesar's will and he has unleashed the force of mob violence.

He appears in only four further scenes and is, arguably, eclipsed by Octavius's cool assurance and control by the end of the play. However, Antony's ruthlessness is underlined by his willing sacrifice of his nephew. He also shows contempt for Lepidus and the integrity of Caesar's will (by siphoning off money to pay for the war against Brutus and Cassius).

At the end of the play, Shakespeare perhaps attempts to recalibrate (重新调整) his presentation of Antony, firstly by having him pardon Lucilius and secondly by the generosity of his tribute to Brutus in the closing moments.

◆ Discuss these differing views of Antony:

> Antony is the most charismatic (魅力超凡) character in the play.
> It is not surprising that he is often played by well-known and attractive actors.
> Antony's main role in the play is as a superb speech-maker.
> Antony [is] a calculating opportunist.

◆ Refer back to the photos of Antony in this book (pp. x, 20, 82, 88, 96, 98, 165, 170). Which one most closely fits your idea of him? Why?

◆ Write a list of the incidents when Antony shows the vicious or cruel side of his character. Pick out a quotation for each incident that sums up his attitude to it.

Now list his acts of kindness or generosity and pick out a quotation for each of them. What conclusions can you draw about him from reading through your lists?

◆ What are Antony's political views? Are they as well defined as those of Cassius and Brutus?

◆ In what ways is Antony a foil to Octavius? What evidence does the play offer that they will work well together and with Lepidus, the other member of the Triumvirate, in the future?

▼ Does this photo of Antony add anything to your understanding of the dramatic function of the character?

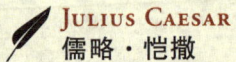

Julius Caesar
儒略・恺撒

Portia and Calpurnia

These are the only female characters in what is known as Shakespeare's 'most male' play. They have several features in common: they mirror Elizabethan attitudes to women; they inhabit a world in which men hold complete power and authority and in which women's lives are subservient. In more recent productions their roles have been highlighted in different ways (see page 194) and feminist criticism has questioned the issue of the importance of gender in the play.

Portia appears in only two scenes. In Act 2 Scene 1 part of her role is to reveal the impact of Brutus's mental turmoil on his domestic life. Portia has sensitively and discreetly witnessed the changes in Brutus, but is keen for him to share his burden with her. She makes clear what a loving wife expects 'By all your vows of love' and, in turn, provokes a tender response from Brutus: 'You are my true and honourable wife'. As testament to her love and devotion she has wounded herself in the thigh, a gesture that wrings pity and admiration from her husband. He begs that he might be 'worthy of this noble wife', noble not only because of her actions but also because she is descended from a noble family: Marcus Porcius Cato is her (and Young Cato's) father and Brutus's uncle. Marcus Porcius Cato was a famous soldier, orator and statesman of high moral standing who committed suicide rather than be captured. Thus, Cato's life has several parallels with Brutus's and Portia refers to herself as a 'woman well reputed' because she is his daughter.

In the scene at the Capitol (Act 2 Scene 4), Portia displays the gender stereotyping so prevalent in Shakespeare's time, confessing that she finds it hard to keep quiet. It is likely that Brutus has shared the conspirators' plan with her and Portia's natural agitation and nervous anxiety ratchet up the dramatic energy of this episode. Her suicide (by swallowing hot coals) is only reported in Act 4. This painful death is further evidence of her nobility and bravery.

'**Calpurnia**' is the first word that Caesar speaks in the play. Perhaps Shakespeare is drawing attention to Caesar's intimate side as well as reminding the audience that the couple are childless. Later (Act 2 Scene 2) she signals the terrifying portents of the storm and relates a striking dream about her husband's death. In entreating him not to go to the Senate house she provides him with an excuse: 'Call it my fear / That keeps you in the house, and not your own.' Momentarily, Caesar listens, only for Decius to sway the decision by mocking Caesar's adherence to his wife's 'dreams'.

◆ In a recent production, Portia was obviously pregnant, in contrast to Calpurnia's childlessness. What do you think of this idea?

◆ If you were given the choice of playing either Portia or Calpurnia in a production of *Julius Caesar*, which role would you choose and why?

◆ Set up a debate within a group of four. Two of you argue that the women in the play are too sketchily drawn to be significant. The other two argue against this view.

◆ Traditionally, the scenes that included the women were considered to be rather limited. More recently critics have highlighted the mixture of both public and private concerns in these domestic scenes. What ideas that have a public significance (for example, political ideas) do you find in these scenes with Calpurnia and Portia?

◆ As a director you decide that Portia's death should not happen off stage – it should be given more prominence, as Brutus's death is. Write the speech she might make before committing suicide.

Characters

▼ As in Shakespeare's time, this 1999 production was all male. What challenges would be presented for a male actor playing Portia in the present day?

▼ A tender moment between Calpurnia and Caesar. How far can this be justified from the script?

The people

The people have a significant dramatic function. Indeed, some critics would consider the importance of the Roman people in the play as rivalling that of Caesar, Brutus and Antony. This is for political as well as dramatic reasons. The Republic is under threat at the start of the play in the eyes of those who are concerned about Caesar's ambition. The Tribunes and the conspirators talk resentfully about Caesar elevating himself above the people on whose support he depends.

Civic unrest is shown at the start of *Julius Caesar* when the crowd gathers to 'make holiday to see Caesar and to rejoice in his triumph', as the Cobbler says. The right and desire of the crowd to do this is challenged by two Tribunes and this leads to lively exchanges and threats. Several individuals (Plebeians 1, 2, 3 and 4) emerge each time the crowd is present, expressing different views. Such scenes would have been familiar to contemporary audiences, as riots frequently broke out when it was holiday time.

Antony's skilful manipulation of the crowd in Act 3 at the funeral of Caesar is demonstrated by the crowd's reactions to his words. Having begun by supporting Brutus, even to the extent of Plebeian 3 shouting 'Let him be Caesar', the crowd begins to assess Antony's words, at first acknowledging that 'there is much reason in his sayings'. From there, Antony works on their natural greed with the promise of Caesar's will, significantly comes down from the pulpit to their level and then works the crowd up to a frenzy of grief, drawing attention to Caesar's body. Without the crowd's reactions, the rhetoric would be empty. It needs to be seen to work. Antony then works on them to feel aggressive towards the conspirators who are responsible for this. He finally reveals what Caesar has promised them in his will and then watches as the crowd departs, intent on the 'mischief' he has encouraged them to. This is directly followed by the shocking scene of the terrorising of Cinna, showing the horrors of mob violence.

CHARACTERS

In more recent productions, members of the cast have been planted among the audience, taking the plebeian speaking parts. The audience then becomes the crowd and hence part of the drama. Arguably this helps to extend the people's involvement in politics to every member of the audience.

- ◆ How would you stage the crowd scenes in your production of the play?

- ◆ Can you think of any other plays or films in which the crowd plays a significant role? What comparisons could you usefully make with this play?

In this play and others, the crowd is often talked of disparagingly (轻蔑地). Flavius calls them 'idle creatures'. Murellus calls them:

> *You blocks, you stones, you worse than senseless things!*
> *O you hard hearts, you cruel men of Rome*

In Shakespeare's play *King Henry IV Part 2* the people are reviled for being

> *the blunt monster with uncounted heads,*
> *The still-discordant wav'ring multitude*

- ◆ Do the people deserve such criticism in *Julius Caesar*? You could tackle this question in a group, with two speech-makers, one saying the people do deserve such criticism, the other saying they don't. The speech-makers should use rhetorical techniques in their speeches (see pp. 185–6). The other members of the group play the crowd, heckling and supporting.

- ◆ 'Without the crowd, this play would be a dry political drama'. Do you agree?

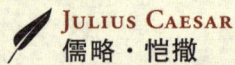

JULIUS CAESAR
儒略・恺撒

The language of *Julius Caesar* 《儒略・恺撒》的语言

Imagery

Some critics have claimed that *Julius Caesar* does not contain much **imagery**: vivid words and phrases that help create atmosphere as they conjure up emotionally charged pictures or associations in the mind. Yet when Flavius describes the removal of decorations from Caesar's statues, claiming that 'These growing feathers plucked from Caesar's wing / Will make him fly an ordinary pitch' (Act 1 Scene 1, lines 71–2), he is using a striking animal image to compare the limiting of Caesar's power to the way a falconer restricts the 'pitch' of a falcon (the height to which it rises before swooping) by plucking its feathers. When Flavius adds that Caesar wants to keep his subjects in 'servile (slave-like) fearfulness', the impression of Caesar as a tyrannical predator is complete.

Shakespeare uses metaphor, simile and personification (拟人). All are comparisons that in effect substitute one thing (the image) for another (the thing described).

A **simile** compares one thing to another using 'like' or 'as'. For example, Cassius contemptuously dismisses Caesar dealing with his fever 'As a sick girl'. Caesar 'doth bestride the narrow world / Like a Colossus'. Brutus, contemplating how to execute Caesar rather than slaughter him, implores his fellows to 'carve him as a dish fit for the gods, / Not hew him as a carcass fit for hounds.' Caesar makes his death inevitable by asserting: 'I am constant as the northern star'.

A **metaphor** is also a comparison, suggesting that dissimilar things are the same. Brutus slights Antony, saying he is so dependent on his friend that he is 'but a limb of Caesar'. Urging the conspirators to be 'sacrificers, but not butchers', Brutus shows a high-minded, ethical approach to the killing of Caesar. Portia, aware of an increasingly distant relationship with Brutus, asks: 'Dwell I but in the suburbs / Of your good pleasure?' To Antony the conspirators' 'purpled hands do reek and smoke'.

Personification turns things into persons, giving them human feelings or attributes. Cassius bemoans the state of Rome 'groaning underneath this age's yoke'. Brutus describes 'conspiracy' as like a person ashamed 'to show thy dang'rous brow by night' and celebrates the assassination of Caesar by declaring: 'Ambition's debt is paid'. For Antony, Caesar's bleeding wounds 'like dumb mouths do ope their ruby lips'.

- Find the sources of the four similes, four metaphors and four personifications cited above. In each case identify the specific comparison being made and write a sentence commenting on the impact of the image.

- Now test yourself with the following images. First, identify whether it is metaphor, simile or personification. Then locate the image in the text and analyse it as outlined above.

    a 'But hollow men, like horses hot at hand, / Make gallant show and promise of their mettle'
    b 'Tiber trembled underneath her banks / To hear the replication of your sounds'
    c 'When you are waspish'
    d 'and put a tongue / In every wound of Caesar, that should move / The stones of Rome to rise and mutiny'
    e 'For I am armed so strong in honesty / That they pass by me as the idle wind'
    f 'There is a tide in the affairs of men / Which, taken at the flood, leads on to fortune'
    g 'sweet Caesar's wounds, poor, poor, dumb mouths'
    h 'The deep of night is crept upon our talk'
    i 'let me not stir you up / To such a sudden flood of mutiny'
    j 'He shall but bear them as the ass bears gold'

- Identify five additional striking and powerful images in the play. Draw them in a bold way that highlights the comparisons at the heart of each one. Collate them into a whole-class display.

The language of Julius Caesar

'Animal' imagery

Images enrich particular moments and can also illuminate key themes. Consider the effect of the following animal images in the play.

- Caesar dismisses the conspirators' pleas to repeal Metellus's brother's banishment by affirming that he will not respond to 'base spaniel fawning' (behaviour like that of an eager-to-please dog).
- As Antony contemplates the civil strife that will follow Caesar's murder, he imagines Caesar's ghost will 'Cry havoc and let slip the dogs of war', linking the frenzied mob violence that he has unleashed to the savagery of unruly hounds.
- Caesar is a 'brave hart (deer)' felled by 'hunters' and 'crimsoned in thy Lethe' (Lethe was the river of oblivion in the underworld), or 'like a deer strucken by many princes'.

Other animal images provide insight into character, and intensify meaning and emotional force. When Brutus muses on 'the bright day that brings forth the adder', his train of thought connects hidden danger with the idea of a snake ... and Caesar. Once Caesar is crowned, 'we put a sting in him / That at his will he may do danger with'. Thus Brutus resolves to 'think him as a serpent's egg ... And kill him in the shell.'

◆ Write a short paragraph exploring each of the above images. Focus on the specific qualities that the animal comparison brings to that image.

Creating atmosphere

Shakespeare often uses language to create atmosphere. Remember that his plays were originally staged in broad daylight so words had to establish setting and atmosphere (see p. 190). A good example of his technique is Act 2 Scene 1, where the language has to suggest a night-time setting in Brutus's orchard for the conspirators' meeting. This darkness gradually gives way to the breaking of dawn (line 106).

◆ Choose a favourite scene. Talk with a partner about its atmosphere (aggressive, fearful, joking, and so on). Compile a 'language list' of phrases or lines from your chosen scene that create the atmosphere.

◆ Use your list to make up a short play with your own plot and characters. Create as powerful an atmosphere as you can in your play by using Shakespeare's words.

Creating character

Most of Shakespeare's characters have a distinctive way of speaking, but their style can change from situation to situation. For example, Casca's language in Act 1 changes from a relaxed, cynical style in Scene 2 (when he is with his patrician friends) to one of fear and apprehension in the storm of Scene 3.

◆ Choose a character, follow them through the play and compile a list of their typical language in different situations.

Rhetoric

Public speaking (or oratory) was hugely significant in ancient Rome. The art of persuasive speaking and writing, known as **rhetoric**, was a skill that all public figures aspired to master. Scholars developed sophisticated and memorable language techniques that were often used to establish and maintain political power. The art of rhetoric was still considered crucial in Elizabethan times and Shakespeare undoubtedly studied it at school.

In all centuries since Shakespeare's time, the art of rhetoric has played a very important part in public and political events across the world. Perhaps one of the most famous public speeches was delivered by Martin Luther King on 28 August 1963. Luther was a major leader of the American civil rights movement and his seventeen-minute speech to over 200,000 civil rights supporters on the steps of the Lincoln Memorial after a march through Washington has become world famous.

Julius Caesar
儒略·恺撒

Largely as a result of the powerful repetition of the phrase, it has become known as his 'I have a dream' speech. In it, King plays significantly on:

- the pattern and repetition of language (for example, 'Now is the time'; 'Let freedom ring')
- the use of balanced phrases and antithesis (对偶) (for example, 'It came as a joyous daybreak to end the long night of captivity')
- paralinguistic (辅助语言的) features (that is, the non-lexical components of the speech, such as the musicality of the rhythm, the preacher's 'call-and-response' technique, the varying of pitch, pace and volume)
- the use of the 'rule of three' (words or ideas repeated three times: 'Free at last!')
- emotive language ('crippled by the manacles of segregation')
- language that makes use of strong sounds (using onomatopoeia [拟声] and alliteration*).

◆ The speech is widely available as a transcript and it can be viewed on the Internet. Working in pairs, analyse a small portion of the speech. See if you can identify other examples of some (or all) of the techniques listed above. Talk together about the kind of impact the speech makes on an audience.

◆ Try your hand at writing your own 'persuasive' speech, modelled on the same core strategies. The choice of subject is entirely yours!

Julius Caesar also contains many examples of rhetoric: speeches that similarly seek to persuade by using striking and memorable vocabulary and language strategies. Language is used to create atmosphere, persuade people, move them to action, seek to change them. It appeals to their reason, emotions and imagination and builds their confidence in the speaker. In the play, rhetoric is used to great effect in several contexts:

- Murellus and Flavius's reprimand (训斥) of the common people (Act 1 Scene 1)
- Cassius's speeches to Brutus in Act 1 Scene 2
- Brutus in soliloquy where he tries to persuade himself that Caesar's death is justified; Portia's emotional speeches to her husband, imploring him to confide in her (Act 2 Scene 1)
- The Soothsayer's cryptic and ominous warnings to Caesar (Act 2 Scene 4)
- Brutus's speech to the common people, 'Romans, countrymen, and lovers'; Antony's funeral oration, 'Friends, Romans, countrymen' (Act 3 Scene 2)
- Caesar's arrogant assertions of fearlessness (Act 2 Scene 2, Act 3 Scene 1).

Rhetoric is discussed in detail in the 'Language' boxes on pages 8, 16, 18, 92 and 120. It uses a range of methods to make language more memorable, in terms of both language selection and its delivery. As well as making extensive use of lists and repetition (see p. 187), it is very precisely structured and ordered. Key phrases and ideas are reinforced through striking imagery, as in 'Our day is gone, / Clouds, dews, and dangers come' (Act 5 Scene 3, lines 63–4). Listeners are directly engaged through rhetorical questions that direct the audience towards the speaker's desired conclusion without the speaker overtly stating it – for example, 'Did this in Caesar seem ambitious?' (Act 3 Scene 2, line 82).

◆ Choose one rhetorical speech from the play (either from the list above, or one of your own). First, identify and annotate its specific 'persuasive' features. Then write a short critical evaluation of how it creates its effects.

◆ Perform or record your own interpretation of the speech in a way that highlights those specific rhetorical effects. Play your version alongside those of other students so that you create a sequence of persuasive speeches that you can compare.

* **alliteration** 头韵，指诗句里两个或多个词的第一个辅音相同，如 sing a song of sixpence，类似中文的双声。

The language of Julius Caesar

Antithesis

Antithesis is the opposition of words or phrases to each other, as in 'Set honour in one eye and death i'th'other' (Act 1 Scene 2, line 86); 'honour' and 'death' stand against each other. The setting of word against word is one of Shakespeare's favourite language devices. He uses it extensively in his plays because antithesis powerfully expresses conflict through the use of opposites, and conflict is the essence of drama. Antony remarks of Caesar after his death 'O mighty Caesar! Dost thou lie so low?' Brutus's argument that Antony should not be killed by the conspirators (Act 2 Scene 1, lines 162–83) contains at least a dozen antitheses – 'head' versus 'limbs', 'sacrificers' versus 'butchers' and so on. These antitheses highlight the debate that Brutus is conducting as he tries to present Caesar's assassination as noble rather than brutal and vicious.

◆ Collect more examples of antithesis. Use them in an essay exploring how antithesis creates a sense of conflict in *Julius Caesar*.

▼ How effectively does this image explore antithesis?

Repetition

The **repetition** that is apparent in the play's language is yet another rhetorical device, used by Shakespeare to create atmosphere, character and dramatic impact. The names 'Caesar' and 'Brutus' each occur over a hundred times in the play. The next most popular words are 'good', 'men' and 'man'. The pattern of repetition reflects some of the play's main concerns: personal identity, the justification and morality of actions, and the appropriate behaviour of men in a patriarchal (男权的) society like Rome.

Shakespeare also repeats language techniques to create particular effects. In the first scene, for example, Murellus fires off a multitude of rhetorical questions as he reproaches the plebeians.

◆ Remind yourself of the 'Language' box on page 8, and then track the repeated use of rhetorical questions through the play. Write a short essay comparing their impact in different situations.

On a grander scale, Shakespeare uses repetition in the public speeches.

◆ In small groups, discuss how Antony's repeated use of 'honourable' in his funeral oration (Act 3 Scene 2) turns the crowd against the conspirators.

◆ Explore the use of repetition in Brutus's funeral oration (also Act 3 Scene 2). Look closely at the ways in which he restates and echoes key words and ideas (for example, 'Believe me for mine honour, and have respect to / mine honour that you may believe.') and his use of the 'rule of three' (see p. 186) and rhetorical questions.

Lists

Another of Shakespeare's favourite language methods is to accumulate words or phrases rather like a list. He intensifies and varies description, atmosphere and argument as he 'piles up' item on item, incident on incident. Brutus uses lists in his funeral oration addressed to the people of Rome (Act 3 Scene 2, lines 13–39): 'There is tears for his love, joy for his fortune, honour for his valour, / and death for his ambition.'

JULIUS CAESAR
儒略・恺撒

Antony likewise lists 'all thy conquests, glories, triumphs, spoils' (Act 3 Scene 1, line 149), and towards the end of his funeral oration (Act 3 Scene 2, lines 211–13) ironically suggests that as a speaker he has 'neither wit, nor words, nor worth, / Action, nor utterance, nor the power of speech / To stir men's blood.'

◆ Lists also help to accentuate the details of the storm (Act 1 Scene 3, lines 59–78) and Calpurnia's description of the omens seen by the guards (Act 2 Scene 2, lines 13–24). In pairs, discuss the effects created by these lists.

Verse (韵文；诗体) and prose (散文；散体)

How did Shakespeare decide whether to write in verse or prose? One answer is that he followed theatrical convention. Prose was traditionally used by comic and low-status characters. High-status characters spoke verse. Comic scenes were written in prose (as were letters), but audiences expected verse in the serious scenes: the poetic style was thought to be particularly suitable for moments of high dramatic or emotional intensity, and for tragic themes.

The Commoners (low-status characters) speak in prose in the first scene although Flavius and Murellus (high status) use verse. However, during Caesar's funeral individual members of the crowd speak in verse, perhaps to underline the emotional intensity of the scene. Another remarkable departure from this prose or verse convention is Brutus's funeral oration (Act 3 Scene 2), which is in prose, although Brutus's language here clearly demonstrates that Shakespeare can use prose just as effectively as verse to express the deepest feelings and the most profound thoughts.

With few other exceptions, the verse of *Julius Caesar* is **blank verse** (无韵诗，素体诗): unrhymed verse written in **iambic pentameter** (抑扬五音步). Shakespeare would probably have learned the technical definition of iambic pentameter at school. In Greek, the word *pente* means 'five'. An **iamb** (抑扬，即前音节轻，后音节重) is a 'foot' (音步)(or group) of two syllables, the first unstressed and the second stressed, as in the pronunciation of 'alas': a LAS.

Iambic pentameter is therefore metrical verse in which each line has five stressed syllables (/) alternating with five unstressed syllables (×), as in this line by Cassius:

× / × / × / × / × /
I know where I will wear this dagger then

◆ Read the line aloud in unison with a partner, pronouncing each syllable very clearly. As you read, beat out the five-stress rhythm (e.g. clap hands, tap the desk).

◆ Now turn to the closing eight lines of Act 1 Scene 3. Repeat what you have just done. Can you find the rhythm? Is it clearly discernible and regular in each line or do you sense some subtle variations?

◆ Choose another verse speech and learn it ready to deliver in a way that emphasises the metre (five beats). Then speak it as you feel it should be delivered on stage.

By the time Shakespeare wrote *Julius Caesar*, he was becoming more flexible and experimental in his use of the iambic pentameter. **End-stopped** lines (lines with a pause at the end [尾断行]) are less frequent and there is a greater use of **enjambement***) (where one line flows into the next).

◆ Find examples of both end-stopping and enjambement in Brutus's speech (Act 2 Scene 1, lines 162–83). Describe the different effects Shakespeare creates using these metrical techniques.

Soliloquy

As in all Shakespeare's tragic plays, he uses the dramatic device of the soliloquy powerfully in *Julius Caesar* – although there are fewer such speeches than in his other tragedies. In order to appreciate the impact of some of the language, try one of the following activities based on Brutus's soliloquy in Act 2 Scene 1 or Antony's in Act 3 Scene 1.

* enjambement 跨行，指一行诗在印刷排版中因过长而无法排成一整行，不得不将长出来的部分排到下一行的情况。

The language of Julius Caesar

'Bare-bones soliloquy'

- In a small group take one line at a time and agree what you consider to be the key word. Write down that key word – just one per line. This will give you a 'bare bones' script of a handful of words.

- Keeping the words in their original order, present this new script in any ways that seem appropriate. Think about using choral speech, echoes, repetitions, sound effects or movement. Share your performance with the rest of the class for comment.

Two-handed soliloquy

- Read through your chosen soliloquy, with each person handing over the reading at each full stop, colon, semi-colon or question mark.

- Now consider ways of performing this speech as if it's a conversation (which it is, in a way, as it's like a piece of internal dialogue or a character debating with himself or herself). Experiment with other ways of dividing up the speech and ways of speaking to create different effects.

- Then think about how you might layer in movement, where you might stand (back-to-back, facing each other, one kneeling the other standing etc.). Share your final response with others in the class.

◀ Match this image to a line of Antony's soliloquy.

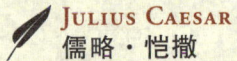

JULIUS CAESAR
儒略・恺撒

Julius Caesar in performance 《儒略・恺撒》的演出

In Shakespeare's time

Julius Caesar was probably first performed in 1599 and seems to have been a popular play from the start. It was almost certainly one of the earliest productions by Shakespeare's own company at the newly built Globe Theatre. There were no elaborate sets on the Globe stage, so Shakespeare had to rely on language to set the scene.

◆ Identify a scene in which Shakespeare has relied heavily on the power of language to evoke a particular atmosphere. Pick out several phrases that you find especially descriptive and share them with a partner, explaining what senses the words appeal to. Design your own set for this scene and write a commentary on your design, making clear which words from the script have prompted your ideas.

At the Globe, plays were performed only in the summer months and in broad daylight in the open air. At about 2 p.m. the audience would gather with food and drink, eager to be entertained. They were not required to be silent or to stay in the theatre – they could come and go as they wanted. This meant that the actors had to cope with significant background noise.

The audience also often found it difficult to hear what was taking place on the stage. The Globe could hold approximately three thousand people: the 'groundlings' (站票观众) stood in the pit (无座观众池) around the stage, while those who paid more were seated on three levels around the pit. Most of the audience could hear well when the actor was at the front of the stage, but it would be dull if all the action happened there. Elsewhere, upstage, furthest away from the audience, and downstage, closer to the audience, only certain sections of the audience could hear. In order to ensure that everyone heard the vital parts of the plot, the same idea was sometimes developed in three different ways in a speech. Shakespeare did this by using different imagery and the accumulation of detail. When such a repetition is present, it may have been a prompt to the actor to move around the stage.

JULIUS CAESAR IN PERFORMANCE

◆ Research further how plays were staged at the Globe in Shakespeare's time. Visit the website for the recreated Shakespeare's Globe in London, or better still go and see a play there!

◆ Having done your research, consider whether there are any features of the stage and layout of the Globe that could be exploited to make a production of *Julius Caesar* particularly dramatic. Make a list, so you are ready to participate in a group discussion.

◆ Look ahead to the short review of the Globe's 400th anniversary production of *Julius Caesar* in 1999 on page 193. Historical authenticity (真实性) was a significant feature and the cast was all male, as it would have been in Shakespeare's time. Using the Internet, research this production in detail, in order to understand the stagecraft and theatrical constraints of Shakespeare's time more fully.

Performances after Shakespeare's time

Today, Shakespeare's words are treated with greater reverence than they were during the centuries after his death. The short survey of performances that follows outlines how freely the script was altered. It also touches on which aspects of the play were stressed, modified or removed.

During the seventeenth and eighteenth centuries, Shakespeare's script was often modified to suggest more strongly that Brutus was the central character and thereby heighten his tragic status. He was, for example, given a more impressive death scene in one production, where he was allowed to kill himself without the aid of Strato. A lengthy and patriotic death speech was also given to Brutus, adding to the sense of him as the fallen Roman hero. There was also a trend to scale down the importance of the 'supernatural' elements.

In the nineteenth century, some productions focused on the recreation of the splendid setting of Rome with lavish scenery and costume. The architecture was carefully designed and the 'public' elements, such as the grand processions and crowd scenes, were handsomely staged.

The text continued to be adjusted to showcase Brutus as a noble and patriotic hero and Antony as a high-minded avenger. This meant that some of the play had to be cut (e.g. Antony's ruthless political activity in Act 4 Scene 1) because it jarred with the overall tone of the production.

William Charles Macready, staging the play in the early 1800s, gave the crowd scenes greater dramatic prominence, which set the trend for late nineteenth-century versions, in which the market-place scene (and Antony) were seen as central to the play.

John Philip Kemble's 1812 production in Covent Garden in London was influential for the rest of the century. He cut the script significantly and altered many of the minor characters, replacing the new ones in the later acts with some from the earlier ones. For example, Artemidorus and the Soothsayer were made into the same character. Brutus was a grand, patriotic philosopher and he was definitely the main character.

◆ Antony's eulogy to Brutus ended Kemble's version of the play. Why do you think Kemble decided to cut Octavius's speech?

Kemble also wanted to create a significant spectacle. His production was notable for its lavish costumes and the vast number of actors that made up Caesar's retinue (随从). Brutus, the classical hero, was played by Kemble in a grand style.

Herbert Beerbohm Tree's production in 1898 emphasised the active involvement of the crowd and highlighted the way in which Antony manipulated them, so that he now became the leading figure in the play. Tree – who thought that Antony provided the 'glamour of the play' – took that role himself. There was also an attempt to instil greater complexity and richness into the presentation of Caesar. Tree's commitment to visual spectacle produced a series of 'Roman daily life' scenes, which he inserted before Shakespeare's opening scene in order to establish a Roman context.

◆ In Tree's production, Calpurnia enters to mourn her husband at the end of the assassination scene. How would this alter the drama at this point in the play?

Julius Caesar
儒略·恺撒

Julius Caesar became a popular play in the United States during the nineteenth century, possibly because the political ideas it explored were close to American political experience at that time. Edwin Booth's 1871 production of the play in New York was especially influential. Interestingly, Booth and his brothers had put on a production in 1864 as a fundraiser. Booth's brother, John Wilkes Booth, played Antony in this production. Only a few months later, he assassinated the American president, Abraham Lincoln.

◆ If you are interested in researching particular productions, see what you can find out about Booth's 1871 production in New York. The characterisation of Brutus was particularly significant. Present your findings to the class.

▲ This painting gave Booth the inspiration for his staging of the assassination scene. How well does it capture the drama of the moment?

Recent productions

The twentieth century saw a return to much simpler stagings of the play. There was still some extravagance, but the dependence on theatrical illusion disappeared and productions concentrated on the clear delivery of the language. Just as Shakespeare probably intended, scenes flowed swiftly into each other and the action was not held up by clumsy stagecraft. Although scenes were often still cut, additional scenes were not added. Orson Welles's landmark 1937 production was subtitled *Death of a Dictator* and was heavily focused on the play's political elements. Welles also took the radical decision to dress the actors in Fascist uniforms and everyday clothes. Importantly, Welles was the first to play Brutus as a self-questioning, ineffectual liberal. For the first time ever in the United States, the scene involving Cinna the poet was kept.

In the last decades of the twentieth century, many productions tried to link the play with contemporary events. Caesar was played as a Latin American dictator, resembled Egypt's assassinated President Sadat and was identified with the freedom fighter Che Guevara (切·格瓦拉). Rome was used to symbolise Germany in the 1930s and East European dictatorships. In the last of these interpretations, a promenade staging (穿行演出，演员可根据剧情在观众中穿行走动), Caesar was followed continually by a secret policeman and TV camera and the actors moved amongst the audience, who found themselves playing the part of the Roman citizens.

◆ Can you think of a contemporary political regime that could be used as a setting for *Julius Caesar*? Debate the advantages and disadvantages of locating a production of the play so specifically.

◆ In the end, this is a play about Rome. Do you agree?

◆ Coleridge, the Romantic poet, praised the impartiality of Shakespeare's politics in this play. Do you think that Shakespeare balances the claims of Caesar and the conspirators, or does he suggest that one side is right and the other wrong?

Describe the impact of the huge head of Caesar behind the action on stage.

Short reviews of more recent productions

- The 1995 RSC production was cut to two hours' running time. A 2.5-metre (8-foot) marble head of Caesar dominated the beginning and ending, and there was a huge amount of visual imagery – buckets of blood, red togas (古罗马宽外袍) and a blood-red crack through Caesar's image in the storm scene. It was a production that emphasised the symbolism of the play.

- In 1999, a 400th anniversary production of the play was staged at the newly finished Shakespeare's Globe in London. Historical reconstruction was its most notable feature with the women's parts being played by men, lavish Elizabethan costumes and a jig (吉格舞, 一种节奏很快的舞蹈) being danced at the end (this detail had been recorded by a member of the audience in 1599). The Soothsayer and the plebeians were among the audience.

Julius Caesar
儒略·恺撒

- In 2001, the RSC again stressed the play's political dimensions, this time by creating a set that resembled the Nazi Nuremberg rallies (see p. vii, bottom). The Fascist references were echoed by the wearing of ceremonial togas combined with jackboots and black shirts.

- The RSC took their 2004 production on tour, using improvised and unconventional venues (see pp. x bottom and 139). The rawness and toughness of the set, reminiscent (引发联想) of industrial Eastern Europe, attracted a young audience. The Roman mob was dressed in fashionable casual clothes, while the soundtrack and lighting were sinisterly threatening.

- The 2005 Barbican production deployed a hundred extras, which gave the mob tremendous energy and power (see pp. x top, 4, 10 and 182–3). Very much a modern-dress version, it opened like a movie premiere based around cool, slick marble and glass. For the battle scenes the fighters wore American-style battle dress and the set was like a vast, devastated warehouse.

- The 2006 RSC production (see pp. v top, vii top, 14 and 39 top) used a minimalist set, just a gravel area surrounded by a pitch-black void. The storm scene was very dramatic, using real water and crackling electricity. The senators wore predominantly red outfits under crisp white togas.

- The 2012 RSC production set the play in an unidentified African state sometime in the last fifty years and had an all-black British cast. There was no interval. The vast statue of a dictator, its back turned to the audience, dominated the back of the stage. Caesar wore a white suit and carried a fly whisk (驱赶苍蝇的掸子); the others wore a mixture of modern dress and desert khakis (卡其裤). The Soothsayer's skin was painted white and the production was punctuated by a beating drum.

- The Donmar Warehouse staged an all-female production of the play in 2012. The key staging idea was that the inmates of a women's prison were putting on a production of *Julius Caesar*. The play opened with the whole cast doing military-style aerobics (有氧运动). Caesar, a prison warder whom they wanted to be rid of, was their instructor. Their weapons were water pistols and the music was punk (朋克摇滚乐). This production also had no interval.

◆ Choose one or more ideas from the above production reviews that you find interesting and describe in detail what special qualities you think they added to those productions.

◆ Some critics feel that setting *Julius Caesar* in a different historical or political period from ancient Rome causes problems for a modern audience. What do you think?

◆ What is gained by the play having no interval? Would you structure your performance like this?

◆ Watch a performance of *Julius Caesar* and write your own review of it.

◆ Comment on the set design of the Dutch production in the photograph below. What ideas from the play lie behind it?

Julius Caesar in performance

Are all-male or all-female productions of the play a gimmick (噱头) or do they make a serious point?

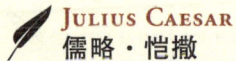

JULIUS CAESAR
儒略·恺撒

Screen versions

There are around fifteen screen versions of adaptations of the play. The 1938 BBC *Julius Caesar* was the first full-length Shakespeare play ever broadcast on television; sadly, it does not survive. Some of the most notable screen versions are described below.

The 1953 MGM version Produced by John Houseman and directed by Joseph L. Mankiewicz, this version was made in Hollywood. Although colour was available, they decided to use black and white for artistic reasons. The set of another movie was reused to create a grand imperial backdrop and there were hundreds of actors involved, making the crowd scenes impressive. There were many contemporary resonances, including the black and white of World War II newsreels. A subtext referenced the rise and fall of the 1930s Fascist leaders Hitler and Mussolini. The film was released at the height of the McCarthy era in the United States, and many parallels can be drawn.

◆ The casting of Marlon Brando as Antony in the film was controversial. Use the Internet to find out why.

The 1979 BBC version This low-budget television version was filmed in a studio with a small cast. There was no Roman grandeur and the emphasis was placed on verse speaking and the quality of the acting. It was only fractionally cut, unlike all other screen versions.

The RSC's 2012 stage production (see p. 194) Set in Africa, this version was adapted and filmed on location and in Stratford. Not only was Africa's turbulent political history referenced, but there were resonances of recent events during the Arab Spring, when dictators were removed by the actions of the people.

Caesar Must Die The Taviani brothers' movie came out in 2012. As in Phyllida Lloyd's 2012 production at the Donmar Warehouse, a prison performance of *Julius Caesar* is the framing device. This time the prisoners are tough Mafia men in the all-male, high-security wing of Rome's Rebibbia prison, auditioning for parts in the production. The roles of Portia and Calpurnia do not exist. Although the movie begins and ends with the prisoners performing the play in colour, the audition scenes in the middle are shot in black and white, which the directors consider to be a less realistic format.

◆ Discuss what is gained and lost by setting a production of *Julius Caesar* in a prison.

◆ There is certainly scope for a new big-budget movie version of *Julius Caesar*. In a group, develop the pitch you will make to a group of media moguls (传媒大亨). You will need to convince them that Shakespeare can pull in big audiences even now. Can you sell this as a political thriller? An outline of your ideas for the setting will be needed and a list of current big-name actors you would like to employ. Another group play the media moguls who will question you closely about your ideas. Will they give you the go-ahead?

◆ If you were given the choice of directing either a stage or a screen version of *Julius Caesar*, which would you choose and why?

▼ A still from the 2012 film *Caesar Must Die*.

Julius Caesar in performance

Stage your own production of *Julius Caesar*

Talk together about the period and place in which you will set your production. Clearly any historical setting other than a Roman one could have wider political resonances. Then choose one or more of the following activities.

- Design the basic set. If your production is going to be school-based, you will need to work with a particular space in mind (either indoors or outdoors). Decide where you want the audience to be seated. Consider whether you want a thrust stage or to present your play 'in the round' or as a promenade performance. Sketch your set or make a three-dimensional model of it. Work out how you will depict the domestic scenes (inside Brutus's and Caesar's homes), the Capitol scenes and the battles.

- Design the costumes. Study some of the ways Caesar and the conspirators have been presented. Think about how you will dress Portia and Calpurnia to reflect their roles and relationships with their husbands. How will you dress the common people?

- Design the props. Three important ones are Cassius's sword (see p. 154), Pompey's statue and Caesar's battle cloak.

- Design a sound-effects programme to accompany any one scene.

- Design a publicity poster. Use illustrations and language that will make people take notice.

- Design the programme. It could include a summary of the plot, a cast list, interviews with the actors, a history of recent productions and photographs from rehearsals.

- Cast the play. Suggest people at your school or college, or from the world of television, theatre or the media.

- Choose any scene from the play and produce your version of a director's prompt book for it. Your prompt book should include detailed notes about the ways in which you want the actors to perform the script, notes on the setting and props, on entrances and exits – anything to help you to bring that scene to life.

▼ For your production, would you choose costumes that locate the play in a particular period or not? Begin your discussion by considering the costumes in these photos.

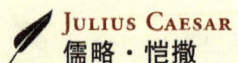
JULIUS CAESAR
儒略·恺撒

Writing about Shakespeare 笔论莎士比亚

The play as text

Shakespeare's plays have always been studied as literary works – as words on a page that need clarification, appreciation and discussion. When you write about the plays, you will be asked to compose short pieces and also longer, more reflective pieces like controlled assessments, examination scripts and coursework – often in the form of essays on themes and/or imagery, character studies, analyses of the structure of the play and on stagecraft. Imagery, stagecraft and character are dealt with elsewhere in this edition. Here, we concentrate on themes and structure. You might find it helpful to look at the 'Write about it' boxes on the left-hand pages throughout the play.

Themes

It is often tempting to say that the theme of a play is a single idea, like 'death' in *Hamlet*, or 'the supernatural' in *Macbeth*, or 'love' in *Romeo and Juliet*. The problem with such a simple approach is that you will miss the complexity of the plays. In *Romeo and Juliet*, for example, the play is about the relationship between love, family loyalty and constraint; it is also about the relationship of youth to age and experience; and the relationship between Romeo and Juliet is also played out against a background of enmity between two families. Between each of these ideas or concepts there are tensions. The tensions are the main focus of attention for Shakespeare and the audience; this is also how the best drama operates – by the presentation of and resolution of tension.

Look back at the 'Themes' boxes throughout the play to see if any of the activities there have given rise to information that you could use as a starting point for further writing about the themes of the specific play you are studying.

Structure

Most Shakespeare plays are in five acts, divided into scenes. These acts were not in the original scripts, but have been included in later editions to make the action more manageable, clearer and more like 'classical' structures. One way to get a sense of the structure of the whole play is to take a printed version (not this one!) and cut it up into scenes and acts, then display each scene and act, in sequence, on a wall, like this:

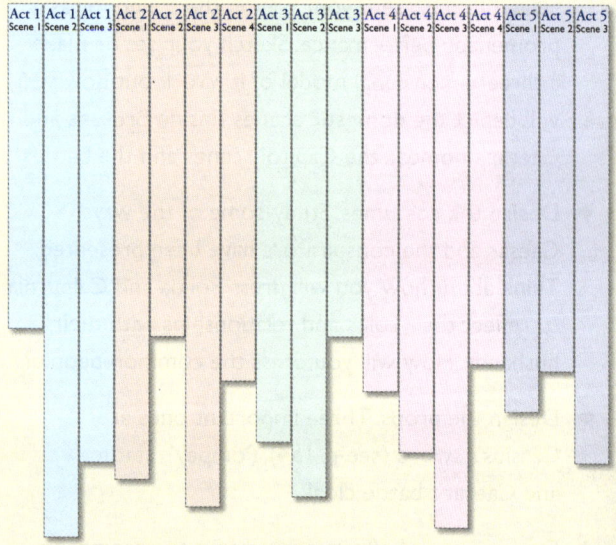

As you set out the whole play, you will be able to see the 'shape' of each act, the relative length of the scenes, and how the acts relate to each other (such as whether one act is shorter, and why that might be). You can annotate the text with comments, observations and questions. You can use a highlighter pen to mark the recurrence of certain words, images or metaphors to see at a glance where and how frequently they appear. You can also follow a particular character's progress through the play.

Such an overview of the play gives you critical perspective: you will be able to see how the parts fit together, to stand back from the play and assess its shape, and to focus on particular parts within the context of the whole. Your writing will reflect a greater awareness of the overall context as a result.

The play as script

There are different, but related, categories when we think of the play as a script for performance. These include *stagecraft* (discussed elsewhere in this edition and throughout the left-hand pages), *lighting*, *focus* (who are we looking at? Where is the attention of the audience?), *music and sound*, *props and costumes*, *casting*, *make-up*, *pace and rhythm*, and other *spatial relationships* (e.g. how actors move around the stage in relation to each other). If you are writing about stagecraft or performance, use the notes you have made as a result of the 'Stagecraft' activities throughout this edition of the play, as well as any information you can find about the plays in performance.

What are the key points of dispute?

Shakespeare is brilliant at capturing a number of key points of dispute in each of his plays. These are the dramatic moments where he concentrates the focus of the audience on difficult (sometimes universal) problems that the characters are facing or embodying.

First, identify these key points in the play you are studying. You can do this as a class by brainstorming what you consider to be the key points in small groups, then debating the long-list as a whole class, and then coming up with a short-list of what the class thinks are the most significant. (This is a good opportunity for speaking and listening work.) They are likely to be places in the play where the action or reflection is at its most intense, and which capture the complexity of themes, character, structure and performance.

Second, drill down at one of the points of contention and tension. In other words, investigate the complexity of the problem that Shakespeare has presented. What is at stake? Why is it important? Is it a problem that can be resolved, or is it an insoluble one?

Key skills in writing about Shakespeare

Here are some suggestions to help you organise your notes and develop advanced writing skills when working on Shakespeare:

- Compose the title of your writing carefully to maximise your opportunities to be creative and critical about the play. Explore the key words in your title carefully. Decide which aspect of the play – or which combination of aspects – you are focusing on.
- Create a mind map of your ideas, making connections between them.
- If appropriate, arrange your ideas into a hierarchy that shows how some themes or features of the play are 'higher' than others and can incorporate other ideas.
- Sequence your ideas so that you have a plan for writing an essay, review, story – whichever genre you are using. You might like to think about whether to put your strongest points first, in the middle, or later.
- Collect key quotations (it might help to compile this list with a partner), which you can use as evidence to support your argument.
- Compose your first draft, embedding quotations in your text as you go along.
- Revise your draft in the light of your own critical reflections and/or those of others.

The following pages focus on writing about *Julius Caesar* in particular.

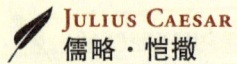

JULIUS CAESAR
儒略・恺撒

Writing about *Julius Caesar* 笔论《儒略・恺撒》

The purpose of this section is to help you to write about *Julius Caesar* in an informed, coherent and convincing fashion. Before you begin to commit to writing down your ideas, remember to keep two key considerations in mind:

1. *Julius Caesar* is a play, so you should always appreciate its form and genre. In Caesar's first scene (Act 1 Scene 2), for example, there is a huge amount of 'stagecraft' built in to the writing (entrances, exits, 'stage business', action and so on). It's all about what the audience sees, hears and experiences.

◆ Look at the script of the first 31 lines of Act 1 Scene 2 in this edition. Try writing about how the language might be brought to life on stage. Speculate about different ways of playing this short episode.

2. *Julius Caesar* is not about 'real' people and 'real' situations, so don't treat it as such. When Shakespeare pays close attention to the presentation of Brutus's home life in the play in Act 2, it's as much about making a dramatic point (the privacy and stability of his home being invaded by the conspiracy) as trying to make it all credible and naturalistic. The play is a dramatic construct and often characters, for example, are vehicles for ideas about themes and structure. Remember Artemidorus? Lucius? The Soothsayer? Shakespeare presents them very sketchily as figures (and they've been played on stage in a variety of ways) but they have crucial roles in the drama.

How many different kinds of writing might you tackle?

You could write about:

- an extract (a key speech, such as Antony's 'If you have tears, prepare to shed them now' [Act 3 Scene 2], or a longer passage of dialogue, such as the reconciliation between Brutus and Cassius in Act 4 Scene 3)
- a key scene (such as the death of Brutus in Act 5 Scene 5)
- a character (Cassius), or group of characters (the 'Triumvirate')
- a core theme (the concept of honour)
- an element of the text re-creatively (that is, rewriting it in another genre or from another perspective or in the persona [人格面具] of one of the characters)

◆ Individually, consider each of these 'types' of writing in turn. See if you can come up with three additional focuses or frameworks for questions besides the ones that are mentioned in brackets above. Then pass your ideas to a partner for consideration. Together, settle on two questions for each category that you think would generate interesting written responses. Keep these in mind as you work through the next section.

Writing about an extract or a key scene

Consider the dramatic effectiveness of the opening 120 lines of Act 3 Scene 1.

1. Locate the extract in the play, and contextualise it. What has just happened? (The conspirators' plot has been settled.) What is about to come? (Caesar is assassinated; the conspirators attempt to justify their actions and bathe themselves in his blood.)

2. Concentrate on exploring the mood or atmosphere of the extract. (Caesar ignores any attempts to warn him and reaffirms that he is 'constant' in his principles. The dramatic intensity escalates as the conspirators stab Caesar. Shakespeare focuses on Caesar's bewilderment at Brutus's betrayal.)

3. How might the lines be spoken – tone, emphasis, pace, pauses, etc. What are key words and images ('constant', '*Et tu, Brute*?', 'death', 'blood')?

4. Think about Shakespeare's stagecraft – how he assembles and groups characters (the big public gathering and the warnings from the Soothsayer and Artemidorus at the start of the scene), the gradual narrowing of focus onto Caesar, the use of entrances/exits and the blocking on stage (how the conspirators close in on Caesar).

5 Link the details of the extract to key themes or issues rooted in the text as a whole (the presentation of Caesar, the motivation of the conspirators, the exploration of death and honour).

6 Show how the extract links to the dramatic construction of the play (a turning point, and a prelude to the rise of Antony and the discrediting of the conspiracy).

◆ Working in a group of six, take one numbered section each of the above essay framework. Plan your answer by researching your specific area of focus. Then divide up a large sheet of sugar paper into six sections. Take turns to fill in the notes you have compiled. Use this large sheet as a resource to help you produce an essay plan of no more than one side that you could include in a revision booklet to be given to students for examination preparation.

Writing about character

Planning an essay on the character of Antony

1 Summarise what Antony does in each act, his interactions with other characters, his decisive actions.

2 Explore how Antony relates to other characters and note down the different ways he treats them. How do they speak to him and about him?

3 Focus on the type of language that Antony uses – the imagery he employs, the tone he strikes, his typical way of speaking. Identify quotations that will back up your points. Link Antony's role to key themes and aspects of the drama.

4 Finally, think about the ways in which Shakespeare shows the development and change within his character over the course of the play.

Writing creatively

Many assessments offer you the opportunity to write about *Julius Caesar* creatively as well as critically. There are a number of such activities which you have been encouraged to try act by act. The great thing is that you can be as imaginative and original within the framework of such responses as you choose to be: *Julius Caesar* is a complex, rich and intriguing text that offers many opportunities for creative approaches.

Summing up

Keep in mind the focus on *Julius Caesar* as a dramatic text. What features of the play as a theatrical performance enhance the impact of key issues? Remember that there is no single, right interpretation – both from you as a critic, but also from a director. How might an audience respond – in Shakespeare's time, and now? How do you respond? What are your own personal responses to the question and how can you justify them?

Possible questions

◆ Below you'll find questions on character, theme, extracts and re-creative tasks. Have a go at one of each, or invent your own!

1 Neither Portia nor Calpurnia has an important role in *Julius Caesar*. What is your view, and why?

2 'Although the play is called *Julius Caesar*, it's really Brutus who is the main character.' Discuss.

3 Discuss the presentation and development of the theme of honour and ambition in the play.

4 Explore the dramatic construction of Act 4 Scene 2.

5 Explore the contrasts between appearance and reality.

6 In role as one of the characters, write about a key incident in the play from your point of view.

7 Brutus's character is full of irreconcilable differences. Explore the presentation of Brutus in the light of this comment.

8 Argue the case for retaining Acts 4 and 5 in a production of the play.

9 Write an additional speech for a character or script a section of dialogue between a character who appears in the play and one who doesn't.

JULIUS CAESAR
儒略・恺撒

William Shakespeare 莎翁年表
1564–1616

1564	Born Stratford-upon-Avon, eldest son of John and Mary Shakespeare.
1582	Marries Anne Hathaway of Shottery, near Stratford.
1583	Daughter Susanna born.
1585	Twins, son and daughter Hamnet and Judith, born.
1592	First mention of Shakespeare in London. Robert Greene, another playwright, described Shakespeare as 'an upstart crow beautified with our feathers'. Greene seems to have been jealous of Shakespeare. He mocked Shakespeare's name, calling him 'the only Shake-scene in a country' (presumably because Shakespeare was writing successful plays).
1595	Becomes a shareholder in The Lord Chamberlain's Men, an acting company that became extremely popular.
1596	Son, Hamnet, dies aged eleven. Father, John, granted arms (acknowledged as a gentleman).
1597	Buys New Place, the grandest house in Stratford.
1598	Acts in Ben Jonson's *Every Man in His Humour*.
1599	Globe Theatre opens on Bankside. Performances in the open air.
1601	Father, John, dies.
1603	James I grants Shakespeare's company a royal patent: The Lord Chamberlain's Men become The King's Men and play about twelve performances each year at court.
1607	Daughter Susanna marries Dr John Hall.
1608	Mother, Mary, dies.
1609	The King's Men begin performing indoors at Blackfriars Theatre.
1610	Probably returns from London to live in Stratford.
1616	Daughter Judith marries Thomas Quiney. Dies. Buried in Holy Trinity Church, Stratford-upon-Avon.

The plays and poems

(no one knows exactly when he wrote each play)

1589–95	*The Two Gentlemen of Verona, The Taming of the Shrew, First, Second* and *Third Parts* of *King Henry VI, Titus Andronicus, King Richard III, The Comedy of Errors, Love's Labour's Lost, A Midsummer Night's Dream, Romeo and Juliet, King Richard II* (and the long poems *Venus and Adonis* and *The Rape of Lucrece*).
1596–99	*King John, The Merchant of Venice, First* and *Second Parts* of *King Henry IV, The Merry Wives of Windsor, Much Ado About Nothing, King Henry V,* **Julius Caesar** (and probably the Sonnets).
1600–05	*As You Like It, Hamlet, Twelfth Night, Troilus and Cressida, Measure for Measure, Othello, All's Well That Ends Well, Timon of Athens, King Lear.*
1606–11	*Macbeth, Antony and Cleopatra, Pericles, Coriolanus, The Winter's Tale, Cymbeline, The Tempest.*
1613	*King Henry VIII, The Two Noble Kinsmen* (both probably with John Fletcher).
1623	Shakespeare's plays published as a collection (now called the First Folio).

Acknowledgements 鸣谢

Cambridge University Press would like to acknowledge the contributions made to this work by Rex Gibson, Mike Clamp and Tim Seward.

Extract from Michael Billington's review of *Julius Caesar* at The Royal Shakespeare Theatre, Stratford-upon-Avon on p. 176 copyright © Guardian News & Media Ltd 2012.

Picture Credits

p. iii: Barbican Theatre, London 2005, © Donald Cooper/Photostage; p. v top: RSC/Royal Shakespeare Theatre 2006, © Donald Cooper/Photostage; p. v bottom: RSC/The Courtyard Theatre, Stratford-upon-Avon 2009, © Geraint Lewis; p. vi: RSC/Royal Shakespeare Theatre 1991, © Donald Cooper/Photostage; p. vii top: RSC/Royal Shakespeare Theatre 2006, © Donald Cooper/Photostage; p. vii bottom: RSC/Royal Shakespeare Theatre 2001, © Donald Cooper/Photostage; p. viii top: RSC/Royal Shakespeare Theatre 2012, © Donald Cooper/Photostage; p. viii bottom: RSC/Royal Shakespeare Theatre 2001, © Donald Cooper/Photostage; p. ix: RSC Tour/Lyric Hammersmith, London 2005 © Donald Cooper/Photostage; p. x top: Barbican Theatre, London 2005, © Donald Cooper/Photostage; p. x bottom: RSC/Lyric Hammersmith, London 2005, © Donald Cooper/Photostage; p. xi top: Barbican Theatre, London 2005, © Donald Cooper/Photostage; p. xi bottom: Barbican Theatre, London 2005, © Donald Cooper/Photostage; p. xii: Barbican Theatre, London 2005, © Donald Cooper/Photostage; p. 2: Shutterstock/ecco; p. 4: Barbican Theatre, London 2005, © Donald Cooper/Photostage; p. 6: RSC/Royal Shakespeare Theatre 1983, © Donald Cooper/Photostage; p. 10: Barbican Theatre, London 2005, © Donald Cooper/Photostage; p. 14: RSC/Royal Shakespeare Theatre 2006, © Donald Cooper/Photostage; p. 20: RSC/Royal Shakespeare Theatre 2012, Nigel Norrington/ArenaPAL/TopFoto; p. 26: Shutterstock/nortivision; p. 34: Barbican Theatre, London 2005, © Donald Cooper/Photostage; p. 39 top: RSC/Royal Shakespeare Theatre 2006, © Donald Cooper/Photostage; p. 39 bottom: RSC/Royal Shakespeare Theatre 1991, © Donald Cooper/Photostage; p. 42: Barbican Theatre, London 2005, © Donald Cooper/Photostage; p. 46: RSC/Royal Shakespeare Theatre 2012, © Geraint Lewis; p. 56: RSC/The Courtyard Theatre, Stratford-upon-Avon 2009, © Donald Cooper/Photostage; p. 62: Barbican Theatre, London 2005, © Donald Cooper/Photostage; p. 73 top: RSC/Royal Shakespeare Theatre 2012, Nigel Norrington/ArenaPAL/TopFoto; p. 73 bottom: RSC/The Courtyard Theatre, Stratford-upon-Avon 2009, Nigel Norrington/ArenaPAL/TopFoto; p. 74: The Granger Collection/TopFoto; p. 76. RSC/Moscow Chekhov Art Theater 2012, RIA Novosti/ArenaPAL; p. 80: Barbican Theatre, London 2005, © Donald Cooper/Photostage; p. 82: Barbican Theatre, London 2005, © Donald Cooper/Photostage; p. 88: RSC/Barbican Theatre, London 1996, © Donald Cooper/Photostage; p. 96 top: RSC/Royal Shakespeare Theatre 2012, © Donald Cooper/Photostage; p. 96 bottom: RSC/Royal Shakespeare Theatre 2001, © Donald Cooper/Photostage; p. 98: RSC/Royal Shakespeare Theatre 1991, © Donald Cooper/Photostage; p. 108: Barbican Theatre, London 2005, © Donald Cooper/Photostage; p. 111 top left: RSC/Barbican Theatre, London 1996, © Donald Cooper/Photostage; p. 111 top right: RSC/The Other Place, Stratford-upon-Avon 1993, © Donald Cooper/Photostage; p. 111 bottom left: Barbican Theatre, London 2005, © Donald Cooper/Photostage; p. 111 bottom right: National Youth Theatre/Bloomsbury Theatre, London 1993, © Donald Cooper/Photostage; p. 114: © TopFoto; p. 116: Belasco Theatre, Broadway, New York 2005, © Joan Marcus/ArenaPAL/TopFoto; p. 122: The Granger Collection/TopFoto; p. 134: RSC/Royal Shakespeare Theatre 2012, © Geraint Lewis; p. 139: RSC Tour, Ebbw Vale, 2004, © Donald Cooper/Photostage; p. 154: Shutterstock/greglith; p. 156: RSC/Royal Shakespeare Theatre 2012, © Donald Cooper/Photostage; p. 165 top: Barbican Theatre, London 2005, © Donald Cooper/Photostage; p. 165 bottom: RSC/Royal Shakespeare Theatre 2012, © Geraint Lewis; p. 169: Shakespeare's Globe, London 1999, © Donald Cooper/Photostage; p. 170: RSC/The Courtyard Theatre, Stratford-upon-Avon 2009, Nigel Norrington/ArenaPAL/TopFoto; p. 171: Shutterstock/Meunierd; p. 172 top: Shutterstock/Jeff Banke; p. 172 bottom: The Granger Collection/

Julius Caesar
儒略·恺撒

TopFoto; p. 173: RSC/Royal Shakespeare Theatre 2012, © Geraint Lewis; p. 175 left: RSC/Royal Shakespeare Theatre 1991, © Donald Cooper/Photostage; p. 175 right: RSC/Royal Shakespeare Theatre 2012, © Geraint Lewis; p. 177 left: RSC/Royal Shakespeare Theatre 2001, © Donald Cooper/Photostage; p. 177 right: RSC/Royal Shakespeare Theatre 2012, © Geraint Lewis; p. 179: RSC/Royal Shakespeare Theatre 2012, © Donald Cooper/Photostage; p. 181 left: Shakespeare's Globe, London 1999, © Donald Cooper/Photostage; p. 181 right: RSC/Royal Shakespeare Theatre 2001, © Donald Cooper/Photostage; pp. 182–3: Barbican Theatre, London 2005, © Donald Cooper/Photostage;

p. 187: Shakespeare at the Tobacco Factory, Bristol 2009, © Donald Cooper/Photostage; pp. 189: RSC/Royal Shakespeare Theatre 1995, © Donald Cooper/Photostage; p. 190: Wikimedia Commons/McKay Savage; p. 192: © Walters Art Museum, Baltimore, USA/Bridgeman Art Library; p. 193: Barbican Theatre, London 1996, © Donald Cooper/Photostage; p. 194: Toneelgroep, Amsterdam/Barbican Theatre, London 2009, © Donald Cooper/Photostage; p. 195: Donmar Warehouse 2012, © Helen Maybanks; p. 196: © Photos 12/Alamy; p. 197 top: RSC/The Other Place, Stratford-upon-Avon 1993, © Donald Cooper/Photostage; p. 197 bottom: RSC/The Courtyard Theatre, Stratford-upon-Avon 2009, © Geraint Lewis.

Produced for Cambridge University Press by
White-Thomson Publishing
+44 (0)843 208 7460
www.wtpub.co.uk

Project editor: Clare Collinson
Designer: Clare Nicholas
Concept design: Jackie Hill